SPARROW'S REVENGE

The Devil's Bridge at Borgo a Mozzano
in the Garfagnana region of Tuscany

Also by Paul Salsini

The Cielo: A Novel of Wartime Tuscany

Second Start

SPARROW'S REVENGE

A Novel of Postwar Tuscany

PAUL SALSINI

iUniverse, Inc.
New York   Bloomington

Sparrow's Revenge
A Novel of Postwar Tuscany

Copyright © 2008 by Paul E. Salsini

This is a work of fiction. All of the characters, names, incidents, organizations, anddialogue in this novel are either the products of the author's imagination or are usedfictitiously.

iUniverse books may be ordered through booksellers or by contacting:

iUniverse
1663 Liberty Drive
Bloomington, IN 47403
www.iuniverse.com
1-800-Authors (1-800-288-4677)

ISBN: 978-0-595-52239-2 (pbk)
ISBN: 978-0-595-62294-8 (ebk)

Printed in the United States of America

For Barbara,
Jim, Laura, and Jack

AUTHOR'S NOTE

When I wrote *The Cielo: A Novel of Wartime Tuscany*, the thought of writing a sequel was the farthest thing from my mind. But after I finished *The Cielo*, the characters remained firmly embedded in my head, and I wondered what they would do next. *Sparrow's Revenge: A Novel of Postwar Tuscany* is the result. Are the characters still in my head and do I wonder about them? Yes.

I have many people to thank for their help with *Sparrow's Revenge*. First, my wife, Barbara, and our daughter, Laura, for their invaluable editing, and our sons, Jim and Jack, for their support. Also, Martha Bergland and Mike Fischer and members of my writing group for their suggestions. And in Italy, my indefatigable driver/interpreter, Marcello Grandini, and, especially, my cousin, Fosca, the inspiration for the indomitable Rosa.

THE MAIN CHARACTERS

In Reboli/San Antonio:

Ezio Maffini, a former partisan, now a schoolteacher
Lucia Sporenza, a young mother
Paolo Ricci, her husband, owner of a pastry shop in Reboli; Ezio's
partisan comrade
Little Dino, her son; his father was killed in the war
Gina Sporenza, her mother
Pietro Sporenza, her father, severely wounded in the war
Roberto Sporenza, her brother, who lives in Florence
Adolfo Sporenza, her brother, a student at the university in Pisa
Rosa Tomaselli, a neighbor
Marco Tomaselli, her husband
Maria Ruffolo, a neighbor and mother of Ezio's lover, Angelica, who
died in the Sant'Anna di Stazzema massacre
Annabella Sabbatini, a neighbor; her husband, Francesco, was killed in
the war
Fausta Sanfilippo, a victim of the Fascists

In Florence:

Antonio Maffini, Ezio's father, a woodworker
Rudolfo Panetto, Antonio's wartime comrade
Franco, a friend of Roberto's

In Pietrasanta:

> Donna Fazzini, a marble cutter
> Rico Fazzini, her father
> Ugo Donatello, a marble factory worker
> Lidia Donatello, his wife
> Angelo Donatello, their son
> Daniella Lisi, his wife
> Little Ugo, their son

In The Garfagnana/Barga:

> Antonio Denato, a fugitive
> Fabiano Guerini, a farmer
> Sabina Guerini, his wife
> Graziella Guerini, their daughter
> Amadeo Mazzella, a police officer
> Calvino Bastiani, a retired banker
> Orsino Nardari, a former race car driver
> Vittorio Izzo, a retired boxer
> *il ragazzo fantasma*, the ghost boy

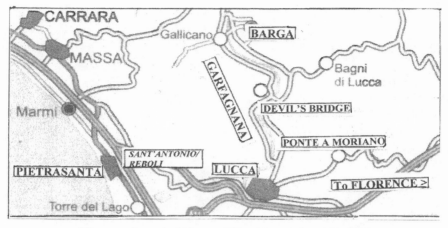

The map shows the location of "Sant'Antonio" and "Reboli"

PART ONE

CHAPTER 1

▼

"Signor Maffini! Signor Maffini!

At first, only the boys were chanting, but now the girls joined in.

"Signor Maffini! Signor Maffini!"

He knew what was going on, but he thought he'd play along with his pupils for a while.

"Signor Maffini!" Rocco shouted. "Look behind you! Look behind you!"

He suppressed a smile and pretended to ignore the clamor by looking down at the papers on his desk.

"Signor Maffini!" Now it was Franco. "It's huge, Signor Maffini, it's huge! It's gonna get you!"

Ezio Maffini had taught the fifth grade long enough to know that the last day of school always brought these pranks. He looked across the desks of the classroom, now in disarray as his pupils jumped up and down, shouting and pointing. Everyone here? No. One vacant desk. Bruno. Of course. Somehow that stocky kid with the chubby cheeks and wild red hair was hiding behind him. He could hear the kid making strange popping noises. How did he get there without my seeing him?

"Signor Maffini!" little Benedetta squeaked. "You better look or it's going to be too late!" The other girls giggled.

Well, he might as well let them go on. The kids were having fun. No harm done.

He put his papers down and looked around the room. The windows, partly open to let in the sultry June air, needed cleaning again. He could barely see the stone houses across from the fields in the back. Beams of sunlight filtering through the dirt cast odd patterns on the wooden floor, making the clumps of dust on the planks even more visible. The faded plaster walls could be brighter, and the soot around the coal stove in the corner needed cleaning. The stain in the corner should be covered up, but unless the tile roof was patched, the rain would still come in and stain all over again.

Last November he had taken down the mandatory crucifix, but the *direttore* stormed in and ordered it put back. Ezio countered by posting a photo of the Italian Communist Party head, Palmiro Togliatti, and a declaration from the party ten years ago during the war, in 1945: "Long live the insurrectionary general strike! Long live the national popular insurrection! Chase out of Italy the hated German! Let the base Fascists and the profiteering plutocrats die the deaths of traitors!"

Even ten-year-olds, Ezio told the *direttore*, should know what happened. In his section on the history of Italy, Ezio skipped over the Etruscans and condensed the Renaissance so that he could talk about the war, about Italy's ambivalent role and about the work of the Resistance. The children sat wide-eyed when he told of his own experiences fighting the Nazis, but he knew that they weren't even born when the war ended and their parents were fast forgetting about it.

He also cut short the hour for mathematics and let the children draw pictures or write little stories and poems. But he didn't dare display their work on the walls, even though some of it was quite good, especially Little Dino's. The stories weren't bad, either. He liked Theresa's about her cat and Domenica's about her grandmother.

"Signor Maffini!"

Ezio stifled a yawn. Another sleepless night, another damn headache that left him exhausted and listless all day.

"Signor Maffini!"

He knew the noise was bothering Giorgio Pilozi in his classroom next door. Too bad. Let the old Fascist suffer.

Maybe he could freshen up the room over the summer. For one thing, he needed to get a new map of Italy. There was a hole where he had cut out Mussolini's picture. Next to it, where *il Duce's* portrait once hung, he needed to get something larger than the photo of the horse race in Siena.

It was hard to believe that he'd been teaching fifth grade in the little brick schoolhouse in Reboli for eight years. Sometimes he thought he should look for a better job, maybe in nearby Lucca or even Florence. His father was always urging him to come back to Florence.

But Ezio liked it here in Reboli. He didn't care that there was little nightlife, few concerts and no theater. He simply needed quiet. A place where he could try to forget, although that was still impossible. And over the bridge, in the tiny village of Sant'Antonio, he could visit friends and especially Maria, his only link to the greatest love of his life.

"Signor Maffini!"

Ezio ran his hand over his thick curly hair and straightened his tie. It was late and time to bring some order to the room. As he was about to call for silence, he saw Little Dino out of the corner of his eye. The smallest and shyest student Ezio ever had, the boy was bouncing in his seat, mouthing the cries of the other students but too bashful to say anything out loud.

Shout it out, Little Dino, Ezio wanted to say. Don't be afraid. Let loose!

But Little Dino was happy enough just to feel a small part of what was going on. It was the same on the playground. He always stood at the back, one foot against the wall, and watched while all the other boys played soccer. And in the reading class he spoke so softly that Ezio had to tell the other pupils to stop snickering.

Only when they were drawing pictures did Little Dino come into his own. Quickly and fervently, he would lean over his desk, not looking up until fantastic creatures in bright yellows and reds almost flew off his paper. The other pupils were amazed.

"How do you do that?" they'd ask. Little Dino's face would turn red, making his freckles even brighter, and he'd smile an awkward little smile and swing his feet, which didn't quite reach the floor. There was one thing Ezio noticed, too. When Little Dino made up his mind to do something, there was no stopping him.

"All right," Ezio said. "Time's up. That's enough for now."

"But Signor Maffini," Rocco shouted. "Aren't you going to look behind you? It's gonna get you if you don't!"

"Look behind you, look behind you!" All of the children were chanting now, except Little Dino, who barely managed a whisper.

Slowly, purposely pausing a couple of times while the children held their breath, Ezio stood up and turned around.

And then laughed so hard he had to sit down again.

Bruno had somehow climbed into the net for the soccer balls that hung from the ceiling and was sitting there proudly. His legs hung over the side and he held two balls against his chest.

"Look at me!" he shouted. "Look at me, Signor Maffini! I'm Nonna Alfonsi!"

Ezio knew he was talking about the oldest, and fattest, woman in Reboli. He also knew that breasts fascinated ten-year-old boys.

The other children hooted as Ezio pulled on Bruno's legs.

"All right, Bruno. That was funny, but now it's time to get down. We have to end the day and get you all home. Your mamas will have your lunch ready."

Bruno tried to stand in the netting and when he suddenly fell forward, his left foot caught in the strands of rope. Now, head almost touching the floor, he swayed back and forth.

"Hey look," he tried to shout, though blood was rushing to his face. "Now I'm Topo the acrobat!"

The room in an uproar, Ezio untangled Bruno's foot and lifted him to the floor.

"Good joke, Bruno." He smoothed the boy's hair and turned to the rest of the class.

"What a way to end the school year, right? Now you've got something to remember all summer."

Ezio felt he had to give a little speech.

"Well," he said as the room quieted down, "we're at the end of the school year. In October you'll be going to school in Lucca, and I don't know if I'll see many of you again. But I want you to know that I'm proud of you. Some of you didn't do quite as well as others." Here he looked at Bruno and Rocco. "But you all tried hard. You're a credit to your families. Mostly, though, I want you to remember what we talked about through the year, that you must always try to do the right thing, that you must always fight against bad things that are happening. Now do you know what that means?"

All the boys suddenly found something to look at on the top of their desks. Two girls frantically waved their hands.

"Elsa?"

"I think if someone does something bad to you," she said breathlessly, "you shouldn't do something bad against them."

"Good! Pina?"

"I think we should look for good things to do for other people." She smiled triumphantly and sat down.

"*Brava!* Now just remember what you learned next year, and the year after that, and all through your lives."

The children were getting restless, so Ezio brought it to a quick ending. "All right, there's one last thing …"

"Signor Maffini!" the children shouted. "Your book! Your book!"

It had become a tradition each year that Ezio would give a copy of his memoir of the war, *A Time to Remember*, to a pupil he thought had shown the most progress.

"Thanks. I almost forgot." Ezio reached into the bottom drawer of his desk and pulled out a slim volume bound in blue.

"Little Dino," he announced, "I want you to have this."

While the other children cheered, Little Dino edged to the front of the room, grabbed the book and hurried back to his desk before Ezio could shake his hand.

"All right, everyone, this is really the last thing," Ezio said. "Come up and return your *sussidiario*. The pupils next year will need them."

The children came up one by one and handed over the heavy books containing all their lessons. He shook their hands and patted them on the shoulder. A few of the girls seemed close to tears. Ezio himself had moist eyes.

"Goodbye, Signor Maffini!"

"Have a good summer!"

"Maybe we'll see you at the soccer field!"

Little Dino was last.

"Little Dino," Ezio said. "And what are you going to do this summer? Big plans?"

"I dunno. Just play, I think." The boy didn't raise his eyes from the floor.

"Well, enjoy the time. Just think, in the fall you'll be going all the way to Lucca for school."

Ezio saw the boy's lower lip quiver.

"You'll like it, I know you will." He tried to sound convincing.

"Signor Maffini?" The boy's voice faltered. "Mama wants to know if you could come for dinner on Sunday?"

"Well, of course, Dino. Tell your mother I would like that very much. You go home now, and I'll see you again on Sunday."

The boy didn't move.

"Aren't you going home?"

"I'm going to Papa's shop."

"All right then. I'll see you on Sunday."

Ezio shook his head as Little Dino went out the door and shuffled down the path.

Turning back to his desk, Ezio stretched his arms. He looked around the room and slowly packed a box of books to take home. He took his time, looking at each of them and remembering his students as they learned about Dante and Michelangelo and Garibaldi. He didn't care so much if they didn't remember the metric system or how Italian politics worked. Just so they were proud of their heritage and their history and that they were good people.

He realized that he didn't want to leave. The end of the school year meant the start of another long summer in which there would be nothing to do but think. "Grieve over my guilt," he called it. He dreaded that, and knew that he was already longing for another school year to begin.

Then he pulled down the windows, careful that the cracked one didn't slam too hard. Closing his classroom door, he almost bumped into Giorgio Pilozi. The old teacher thrust his arm out and made an obscene gesture. Ezio returned it in kind.

CHAPTER 2

▼

The cobblestone streets and alleys, dating back to Reboli's medieval times, were nearly deserted as Ezio climbed the steep Via Bellini. He sometimes thought that other countries scheduled the school day better, giving students a short break for lunch, then resuming classes in the afternoon. This being Italy, classes ended at 1 o'clock to allow the children to go home for *il pranzo*, which their mothers would have waiting. Then, full of pasta, they could rest along with everyone else and go out to play. Ezio thought it would be better if they spent the time in school learning some history or reading about famous writers and painters.

This was his favorite time of day and this was his favorite street in Reboli. His heels echoed on the stones as he passed shops that were closed for the siesta. Signora Renaldi had spread newspapers over the wooden crates of her fat luscious tomatoes outside her tiny shop. Signor Stentini's golden flowers were sheltered from the midday sun by the little awning over his door. The lilies were almost translucent in front of the copy of a Della Robbia blue-and-white Madonna on the wall of the Bandini house. Signora Franconi's fat gray cat slept with one eye open next to a pot holding bright red geraniums.

Rounding a corner, he saw Rocco and Bruno still dawdling.

"Signor Maffini!" Rocco shouted. "Look at us!"

"We're up here!" Bruno yelled.

Waving their arms, Rocco and Bruno stood atop the Panzer tank that the city refused to destroy after the war. Abandoned during the Germans' hasty retreat to the north, it stood as a grim and eternal reminder of occupation, warfare and atrocities. "We must never forget!" were the only words on the plaque in front of the turret.

No, we must never forget the fifty-four soldiers from Reboli killed in the war, Ezio thought. He had looked up the number.

We must never forget the untold number of women and girls raped by the Nazis.

We must never forget the seventy-eight homes destroyed by bombs as the British tried to flush out the Germans.

We must never forget the ten innocent men hanged at the bridge because the partisans had killed a German soldier.

And, he thought, we must never forget the thirteen brave young men and three young women from Reboli who joined my band of partisans in the closing months of the war.

Watching Rocco and Bruno playing on the cannon, Ezio wondered if the tank had any meaning at all for these boys. To them, it was just another place to play. Was he the only one in Reboli who was still haunted day and night by the horrors of the war? Why couldn't he put it in the past like everyone else?

"You have to move on," his friend Paolo Ricci had told him again the other night over linguini at Sabbatini's *Trattoria*. "It's ten years since the war ended. We've got other things to worry about. Better jobs. Getting some new industry here. Repairing the streets. And things aren't really so bad, are they? Forget the war, Ezio. Forget it."

At least Paolo would still remember the war. They had fought together in the Resistance; Ezio used the name of Sparrow and Paolo was Owl. They had laid traps and landmines against the Germans and watched their comrades die horrible deaths. And after the horrific massacre at Sant'Anna di Stazzema, in which Ezio's beloved Angelica was killed, Paolo had tried to comfort him. Over the years, as Ezio became a schoolteacher and Paolo took over a pastry shop and became Little Dino's stepfather, the two men had remained close. But Ezio harbored deeper feelings that Paolo could never understand.

"This is Italy, remember?" Paolo would say. "We live for the day."

"I can't forget what happened."

"Can't or won't?"

"Both."

The narrow Via Bellini suddenly burst into the huge sunlit piazza in front of the Chiesa di Sant'Ignazio, which was empty save for two elderly nuns scurrying to ready the sacristy before vespers. Ezio dropped his box of books on the stone bench opposite the graceful bronze fountain in front of the church and let his weary body rest for a moment. The rose window of the church looked black in the afternoon sun. He could go through those heavy wooden doors to see what it looked like from the inside, but he avoided churches as much as possible. He had not been in a church since his mother's funeral four years ago.

Ezio leaned back and closed his eyes.

"Hey Ezio! Sparrow!"

Ezio smiled as Paolo emerged from the *gelateria* holding Little Dino by the hand. Both licked chocolate ice cream cones.

"Hey Paolo!" Ezio cried as they approached.

"Little Dino wanted some *gelato* so he came to my *pasticceria* and I said I'd get him some."

"Right. Little Dino wanted some *gelato* so he came to your pastry shop and you said you'd get him some. Not you?"

"Me? You know I don't eat ice cream," Paolo said, licking his cone. "Not more than twice a day anyway."

"I hate to tell you this, Paolo," Ezio said as he patted his friend's belly, now starting to sag over his belt, "but it's starting to show."

"Not something you have to worry about." Paolo punched Ezio's hard abdomen.

"Sit," Ezio said. "Finish your ice cream here."

Little Dino found space on the next bench and Paolo lowered his voice. "Thank you for giving Little Dino your book. He won't be able to read it, but I'll read it to him. It will remind me of our old times."

"Don't thank me," Ezio said. "He deserved it."

"How did Little Dino do this year, Ezio? He tries so hard with his homework, but some things just don't come. And he's so afraid of making a mistake. Sometimes he starts to cry and Lucia has to help him."

"He did fine, Paolo. Don't worry about him. Some kids are better than others in some areas. I think Little Dino is going to be a great artist some day. Maybe with paints, maybe with wood, maybe with stone. I don't worry about the quiet ones."

They both studied the boy.

"You know," Ezio said, "he looks more like Dino every day. The nose, the freckles ..."

"And the ears," Paolo whispered.

"Yes, that, too. You've been a good father for Little Dino, Paolo."

Paolo smiled and licked his ice cream.

"How's the shop?" Ezio asked.

"Pretty busy. People seem to like the new chocolate *cannoli* we're making. And you? Happy to have the summer off? God, I would love to have a summer off."

Ezio could feel Paolo staring at him. Paolo had asked him recently about the lines under his eyes and why he didn't smile much anymore. Ezio brushed it off. "The life of a schoolteacher," he said.

"Sparrow, Sparrow, Sparrow," Paolo said. "It'll be good to see you more often now."

"Owl, Owl, Owl." Both men smiled, remembering the names they had used when they were fighting the Germans in the hills. There was no need to talk about it. Instead, they focused on Little Dino, absorbed in his ice cream cone and swinging his legs.

"Any plans for the summer, Sparrow?"

"No. Maybe read a little."

"That's all?"

"Maybe go biking a little."

"But mostly stay in your rooms?"

"Yes."

Paolo tried to look into his friend's eyes, but Ezio had shut them tight.

"Do you think that's a good idea?"

Ezio didn't answer, just kept his eyes closed.

"Hey," Paolo said. "I have an idea. Want to help me in my *pasticceria*? I could use some help. Really. People take vacations. It's very busy in summer."

Ezio laughed. "Can you see me making *connoli* or *biscotti* or, what are they called, the flaky ones?

"*Mille foglia.*" Paolo laughed, too. "Yeah, I guess you're not smart enough to work in my pastry shop."

"Well," Ezio said, "you know what they say, those who can, do, and those who can't, teach."

"All I know, Sparrow, is that Little Dino and all the other kids are lucky to have you as a teacher."

They were silent for a long time. In the middle of the square, the statue of the town's most famous son, Francesco Reboli, who helped Garibaldi lead an army into Austria in 1866, glowered under a sheet of pigeon droppings.

"Have you ever noticed," Ezio said, "how many statues Italy has erected for military heroes? They're in every city and village."

"I haven't traveled that much," Paolo said. "I guess I've never noticed."

"War. That's what all these statues memorialize. War."

Paolo, afraid Ezio was going to start another rant about how everyone needed to remember what happened ten years ago, changed the subject.

"So," he said, "did Little Dino ask you to dinner Sunday? And you're coming, right?"

"Wouldn't miss it. Thanks."

"Roberto's coming over from Florence and Adolfo's coming up from Pisa."

"Roberto still working?"

"You know Roberto. He works four or five weeks and then says he wants to take some time off. Adolfo's doing well at the university, though. Now he says he wants to be a teacher like you. You know you're his hero."

Ezio allowed himself a small smile. Maybe he'd had some influence. "It'll be good to see them again."

The two old friends stretched their legs in the sun. Paolo finished the cone and popped the tip into his mouth with an elaborate gesture. "Maria's bringing chicken."

"Love Maria's chicken."

"Rosa's bringing her ravioli. Marco's coming, too. And Annabella's bringing something or other."

"Wait. I thought this was going to be just your family."

"We thought we'd get the Cielo *gruppo* together."

"The *gruppo*? Really?"

As Paolo looked intently in the other direction, Ezio thought again how fortunate he was to have *il gruppo di Cielo* in his life. These were the people who offered support even if they didn't understand him.

It all started during the war when German SS troops ordered Sant'Antonio evacuated and all of the villagers fled to old houses in the hills. Those who had gone to a farmhouse called the Cielo, which meant heaven, found it instead to be a purgatory. Yet they learned to put aside the petty conflicts they'd had in the village, endured a Nazi raid, and watched terrified as a band of partisans fought German soldiers just outside. Ezio was one of those partisans.

But not all of the villagers survived, and when they came together, they never spoke about what they had suffered. A small embrace, a knowing glance, a hand tightly grasped were all that were needed to remember those times.

For the last ten years, the ten or so remaining neighbors who had been trapped in the Cielo got together for a party on the anniversary of their liberation. At first, it was at Rosa's house, but lately it had been at Paolo and Lucia's.

"But this isn't the anniversary," Ezio said. "Everyone left the Cielo in September. This is only June."

"We just thought getting together would be nice." Paolo still didn't look at his friend.

Ezio put his hand on Paolo's shoulder. "All right, Paolo. Tell me. Why are you and Lucia having all these people over? Just to see me? To talk to me?"

"Just a little get-together."

"Paolo ...?"

"All right, all right." Paolo turned to face him. "Some of us are worried about you."

Ezio's eyes blazed and he was about to push his friend away. But then he put his hand on Paolo's arm.

"I'm worried about me," he said softly.

For a while, they stared at the statue in the center of the piazza. The elderly nuns emerged from the church. Shopkeepers around the piazza pulled metal gates away from windows and doors. Knowing someone would soon provide dinner, a gathering of pigeons swooped down on the cobblestones. Reboli returned to life. Ezio looked over at his friend.

"What brought this on, Paolo?"

Paolo hesitated. "It's just something you said to Maria last week. Probably nothing at all. And you know how Maria gets excited about things and lately she doesn't hear very well either."

"What was I supposed to have said?"

Paolo lowered his voice. "You told her about the headaches you've been having lately. And the nightmares. And then you said something about wishing you could join Angelica. I'm sure you didn't mean it. Right? Right?"

Ezio stared at the Duomo's rose window. He wondered if the colors looked brighter at sunset. He wondered who designed the window, in fact, who designed the church. Four hundred? Five hundred years ago? Where did they get the marble? Pietrasanta, probably. Or maybe Carrara. One of those places.

"Ezio? Sparrow? Did you hear me?"

Ezio closed his eyes. "I heard you."

"And?"

"Paolo, I don't know what to do. Sometimes I get so very sad. I can't sleep. I have these terrible headaches."

"More now than before?"

"Yes."

"Why, Ezio? Why now?"

"I wish I knew, Paolo. Part of it is because no one seems to remember the war anymore ..."

Paolo grimaced but didn't say anything.

"But lately I'm reminded of Angelica so often. I pass a woman wearing a yellow dress. Or one with long blond hair. Or one holding the hands of two little boys. Or when I smell the smoke of a cigarette. Or when I hear hunters firing rifles in the hills. The other day I saw a black cloud rising over that hill toward Sant'Antonio and I ran up to see what it was. It was only some farmers burning some brush. Everywhere. The massacre is everywhere for me.

"And then sometimes I have the same nightmare. I see the smoke, the fire. I hear the gunshots. But I can't do anything about it. It's like there's a glass wall in front of me. I pound on it but it doesn't break. And then, the strangest thing, there's always a man standing by watching, and then he runs away."

Paolo pointed to two windows above his *pasticceria*. "Have you seen the *dottore* again?"

Ezio hesitated. "I've seen him. He doesn't know what to do. He doesn't know if the headaches cause the nightmares or the nightmares cause the headaches. He gave me some new medicine. All he told me was to avoid stress."

"Ah, stress. Like maybe you're obsessing over ..."

"Don't lecture me again, Paolo."

"I'm sorry, Ezio."

"Thank you, Paolo. But there's nothing you can do."

Paolo sighed. Once again, he felt helpless. Maybe the gathering Sunday would help.

"Well," he said, "I'd better get back to the shop. Little Dino!"

Somehow, Little Dino had climbed off the bench and was nowhere in sight.

"This happens all the time," Paolo said. "He just goes off on his own, disappears. He can be so shy and quiet, but sometimes he can be so stubborn, so determined to do something."

"He can't have gone far," Ezio said. "Little Dino! Where are you?"

After Ezio and Paolo scoured the piazza, with Paolo becoming frantic, they found Little Dino at the portico of the church, examining a pillar.

Paolo patted him on the head. "Little Dino. What are you doing now?"

"Look, Papa, see how this crack goes up and up and then it disappears. And there's another one on this other pillar. Look, I'll show you."

"You're always finding things I never even see," Paolo said, pulling out a red handkerchief and wiping chocolate ice cream from the boy's face. "Ready to go home? Your mother will be waiting for you."

Ezio shook the boy's sticky hand. "Have some fun today, Little Dino."

Paolo grabbed his friend's shoulders. "You're always telling other people that, Ezio. Why don't you have some fun yourself?"

Ezio forced a smile. "I'll try, Paolo. I'll try."

Ezio gave his friend an extra long embrace.

"Thank you, Paolo. Till Sunday."

Paolo and Little Dino walked hand in hand back to Paolo's shop. Ezio went back to the bench.

Across the cobblestones, Signora Antonelli and Signora Piazini crossed the piazza. The ancient widows, swathed in black dresses, black stockings and black shoes, chattered away until they saw Ezio. Then they looked at him sadly and walked on.

"*Povero sfortunato*," he heard one whisper. "Poor boy."

He knew what the gossips were thinking. Why wasn't he married? Such a nice man, such a good teacher for the children. Yet he has no woman to take care of him. He needs a woman. Now if he could only get interested in Signora Antonelli's daughter, or Signora Piazini's daughter, or Signora … They would make a good match, have lots of children. But sometimes he looked so sad …

There was a time a few years ago when it seemed as though every woman in Reboli was determined to match her daughter with this handsome eligible teacher. Having failed, most now just shook their heads and smiled a sad smile when they saw him.

"*Povero sfortunato*."

Everyone in Reboli knew about Ezio's loss at Sant'Anna. Many had themselves lost relatives and friends there. But that was eleven years ago. And the war ended more than ten years ago.

Ezio watched the women disappear down Via Bellini. He hoisted the box of books onto his shoulder again and made his way home.

CHAPTER 3

▼

Ezio climbed the stone stairs to his rooms on the third floor. Except for Signora Rezzo down the hall, who seemed to have many male visitors into the night, it was a quiet place and he didn't have to talk to anyone except for a pleasant "*buon giorno.*"

Putting down his box of books, he opened the windows to let in some air and sunlight. In the distance, he could see the bell tower of the Chiesa di Sant'Ignazio. The rows and rows of red tile roofs glimmered, and the hills beyond them shone lush and green. Across the alley, the sign for the *farmacia* blinked, two of its letters missing. Vespas screeched and roared. Below the window, an old man shouted at a boy who was making a racket with a stick and ball.

He reached under the bed. The brown cardboard box once held dress shirts his mother had given him when he began teaching. Now, it was filled with his wartime journal, neatly labeled folders containing newspaper clippings and a long ivory-colored envelope.

As he did about once a week, Ezio sorted out the box. He knew he wouldn't find anything new, but he felt comforted holding reminders of something he knew he could never forget.

The journal was the basis for *A Time to Remember*. During the two years that he led a band of partisans in the nearby hills, Ezio tried to write something every day. He wrote about how they desperately needed arms and supplies, how they cut the Germans' communications systems, how they diverted railroad tracks. He wrote about his brave comrades, Paolo and Dino and all the rest. He wrote about their confrontations with the Nazis, especially the final one in which Dino was killed.

No one wanted to publish the book, so he found a small press in Florence and had a hundred copies printed. He gave some to his father and some to libraries, but he knew that almost no one wanted to read about the war anymore.

Ezio put the journal aside and started going through the gray folders.

The folder labeled *Tenth Anniversary*. Inside were a half-dozen tattered newspaper articles dated 12 August 1954.

"A few people remembered the tenth anniversary," Ezio thought. "How long will they remember?"

He quickly read one of the clippings: SS officers descended on Sant'Anna di Stazzema from four directions. People herded into basements, into stables, into barns. Everyone killed, every building set on fire. More than one hundred women and children forced into the square in front of the church. Everyone shot to death, their bodies burned. Total of five hundred sixty slaughtered. A memorial has been created.

Ezio put the folder down, paced to the window, watched the Vespas for a while and then returned to the box.

The folder labeled *Reder*. A paper clip fastened a half dozen clippings: "Major Walter Reder captured by United States Army troops for ordering the massacres at Sant'Anna di Stazzema and Marzabotto. Reder released because of war injuries. Reder arrested again, held in internment camp in Germany. Reder extradited to Italy. Reder tried by military court in Bologna. Reder sentenced to life imprisonment in Gaeta fortress prison on coast north of Naples. Former SS comrades gather hundreds of thousands of petitions seeking his release ..."

"Bastard! Let him rot in prison." Ezio put the clippings neatly back. "They get the majors and the colonels. What about the soldiers who did the shooting? What about the bastards who burned the houses? And what about the Italian Fascists who helped them? Where have the Fascist judges hidden all the records? When are we going to have justice?"

The folder labeled *Resistance: Statistics*. At the end of the war, one clipping said, more then 185,000 men and women were involved in the Italian Resistance.

Ezio was proud of that figure, but then read on: "There were 29,000 casualties."

"Eleven from my little *banda* alone," he thought.

The folder labeled *Retribution*. Mostly, the clippings were about an incident in a jail at Schio, in far northern Italy, on July 6, 1945. A group of masked men, later identified as former partisans, broke into the place and killed fifty-four people, most of them jailed only because they were supporters of Fascism.

"Yes, but what else was going on then?" Ezio said aloud. "There was civil war. These partisans were seeking justice!"

The folder labeled *Fascists: Amnesty*. Not much was in it. An editorial from a Communist newspaper from 1946. "We ask why our leader, Togliatti, has granted a blanket amnesty, except for prominent Fascists, for the crimes they have committed. Does no one remember how these Fascists helped the enemy throughout the war? How they murdered civilians and our comrades in cold blood? How they massacred hundreds of people at Marzabotto and Sant'Anna di Stazzema? Does everyone have amnesia?"

"Yes!" Ezio cried. "Yes, everyone has amnesia."

Ezio threw the clippings down. Once again he was tempted to tear them up, but he put them back into their folders.

"Throw those clippings away!" Paolo had told him more than once. "You have to forget!"

He opened the long envelope and took out a piece of pink paper, torn in three places. There was only a faint fragrance lingering. That's why he kept it in the envelope.

> 10 August 1944
>
> My darling,
>
> I don't know where you are now, so I'm sending this to my mother. I hope you are able to get it sometime. I know she will keep it for you because she knows all about you and me. Remember when you met her here last? At Easter? She may not approve of what we are doing but she would do anything for me.
>
> Oh, Sparrow, I am so afraid. Everyone here is frightened, and Sant'Anna di Stazzema is so crowded now. People have come from all over because they think it's safer here than anywhere else. You know how high in the mountains we are. Now we are told the Germans want us to evacuate. But of course we will refuse. Where would we go?
>
> We've also heard the Germans found out that we were helping you and your *banda*. We hear they plan some sort of retribution even though you have all left. We don't know what it will be, but everyone has some sort of theory. Some people think it will be terrible. I don't know. Do you think it will be? Oh, Sparrow, I hope not. Then you can come back and we can be together again.
>
> Little Carlo and Nando say they miss you, too. I haven't heard from their father. I can only assume he was killed in Russia.

Sparrow, if something does happen to me I want you to remember our love always. Remember our walks in the woods and remember the times in the dark of night when we shared so much. I know you will.

Yours always,
Angelica

"If something happens to me. If something happens to me." And two days later, the worst possible thing did happen to her. "And where was I? On some distant hill. I should have gone back. I should have gone back." Ezio wiped his eyes and put the letter back in the envelope.

He stroked the copper wire bracelet on his right wrist. The wire was smooth and glistened from so much rubbing over so many years. He remembered the hilltop where he had found strands of copper wire and where he and Angelica wove bracelets and exchanged them. He remembered the night when they made love and their bracelets became entangled. They were laughing so hard they had to stop. He never took his off.

Many of his friends urged him to look for another woman. He tried a few times. In each case, he kept comparing the woman to Angelica and the relationship ended.

Finally, Ezio picked up the folder marked *Occhio unico*. The cover was decorated with a huge eye.

"Little Dino could have drawn this better than I did," Ezio thought. The folder was empty.

"Old One-Eye. Someday we will have justice!"

Ezio put the cover on the box and held it on his lap. He remembered what Paolo had said when he told him about the box.

"A bunch of clippings about the massacre? What are you saving them for? Is this a Revenge Box?"

"No, no, it's just ..."

"What?"

"I just can't give them up. They mean too much to me."

"Ezio," Paolo said, "let it go. Please. This isn't good for you. Let it go."

Considering that the people in *il gruppo di Cielo* now considered him suicidal, he would never tell anyone, not even Paolo, about his last conversation with his doctor.

"Ezio," the doctor had said, pulling up a stool so that he could face him, "you know that I've been treating you for, let's see, about eight years. Sometimes the medication seems to help the headaches and the nightmares, sometimes not. I wish I could do more."

"I appreciate what you've done," Ezio had said.

"Well, I think I have some good news. Last week I went to a lecture in Lucca. It was given by a new doctor who is just setting up his practice. He's a young man, but very bright and he seems very compassionate. I talked to him afterwards, not about you, of course, but in general terms about someone with your condition."

"That was very kind of you."

"Ezio, I think you should see this doctor. I can give you his address and you can make your own appointment. Tell him I referred you to him."

"And what would he do different from you?"

"You've talked to me about your feelings of guilt, Ezio. How you left this woman you loved because you wanted to protect her. How you didn't go back to her when you learned there would be some sort of violent action. And now you feel guilty. I think that's natural, and I wish I could go through those feelings with you, that I could help you. I can't. I don't have the training. But this doctor has studied in New York. He has made certain things his specialties. His lecture was about how feelings of guilt can cause physical ailments, things like headaches. I found it very interesting. You know, a lot of advances have been made in psychiatry in recent …"

"Psychiatry? You think I'm crazy?"

"No, no, Ezio, no. Sit down, please. Of course I don't think you're crazy. But I think you need more help than I'm able to give you. I don't know what new treatments they have. I know they rarely use electroshocks now. Instead …"

Ezio was halfway down the stairs before the doctor could finish his sentence.

Now, he sat on the bed and gripped the box. "I'm not crazy! I know I'm obsessed. I admit that. But it's because I lost my great love. And, yes, it's because of guilt. I know I should have stayed there. And I know I should have gone back to protect her. But I didn't. I didn't. I know all those things. I don't need a damn doctor to tell me that. What the hell would he do anyway? This isn't my 'Revenge Box.' How can I take revenge if there's no one out there to avenge? How? How?"

Except *Occhio unico*, of course, and he was in Germany.

Ezio put the box back under the bed. His head was throbbing. He closed the shutters, put a cold damp towel on his forehead and lay on the bed. He soon drifted to an anxious sleep. At first he mumbled, "No, no, no."

And then: "If only … if only …"

CHAPTER 4

▼

Balancing a gigantic bowl of steaming ravioli in one hand and leading her husband, Marco, slowly by the other, Rosa Tomaselli was the first to arrive at Paolo and Lucia's for Ezio's party.

"I just brought a few ravioli," Rosa said after kissing Lucia lightly on both cheeks. "I don't have much time to make them anymore."

"A few?" Lucia said, taking off the hand towel that covered them. "Rosa this looks more like three dozen."

"Actually four."

"*Grazie*, Rosa. Everyone says you make the best ravioli in Sant'Antonio."

Rosa brushed aside the compliment, but she knew it was true. She used nutmeg when all the other women in the tiny village used cinnamon. It was a recipe she inherited from her mother, who got it from her mother and who knows who before that. Even in a village as small as Sant'Antonio, her recipe was a secret.

"*Grazie* to you, Lucia. And thank you for inviting us all. It's good for *il gruppo di Cielo* to get together when it's not the anniversary. But I don't know if we can help Ezio. I think he has to work this out by himself. *Povero sfortunato*."

"Paolo talked to him the other day. Paolo is more worried now than ever."

Rosa sighed. "When will he ever forget? *Povero sfortunato*."

Rosa led Marco to the overstuffed chair near the window so that he could see the new house being built down the street. When the new family moved in, Sant'Antonio would have eighty-four residents. Slowly, after ten years, Sant'Antonio was returning to life. New chestnut trees were replacing those destroyed by bombs along the highway. Two new houses were just finished at the eastern end. Leoni's *bottega* had a new sign and Manconi's butcher shop a new awning. But shells of houses, deep holes and shattered trees still scarred the nondescript little village.

Rosa put Marco's cane at his side, combed his hair and straightened his glasses. She smoothed the apron over her blue dress.

"*Allora*. Another beautiful sunny day. Everything all right here, Lucia? How's your Mama? Your Papa?"

"Mama's fine. She's upstairs with Papa."

"Every time I look up, I see him looking out the window."

Lucia took plates and glasses down from the shelves. "He doesn't say much. Mama tries to get him to talk but he doesn't seem interested in anything."

"Gina's a saint, Lucia. And so are you. Running the house. Doing all the cooking, the cleaning, the garden."

"I don't mind. Paolo even does some cooking when he comes home. Little Dino helps me when he comes home from school in the afternoon. He's very good at cleaning and weeding."

Lucia looked out the kitchen window and watched her husband and son under the huge mimosa tree. Little Dino had put a bunch of flowers on the bench and was engrossed in drawing them on a sheet of white paper. Paolo sat across from him, handing him crayons.

"We'll be eating soon!" Lucia called out to them.

Where does Little Dino get that talent? Lucia wondered. Certainly not from me. Well, maybe his father did have some artistic abilities. She remembered when he found some poppies and *strigoli* and carefully wound them into a beautiful crown for her after they had made love near the stream in the forest.

"My princess," he said, and he bowed. "And I'm your prince."

That's how Dino always talked. No wonder she fell so hard for him. But she hadn't known him long enough, just a few months in the summer of 1944, to discover what he was really like.

Paolo was there when she first met Dino. She was only sixteen and Dino was barely eighteen. She was looking out the upstairs window of the Cielo, where her family and others had been trapped after the evacuation from Sant'Antonio. Dino and Paolo had deserted the Italian army, and it was raining. Paolo had hurt his foot, and so she found an old sheet, no, a nightgown, and bandaged it. Dino liked her name. He said Lucia was like a light in the window. She liked his freckles.

And then, after the secret meetings in the woods, Dino was gone. Ran off with Paolo to join the partisan *banda* led by Sparrow. And then her young prince was killed in a battle between the partisans and the Germans right outside the farmhouse.

Little Dino was born seven months later.

Lucia opened a drawer and pulled out knives and forks. Years ago, memories of Dino would have made her angry. Now, she had no more bitterness. And when she visited his grave, near that farmhouse on the hill, she sometimes brought *strigoli*. If she felt regrets about losing her teenage years to motherhood, she did not talk about them to anyone, not even her mother. And she had come to love Paolo very much.

"*Permesso?*" Maria Ruffolo was at the door.

"Let me, Lucia." Rosa was already at the door and helping her friend over the threshold. Rosa may have been small, but she had the strength of someone who could strangle chickens as easily as she could roll out pasta dough. "Slowly, slowly, Maria. It's all right. Hold on to my arm. Take your time."

Gasping for breath, Maria eased into the chair opposite Marco, who was now dozing off, his head on his chest. Rosa wiped perspiration from her friend's forehead and smoothed the gray braid around her head.

"Maria! You should have called and I would have come over to help you! You shouldn't walk all that way by yourself."

Maria lived next door, separated only by a path from Lucia's house.

"My legs get worse every day. *Santa Maria!*"

Slowly, Maria regained her breath and tried to loosen the black cotton dress that was sticking to her robust body. In the last few years, Maria's complexion had become even more spotted, her eyebrows thicker and her mustache more prominent. Yet when she smiled and her eyes glistened, friends thought she was as beautiful as she was fifty years ago.

As always, she fingered the photo, encased in plastic, that hung on a cord over her abundant bosom. The photo showed a young woman and two young boys.

"I made some chicken," Maria told Lucia when she could speak again. "But I couldn't carry it. Could Little Dino go over and get it? It's in the big pot on the stove."

While Little Dino was dispatched, Paolo came in from the back and Gina helped Pietro down from upstairs. Pietro's eyes were vacant, and he said nothing. Pietro had never recovered from the war.

On the surface, Gina looked the same as she had for years. She still wore white peasant blouses and red skirts that reached to the floor. With the help of dyes she found in Reboli, her curly hair was still blond. Her makeup was thicker now, but it couldn't conceal the lines around her eyes, which always seemed tired. The loss of a child during the war and the constant care for her husband were taking a visible toll.

Then another guest arrived. Annabella Sabbatini carried a tray of cookies, which Rosa took after kissing her.

"*Cara mia, cara mia*," they both said, hugging each other. Tall and, as usual, impeccably dressed and manicured, Annabella smiled wanly.

In the midst of all the hugging and kissing and back slapping, no one noticed Ezio slip through the door until Paolo spied him.

"Ah! Here's the guest of honor!" Paolo held Ezio by the shoulders.

Ezio returned the embrace and kissed Lucia. She smoothed his hair and looked hard into his eyes.

"How are you, Ezio? You stay away too long."

"I'm all right, Lucia. Looks like you've invited half of Tuscany today."

"Just *il gruppo di Cielo*, Ezio," Lucia said. "And we're not all here yet. Roberto and Adolfo will be late, but we'll start dinner."

With the pungent smells of ravioli and roasted chicken filling the house, Lucia took command and ordered Paolo and Ezio to carry the dining room table out to the back. "We'll have more room out there."

Outside, under the shade of the mimosa tree, the ravioli and the chicken and the salad made the rounds of the table two, three, four times, and three Chianti bottles were soon empty.

The talk was of new babies and weddings and funerals in the village, of new factories opening in Reboli while Sant'Antonio remained the same, of the priest's sermon last Sunday and the new pasta brands at Leoni's.

What no one talked about was Ezio. There were a few quick questions about teaching and his pupils, but the villagers avoided any acknowledgement of his obsession with the Sant'Anna massacre. How strange, he thought. They ask me here and they all come to make me feel better but they don't want to talk about it. That was all right. He didn't want to talk about it either. He remembered something from a psychology course he took at the university. The avoidance theory. That must be it. They didn't want to talk about his obsession because they couldn't cope with the massacre themselves. Nice theory. Maybe true, maybe not. Or maybe they had been able to put it in the distant past. Unlike him.

How could they ever understand? They had never gone to a village high in the hills where the flames were still smoldering and the smoke was rising and the stench of burned bodies was still overpowering. And where Ezio had frantically clawed through the embers in a fruitless search for his beloved Angelica.

And how could they possibly understand the guilt he suffered? Maybe that new doctor in Lucca would be able to offer an explanation, but Ezio had no intention of finding out.

"Ezio!" It was Lucia. "Are you all right?"

Ezio shook his head. "Sure. I'm fine. Just daydreaming, I guess. Too much of Rosa's ravioli."

Ezio couldn't help smiling at Lucia and Paolo, sitting across from him, with Little Dino silently munching on a chicken leg between them. What a remarkable woman Lucia has turned out to be, Ezio thought. Only twenty-six years old and pretty as her mother. Gina was at the end of the table, spooning bits of chicken into her husband's mouth.

"You know what this reminds me of, Lucia?" Ezio said. "The times we first got together after the war. Remember?"

"I remember, but it's not quite the same, is it?" Lucia said, looking at the other end of the table where there was a similar scene. Rosa was helping Marco cut up a big fat ravioli into quarters but tried to conceal her efforts from the others.

Having declined the chocolate *cannoli* that Paolo had brought from his *pasticceria*, Ezio thought he should spend a little time with Rosa and Marco and pulled his chair next to them.

"Ezio, Ezio!" Rosa said, gripping his arm. "You need to eat more. I can feel your bones."

"All right, all right," he smiled. "I'll try to eat better. How are you, Rosa?"

"Oh, you know. I'm all right." She glanced at her husband.

Ezio raised his voice. "Marco! How are you?"

Marco lifted his head and stared at the man before him. For a moment his eyes seemed to hold a flicker of recognition, but then they were blank again.

Rosa put her hand on her husband's shoulder. "He's the same, Ezio."

"What are you saying?" Marco suddenly shouted.

"I said you were fine!"

"Don't yell at me. I can hear you!"

"You see, Ezio. When I talk normal, he complains that he can't hear me. Then when I raise my voice, he yells at me. *Santa Maria!*"

"You have a lot of patience, Rosa."

"He's a good man, Ezio. This is a terrible thing that is happening to him."

Ezio did not to know what to say to a man who had been so vigorous only a few years ago.

"Do you go hunting?" Marco suddenly shouted.

"No, no I don't," Ezio said.

"I went hunting today! I got some rabbits!"

Rosa smoothed her husband's hair, white and wispy. "He didn't go hunting today," she said softly. "He hasn't been out of my sight all day, all week. Marco, do you know who this is?"

Marco looked at Ezio. Again there was a faint and fleeting hint of recognition.

"It's Ezio, the partisan. Remember up at the Cielo? The farmhouse where we stayed during the war? With the other people from the village? Ezio came to see us."

That was about all Rosa wanted to say about the Cielo and the war. Marco would become nervous if she reminded him of their stay at the farmhouse. She wished she could tell Marco how brave he had been during the German raid, and everything else that had happened there.

"Francesco!" Marco pointed at Ezio.

"*O Dio*," Rosa said. "Now he thinks you are Francesco." She made the sign of the cross and looked nervously for Annabella, who was getting something in the kitchen and fortunately hadn't heard anything.

"No," Ezio said, "I'm …"

"Francesco," Marco interrupted. "You come tomorrow. We go hunting!"

Rosa patted her husband's arm. "Marco, Francesco is dead," she whispered. "He died in the war. Don't you remember?"

Marco looked confused and rubbed his hands frantically together. Rosa wiped some spittle from his chin.

"Ezio, I think Marco is getting upset. I'll take him into the kitchen."

Rosa helped the old man up and into the house, waving to the others as she closed the door.

Ezio sat down next to Maria. "Poor Marco," he said.

"Poor Rosa, too," Maria said. "She's a saint."

Ezio stroked Maria's arm and smiled. "I thought that's what everyone said about you, Maria."

"Well, they shouldn't say that. Just because I pray a lot doesn't make me a saint."

Maria looked down at the photo encased in plastic on her breast. Immediately, tears welled in her eyes. Ezio held her hand and they were silent for long minutes.

Ezio could barely bring himself to look at the photo. Angelica. Maria's daughter. The greatest love he had ever known. Angelica's two boys.

"You know, Ezio," Maria said quietly. "This is all I have left of her. She sent it with that letter I gave you. I suppose I should have given this to you, too, but I can't part with it. I can't part with it."

Maria lifted the photo to her lips and kissed it. She had done this so often over the years that the plastic had worn away.

"It's all right, Maria. I have my memories. I don't need a photograph. I can see Angelica like it was yesterday."

"When I'm gone, you can have it, all right? Is that all right, Ezio?"

Ezio grasped Maria's hand tighter.

"Ezio, you know that I think about Angelica and Little Carlo and Nando all the time. And I pray night and day for them. That's all right for me. I don't have much time left. But you, Ezio. I know how you are thinking about her, too. All the time. That's not good, Ezio. You have to forget. That was eleven years ago. You have to find someone else."

Ezio bent his head to Maria's hands. "I can't, Maria, I can't."

Maria stroked his hair. The others at the table tried not to notice and started quiet conversations among themselves. The shade from the mimosa tree now extended all across the yard. Lucia started clearing the plates and was soon joined by Annabella. Gina helped Pietro, who had remained silent throughout the meal, into the house where she found Rosa washing the dishes. Marco dozed in a nearby chair.

"Pietro and Marco," Rosa said. "Two men old before their time."

"At least you have a husband, Rosa," Annabella said. She did not say it bitterly. It was just a fact.

Rosa put down the dish she was wiping and grabbed Annabella's arm. "Oh, I'm sorry, Annabella. I shouldn't have said that. Forgive me."

"It's all right," Annabella said. "Sometimes I can't get Francesco off my mind."

CHAPTER 5

▼

Lucia's brothers, Roberto and Adolfo, turned up almost simultaneously as the women were drying dishes and Paolo, Ezio and Little Dino were bringing chairs back into the house. Gina rushed to meet them, guiding Pietro by the hand.

"So, you finally come home," Gina said, alternatively kissing and pinching their cheeks. "How long has it been? Four weeks?"

"We were here three weeks ago, Mama," Adolfo said.

"Three weeks! That's a long time," Gina said. "Why do you have to study in Pisa, Adolfo? You don't need all that education. And Roberto, I don't know why you moved to Florence. You could find work here. What's so great about Florence anyway? Sant'Antonio is a nice town. And your father misses you. Come, give him a kiss."

Bending over his cane, Pietro looked up blankly and smiled at his sons.

"Sorry I'm late," Roberto said. "I don't know why that train from Florence runs on time all the time. I had to catch the next one."

"And I'm sure you would have made it if you had gotten out of bed on time," Lucia said, giving her brother a hug.

Roberto and Adolfo exchanged more hugs with Ezio and Paolo.

"We've saved some of Rosa's ravioli and Maria's chicken for you," Gina said. "You can eat out in the back."

While Roberto and Adolfo devoured the ravioli and chicken, Ezio and Paolo leaned back in their wooden chairs and looked at the stars, now filling the heavens beyond the half moon. "There's nothing like a starry night in Tuscany, is there?" Paolo said to no one in particular. Cigar smoke circled into the air.

Roberto swiped a chicken leg from Adolfo's plate. "So, little brother, are you learning anything at that university? You've been there long enough. When are they going to throw you out?"

"As long as I pay my money, they're going to keep me." Adolfo pushed his hand away. "And what about money, Roberto? Are you ever going to keep a job? You don't last more than six weeks."

"Hey," Roberto said. "I was at the plastics factory for three months. Three months! Drove me crazy."

"So what do you do in Florence all day, Roberto?" Paolo asked. "I never thought I'd have a brother-in-law who couldn't make up his mind about what to do with his life."

"Oh, I am very busy, Paolo, very busy. I go for my coffee and sweets in the morning. Then I sit along the Arno. Or I sit in Piazza della Signoria and watch the pretty girls go by. You know, there are more and more foreign girls coming now. You should see those French girls!"

Roberto rolled his eyes.

"Then I go get a *panini*. Then I go home and take a rest. Then I sit some more by the Arno. Or I take a walk to some place in Florence where I haven't been. Then I have something to eat with my friends. And then I go to my favorite *osteria* and play *briscola* and *scopa* and drink some wine or beer or grappa. Sometimes I go with my friends to the cinema. We saw *La strada* the other night. That Fellini. He's a genius. And if I'm lucky, I find a girl to bring home with me. See? I'm very busy."

"You need a vacation," Adolfo said. "I'm getting tired just hearing about this."

"Hey, don't laugh, little brother. I'm happy." He reached for the grappa bottle.

Ezio had to smile when he looked at the two of them, still so much alike. Roberto, now twenty-four, was four years older, but he and Adolfo seemed like twins. Adolfo was always more serious. Roberto was the one who got them in trouble when they were kids.

"And these friends, Roberto?" Adolfo was saying. "They're good men?"

"Of course, of course. Well, most of them."

"And the others?"

"The others. It's interesting what they talk about." He lowered his voice. "I'm pretty sure one of them is a Fascist."

"Roberto," Paolo warned, "why are you hanging around a Fascist? Don't you have better friends than that?"

Roberto leaned over and whispered, "The guy is rich. His father owns the plastics factory. He picks up the check every night."

"Well, just be careful," Paolo said.

Roberto put down his glass.

"I will. But you know the other night this guy had a little too much grappa and you know what he was talking about? He said someone had seen *Occhio unico* again."

"Shit!" Paolo said, slapping the arm of his chair. "Old One-Eye? You're kidding."

Roberto lit another cigar. "That's what he said. I don't know. It's just what he said."

"I don't believe him," Adolfo said. "*Occhio unico* hasn't been seen in years. He went to Germany, didn't he?"

"That's what everybody said. But this guy said someone had seen him."

Everyone looked at Ezio, whose face had grown as white as the tablecloth. But his eyes blazed brighter than the cigar in his hand.

"*Occhio unico* was seen?" he finally said.

"That's what this guy said."

"Where? When?" His voice came from some lower reaches of his body.

"I don't know," Roberto said. "That's all this guy said."

Ezio stood across from Roberto, his hands on the table. "Roberto. Remember how I rescued you and Adolfo when you were lost in the forest during the war?"

"Well, yes, of course."

"Remember how I didn't tell your Mama it was your fault?"

"Yes."

"Well, Roberto, now you can do something for me."

Roberto cowered in his chair. "What?"

Ezio could feel a headache coming on and knew he had to go home and get into a dark room fast. "If I come to Florence, will you introduce me to your good Fascist friend?"

"He's not my good friend, Ezio. He's just a guy who comes to the osteria and pays our bills."

"Well, that's enough. You can point him out, right?"

"Well, sure."

Ezio was sweating. "I'll come tomorrow. Where will we meet?"

"Tomorrow? All right. At Osteria del Ponte. You know where that is?"

Ezio was trembling now. "Yes, of course. In Oltrarno. Near Ponte Vecchio. What time?"

"Uh. 10 o'clock. Could you move away, please?"

"All right. I'll meet you there. Don't be late."

Holding his hand on the side of his head, Ezio ran into the house, said his good nights to the women and opened the door. Paolo stopped him. "Ezio! I don't know what you're planning to do, but count on me to help, all right? After all we've been through, I want to be with you in this, all right?"

Ezio held his friend's shoulders. "Thank you, Paolo. I'm not going to be able to do this alone. I'm going to need help."

Adolfo put his hand on Roberto's arm. "Me, too, Ezio. I'd love to get away from the university."

"I don't know what you're going to do, Ezio, but it looks like something bad," Rosa said, and the other women murmured. "Let us help you, Ezio! And please be careful!"

"Pray, Ezio, pray," Maria called out. "And I will pray for you."

Ezio nodded to the others as he ran down the steps, got on his bicycle and headed for the bridge to Reboli.

"Well," Rosa said as she watched the fleeting figure from the window, "isn't it good that we all got together tonight to help Ezio?"

"Oh, we might have helped him, Rosa," Paolo said. "At least now he's going to do something about this obsession of his."

CHAPTER 6

─────────────▼─────────────

The bike ride from Reboli to the station outside Lucca the next morning took more than an hour, and Ezio almost missed the train to Florence. As usual, it was crowded with students and office workers, old women and babies. He felt better now; with the help of cold towels and a dark room, the headache had gradually passed by morning.

He found the last seat, next to a huge man who smelled of garlic. It was a window seat, and for a couple of hours he could watch the signs for the towns and villages and cities speed by. Montecatini, Pistola, Prato. The Tuscan countryside never looked so beautiful, but Ezio was too absorbed in his thoughts to enjoy it.

Occhio unico was seen. He couldn't believe it. The most notorious Fascist collaborator in all of Tuscany during the war. The man with only one eye who led the SS to Sant'Anna and helped with the massacre. The one who everyone said fled to Germany right afterwards. Was he somewhere near here now? And why?

The train slowed as it entered Florence, finally wheezing to a stop. Stazione Santa Maria Novella bustled with travelers, and Ezio pushed his way out. He didn't know why he took a morning train since he wasn't going to meet Roberto until night. He just wanted to make sure that nothing happened to prevent their meeting, and he wanted to be as close as possible. Besides, it would give him a chance to visit his father. He hadn't seen him since Easter. "Come for a visit," Antonio Maffini had written his son only a month ago. "I miss you."

On the way to see his father, Ezio detoured to Via Cavour and made the stop that was always his first when he returned to Florence. The Museum of San Marco. Even as a child, he found comfort in the Fra Angelico frescoes, and now he stood before the *Annunciation* for a long time, finding peace in the tranquil, if silent, communication between the angel and Mary.

"My angel," Ezio thought. "My Angelica."

Dodging buses and cars and ignoring the red lights, he walked down Via Cavour to the hulking fortress of the Marucelliana library. He climbed the stones steps to the massive reading room. Students filled the long tables and he went to the ceiling-high shelves. There were only a few books recounting the activities of the partisan movement in Tuscany. His own memoir, *A Time to Remember*, looked like it had never been opened.

"I should tell that to Giorgio Pilozi when classes start again," he thought. "The old Fascist would be pleased that it's being ignored."

Ezio walked over to Via Tornabuoni, crowded now with tourists. "Where do people get the money to buy this stuff?" he thought as he looked into a shop window showing men's suits, shirts and ties.

Ten years ago, Ezio had friends who might have thrown a brick through one of those windows. Now, he could only pity the people who bought and sold the expensive clothing, paintings and silverware on this, the most fashionable street in Florence.

Near the Uffizi, he sat on a bench and looked across the river. Ezio remembered his father teaching him to swim in the river when he was a boy, but no one ventured into the murky waters now. With recent rains, the Arno was higher now in summer, and its color a sickly green.

"Some day," his father often said, "the Arno is going to flood again and it's going to be a terrible thing." Others would scoff. "It hasn't flooded since 1844," they'd say. "It's never going to flood again." But every time it rained, Antonio would check on the river.

He should come back to Florence more often, Ezio thought. His father was getting old, and might need help soon. He thought of the last time he saw his mother, a week before she died.

Marita Maffini had never been the same since the war. With her husband fighting with the partisans north of Florence and her son leading another partisan band northwest of Lucca, she was alone. Like everyone else, she suffered through the food shortages and the air raids and then the bombings. But the worst was just before the Germans fled Florence, just eleven years ago, in August 1944. The city was in turmoil. Everyone was told to seek shelter. With her neighbors, she took a few things into the basement of the Pitti Palace and huddled in the dark for days. It was crowded, dank and smelly. There wasn't much food and people were screaming and bickering. Sometimes the Allied artillery was so close she could hear it whistle.

She was never the same after that ordeal. She became frightened of everything and everyone. When her husband returned from the war, she remained in the back of the shop, spending days in bed and refusing to eat the meals Antonio carefully prepared. Year after year, she slowly declined, and she hardly knew Ezio when he last visited. Marita Maffini willed herself to die so often that one day she did.

Ezio never told his mother what happened at Sant'Anna di Stazzema. And he had told only his father about Angelica. War, Ezio thought. No one had been spared. Except, he realized, the Fascists like *Occhio unico* who had collaborated.

Before the war, he could have walked to the Oltrarno on the bridge called Santa Trinita, often considered the most beautiful bridge in the world. The Germans thought otherwise. It was among five they destroyed to prevent the Allies from crossing the Arno. Ten years later, construction of a new bridge had yet to begin. Not all of Florence was recovering like the shops on Via Tornabuoni.

The Germans had left only Ponte Vecchio alone, supposedly because Hitler liked its medieval architecture. Ezio walked across it now, finding the little goldsmith shops busy again. In the middle, the bust of Benvenuto Cellini frowned on the hordes of students who played their guitars and yelled to each other in foreign tongues.

Elbowing his way to the other side, he made sure the Osteria del Ponte was still open. Yes, until midnight, the sign said. He walked along the street named Borgo San Jocobo, turned down Via Presto di San Martino and entered Piazza Santo Spirito. As a boy, this was where he and his friends played soccer in the summer, and he was always late for dinner. Later, they brought their girls here and took them on long walks along the Arno. It was here that they had their first cigarettes, here where they whispered about the things they were doing in their bedrooms.

The piazza was still the center of activity for the neighborhood. An elderly man hobbled across and sat next to an elderly woman on a stone bench. A girl bicycled through to the other side. A young couple played with their baby near the fountain.

Wedged between a shoe shop and a mosaic shop on the opposite side, Maffini Woodworking had been in the family for three generations. But since Ezio had no talent or inclination to continue it, Antonio Maffini was looking for someone to take over the business when, in a few years, he would quietly retire.

Through the open door, Ezio saw his father inside the shop, carefully smoothing a length of pine with a plane. Years after the war ended, people still needed doors and frames, often custom-made to fit spaces distorted by bombs and shells.

"Papa!"

"Ezio! You didn't tell me you were coming! I could have prepared!"

Antonio took off his carpenter's apron and wiped dust and wood shavings from his hair and beard. "Give your father a big hug."

"I'm sorry I didn't let you know, Papa," Ezio said, returning his father's embrace. "I just decided to come."

"Then it must be important. Let's go outside and talk."

There was no need to lock the shop. Antonio could see the door clearly from the bench in the piazza. Antonio looked into his son's eyes. "How have you been, Ezio? You look tired."

"Yes. You know. The same problems."

The two men looked across the piazza at the stark plaster façade of a church that everyone said was begun in the fifteenth century by the great Brunelleschi. No matter that he didn't finish it. Although he lived and worked only a few yards away, Antonio never went inside.

Ezio thought his father had aged since he had last seen him at Easter. His eyes looked tired, and Ezio noticed that Antonio rubbed the side of his neck a lot. "And how are you, Papa?"

Antonio quickly took his hand from his neck. "Oh, a few kinks in my hands now and then. It's harder to use the plane sometimes. My back gets tired standing all the time. And my neck. But you know, I feel good. I've got a lot of work. I'm busy."

"Still haven't found someone to take over the shop?"

Antonio sighed. "No, no one. The young guys today just want to have a good time, find some girls, go to the *osteria*."

Ezio couldn't help think of Roberto. "Are you still lonely?"

"It's been four years now since your mother died. I still miss her. I miss her very much. But I keep busy."

No one could doubt that they were father and son. Ezio was taller now, and still slim. Antonio had developed a small stoop, but his chest and belly remained firm. Both men had black curly hair, strong noses and piercing blue eyes that twinkled when they smiled. Both wore glasses with heavy black frames. While Antonio had a beard flecked with gray, Ezio tried to shave every day.

"I worry about you, Ezio. It's time you found someone. You're thirty-four years old."

"Thirty-five."

"Thirty-five. Ezio, you'll never find another woman like Angelica, you know that, I know that. But there are a lot of beautiful, wonderful women out there."

"I know, Papa. I'm not ready yet."

"*Allora*," Antonio sighed. As the sun began to cast shadows over the piazza, they watched as four boys kicked a soccer ball, much like Ezio and his friends did many years ago. The fountain in the middle looked much smaller now. So did the entire piazza.

"And the headaches? Are you still having them?"

"More often, terrible ones."

"No help from the doctor?"

"No."

"I'm sorry, Ezio. The war did terrible things to you."

"Not just the war, Papa! It was ..." He looked away in silence.

"The massacre. I know, I know."

"And not just the massacre, Papa."

Ezio crouched down and put his face in his hands and his father looked away. He wanted to tell his son again that he had to remove the stress in his life, that he had to forget. But he had said these things so many times that he knew it would make Ezio only more upset.

"You haven't told me yet why you have come, Ezio," Antonio said finally. "You had a reason to come without telling me."

Lowering his voice, Ezio told his father that Roberto had a friend who reported that *Occhio unico* had been seen.

"And I'm going to meet this person at an *osteria* tonight."

"Ezio! No! That can't be true! One-eye is in Germany!"

"That's what he said, Papa. I couldn't believe it either. Maybe it's not true. Maybe this was just a guy who was drunk and said anything."

"But Ezio," Antonio said, "what does this have to do with you? You're not thinking of trying to find him, are you? Oh, Ezio, don't tell your father that."

Ezio turned to look into Antonio's eyes. "Papa, sometimes when I have headaches I have nightmares. I see the fire and the smoke and then I always see a dark figure running away. I was thinking about it on the train. It was *Occhio unico*. The man who helped the SS!"

"Ezio!"

"Papa, don't you see? If I'm haunted by the massacre, if I have these terrible headaches, it's somehow because I know that some of my countrymen were involved. But ever since the war, Italy has let these criminals go free. In effect, we have been saying that it was all right if you helped kill five hundred and sixty innocent people. Is that right, Papa? Is it?"

"No, no, of course it isn't."

"No one wants to talk about it. Every time I try to talk about the massacre and the other atrocities, people turn away or talk about something else. No one wants to get angry about what happened. No one wants to investigate anything."

"The United States Army did."

"Ha! You heard their conclusion. They said it wasn't a war crime because Sant'Anna was helping the partisans and the people were told to evacuate. Well, yes, they had been helping the partisans …"

"Especially one of them."

"Yes, especially one of them. Angelica was my angel. I know what you're thinking. Yes, I want to do this for her, but I want to do it for justice, too."

Antonio looked hard at his son. "Justice, Ezio?"

"Yes, justice."

"Or revenge?"

Ezio thought of the box under his bed.

"Papa, I want to call it retribution."

Now Antonio looked into Ezio's eyes. "And maybe because of guilt?"

Ezio blanched. He knew exactly what his father meant. Antonio and Paolo were the only ones who knew that Ezio's *banda* had left Sant'Anna a few days before the massacre, and even when Ezio learned that the Germans were about to descend on the village, he refused to go back. He had only twenty men and the Nazis had hundreds. He couldn't send his men into what surely would have been a slaughter. But Ezio had never forgiven himself for that.

"Yes, Papa," he said quietly, "guilt, too."

"Ezio, I agree with what you're saying. That was a terrible, terrible thing that happened, and you're right, Italy hasn't done enough to investigate Sant'Anna or the other massacres. But if you start looking for people like *Occhio unico*, it could be very dangerous. There are a lot of people who still sympathize with the Fascists and would do anything to protect them. They still hate the partisans. And you're still a Communist, right?"

"Of course. I take after my father."

Antonio smiled.

"But, Ezio, what can you do? Even if *Occhio unico* is around, he would have a different identity now. What could one person like you possibly do?"

"I can start something. I can get other people to help me. But if no one will, Papa, I will do it by myself."

Antonio looked at his son. "I raised you right, Ezio. But, please, be careful."

CHAPTER 7

▼

The room was so dark, and the smoke so thick, that it took Ezio about three minutes before he was able to make out who, or even what, was inside. Then through the haze he saw in one corner what appeared to be an improvised shrine to Sergio Cervato. The *osteria's* owner had put up not one but three posters of the leading player on the *Fiorentina Serie A* soccer team and draped them with strips of purple and white satin. On the ceiling, he had rigged a spotlight to shine on the tribute.

A shrine in the opposite corner was draped in black, and above the huge photo of eleven smiling soccer players were the words *Torino, la storia immortale*. Ezio didn't need to be reminded of one of the worst days in Italian history. The country's best soccer team, on its way to its fifth straight championship, was wiped out in a plane crash near Turin on May 3, 1949.

Along two tables in the middle, members of what looked like an extended family passed fruit and cheese around in the final stages of their meal. They didn't look like they'd be leaving anytime soon. Ezio counted at least three Nonnas and perhaps two Nonnos, a half-dozen children and a variety of ages in between. One tousle-haired boy ignored his mother's commands and chased a girl around the room.

In a far corner, four elderly men focused intently on their cards. Probably playing *scopa*, Ezio thought. In another, two young couples, oblivious to everyone else, engaged in some pretty heavy petting.

In the fourth corner, Ezio saw Roberto among a group of seven young men who seemed to have enjoyed a few grappas too many.

"Hey, Ezio!" Roberto shouted. "Over here!"

The men could have been Roberto's cousins; all were in their mid-twenties, with short black hair, tight black shirts open at the neck to reveal gold medallions on heavy chains, tight black pants and black shoes.

Ezio thought of himself at that age. Instead of a medallion around his neck, an ammunition belt was slung across his chest. Instead of sitting around drinking grappa in an *osteria* at night, he and his friends were holed up in a cave deep in the Apennine Mountains. Instead of watching girls in piazzas during the day, his band of partisans would be laying traps for the Germans.

These men weren't even teenagers during the war, he thought. What could it mean to them?

He tried to determine which of them could be a Fascist. The introductions went quickly and Ezio soon forgot most of the names.

"This is my friend, Ezio," Roberto said over and over. "He was born here but now he lives in Reboli.

'Reboli?" one of the men asked. "Past Lucca? Near Pietrasanta?"

"Yes, that's the place."

"Do you work there?"

"Yes," Ezio said quickly, "I'm a journalist." He ignored Roberto's surprised stare.

Ezio had decided during his walk from his father's house that he needed a reason to ask questions about Fascists. Briefly, he thought he might pose as a policeman, but many people did not respect the *polizia*. Perhaps he could be a doctor. That would allow him to ask personal questions, but he didn't know what kind of medical questions to ask. Perhaps a priest? No, people would quickly see through that. Or he could tell the truth, that he was a teacher. But people would wonder why a teacher would ask questions about Fascists. No, he would try to fake being a journalist.

"So what paper do you write for?" the man next to Roberto asked.

"It's a small paper," Ezio stumbled. "We are owned by *Movimento Sociale Italiano* so our articles are mainly about the Italian Right, especially in our part of Tuscany." He did not dare look at Roberto, who seemed to be enjoying this very much.

"And what brings you to Florence?" The questioner looked like the oldest of the group. He was the only one who was clean shaven; the others had varying degrees of facial hair.

"Here to see my father," Ezio said. "Just for a visit. But Roberto said I should drop by and meet some of his friends."

Roberto poured another grappa and didn't look up.

"You say you write about the Italian Right," the man said. "Do you mean the new Fascists? Do you write good articles about them?"

"Of course. I've talked to a number of neo-Fascists and have reported on how the *Movimento Sociale Italiano* is gaining strength again," Ezio said. "I'm sorry, what was your name again?"

"Franco."

"Franco." Ezio shook his hand.

"You must have written very interesting articles," Franco said.

A bearded man next to Franco nudged him. "Hey, Franco. Let's not start talking politics again, OK? Let me tell you about that *prostituta* I brought home last night."

"Yeah, Alfonso, tell us about her," four other men shouted. "Tell us …"

"Hey," Roberto interrupted. "No dirty talk in here, all right? My friend Ezio lives in Reboli. He doesn't know what goes on in Florence."

For the next hour, the conversation went from soccer to women to soccer to the new shirts in the shops on Via Tornabuoni to women to soccer to the new Fiat 600 and back to soccer. Bets were taken on the *Fiorentina's* chances in the Italian championship in the next season. Roberto was among five of the eight who bet a week's wages that the *Fiorentina* would take it.

"But you're not even working!" three of the men said.

"Never mind. I'm going to win this bet," Roberto said. "Anyway, by next November, I'll have a job again."

As the night wore on, a few of the men started to drift out the door. "Some of us have to work tomorrow," one of them said pointedly. Roberto paid no attention.

More talk, now slurred and halting, of soccer and women and women and soccer. The extended family had left long ago, with babies and children slung over their fathers' shoulders. The *scopa* players had thrown down their cards and went arguing into the night. The young lovers sought more private accommodations.

Finally, even Roberto got up. "Good night, Ezio. You picking up the check, Franco?"

"Looks like it," Franco said. "Everyone else has fled."

"Thanks, old friend," Roberto said as he stumbled out.

Only Franco and Ezio remained. Neither had drunk much grappa, and the bottle was half empty before them.

"I'd better be going, too," Ezio said. "My Papa might get worried." But he made no effort to leave.

"Let me finish this," Franco said, holding his glass up. "What article are you working on now?"

"Can't tell you much," Ezio said. "But it's the biggest article I've ever written."

"Really?"

"Yes."

Was this guy going to bite? Ezio wondered. His stomach was churning and he was starting to perspire.

"Can you tell me anything more?" Franco asked.

Ezio lowered his voice. "Sant'Anna di Stazzema. The whole story has never come out."

He could feel drops of sweat running down the back of his neck. He silently prayed that Angelica would forgive him.

"Oh, we know that. After it happened, everyone called it a massacre, blamed the Germans. There's a whole other side."

Ezio wanted to get up and throttle the arrogant bastard across the table. What the hell was he talking about? Goddamn Fascists! But he had to get more information.

"Yes." He hoped Franco didn't notice that his voice was shaking. "There's always another side."

The two men stared at each other, each tracing the rim of their glasses with a finger. Shadows made Franco's face look thin, and Ezio noticed a scar from his chin to his right ear. Ezio remained silent, daring Franco to say something. He finally did.

"Do you have all the information you need for your article?"

"Almost. I want to talk to one more person. I know there's a man who took the major part in the activity and I know the damn Communists drove him into seclusion. But now I've heard that he's been seen again. Just have to find him."

"Just that one more person?"

"Yes."

"And then the whole story of Sant'Anna di Stazzema will be told?"

"Yes."

"How do you know he's been seen again?"

Ezio realized that his answer could put Roberto in jeopardy. "Our newspaper has many sources," he said. He looked into Franco's eyes, trying to see if the man believed any of this. He couldn't tell.

More silence. This time broken by Ezio.

"Do you think you know anything about this?"

Franco turned over the medallion of the Virgin Mary around his neck. On the back, the letters MSI.

"So you're a member of the *Movimento Sociale Italiano*?"

"Four years."

"You must be very proud." Sharp daggers were digging into his stomach and Ezio held on to the wooden table so that he wouldn't get up and strike the man.

"It's been one of the best times of my life," Franco said, downing the last of the grappa. "I've met some great people, and I've learned some very interesting information. If only the rest of Italy could realize what really went on during the war. If only …"

"But, don't you see? That's what I'm trying to do." In the back, the *osteria's* owner began to put out the lights. Ezio hoped the darkness concealed how his hands were shaking.

"Is it?"

"Of course. I'm a journalist, and I work for a paper that's sympathetic to the cause. I want to get the whole story out there. People don't know what really happened." Ezio's shirt clung to his chest and back. "If I found this man and told his story, then everyone would know."

In the gathering darkness, Ezio squinted at the man across the table, trying to read his mind. He knew Franco didn't believe his story. Why was he leading him on?

Franco played with his glass some more. "I think I may be able to help you, Ezio."

"Then you'll be able to tell me where I can find this source?"

"I don't have the authority to tell you that. But let me talk to some people. Maybe they will give you a name of someone who can lead you to this man. This is very dangerous, you know. The Communists are looking for this man, too. You're not a Communist, right?

Ezio faked a laugh. "Do I look like a Communist?" His knees were shaking now.

Franco smiled. "I'm certain," he said slowly, daring Ezio to blink, "that Roberto wouldn't have any Communist friends."

"So you'll give me a name?"

"I will get back to you."

"When?"

"Tomorrow."

All the lights in the place were out now.

"What time?"

"5 o'clock."

"Where?"

"Piazza Maria Novella."

Franco pulled a batch of *lira* from his pocket and threw it on the table. The *osteria* owner shoved Ezio and Franco out the door.

After a fitful day in which he alternately paced in the Piazza Santo Spirito and walked up and down the banks of the Arno, Ezio went to the Piazza Maria Novella. He was an hour early.

Under the obelisk to the right of the church, he watched travelers hurry to the train station and shoppers emerge from establishments around the square. Piazza Maria Novella was never his favorite place in Florence. Too crowded, too dirty, too many pigeons. Now there were foreigners everywhere, picking the pockets of tourists who had lingered too long in the seedy bars.

At 5:10, Ezio began to worry. Maybe he should walk around the square. Maybe Franco couldn't see him here.

At 5:20, Ezio walked to the other obelisk.

At 5:30, he began pacing back and forth between the two.

Then at 5:47, he saw Franco emerge from Via Nationale. He saw Franco light a cigarette and then another man approached him. They talked quickly and they both looked over at Ezio. Then the other man vanished. What is going on? Ezio thought. He strode to the edge of the piazza. Franco looked up.

"*Ciao*," Franco said. No apology.

"*Ciao*," Ezio said. "Were you able to find any information?"

Franco reached into his pants pocket and pulled out a slip of paper.

"Here. This man may be able to lead you to the source you're seeking."

When Ezio looked up again, Franco had disappeared into the crowd. As soon as he looked at the piece of paper, Ezio knew he would need help.

CHAPTER 8

▼

It was so late when Ezio returned that his father was snoring loudly in the back room of the shop. He pulled out the cot that Antonio kept in a closet and eased onto its thin mattress. He had been so upset for the last hours that he thought he would never get to sleep. And he didn't. The mattress acquired more lumps, the air became more stifling, and the hourly church bells more deafening as the night wore on.

"*Occhio unico, Occhio unico.*" He couldn't get the name out of his head.

While it was still dark, he quietly unlatched the door and went out into the deserted piazza. The bells in Santo Spirito rang twice. Ezio collapsed onto the same bench he had shared with his father yesterday and stretched out under the moonlight. He must have fallen asleep because when he awoke the first glimmer of sunlight lit the top of Santo Spirito. He hurried back to bed and was dozing again when his father called out to him.

"Ezio! It's after 8 o'clock. Are you going to stay in bed all day?"

Rubbing his eyes, Ezio joined his father in the kitchen.

"Did you sleep well?"

"Yes, Papa, of course." No point in worrying his father.

"And did you meet this man last night? What did he say?"

Ezio recounted his conversation with Franco and retrieved the piece of paper from his pocket. "Look at this, Papa."

Antonio studied the paper. "Amadeo Mazzella? Garfagnana? Ezio, what does this mean?"

"It means that a man who can help me find *Occhio unico* is named Amadeo Mazzella and that this Mazzella is somewhere in the Garfagnana. Maybe One-Eye, too."

Antonio slapped his forehead. "Oh, well, then, my innocent boy, you just go on up to the Garfagnana and yell out 'Amadeo Mazzella, Amadeo Mazzella' and he'll come running down from the mountains."

Antonio shook his head and walked away.

"Papa, I know this isn't much," Ezio called after him. "But it's more than I had yesterday. I know it's only one step, but it's a start! Look, everyone thought *Occhio unico* had fled to Germany. But they didn't know for sure. They just thought that since he escaped from Sant'Anna he must have gone to Germany."

Antonio turned around and pointed a measuring stick at his son.

"All right, let's go through this. First, there must be dozens of Mazzellas around. I know at least four or five right here in the Oltrarno, and one of them is called Amadeo. But he's twelve years old so I don't think he's the one. Second, if this One-Eye is still around, I bet he goes by another name. Third, the Garfagnana stretches for miles up from Lucca. High mountains, forests nobody can get through. Many little towns, many little villages. And all the farms and caves in the mountains. Where could you possibly start?"

"Shit! Shit! Shit! I don't know, Papa! I don't know!" Ezio went out into the piazza, sat on the bench and put his head in his hands. In a few moments, he felt his father's hand on his shoulder.

"Look, Ezio. I understand. I do."

"I don't think anyone can."

"Ezio. You weren't the only one who fought in the war. Remember, as old as I was, I was at Monte Morello."

Ezio lifted his head. "I'm sorry, Papa. I'm just frustrated. I don't know where to start. I need help!"

Antonio thought for a long while, then sat down next to him. "Ezio, let me take you to someone who knows more about all this than I do. His name is Rudolfo. Rudolfo Panetto. He lives near Santa Croce. We were together on Monte Morello with Lanciotto Ballerini."

"Ballerini? The bearded man in the picture on your wall?"

"That one. A hero, Ezio, a true hero. Rudolfo would do anything to honor Ballerini's memory. I will take you there tonight. I have to finish three door frames today."

The bars and cafes around the Piazza di Santa Croce were already crowded when Antonio and Ezio turned down Corso dei Tintori and found No. 5. They climbed the time-worn stairs to the fourth floor of the massive apartment building and knocked on the third door.

"Rudolfo! It's Antonio. Antonio Maffini."

Antonio and Ezio could hear some muffled rumbling, a chair falling over and finally the chain being pulled from the door.

"Antonio! Antonio! Come in, come in! And this is Ezio? *Molto bene! Spendido!* I haven't seen you in so many years. You look just like your papa. Your father is very proud of you, I can tell you that. What a pleasure!"

Ezio shook the old man's gnarled hand. "And it's a pleasure to see you again, sir."

Rudolfo cleared a pile of books from an old leather chair near the window. The room, reeking of cigarette smoke, was cluttered with newspapers, books and magazines. A path had been cleared from the living room chair to the kitchen and to the bathroom. The three settled down, Antonio in the leather chair, Rudolfo on a folding chair and Ezio in a tiny space Rudolfo had cleared on the floor.

Rudolfo turned to Antonio. "Let me look at you, Antonio. You never change. You still look like you did on Monte Morello."

"Oh, I don't think so, Rudolfo. Sixty-eight the last birthday. We were old then, and we're older now."

Antonio had to admit that Rudolfo had changed. In a war that required youth and stamina, he had been about sixty when he joined the partisans and must be well past seventy now. The years since the war had taken their toll. His left leg shattered by a landmine, Rudolfo walked carefully with a cane. But more than that, he had lost weight since the last time Antonio had seen him, and his plaid flannel shirt hung loosely over his pants. He still wore a red bowtie. Antonio had never seen him without it.

"Cigarette?" Rudolfo pulled out a pack from his shirt pocket. The thumb and index finger of his right hand were brown with stains.

"Thanks, Rudolfo, but I've never been able to touch that." Antonio watched as Rudolfo sat back and blew the smoke to the side.

"It's so good to see you again, Antonio. I think about that time so often."

"I do, too, Rudolfo. It seems so long ago."

"Some things I remember. Some things I've forgotten." Rudolfo let the smoke rise to the stained ceiling. He dug through a pile of books and pulled out one with a dark blue cover. "Here, you see, Ezio, I have read your book. Your father gave it to me. It's very good. It tells a lot about what partisan life was like. We must all be grateful that you wrote it."

Ezio smiled. "Thank you, sir."

"You were very brave, Ezio," Rudolfo said. "You saved a lot of people. You helped win this war. Remember that."

"I wish I could have saved more."

"So what brings you here today, Antonio? You've got a reason."

Slowly, Antonio told his wartime comrade about his son's obsession with the massacre at Sant'Anna and how he had heard that *Occhio unico* had been seen.

"*Occhio unico*?" Rudolfo shouted. "You have to be joking! Collaborator *Numero Uno*. Nobody has seen him for years. I can't believe he's still around."

"What do you know about him?" Ezio asked.

"I don't know anything. Just that he has one eye. Nothing more than that. There are lots of stories. That he fled to Germany. Maybe even Argentina. That he's dead. I don't know what to believe. Bastard. I haven't thought of him in years."

Rudolfo watched the cigarette smoke rise to the ceiling. "So what do you want from me? I don't know where he is."

"Ezio actually has been given a name, Rudolfo. Someone who is supposed to know where *Occhio unico* is. Show it to him, Ezio."

Ezio handed the piece of paper to Rudolfo.

"Amadeo Mazzella? Garfagnana?"

"Ezio thinks this man can lead him to *Occhio unico*," Antonio said. "He thinks this Mazzella is somewhere in the Garfagnana. But where? I've tried to explain to Ezio that this is an impossible task. Still, if you know of anyone who can help him, I thought we could do it in honor of Lanciotto. One more thing for him."

Antonio pointed to the photograph on the wall. It was the same poster that hung in Antonio's room. A handsome, dark-haired man with a thick beard stared into the camera as if daring anyone to defy him.

"My last thing, I'm sure."

"Don't talk like that," Antonio said.

"Oh, I know there isn't much time left for me," Rudolfo said. "But let me see what I can find." Pushing papers aside with his cane, Rudolfo limped to a small file cabinet in a corner, unlocked it and pulled out some brown envelopes stuffed with papers and newspaper clippings. He opened the one labeled *Fascisti*.

"Let's see what's in here."

Rudolfo fumbled through the papers and clippings, some of them so fragile they tore when he unfolded them. "I don't think there's anything here," he said, but he continued to open little pieces of paper.

"You've got quite a filing system," Antonio said.

"Oh yes, I know where everything is. Oh, this may be something." He found a slip of paper attached by a paper clip to a report.

"After the war," he told Ezio, "there were many people, former partisans and some other people, who were very active in tracking down the collaborators. This is a list of places where there were active anti-Fascists groups. But now, who knows? Let's see …"

He put his tobacco-stained thumb on each name.

"Pascaglia … no, everyone there has died.

"Camaiore … after Fredi died, no one is interested.

"Bagni di Lucca … no, no one left.

"Pietrasanta … yes, I've heard there are still people there. But, Ezio, I'm sorry. I've lost touch. Or maybe my memory isn't so good anymore. I don't know any names. What you should do is go to the Casa del Popolo. People there will know."

"Pietrasanta," Antonio said. "Only a few miles from Sant'Anna. Of course there would be people there."

Ezio got up. "I'm going. I'm going tomorrow."

"And maybe at the Casa in Pietrasanta," Rudolfo said, "they can tell you more about *Occhio unico*."

CHAPTER 9

▼

Donna Fazzini reluctantly put the book back into her satchel. She was so engrossed in the new novel by Vasco Pratolini that she didn't realize it was almost time to go back to work. Other workers were gathering their things, too. During the siesta she liked to sit in the Piazza del Duomo, one of the loveliest places in Pietrasanta, have a cup of coffee and read. It was always quieter in the shade near the cinema and the Column of Liberty, away from the bustle of the cathedral and the architectural museum. But now it was time to walk the short distance back to the factory.

Inside, she edged through the rows of giant half-finished statues, wooden frames, tables with cutting tools and buckets of marble dust. She rather liked the clean, if pungent, smell that pervaded the vast room. At her work station she put on her cap and pushed it down around her brown curls. She pulled up the collar on her denim shirt and fastened the top button. She was drawing her leather gloves from her overalls when Fabrizio came up from behind and put his arms around her.

"Hey, Donna, you're making progress. I can see two more pieces of the rope. How long is it going to take you to finish it? Ten years?"

"Only two," she said sweetly, pushing him away. "By that time you should have the frame made for your David."

"I take a long time because I'm good. I'm the best marble cutter in all of Pietrasanta," Fabrizio said, pulling on his gloves and moving to a huge block of uncut marble. "Hey, Donna, want to come over to my place tonight? We can have some fun."

"Not tonight, Fabrizio. You'll be too tired."

"Want to bet? I can always get it up for you, Donna."

Donna smiled and pulled out her goggles. She watched the other workers come back into the factory. Men, all of them. She had been working at the

Stupendi Marbleworks longer than any of them, having started during the war when there weren't any men around. If the factory went by seniority, she would have been the foreman, but old Signor Tassi would never let a woman tell fifteen men what to do.

It was the same in all the other marble factories in Pietrasanta. Only a few women were hired to make reproductions of famous statues out of marble from nearby quarries. Marble had been the main industry in the town for centuries and now that the tourists were returning to the seaside resorts, they often ended their trip with a visit to the factories. They would take a small copy home or order a big one shipped.

For the last few days Donna had been having trouble adjusting the nails of the wooden frame so that she could focus on another area of the statue. The Waking Slave was always a hard one to copy, big as life and with many intricate details. Today, the frame seemed in the right place, so with her drill Donna was able to remove more tiny pieces from the ancient marble. She became so involved in her work that she was surprised when she saw the other workers putting their tools aside and cleaning up.

"You sure about tonight, Donna?" Fabrizio called over the three Davids that other workers were reproducing. "We can have fun!"

"I'm sure," Donna said. "Have a good time with Giulietta or whoever you're with tonight."

"You think I'm going to tell you!" Fabrizio laughed.

Donna took off her goggles and glanced at a small mirror hung on the dirty wall. Except for the space around her eyes, her face was as white as the marble of her Waking Slave. "I look like one of those aliens in the magazines," she thought. She took off her cap and shook out her hair. With the others, she clomped around the shop attempting to get the fine dust off her clothes and heavy boots. She finally gave up and headed out the door.

All the other marble factories were closing, too. Piazza del Duomo was suddenly filled with people enjoying Pietrasanta's evening sun or dining under the umbrellas in front of Palazzo Moroni. She crossed the piazza and walked to the outskirts. She liked to walk home through the sprawling cemetery, fascinated by the art that went into the tombstones. She passed quickly by the one with a skull on top, paused before the tearful Madonna, wondered again about the father standing behind his kneeling son and smiled at the sepia photograph of an infant. She stood for a long time before the wall listing Pietrasanta's victims of the war and then knelt at her mother's grave. Marianna Fazzini had died five years ago.

Then, brushing off her overalls, she strode along the dirt road and arrived home in thirty minutes. It wasn't much of a home. Just a converted old stable, actually. The Fazzini family had lived there for three generations, and somehow they didn't mind that it had only two bedrooms, a kitchen and a bathroom. The kitchen was large enough for the gatherings of her father's old partisan compatriots who came once or twice a month to share memories and, more important, new information about people they were tracking.

Since Marianna's death, only Rico Fazzini and his daughter were left at home.

Rico was waiting for her at the kitchen table.

"Late again," he complained. But he was smiling.

"Not late at all, Papa. Actually early. You could have put the soup on if you were that hungry." She kissed her father.

"I just got home from the Casa del Popolo. Anyway, I don't know how to make soup."

"Oh, Papa, you always want someone to wait on you." Donna put down her satchel. She took out a cast-iron pot from under the stove, poured a batch of beans that had been soaking overnight into a pot, added water and lit the fire. She threw in some olive oil, chopped a couple of carrots and two sticks of celery, diced two tomatoes and an onion, and then added garlic and sage.

"We're going to have enough for days," she said. "But I need to wash up first."

The breeze that rustled the curtains on the bathroom windows also brought the smell of pigs from outside. Taking off her dusty work clothes, she could see her father's garden thriving in the hot June sun, the bean and pea plants thick with leaves, the tomatoes ripened to a deep crimson and the corn stalks getting higher. She took her time scrubbing her face, her neck, her arms, her breasts. Not bad for a woman going on thirty-three, she told herself in the mirror.

Wearing a red silk robe, she returned to the kitchen where Rico was smoothing out the checkered tablecloth and putting dishes on the table. He managed to open a bottle of red wine with his right hand. His left arm had been left paralyzed by a German sniper. "Did you get much done today?"

"I was pleased with myself," Donna said. "I think I've solved the problems."

"I can't imagine why people want life-size statues of David or the Waking Slave or the Pieta. What kind of homes do they have in America?"

"Not in their homes, Papa." She scooped the thick soup into two bowls and added chunks of bread. "They put them in their restaurants or gardens and then they can boast to their friends how cultured they are, that they have a real Michelangelo statue from Italy."

"And those people, from New York or New Jersey or wherever they're from, they believe that?"

"People believe what they want to believe, Papa. We're not going to tell them anything different."

"I can't imagine," Rico said, "someone wanting a big statue of David around with such huge hands and feet ..."

"And a tiny ..."

The father and daughter burst out laughing. Rico, who unlike his daughter wasn't afraid to show his emotions, laughed so hard he had tears streaming down his face. "Stupid Americans!" they cried.

"Ah, Donna, you're a good girl," Rico said, holding her arm. "Are you going out tonight?"

Donna smiled at her father. "Not tonight, Papa. I'm going to stay home with you and read my book."

"I'm glad."

Donna was washing dishes and Rico was drying when Rico said, "Luigi was at the Casa del Popolo today. I talked to him."

"You did? You waited until now to tell me?"

"I didn't want to spoil your dinner. He didn't have good news. He's learned that Ferdinando is now in Argentina."

"Damn!" Donna dropped a soapy plate on the floor but it was so heavy it didn't break.

Rico picked it up. "He heard it from Tommaso who heard it from Georgio."

"They're sure? Ferdinando hasn't just gone to Trieste? I thought that's where he was supposed to go."

"They're sure," Rico said.

"Damn! They're still escaping. And we'll never find the big one."

"We can't give up hope, Donna."

"What? We're going to look for him in Germany?"

CHAPTER 10

▼

The rickety bus from Florence to Pietrasanta seemed to stop at every little town and village on the way, and Ezio became more agitated with every passing hour. He knew he was getting closer to the scene he had tried to avoid for eleven years. Once, three months after the massacre, he and Maria had taken the same bus, intending to go to Sant'Anna to see if there was any remnant of Angelica's home. But when they got to Pietrasanta, they couldn't bear to go to the village, and took the next bus back to Sant'Antonio.

By the time the bus neared Pietrasanta, Ezio could feel another headache coming on and he began to sweat. An elderly woman offered to get him a drink of water at the stop at Camaoire and he took it gratefully. He closed his eyes when the bus passed the road leading to Sant'Anna.

When they arrived at the dingy bus station, it was almost morning and he had to settle for a room in a shabby *pensione* a few streets from Piazza del Duomo. The place was small and had only four rooms to rent. His was in the back, so close to the alley he could smell the garbage piled up outside. The water was cold and the bed lumpy, but he was too tired and sick to complain about anything.

He closed all the curtains and put cold damp towels on his head. He waited and waited, dozing off occasionally.

And then a nightmare. The worst he had ever experienced. The flames, the smoke, the smells. All magnified. He could hardly see Angelica and the boys. There was a thick wall of glass in front of them. He pounded on the glass, but it wouldn't break. He screamed, but there was no sound. He could see a dark figure at the side, watching. Then the figure ran away. And Ezio awoke, soaking on his lumpy bed.

He realized that he had forgotten his pills so he tried to remember what the doctor said. Count. Slowly.

One. Two. Three. Four. Five. Six.

And he tried to breath normally.

One. Two. Three.

Gradually, the pain eased, and he opened the shutters to a gloomy day. Somehow, he had made it through the night and much of the next day, and it was now late afternoon. He had to get some air. He pushed his way out of the room and threw his heavy room key on the desk where the elderly clerk was absorbed in a magazine featuring barely clad women.

"Do you know where the Casa del Popolo is?"

The clerk looked up and eyed Ezio for a long minute.

"Via Fumina."

The old man returned to his magazine, but as soon as Ezio went out the door he picked up the telephone.

It was raining softly and Ezio held his face up to receive the cool drops. He was still in a daze but saw that the streets led to the piazza. Narrow streets with white dust on the pavement. He remembered that Pietrasanta was famous for its marble factories. He'd read that Michelangelo thought the marble at Carrara was better, but he used some from here.

He looked in one grimy window, amazed as the workers chipped away at huge chunks of marble to make copies of famous statues. The David. The Pieta. The Waking Slave. He watched one of the workers who was smaller than the others, even feminine.

After wandering into the piazza in front of the Duomo, he found Via Fumina and almost tripped on its cobblestone pavement. The Casa del Popolo was just a storefront, and it looked dark inside. But when he opened the door, he found a dozen men seated around tables in the huge dining room. It was near the kitchen, and the strong smells of garlic, tomatoes and smoked cod spread throughout the room.

But the focus now was not on food. Through clouds of cigar and cigarette smoke, Ezio could see a tiny television set on a table at the far wall. It screeched and sputtered, and white lines frequently obliterated shaky figures on the screen. Silently, the men leaned forward. They could have been in church.

"What is this?" Ezio whispered to a man standing near the door.

"It's something called *Double Your Money*," he said, "and the people on the show are trying to answer questions and make a lot of money."

"Who's that man?"

"His name is Mike Bongiorno, he's the host. Everyone in Italy knows him."

"Not me."

"This show is so popular everything stops when it's on. It's incredible."

"I'm glad I live in Reboli," Ezio said. "We don't even have television there yet."

"You live in Reboli?" the man said. "Well, welcome to Pietrasanta."

The man took him into the adjoining room where posters on the wall made clear that this place was built by and for Communists. Photos of Communist leaders and of demonstrations lined the walls, a small display of weapons used during the war was in a glass case and a plaque honoring partisans who had died hung in a flag-draped shrine. Off to a side was a drawing of a man wearing a knitted cap and dark eyeglasses. He had a beard and long hair. Underneath, the words *Occhio unico*. It was the poster Ezio had seen in other Casas throughout Tuscany since the war.

"My name is Rico, Rico Fazzini," the man said. He shook Ezio's hand.

"Ezio Maffini. I just got here last night."

"Beer?" Rico pulled a bottle down from the shelf behind the bar.

"Thanks."

"They call me the manager here. That means I pick up empty beer bottles and sweep the floor."

Ezio liked the looks of this man who reminded him so much of his father. Tall, curly black hair flecked with gray, a mustache that drooped down to his chin. Ezio noticed, however, that the man's left arm appeared useless.

"Sit down," Rico said. "You look tired."

"I guess I am a little. Long bus ride. Didn't sleep well last night at the *pensione*."

They settled into a booth near the bar.

"Nobody sleeps well in a *pensione*."

Rico turned so he could face Ezio, letting his left arm lie limply in his lap. "The arm? A little souvenir of the Germans. I guess we all have souvenirs of the war."

"Yes." Ezio took a drink and set his bottle down. "Yes, we do."

Rico stretched back in the booth. "I was in a *banda* just west of here. There was some terrible fighting about eleven years ago, just this time. The Germans occupied Pietrasanta and we didn't liberate it until September 1944. This happened then. A German sniper. Up on a rooftop just as we were coming down that street over there."

Ezio told Rico that his father was also in the Resistance and had served with the legendary Lanciotto Ballerini north of Florence.

"Ballerini?" Rico slapped the table with his good right hand. "No! He's my hero! Your father fought with Ballerini? Ezio, it's an honor to meet you!"

Ezio said Ballerini was his father's hero, too, and then casually mentioned his own *banda*.

"You led a *banda*?"

"Just a small one," Ezio said. "We had a lot of confrontations with the Germans, the SS even. We lost some good men. I lost some good friends. We weren't far from here in August 1944. Near Sant'Anna di Stazzema."

"A terrible tragedy," Rico said. "We lost my brother and his entire family, my wife's sister and her entire family, and so many other people that we knew."

"Everything ended for me at Sant'Anna."

Rico reached over and held Ezio's arm. "You don't have to talk about it if you don't want to."

"I lost ..." Ezio couldn't continue.

"Someone very special?"

"Yes." Ezio fingered the wire bracelet on his wrist.

"I'm sorry."

"I can't talk about it."

"I understand."

Ezio closed his eyes and Rico was silent. The men in the next room whooped as a contestant apparently won a considerable amount of *lire*.

"I was told to come here," Ezio finally said, "by a man in Florence. That's where my father lives. Well, it's a long story. Anyway, I was told that people here at the Casa del Popolo might be able to help me."

"Help you?"

Ezio paused to make sure the men in the next room were still absorbed in the television program and lowered his voice.

"It's about *Occhio unico*."

They both glanced at the poster on the wall and Rico quickly leaned forward. "What? What did you say?"

"One-Eye, yes. I think I have some information."

"What kind of information?" Rico was breathing heavily.

"He's been seen."

"No! He's in Germany!"

"I'm told he may be in the Garfagnana."

Rico grabbed Ezio's hand. "I don't believe this. Ezio, he's in Germany. The monster fled after the massacre. We all know ..."

"Are you certain?"

"Well, no, but everyone has always said ..."

Ezio started to tell Rico the story of his trip to Florence and how he had obtained this information, but Rico interrupted him.

"Wait! Don't say anymore. This is too important and I'm too excited. I want my daughter to hear this, too. Oh, my boy, you don't know what this means to me. To us. My daughter will be so excited. And the others here."

Rico's eyes were filled with tears. He gripped Ezio's hand even harder.

"Come," he said. "We'll go to my house now. Donna should be there. And tomorrow you need to talk to the others. They're not here now, they go to bed early. They don't even stay for *Double Your Money.*"

Rico put the beer bottles away and told the men in the other room that he was leaving. They should lock up.

"Imagine," he said as he guided Ezio out the door. "*Occhio unico!*"

CHAPTER 11

▼

Donna Fazzini was surprised that her father was not there when she got home. He must be staying late with his friends at the Casa del Popolo, she thought. That was all right. It gave her time to clean up and change before she started dinner.

Her hair down and wearing her red silk robe, she had put the bean soup on a low burner to warm up and gone back to her Pratolini novel when she looked out the window and saw her father walking up the path with another man.

"Great," she said, putting down the book. "Who's he bringing home for dinner this time?"

But when Donna saw the man who accompanied her father, she ran into her bedroom, stripped off the red robe, pulled her light blue dress over her head and tied her hair back with a ribbon. She moistened her lips and pinched her cheeks. Knowing his daughter, Rico guessed exactly what she was doing and gave her a little time by showing Ezio the garden. He and Ezio came in the door just as she entered the kitchen.

"Donna, we have a guest. This is Ezio Maffini. His father fought with Ballerini. He's come all the way from Reboli."

Donna was clearly impressed, less with the Maffini family history than with Ezio himself. Tall, broad shoulders, curly black hair, black eyes, a ruddy complexion, a nice smile. Excellent teeth. No one at Stupendi looked like this. She shook his hand.

"Welcome to Pietrasanta. I'm Donna Fazzini. Well, actually, Madonna, but no one calls me that."

"Madonna, like the Virgin Mary?" Ezio said.

"I'm afraid not." There was not a hint of embarrassment in her voice.

Ezio was also impressed. A soft round face. Brown curly hair. Nice hands, but with a little white under her fingernails. He liked the way her eyes crinkled and her inviting half-smile. And the blue dress fit perfectly. For a fleeting moment, her blue dress erased the memory of a yellow dress. But only for a moment.

Rico let them stare at each other for a minute. "Well, Donna," he said, "You're not going to believe what Ezio just told me."

"What?"

Ezio tried to say something but Rico held on to his arm. "Wait, Ezio. Wait. Donna, I told him I wanted you to hear the whole thing. But I want to have time. First, let's have something to eat."

"Yes, of course," Donna said. "Sit down, Ezio. We're having soup. Again. Left over from last night, I'm afraid. I may be able to cut a piece of marble into a life-sized statue of David, but I can't cook."

"Don't listen to her," Rico said. "She makes wonderful soup."

Donna shrugged. She broke up pieces of hard bread and tossed it into the bean soup, then put a plate of sliced tomatoes on the red tablecloth along with cheese and plums from the tree in back. Rico took a bottle of red wine from the shelf.

"This, Donna, is an occasion. When have we ever had someone so distinguished visit us?" He raised his glass. "Here's to Lanciotto Ballerini and here's to Ezio Maffini and here's to all the partisans!"

Ezio raised his glass but protested. "It's my father you should be toasting. He can tell you many stories and he was very brave. I just served with a few men and we didn't have many battles with the Germans."

"He's being modest, Donna. He won't tell me much about it, but he was the leader of a *banda* north of here and he lost some good men in battles. May I tell her more, Ezio?"

"It's all right."

"Donna, Ezio lost someone very special at Sant'Anna."

Donna put her hand on Ezio's. "I'm so sorry," she said softly.

Rico raised his glass again. "May we never forget the victims of Sant'Anna."

"No," Ezio said, and Donna wondered about this someone very special as she put down her glass.

Ezio poured another helping of soup into his bowl and complimented Donna, who blushed slightly. Rico began telling stories of his days in the *banda*, and Ezio added a few of his own, especially of the sabotage they had accomplished and the Nazis they had killed.

"My partisan name was Sparrow," Ezio said. "All the partisans in my *banda* had the names of birds."

"My *banda* wasn't so clever," Rico said. "My name was Cabbage."

Ezio cleared the table while Donna started washing the dishes. Ezio liked it here, the simple room, the big garden, even the pigs snorting in their pen. Far different, he thought, from his lonely rooms in Reboli.

Donna suddenly stopped washing the dishes. "Ezio Maffini! Ezio Maffini! I knew there was something familiar about that name. You wrote *A Time to Remember!* Papa, he wrote *A Time to Remember!*"

Ezio stopped drying a glass. "You mean you've read it? Where did you ever find it?"

"From a little old bookstore here," Donna said. "I get all my books from there. Somebody had owned it before, I guess. Ezio, it's an excellent book. Isn't it, Papa?"

"It's a wonderful book," Rico said. "A fine book. You should be very proud."

He slapped Ezio on the shoulder with his good right hand. Ezio smiled.

Rico wiped off the table and rearranged the chairs. He could hardly contain his excitement.

"Well, Donna, let's get to Ezio's story. I told you you're not going to believe this. He says someone has seen *Occhio unico.*"

Donna put her hand to her mouth.

"In the Garfagnana, Ezio says."

Donna held on to the back of the chair. "You'd better start at the beginning, Ezio. This is impossible."

"Yes, Ezio," Rico said, now opening a bottle of grappa. "Sit down. Let's hear your story. More than you told me at the Casa del Popolo. Start at the beginning."

Ezio trusted these two people he barely knew, and although it took a long while, he began by telling of his love for Angelica, how she and her little boys were massacred in Sant'Anna, and how he had been tormented by the loss ever since. He told them he had wanted to take revenge for a long time, but since he thought *Occhio unico* had escaped to Germany, how could he do that? But then last week he heard that *Occhio unico* had been seen and he went to Florence to get more information.

"And I met someone in an *osteria* there, a man by the name of Franco, and I told him I was looking for *Occhio unico*. So the next day he gave me a slip of paper that had a name and the word Garfagnana."

"Ezio!" Donna cried. "Why on earth would he give you that information?"

"I told this Franco that I was a journalist and I was doing an article for a Fascist newspaper about the neo-Fascists and wanted to tell the story of Sant'Anna."

"You're a journalist?"

"No, no, I'm a schoolteacher. But I had to have a reason to ask questions."

Donna laughed. "And he believed you?"

"Yes. Well, I think so."

"You must be a good actor. But then, you sort of look like a journalist."

Ezio smiled. "Oh, and what do you think a journalist looks like?"

Donna looked him up and down. "Oh, someone young, handsome, earnest, articulate."

Ezio's face reddened. "Anyway," he said, "as soon as he gave me this slip of paper, I knew I needed help. I mean, where would I start looking in the Garfagnana? So I asked my father, he has a woodworking shop in Florence, and he took me to a man who had fought with him in Ballerini's *banda*. That man, Rudolfo, said there were people here in Pietrasanta who were also involved in looking for the collaborators of Nazi atrocities. He told me to go to the Casa del Popolo. And so here I am."

Rico looked at his daughter. Donna's face was drained of color, but her eyes sparkled with excitement.

"Ezio," she said, "what is the name that this Franco gave you?"

"Amadeo Mazzella."

"Amadeo Mazzella, Amadeo Mazzella, Amadeo Mazzella," Rico said. "Sounds familiar. But I can't quite remember."

Donna thought a long while. "No, I can't either.... Wait ... I think Mazzella was that man who was active in the Fascists after the war and went around organizing. Remember that big fat man who always smelled of garlic, Papa? He was always stuffing himself in the *trattoria* in the piazza. Didn't we hear that he moved to Castigione?"

"Right, that one. But I think it was Barga."

"Both in the Garfagnana!" Ezio cried.

"Ezio," Donna said. "Please don't get your hopes up. I said we heard he went to these places. We're not sure. We haven't had a report on him in years."

"But still ..." Ezio said.

They sat silently. Rico filled Ezio's grappa glass again but Donna put her hand over hers. Then she put her hand on Ezio's.

"I'm afraid to ask this," she said. "So you have a name of a place where *Occhio unico* may be and you have the name of a man who might point you to him. What then? You're not going to look for him, are you?"

"Well, of course," Ezio said. "Why do you think I'm here?"

"Ezio!" Rico and Donna shouted together.

"You don't think I should?"

Rico and Donna looked at each other for a long while.

"Yes," Donna said softly. "We think you should."

"Good," Ezio said, putting his glass down. "You know, I've been tormented by the massacre for so many years, and I haven't known what to do about it. No one, not even my best friend who was in the *banda* with me, wants to remember anything about the war. I didn't know other people still cared. Why do you? What has made you still involved when this has seemed so hopeless?"

Rico looked at his daughter. "Let Donna tell you some stories," he said.

With the sun setting, Donna lit the lone light in the kitchen. Her father poured more grappa and invited Ezio to settle back in the big green armchair. Donna sat opposite him in a straight-backed chair.

"Ezio," Donna said, "I'll start at the beginning, too. The man who was the main collaborator at Sant'Anna, the man who is now known as *Occhio unico*, lived in Pietrasanta. His name then was Angelo Donatello. Isn't that a beautiful name for such a monster?"

"My grandfather's name was Angelo," Ezio said.

"And Donatello? Like the sculptor." Rico shook his head.

"We didn't know him then," Donna said, "but we have heard many stories about him since the war. His father actually worked at Stupendi in the 1930s but he was killed in some sort of accident. The father was a big Fascist, too. People say Angelo was a bully even in school. He was one of the first men here to join the Blackshirts and he was sent to Ethiopia in 1935 when Italy started that stupid war.

"Somehow, he was badly wounded there and he came back with a big hole where his left eye was. He used to sit in the piazza in front of the Duomo all day. Wore his Blackshirt uniform but also this crazy cap, wool, bright colors. He refused to wear an eye patch because he wanted everyone to see what he had suffered. Children would run away screaming when they saw the hole where his eye had been."

"*Occhio unico*," Ezio said.

"Anyway, he couldn't rejoin the army when the war broke out but he was very active in the Fascists. There were a lot of Fascists around here then. The rest of us had to be careful of what we said.

"And if they weren't actually Fascists, a lot of people were sympathetic to the Germans. They liked what Mussolini had done and wanted victory. But then as the war went on, most people just got tired of it. They were terrified when the British started bombing and so many towns and villages were being evacuated. Then the Germans started going crazy. They killed people, they raped women, they burned whole villages without reason.

"Mama and I were very afraid. Papa had joined the partisans, so Mama and I were alone here. We heard these terrible things that the Germans were doing but we didn't think they would ever come here, out in the country."

Donna paused and closed her eyes.

"You don't have to tell this part, Donna," her father said.

"No, I want to. Ezio should know." She went to the sink for a glass of water.

"One day," she said, sitting down again, "four German soldiers came here. They wanted to know if we knew any partisans. We said we didn't. They wouldn't listen to us. They hit Mama and pushed her around. She started screaming and ran into the bedroom. Then one soldier started beating me around the face. The other three grabbed me and held me down."

Donna paused and closed her eyes again.

"All four of them did it. All four. Right here on this floor."

"Donna ..." Rico said.

Ezio looked helpless, unable to say anything. He stood up, put his hands in his pockets, took them out, walked to the window, came back, sat down, got up, walked to the window and came back and sat down again.

"Donna, I'm so sorry."

Donna looked up. "It's all right. I can talk about it now. You see that my voice is steady. But you can see that I have a personal reason for wanting to find any Fascists who helped the Germans."

The tiny house was silent. Only the snorting of the pigs could be heard.

"Then in the summer of 1944," Donna said, "we all knew that the Allies finally were coming north and the Germans were retreating. But then the brutalities became even worse. The partisans were fighting terrible battles all over and the Germans couldn't control them. So they had to get at the people who were helping the partisans. We all knew that there were some people in Sant'Anna helping the partisans, but Sant'Anna was so isolated we didn't think the Germans would ever be able to get there. People were coming from all over because they thought it was safe there."

"Yes, I knew that," Ezio said.

"Around August 9 or 10, we heard that the Germans were going to invade Sant'Anna. We couldn't believe it. We knew that they had to have help. And we knew that the help had to come from some people right here. We tried to get word to Sant'Anna, but we couldn't.

"It was only later that we found out that fifteen men from here were involved, and the leader was Angelo Donatello. There are lots of stories about what he did. Some say he went up to Sant'Anna beforehand and scouted all the little hamlets there. Some say he told the Germans the people of Sant'Anna were helping the partisans, even though the partisan group had left by then."

"Oh my God," Ezio said. "That was our *banda.*"

"But there's no question that Donatello led the Germans to Sant'Anna. He wore a goddamn mask so he wouldn't be recognized! He carried their weapons. He told them where to go. He told them what path to take. He didn't do the actual shooting, but he stood there and he saw everything. And he was there the entire time!"

Donna wiped her eyes before continuing. "A few months later, the United States Army conducted an investigation."

"I know about that," Ezio said. "It was a sham."

"A whitewash. But Donatello had disappeared. By then some of us had organized. Just like you, we wanted to seek retribution for this horrible thing. Especially since Italy wasn't doing anything. Nothing. At one point we had people here and all over Italy who kept in contact with each other about what we had found. There were those fifteen men involved here but there were collaborators for the other atrocities, too. Some of them went to Germany, some to Austria, and we just learned that one went to Argentina. And Donatello, well, we all believed he escaped to Germany."

"Gone, but not forgotten," Rico said. "That's why there are posters in every Casa in Tuscany just in case he should turn up again. We figure he'd be wearing glasses and let his hair and beard grow long now."

Rico leaned back in his chair and closed his eyes. Donna and Ezio stared at each other for long minutes. For Ezio, the war that had always been so close to him was now even closer. And now he knew that he was no longer alone.

"Well, there's one more thing you should know about Angelo Donatello, this man they now call *Occhio unico*." Donna said. "He sent his wife and son to Sant'Anna the day before the massacre. That's something we have never understood. But that's how evil the man was. Or is."

CHAPTER 12

───────────▼───────────

Rico yawned and stretched his legs, then his right arm. His left remained in his lap. "I need to go to bed, Ezio. I'm not a young man like you. I don't know if we can help or not. Remember, we were old then and we are all very old now. Especially me. We all fought in the war and some of us never recovered. The only thing I can do is get my friends together and you can ask them if they know anything. They will be very interested in this new information you have. So ... tomorrow afternoon at the Casa del Popolo."

He yawned again. "I'm going to bed. You should, too, Donna. You have to go to work tomorrow."

"No, Papa, it's Saturday. I don't have to work. And I'm going to the Casa, too."

Rico looked at Donna and then at Ezio and then at Donna again. He smiled. "Yes, and I can guess why."

He winked and kissed Donna on the forehead and shook Ezio's hand. "I will see you tomorrow afternoon."

Donna kissed her father, and he shuffled off to his bedroom.

"So that's the story," Donna said, putting the glasses in the sink. Ezio went up behind her, but hesitated before putting his hands on her shoulders.

"Donna, I don't know what to say. What a terrible, terrible thing that happened to you. I ..."

She turned to face him. "Thanks. You don't have to say anything. It was more than ten years ago. I was in shock at first. Then I cried a lot. Then I was so angry. Now, it's something that happened and I can't do anything about it. I can't change the past."

"I'd like to change the past," Ezio said quietly. "I wish Sant'Anna had never happened."

He turned to the window and looked out at the moonlit landscape.

"We can't change that, Ezio, as much as we'd like to. All we can do is try to find the people who did it."

She suggested that they go out in the back and sit on the wooden benches that overlooked the garden. With a full moon, the corn stalks looked like rows of stately soldiers at parade rest. The vineyards across the fields glimmered a dark green. Moths buzzed around the light above the door.

"So you're a schoolteacher," Donna said. "I loved my teachers. I imagine you are a very good one, your face is so kind, you must be, too."

"Kind sometimes. But I can be tough, too. The students like that."

"A big school?"

"No, just a small one in Reboli. A few years ago they changed its name to the Dante Silva School after a former teacher who was killed in the war."

"The names of war heroes are everywhere," she said. "And how did you get from Florence to Reboli?"

"I had gone to university in Pisa. After the war I didn't know what to do. I wanted to do something good. So I decided to become a teacher. It's been good. And you? What do you do?"

Donna smoothed her dress over her knees. "During the war, they were looking for workers in the marble factories here. At first the factory, Stupendi, the same one where *Occhio unico's* father worked, didn't want to hire a woman, but then they didn't have a choice. I got on as an apprentice, and then they hired me. I've been there almost twelve years."

"I've seen some of the Stupendi statues," Ezio said. "They're very good. Hard to tell from the originals."

"Sometimes, the work is good. Sometimes, it's boring. But I'm lucky to have work now."

"What do you do to help the boredom?"

"I love to read," Donna said. "Right now I'm reading the new Pratolini novel. *Il quartiere.*"

"*Il quartiere!* I love that book. When I was growing up, I walked all over Florence so I recognized everything he writes about."

"I've never been to Florence," she said, almost wistfully. "I've never been anywhere."

"Actually," Ezio said, learning forward now. "I grew up in Oltrarno, which they call the 'other side' because it's south of the Arno. It's a working class neighborhood, not as poor as the neighborhood of San Croce, like in that book, but pretty much the same."

"When I think of Florence, I think of the Duomo and the Uffizi and the Palazzo Vecchio, the historic buildings."

"A lot of people do. But many people just live and work in Florence. The boys in that book? I could have been one of them."

"Oh, really? Which one? No, let me guess." She was teasing now. "Carlo? No, he's too hot-headed. You don't look hot-headed. Valerio? No, too wishy-washy. Not Gino certainly. Poor boy. No, you would have been Giorgio, the good one."

"I'm not sure about Giorgio. He was so good he married Maria even though he knew she had been with other men."

"You'd never do that?"

Ezio's face grew red. "Well, I ..."

"There's another thing I like about him," she said hurriedly. "He's the anti-Fascist."

For the next half hour, Ezio and Donna talked about their childhoods, what they did in school, where he lived, what books they had read, what movies they had seen.

"I love Fellini," Donna said. "And de Sica."

"For me, Rossellini is the best," Ezio said. "I've seen *Open City* about a half dozen times."

"Too bad his reputation was ruined by that American actress."

"Just in America," Ezio said. "We love Ingrid Bergman here."

They both laughed. For the first time in years, Ezio felt comfortable talking to a woman, a woman who seemed to be his own age. And they liked the same things. Imagine. She was reading Pratolini, one of his favorite authors. He wanted to talk to her more about books and movies.

"Something wrong?" Donna asked. "You're staring."

"Oh, sorry, sorry. I guess I was just thinking about something."

"It's all right," Donna said. "Tell me about your family."

Ezio told Donna about his mother getting so sick in the days before Florence's liberation and how she eventually died. Now, there was only him and his father, one of the best wood workers in Florence. "And your family?"

"Just me and Papa, too," Donna said. "My mother died five years ago of a heart attack."

They remained silent, deep in their own thoughts, as the moon cast a bright but eerie light on the landscape.

"Ezio," Donna said, "what you're planning to do is very dangerous. These Fascists have been known to do things and get away with it. They track people down. They know everyone in families. Your father works with saws and machinery, right? There could be an 'accident' and nobody could prove they were involved."

"Donna! You don't think that they …"

Donna went back into the house and took a notebook out of a cupboard drawer. Returning to the bench under the light, she began to read. "On August 23 two years ago, a man riding his bicycle on Aurelia Nord was struck and killed by a passing car. The driver was not found. The man was one of ours."

She paused and looked out past the corn stalks. "Did you hear something?"

"No."

"I thought I heard something across the field."

"I didn't hear anything."

"I must have been mistaken. Papa says I'm paranoid. Maybe I am."

She read from the notebook again. "On February 18 last year, a man's body was found in the marble quarry north of here. He was one of ours. On March 5 of this year, one of Papa's friends, a man who had been very active in our movement, disappeared and hasn't been seen since. Do you want me to go on?"

"No," he said quietly. "I understand."

Donna closed the notebook. It was so quiet they could hear the moths buzzing around the light. "Ezio, have you thought about what you would do if you did find *Occhio unico*?"

"I guess I haven't. I just want to find him."

"Well, I've thought about it. The others in the group haven't, but I have. We've never actually caught one of these bastards, so we don't know. I suppose we could take him to the authorities, but what good would that do? They had some trials after the war but even those who were convicted got amnesty."

"National reconciliation, that's what they called it," Ezio said bitterly.

"And a lot of us aren't reconciled."

"What about just exposing them?" Ezio said. "Let everyone know that Angelo Donatello and the other bastards helped kill their relatives and friends at Sant'Anna. That would get people angry, right?"

"Ezio, I don't think you understand how people think around here. Like you said, they don't think much about the war anymore, not even the massacre. It's in the past, just like my rape. They want to live their own lives now. They want to take trips to the seaside, get nice things for their homes, maybe even a television set. You know Italians. They want to put a good face on things. The old *bella figura*."

"Partisans had a way to deal with these bastards after the war. They didn't need to haul them into a court. They administered their own justice."

Donna put her fingers to his lips. "And look at the reaction to that, Ezio. That stuff just turned people against the partisans. You know that."

"I don't know what to think, Donna, I just don't know. All I know is that we can't—at least I can't—let these Fascists go free forever. I have to do something, I have to do something."

"Ezio, it's late," Donna said, getting up. "We can't solve these problems tonight. I'll see you at the Casa del Popolo tomorrow."

Donna kissed Ezio lightly on both cheeks. For a moment, he wanted to draw her near. Then a glimpse of a yellow dress flashed through his memory and he moved away.

"Good night, Donna."

"Good night, Ezio. Please. Be careful. You know what I said."

Lit by moonlight, the streets were quiet as Ezio walked back to the center of Pietrasanta. He felt lighter than he had in years, but also more confused. He didn't want to think about his feelings now.

"No matter what happens," he thought, "I have met a wonderful woman."

CHAPTER 13

▼

The television set was off but the room was still blue with smoke when Ezio arrived at the Casa del Popolo the next afternoon. He saw Donna reading in a corner and Rico with three other men at a table in the center of the room.

"Ah, Ezio!" Rico said, getting up and slapping him on the back. "I want you to meet my friends. And they want to meet you." The other men all rose slowly to their feet, holding on to the table.

"Ezio, this is Signor Filippo Parisi."

A short, stooped man who looked like a gnome bowed and extended a gnarled hand.

"And Signor Leonardo Ciamino."

Tall and broad-shouldered, Ciamino wore a military cap with three insignia.

"And Signor Orfeo Tolosi. We call him *Il Rospo*—the toad. Look at his fingers." It was true. The fingers were webbed together, as Ezio discovered when he shook the man's hand.

"I haven't told them why you're here," Rico whispered in Ezio's ear. "But they're excited that the son of a man who fought with Ballerini is here and they want to tell you their own stories."

Although he was eager to get to the subject that brought him to Pietrasanta, Ezio told the men he was pleased to meet them and would like to hear stories of their partisan lives during the war. The extensive tales of daring and heroism that followed grew more and more spectacular as each vied with the others to describe the most courageous partisan band and the most stupendous victory.

"Remember the parades they gave us after the war," Filippo said, filling his glass with grappa. "The bands, the pretty girls waving their flags."

"They had a mass in the church," Leonardo said. "They dedicated the plaque at the cemetery."

"We were heroes then," *Il Rospo* said. "Here's to the heroes!" He raised his glass.

"Yes," Rico said. "Heroes. People remembered what we had done for them during the fighting. They remembered the Germans we killed. They remembered that it was us, the Communists, who led the Resistance."

"Now they don't remember," Leonardo said. "They don't remember at all. They don't want to think about the war."

The four veterans remained lost in their memories.

"It's worse than that!" *Il Rospo* shouted. "Some of these people want to be Fascists again! Why do they want to do that? After the war people were grateful to the Resistance. We brought those Fascist bastards to trial. We found the collaborators and got them sent to prison. We were going to have justice!"

"And then," Leonardo said, "it all ended. Just like that. That constitution after the *Democrazia Cristiana* won control? That changed everything. We went from the left to the right. And then those neo-Fascists in the *Movimento Sociale Italiano* became powerful."

"Not only that," Rico said. "Everyone was afraid of the Communists! The Communists! Hell, we were Communists during the war, we were Communists after the war, and we're still Communists! But suddenly nobody wanted anything to do with us. *Boh!*"

Ezio knew this history lesson as well as anyone in the room. He also knew that things were not as simple as they would like to believe. Italian politics had always been complicated, never more so than in the postwar years. Still, he found it interesting that unlike so many other people, these old partisans had so much anger ten years after the war. No wonder they were still seeking the collaborators of Sant'Anna and the other massacres. He walked over to Donna and put his hand on her shoulder.

"No history lesson for you today?"

"I'll wait until after they finish their stories," she said, closing her book. "They come here every week and say the same things. It's too bad, but it's a fact of life. Italy isn't the same now as it was after the war."

"That's what I've been thinking," Ezio said. "It's going to be hard to find people who care anymore."

Back at the table, the stories continued. And then Leonardo was discussing the trial against some of the collaborators right after the war. The mood then was to punish them, but now many sentences had been commuted. The Fascists were free.

"Too bad they didn't catch Angelo Donatello before he escaped," he said.

"*Occhio unico* might have been tossed in jail then," Rico said, "but by now he would be out walking the streets just like you and me."

Hearing the name, Ezio returned to the table. Rico raised his hand. "Wait. Ezio here has some information." He lowered her voice. "One-Eye has been seen again."

"Whoa!" Filippo said.

"I don't believe it!" Leonardo exclaimed.

"Where? Where?" *Il Rospo* shouted.

Rico explained that Ezio had talked to a man and gotten a slip of paper with the word Garfagnana written on it.

"The Garfagnana? North of Lucca?" Leonardo said. "Why would Donatello hide in the Garfagnana?"

"Caves," Filippo theorized. "There are caves all over there. And little farms and huts. He could stay there for years and never be found."

There were then lengthy arguments about how long someone could stay in the mountainous, treacherous area of the Garfagnana without being discovered. They finally agreed that it would be possible, but only with a lot of help from Fascist supporters.

"There's more," Rico told his three comrades. "Ezio also got the name of someone who might tell him where *Occhio unico* is. Amadeo Mazzella."

"Mazzella!" all three shouted at once.

"The Fascist fat guy?"

"The one who ate all the time?"

"The one who was organizing Fascists all over here?"

They all talked at once, but when it all came down, no one seemed to know any more than Rico about this Amadeo Mazzella. Like Rico, they thought Mazzella had gone to Castiglione or Barga.

Ezio tried to hide his disappointment. "It's all right. I'm going to go up there. I'll go to Barga and if I don't find him there, I'll go to Castiglione."

"You're going to go there?" *Il Rospo* said.

"Yes. I'm going to go there."

"But Ezio," Fernando said, "what are you going to do if you find Amadeo Mazzella? You're a Communist, right? He's a Fascist. He'll be protecting *Occhio unico*. This has to be a trap. That guy who gave you the name, he's sending you to the wolves."

"I know that's possible," Ezio said. "But I've got to do this."

"And," Donna interrupted, "he's not going as a Communist. He's going as a journalist."

Ezio smiled and held her hand. "Right, a well-known journalist from Reboli."

They wondered if Ezio even knew where the Garfagnana was.

"Of course, I know," Ezio said. "Biking up from Lucca along the Serchio to Barga is one of my favorite things during the summer. I know all the towns on the way. I usually stop for lunch at the Devil's Bridge at Borgo a Mozzano. I know the Garfagnana well."

"Well," Filippo said, "see if you can get some help there. See if there's a Casa del Popolo. I think they have one in Barga, I'm not sure about Castiglione."

They then started talking about the small group of Communists in the area who had sought collaborators in the past.

"Muzio! Remember him?" Filippo said.

"Ricardo," Rico said. "He was sick the last I heard. Maybe he's dead."

"Del Rosso was active," *Il Rospo* volunteered.

"And Edidio!"

"And Innocenzio!"

"And if I find these people?" Ezio asked. "How am I going to get them to believe me?"

"Tell them Cabbage sent you," Rico said. "Everyone knows my name."

"And Radish," Filippo said.

"Cucumber," *Il Rospo* said.

"Tomato," Leonardo said.

All four of the comrades said they wanted to join Ezio but they just couldn't. They were all in their seventies or eighties, none of them was in good health and they couldn't go as far as Camaiore, much less Barga.

"That's all right," Ezio said. "You've been very helpful and.I thank you very much. I'll be fine."

All of the men had tears in their eyes as Ezio shook their hands and walked to the door.

"*Buon viaggio!*" they cried. Rico held Ezio's shoulders and kissed him on both cheeks.

Donna, who had remained silent through much of this, caught up with Ezio at the door and put her hand on his arm.

"Wait. I'm going with you."

CHAPTER 14

As the rusty Fiat pulled out of Pietrasanta the next morning, Ezio smiled and almost laughed out loud.

"You're very pleased with yourself, aren't you?" Donna said as she put her hand on his on the steering wheel.

"I feel like one of my pupils skipping school." He laughed again, but then saw how close her hand was to his wire bracelet.

Both of them were thinking about what happened outside of the Casa del Popolo the day before.

"Donna!" her father had cried. "You can't go to the Garfagnana! What are you thinking about? What would you do there? It's bad enough that Ezio is going, but you're going to be in danger, too."

"I can take care of myself, Papa," she had said with a half-smile.

"And how can you get time off from the factory?"

"Papa, I've been there long enough I can take some days off. They owe me."

"And what will people think, you going off with … with a man?"

"Let them think what they want. Papa, it's 1955! I'm almost 33 years old! Things are different now, even in Italy. Are you worried about Ezio and me being alone together?"

"Of course I am." He wiped a tear from his eye. "I just wish your mother was here."

"Papa, I can take care of myself." That half-smile again. "And you can, too. There are plenty of vegetables in the garden, you can go to the *bottega* to get whatever else you need. You won't starve."

Rico finally agreed to let Donna go with Ezio only if they took the 1948 Fiat that had stood unused for years outside the shed in back of their house. In the morning, it took a half hour to get the car started, and once the smoke died down and the banging stopped, Ezio kept the motor running so it wouldn't stall again.

Donna kissed Rico good-bye, and when they rounded the dirt road that led to the highway, both turned to wave back at the lonely man on the doorstep.

The route took them past scattered villages and towns on their way to Lucca. The sun was warm, the sky cloudless, and honeysuckle and the last of the spring poppies were in bloom all the way. When they turned past Camaiore, the Apuan Mountains soared to the left, to the right and up ahead. They were surrounded by thick emerald green forests, broken occasionally by cliffs of granite that stretched to the sky.

"Impossible," Ezio said.

"Are you thinking what I'm thinking?"

Ezio slowed the old car to thirty miles an hour. "No one could survive in the mountains for long even here. And the forests are even more dense in the Garfagnana."

"But *Occhio unico* seems to be doing it."

"That's hard to believe," Ezio said. "I know there are stories about people who never come down from their farms, but I don't know how anyone could live in a cave in forests and mountains like this."

"I've heard a few stories," Donna said. "Papa told me about an old man who was born in a tiny hut in the mountains, stayed there all his life eating food from his garden and the rabbits and chickens that he raised. He never left the place, never went to the village down below. He was found dead by hunters months after he died. Probably ninety years old."

"Very sad."

"Well," Donna said, "he was probably very happy. At least he didn't know what was going on in the world."

"It's like," Ezio said, "the story of *il ragazzo fantasma*."

"Ezio, do you know the story of the ghost boy, too?"

"Doesn't everyone?" Ezio said. "It's a legend. My pupils love to make up stories about him. They like to scare the little kids. '*Il ragazzo fantasma* is gonna get you,' they say. But they're just made up. They've never seen him. I don't know of anyone who has actually seen him."

Ever since the Sant'Anna massacre, fantastic stories spread through the mountain villages like the fireflies that lit the evening skies. There were unbelievable tales of people saved only, it was said, because of the intercession of their patron saints. The woman who had taken her children to Camaiore the night before to see a doctor. Saint Zita was credited. The grandmother who had gone to Seravezza to visit her grandchildren. Saint Catherine. The man who had taken his daughters to harvest wood. Saint Martino. Of course, people didn't mention that the man's wife, who stayed at home, was killed.

And there were those whose lives were ended because of cruel fate—or because, the gossips said, they had done something bad. The woman who had pilfered money and went to Sant'Anna to give it to her sister. The widow who had an old gentleman friend there. The two young girls who had run away from home.

There were also stories of people who had escaped when the Nazis arrived. They had run into the woods or hid in distant caves and stables. But no story was more fantastic than that of *il ragazzo fantasma*. As the years went on, the story of the ghost boy became more and more embellished, but at the beginning, this was what was said:

A mother and her son, maybe about nine or ten years old, were hiding in a stable when the SS descended on Sant'Anna. Hearing the soldiers approaching, the frantic mother shoved her son into a pile of hay and lay on top of it. The soldiers pushed open the door and shot the woman dead. Then they set the place on fire and soon there was nothing left but ashes.

Somehow, the boy dug himself out from under his mother's body and crawled into the woods. But he was so badly burned, and his fright was so great, that he never left the forests again, going from one mountain to another. Eating berries or ears of corn or stealing whatever he could find from farmers' garbage bins, he was supposed to be have hid in the forests all these years.

Because the woman's body was so badly burned, she was never identified. But villagers knew that everyone else in Sant'Anna was accounted for, and so the story spread that this was *Occhio unico's* wife. But no ashes could be found for the boy. So where was he? Could *il ragazzo fantasma* be *Occhio unico's* little son? In the cold of a winter's night, when the moon was full, old grandmothers would tell their grandchildren the story of the ghost boy and whisper, "You'd better behave, or *il ragazzo fantasma* will get you."

"Donna," Ezio said, "have you ever seen this ghost boy? If this is *Occhio unico's* son, he's not a boy anymore, is he? It's been eleven years. He must be almost twenty now."

"No, but I've heard of people who have seen him running in the woods. He doesn't have any hair and his face is blotched in many colors and his clothes are just tatters. And you know, One-Eye's son was a small boy. Like his father and, I've heard, like his grandfather. So he might be almost twenty but he'd still look like a boy."

"Where have they seen him?"

"Near Pescaglia. At the river near Vergemoli. Near Castelnuovo."

"Ah, Castelnuovo. In the Garfagnana. Well, maybe we'll run into him."

"Don't laugh, Ezio. I feel very sorry for this boy. What a terrible life."

"I'm not laughing. I just don't believe it."

Donna leaned against the window and closed her eyes. Ezio's smile gradually faded. Enough talk about ghost boys. He wondered about his sudden interest in this woman who was sitting at his side. He may have been with other women, younger women over the years, but he had never loved one of them. Angelica's memory was still too strong. With his hands gripping the steering wheel, he looked down at the wire bracelet on his wrist and drove on to the side of the highway.

"Everything all right?" Donna asked as Ezio got the Fiat back on the road. "Why the frown? What are you thinking about?"

"Nothing." He tried to smile. "Nothing."

"Well, something bothers me. This Franco who gave you the name. Do you really think he believed you when you said you're a journalist? Be honest."

"Of course he believed me. Why wouldn't he?" Ezio's voice was far from confident.

"Because he wants you to meet this Amadeo Mazzella who will … who will …"

"What?"

"Ezio, I told you these Fascists are organized. They have networks …"

"Just like you do …"

"Yes, but they are even more organized. Someone might have followed you to Pietrasanta, or at least let their friends in Pietrasanta know about you. Did you see this Franco talk to anyone else?"

Ezio thought for a moment, and then remembered. "There was a man he talked to in the Piazza Maria Novella."

"What man? What did he look like?"

"I don't know. Just a man. He had long hair, and I think he had a mustache."

"Not a very good description, but how were you to know, right?"

Ezio blamed himself. "I'll pay more attention from now on."

"But that's not the most important thing."

"Which is?"

"Don't you see?" Donna said. "If someone tracked you to Pietrasanta, your cover would be blown. Why would you come to Pietrasanta and not go to the Garfagnana? And more important: They would know you're one of us."

After years of scholarly work at a university, after years of planning strategic maneuvers as a partisan, after years of teaching, Ezio suddenly felt more ignorant than any of his fifth-grade pupils. How could he be so naïve? He wiped the sweat from his forehead.

And now it wasn't just him. He was also putting this lovely woman at his side in danger.

"Ezio, have you seen anyone here who might be following you?"

"No. Do you think someone was watching us at the Casa del Popolo?"

"No, no. They wouldn't dare go into that place. But they could have been outside."

"And who is they?"

"All sorts of people. Bagnini the florist. Agnese the postman. Luciano the chief of police. My boss at the factory ..."

For the next dozen miles, the only sounds were the Fiat's sputtering engine. Gradually, the sky became overcast, and the flowers along the roadside were no longer bright. They were now at the top of the winding hill and could see tiny villages, spread out like toy landscapes, far below them.

Ezio broke the silence. "Donna, there's something else I have to tell you."

"More?"

"You need to know my other reasons for finding *Occhio unico*."

"What other reasons could there be? The man is a monster!"

Again, Ezio thought of the box under his bed.

"No. Let me tell you. I want you to know." He took a deep breath. "Our *banda* settled in outside of Sant'Anna in the spring of 1944. It was a good location, and we could scout the mountains easily from there. The people loved us, most of them, and they helped us. Gave us food, supplies. That's how I met Angelica."

"You don't have to tell me everything, Ezio."

"No, I want to. We fell in love right away and we were so happy. Her boys liked me, I liked them. Yes, we both knew it was wrong. Her husband was off in the war, probably on the eastern front. But we were so much in love."

He paused, and Donna waited.

"There seemed to be a lull in the war and everything was going well. Then the Germans found out the people were helping us. We knew they would kill anyone helping a partisan. They'd done it everywhere else. I didn't want to leave, but we had to. Don't you see, Donna?"

"Of course I see, Ezio. What else could you do?"

Ezio knew he was trying to convince himself more than Donna. "We couldn't stay there and put those people in danger. We had to go. Angelica looked so sad when we said good-bye. I can still see her face. We moved miles away."

Donna waited while Ezio drove silently through the hills.

"But that's not all."

"Oh, Ezio …"

"We had a good source, a priest, who sent us messages almost every night on his radio transmitter. Well, he told us that the Germans were going to attack Sant'Anna even though we had already left. They were still going to take retribution for what the people had done for us. I told my *banda* what was going to happen. Everyone wanted to go back there and fight. We had to go down there, they said. We had enough arms. We couldn't let this happen. We couldn't let those people who had befriended us die. That's what they said. We had a big argument."

"What did you say?"

Ezio clenched the steering wheel. "We had only twenty men. They had hundreds. We would have been slaughtered like everyone else. We had to keep fighting where we were. I said … I said … Donna, I said no, we couldn't go back. And so we didn't go."

Ezio's shoulders were shaking and Donna held the steering wheel.

"Ezio, of course, you couldn't go back. What good would it have done?"

"I know that in my head, Donna. But my heart tells me differently. And for eleven years I've held this guilt inside me. Sometimes I think I was a coward."

"Oh God, Ezio! How can you think that? Look at what you had been doing. Look at the fights you had with the Germans. The communication lines you cut. The landmines you set. The railroad lines you demolished. You saved people, Ezio. You probably saved hundreds of people, just you and your *banda*. And you continued to save them because you didn't go to Sant'Anna."

"I know that, Donna, but …"

"No buts, please, Ezio. You did what you had to do."

"I keep thinking if only I had stayed. Maybe I could have taken Angelica and the boys out of there, to someplace safe."

"Where, for God's sake? Sant'Anna was the safest place on earth then."

"Or if only I had gone back when the priest warned us. Maybe I could have protected her somehow."

"Ezio, you know you would have been shot in an instant."

"I know, I know."

"Ezio, look at it this way. We can't go through life saying 'if only.' If only I had run into the bedroom maybe I wouldn't have been raped. If only Papa had been on the other side of the street maybe he wouldn't have been shot.

If only the United States Army had found the Fascists guilty at Sant'Anna maybe One-Eye would have been brought to justice. It's useless to think what might have been. It happened. We have to live with it."

"I know, I know."

"Oh my God, you've been suffering like this for all these years?"

"At first I guess I was in shock. After the war I stayed in Florence with my parents, then I went back to Pisa to finish my studies. Then I found out about the teaching position in Reboli and I've been there since. Thank God I've got that. During the school year I'm busy and I don't think about it so much. But it's bad in summer. I get bad headaches, I have terrible nightmares."

"Oh, Ezio, I'm sorry."

"I told my doctor about this. He's tried to help, gives me medications. Sometimes they help, sometimes not. Do you know what he said the other day? He wants me to see a psychiatrist in Lucca."

"Oh, Ezio!"

"I'm not going to, Donna. I'm not crazy."

"Ezio, Ezio, of course you're not crazy."

"But you think I should see this guy?"

For a long time, Donna picked at the marble dust under the fingers of her left hand. "Ezio, I don't know anything about psychiatry. I know it helps some people …"

"What can he tell me that I don't already know? I know I'm obsessed and I know I have these guilt feelings. He can't do anything about that. What do you think I should do?"

Now Donna picked at the marble dust on her right hand. "Ezio, I've only known you for two days. I don't know what to tell you. I wish I did. I wish I could help." She put her hand on his. "There are no easy answers in war, you know that. I'm so sorry, Ezio."

"So you see," Ezio said, "that's why I have to find *Occhio unico*. Not just for justice. Not just to revenge what happened at Sant'Anna, but to finally let go of all this guilt, all of this … this shit … that I've been carrying around for so long."

Donna knew she didn't have to say anything to the tortured man next to her. She just held his hand tighter.

Deep in thought, Ezio almost struck an old man riding a bicycle just ahead of them. Ezio swerved the car and drove onto the gravel at the side of the road. While the man rode on, making a fist and cursing loudly, Ezio inspected the Fiat's tires. He didn't see the car that suddenly stopped a quarter mile behind them.

CHAPTER 15

▼

For miles, they rode along in silence. Gradually, Ezio regained his composure and Donna settled back and closed her eyes. With the temperatures rising quickly, Ezio opened the windows of the Fiat, letting in some air but also tiny white sand from the nearby marble quarries. When they had driven about thirty miles away from Pietrasanta, they both noticed the sign: Sant'Antonio.

"I want to stop in Sant'Antonio," Ezio said. "I want you to meet some people."

"Who?"

"Lots of people. I like to call them my family."

"Your own family is just you and your Papa, right?"

"Oh, I have some distant cousins who moved to America before the war. We get Christmas cards from them. They're in Chi-ca-go. What an ugly name for a city."

Donna laughed. "I don't know where the Americans get these names. I heard another one recently. Minn-e-a-po-lis. What do you think that means?"

"Sounds like something you'd want to avoid eating. Wait. One of my cousins moved. Now he's in Sche-ne-ct-ad-y. I think that's near New York."

"Pitts-burgh!"

"Mil-wau-kee!"

They both howled.

"Well," Ezio said, "I suppose they'd have trouble pronouncing Castelnuovo di Val di Cecina."

"Or, let's see, how about Marciano della Chiana?"

"At least," Donna said, wiping tears from her eyes, "our names roll off the tongue instead of getting stuck in the throat."

The breeze was now so stiff that both Ezio and Donna rolled up their windows, which made the inside of the car only hotter.

Ezio took out a handkerchief and wiped his forehead. "And your family? Just you and your Papa, too?"

Donna waited a moment. "We had a lot of relatives at Sant'Anna. Now there's nobody."

Ezio wanted to reach over and hold her hand, but he kept it on the steering wheel.

"I'm sorry," he said.

"I am, too." She looked out the window for a long time. They passed another sign saying Sant'Antonio.

"So tell me about the people in Sant'Antonio. Why are they your family?"

"It started during the war. After our *banda* had left Sant'Anna, we were on the mountain just north of here. One night I was on patrol and I found these two boys, brothers, who were lost. I took them back to the farmhouse where they were staying and I met all these wonderful people."

"They were staying in a farmhouse?"

"They were all from Sant'Antonio, the village we're coming to. Part of an SS division had descended on Sant'Antonio and ordered everyone evacuated. The people thought they'd be sent north on the trains ..."

"And we know what would have happened to them then."

"Exactly. So the priest, the same priest who was our informant, told everyone in the village to go up to some of the empty farmhouses in the hills and hide out there until it was safe to come back down. They thought it would be only a few days but it turned out to be about three months."

"I can't imagine."

"The farmhouse this group went to was called the Cielo."

"Heaven."

"More like purgatory. There were eighteen people there, including five children."

"Good God! I can see why it was purgatory."

"Well, as I said, I found these two boys and took them back to the farmhouse. And that's when I met all these people. They sort of adopted me, I guess."

"Who were they?"

"Let's see. Rosa and Marco, an older couple, were there, and Annabella and Francesco, about their age. Two elderly sisters, Maddelena and Renata, and two old cousins, Vito and Giacomo. Dante Silva, a schoolmaster. In fact, he used to teach at my school, and now it's named for him."

"He's dead?"

"Yes, I'll come to that. I know this is complicated, Donna. But there was also the Contessa, who wasn't a contessa, just a little eccentric, and Fausta, who was a Fascist ..."

"Ezio, you're making this up!"

"No, I swear. And they were hiding an escaped prisoner of war, too."

"Oh, my God, they could all have been killed."

"They were all so brave. Well, there's more. There was Gina, who had the five children. Lucia was the oldest, about sixteen, I think, then the boys, and another girl, and the baby, Carlotta, three months. The boys had gone to Sant'Antonio to get medicine for her because she was so sick, but it didn't do any good. She's buried just outside the farmhouse."

"What they all went through ..."

"There's more to that story. Nobody knew it, but Lucia had met this young guy, Dino, who had deserted from the army and they were having an affair. She wasn't supposed to leave the Cielo, but she'd run off to meet him. But then Dino joined our *banda* and was killed in a confrontation we had with the Germans just outside the farmhouse. After the war Little Dino was born. I hope you can meet him. He was in my class last year. The shyest kid I've ever known, but very smart."

"Well, that's quite a list."

"There was one more. I saved her for last. Maria. I knew Angelica's mother lived in Sant'Antonio, but the only time I met her was when she came to visit Angelica at Sant'Anna and I was there."

"So you met the mother of your lover, whose husband was off in the war? What did Maria say?"

"Maria cared about her daughter's happiness more than anything else. And, of course, there was a war going on. People do things."

"You don't have to explain anything to me, Ezio."

The landscape was flat now, with hills far in the distance. Donna could make out ruins of farmhouses in the hills and wondered if one was the Cielo.

"So all these people are still in Sant'Antonio?"

"Not all of them. Francesco and Dante were killed. Their bodies were brought back and they're buried in the cemetery outside the church. And others have died since then. Maddelena. Her sister, Renata. The cousins, Vito and Giacomo. The Contessa. All of them buried in the cemetery along with the priest."

"He died, too?"

"Killed by the Germans when he was trying to send a radio message to us. He'd been helping us for years."

"There were many unsung heroes in the war," Donna said quietly. "Too many to count. Too many we don't know about. So these friends, these survivors, are your family now."

"They like to call themselves *il gruppo di Cielo*. The Cielo group. But it's really a community. They suffered together but they never talk about it. They have a party on the anniversary of the day they were allowed to return to Sant'Antonio. But just the other day they got together because they were worried about me."

"I can see why. Where do they meet?"

"The party had been at Rosa's, but her husband isn't very well now, so it's at Lucia and Paolo's."

"Paolo? So Lucia got married?"

"Yes. To Dino's best friend."

"Oh, that's such a nice story. Dino's best friend married her?"

"Paolo is the kindest, most generous man I've ever met. And the thing is, he loves Lucia very much, she loves him, and he's a great father to Little Dino. And now he's my best friend, too."

She put her hand next to his on the seat. "I'm glad you have someone to talk to, Ezio."

"I've needed it. But I really want you to meet Maria."

"Really? Would she want to meet someone who is a ..." Donna struggled to find the word, "... a friend ... of yours?"

Ezio turned to look at her. "Yes. Maria would very much like to meet my ... my good friend." He put his hand on hers.

At that moment, on the right, they passed a steel bunker, once used by German snipers to attack partisans on this very road. It could have been hidden by overgrown bushes. Instead, someone had been carefully keeping it visible, a constant reminder for anyone driving by. They were almost in Sant'Antonio now and a few boys were riding bikes, and old women were carrying shopping bags to town.

"But wait," Donna said. "I think we've forgotten someone. Fausta? Fausta the Fascist? Is she still alive?"

"She's not a Fascist anymore. She came to her senses at the Cielo. In fact, she was trying to fend off the Germans when they attacked that day and Dante tried to protect her. And that's how he was killed."

"Oh my. Another hero."

"She lives in the Contessa's house now. Just her and her cat. Doesn't come out at all."

"But she was a Fascist during the war?"

"Actually, she was a leading member of the *Fasci Femminili* in the area."

"Really? I knew some girls in that. You should have seen us fight with them. I mean really fight!"

Ezio smiled. "I don't doubt that at all."

Donna's brow furrowed. "Ezio? Do you think Fausta would know anything about this Amadeo Mazzella and how he could lead us to One-Eye?"

"Fausta? I can't believe that. It's been eleven years since she was a Fascist."

"It wouldn't hurt to ask her, though, would it?"

CHAPTER 16

───────▼───────

Since the war, with more jobs, with wages a little higher and, above all, with a desire to show one's status, more people in Tuscany were buying cars, and, of course, the Turin-based Fiat was the most popular. The only highway through tiny Sant'Antonio might see as many as fifteen or twenty cars go through on a given day, and children would stop and watch. Occasionally, they threw a tomato at a car, yelping when the shiny black doors were suddenly splattered red.

Almost no cars turned down the side road where Lucia Sporenza and her family lived, however, so when Ezio and Donna's battered Fiat sputtered down the gravel road, curtains suddenly opened in the half-dozen houses along the way. And when the car whimpered and died in front of the Sporenzas, the neighbors quickly ran out.

Since Marco was napping, Rosa, next door on the left, was the first, hugging Ezio as he tried to wipe the white dust from his shirt, his pants and his hair. Maria, on the right, struggled with her swollen legs down the steps and into Ezio's arms. Annabella came running from two houses away. Lucia herself rushed out the door, wiping her hands on her apron, followed by her mother.

Then they saw Donna.

Ezio let them admire his friend, enjoying their curiosity, and after an awkward silence, finally introduced her.

"Donna Fazzini, this is Rosa Tomasselli."

Rosa shook her hand politely, not sure what to make of this new person.

"And Annabella Sabattini, another friend."

Annabella also shook Donna's hand.

"And Gina Sporenza, and her daughter, Lucia Sporenza. Lucia's the mother of Little Dino."

"I'm so glad to meet you," Lucia said.

"And this is Maria Ruffolo. Maria, this is Donna Fazzini."

Tears in her eyes, Maria took Donna's hands and drew her near.

"Donna, Donna. Like in Madonna, right?" Maria said. "Oh, Ezio, what a lovely person you have brought to see us."

Donna kissed her cheeks. "Ezio has told me about your loss. I'm so sorry."

Ezio kissed Lucia. "Is Paolo at the *pasticceria*?"

"Yes." Lucia returned the kiss. "He had to stay in Reboli to make more *cannoli* during the siesta today. And Little Dino is at Fausta's. He weeds her garden every Friday. She gives him five *lira* and he thinks he has a million."

Lucia led the group into the house, Maria holding Donna's hand, and Ezio coming last. Inside, in the living room, Gina, Rosa and Annabella sat on straight-backed chairs, Maria in the only overstuffed chair and Ezio and Donna on the worn couch on which Lucia had placed a colorful afghan. Lucia stood at the door to the kitchen. Clearly, they were all waiting for Ezio to explain this fascinating creature who had come to Sant'Antonio. Only days ago he had left in a fury. Now he was back with an attractive woman at his side. Could she have taken his mind off the massacre?

It took Ezio a while to tell the story, and he had to repeat it several times, especially for Maria, who seemed not to be listening but simply looking at Donna.

Finally, the story was out. How Ezio had gone to Florence the day after the party at Lucia's last Sunday, how he met the man who gave him a name of someone who might be able to direct him to the main collaborator of the Sant'Anna massacre, how he had gone to Pietrasanta and met Donna, and how he and Donna were on their way to the Garfagnana, where they hoped to track down this man.

"And, you know," he concluded. "I think I know now who that man is who runs away from the fire in my nightmares. I think it's the Fascist collaborator of the massacre. And you know something else? I haven't had a headache or a nightmare since ..."

"Since?" Rosa asked.

"Since I met Donna."

Suddenly, there were triumphant smiles on the faces of five women who had worried and suffered through Ezio's headaches and nightmares for so long. Ezio may not have forgotten the massacre, but now he had someone to help him. Unable to hold their curiosity any longer, they immediately began to question Donna, although at times it sounded more like a police interrogation.

What does her father do? (A partisan! Like Ezio!) What about her mother? (Here, they all made the sign of the cross, and Maria murmured a prayer.) Did Donna work? (They couldn't believe that a young woman would have to work in a marble factory and decried what was happening to femininity in Italy.)

And then more important matters. How well could she cook? (Ezio, they said, needed to put more meat on his bones.) What were her favorite dishes? How much olive oil did she use? Tomatoes? Garlic? (Rosa volunteered to give her her secret ravioli recipe.)

Donna took all of the questions calmly, answering each carefully and fully, without condescension and showing an interest in the questioners as well.

Then came the crucial question, and Rosa asked it. "Since you are thirty-two years old, how is that you have not gotten married?"

As always, Donna answered matter of factly. "I have had men in my life," she said, "but I have never found one I wanted to spend the rest of my life with."

If the women hoped that she and Ezio would then hold hands, or even exchange glances, they were disappointed. Donna smiled at the women, one by one, and Ezio seemed absorbed in the wedding photograph of Gina and Pietro on the opposite wall. No one could think of anything else to say.

"Well, what am I thinking of," Lucia suddenly said. "Would you like some tea, some coffee, a few cookies? Annabella brought me some just yesterday."

"That would be lovely," Donna said.

"I'll help you," Rosa said, getting up quickly. "So will I," Gina and Annabella said together, leaving Maria sitting across from Donna and Ezio, each simply smiling at one another. When Maria fingered the photograph of Angelica and her children on her breast, Donna asked her about it, and then rose to kiss Maria on her graying hair.

In the kitchen, there were many whispers.

"Oh my," Annabella said. "I'm so excited I can hardly pour this coffee."

"She's a lovely, lovely girl," Gina said. "And that dress! Such a pretty blue."

"Mama," Lucia said, "that's the kind of dress I was telling you about last week. Can you make one for me?"

"If she works in a factory, maybe that's the only dress she has," Rosa said.

"Did you notice how small and soft her hands are?" Annabella said. "She must wear heavy gloves in that factory."

"And Ezio looks so happy," Gina said.

"Do you think? Do you think?" Lucia asked.

"I'll tell you one thing," Rosa said, lowering her voice. "That girl has had a hard life. Going through the war. Losing her mother. Working in a factory. *Santa Maria!*"

The women shook their heads.

"Look at her eyes," Rosa said, pouring coffee into tiny cups. "Look at how sad they are. Something terrible happened to her. And that's why she hasn't gotten married."

"Rosa, how could you know that?" Annabella said. "You always think you know everything."

Rosa smiled, but said nothing.

When the women paraded into the living room, bearing coffee and homemade cookies, there was a great deal of scrutiny about Donna's eyes, but they were now, in fact, twinkling, and so Rosa's theory was immediately discounted.

When the coffee pot had emptied, and the cookie tray was clean, Ezio stretched and said it was time to go. After kissing everyone one more time, Ezio and Donna went outside to their car. Ezio stopped Donna before she got in.

"Look up there," he said. "You can see it."

"Where?"

"On that high hill, the highest one. Look, see the red building about the center of the hill?"

"Where? Oh there."

"Now look straight up and then to the left a little at the top. See the yellow spot?"

"Mmmm. I guess I do."

"That's the Cielo."

"Really? It's still there? Who lives there now?"

"Nobody. Some people lived in it for a while but then they moved to Reboli. It's been abandoned for years. The roof has caved in and there's a lot of water damage. But if someone fixed it up, it would be a great place to live, don't you think?"

Donna looked at him. "It sounds as though you've been thinking about it."

"I'm not great with my hands, but I did help my father in his shop when I was in school and I guess I could nail two boards together."

"A place high on a hill. The Cielo sounds like heaven to me."

As Ezio helped Donna into the Fiat for the short ride to Fausta's house at the other end of the village, Maria stood between Gina and Lucia, holding their hands.

"I knew if I prayed to the Madonna my prayers would be answered."

CHAPTER 17

In 1944, when the people of Sant'Antonio returned to their village after the Germans fled, many houses were uninhabitable. British bombs had destroyed some of them, German soldiers wrecked others. Fausta's little house was among the casualties, but the Contessa's escaped harm.

The Contessa, a widow who was not a contessa at all but liked to wear fancy jewelry, invited Fausta to live with her. No two more contrasting women could be found. The Contessa, frail and flighty, Fausta, strong and silent. At first, they kept to their rooms, fixing their own meals and passing each other silently in the halls. This could have gone on for years, but then little Chiara entered their lives. She was small and white, a month-old kitten that had been abandoned by her mother. She was also deaf, presumably from getting too close to one of the landmines that were still exploding.

The Contessa screamed when she found the kitten whimpering on her doorstep. She had never owned a cat before. Hearing the noise, Fausta came running, scooped up the kitten and hugged her to her bosom. The kitten's purr could be heard in the next room. They found a tiny bottle and took turns feeding her fresh milk they got from Anzio's cows down the road. They called her Chiara because she was so bright. And they sat together taking care of her.

From then on, the Contessa and Fausta shared not only their meals but also their stories and their thoughts with each other. They sat for hours, one or the other holding Chiara on her lap. They read voraciously, often to one another. Two women, so very different, and so much in need of one another.

Fausta was devastated when the Contessa's heart just stopped and she died in her sleep one night four years ago. And from then on Fausta rarely went out. She saw only Paolo and Rosa occasionally, and Little Dino on Friday afternoons.

As much as the Contessa had kept the inside of the house immaculate for her collection of antiques and inherited things, she had not taken care of the outside. Now, pines and bushes and mimosa trees smothered the front, making the tile roof barely visible. In the back, however, Fausta, with Little Dino's help, had maintained the Contessa's ancient roses and orchids and irises.

When the sputtering Fiat pulled up in front of the house, Little Dino dropped his garden shears, ran to the fence and then stopped short, shyly waiting inside the gate until he saw that it was his teacher. Then he ran to the car.

"Little Dino! Working hard?" Ezio said, helping Donna from the car.

Little Dino smiled.

"Little Dino, I want you to meet my friend, Donna Fazzini."

Little Dino's smile grew wider.

"Dino," Donna said, and she shook his hand. "I'm so happy to meet you. Your teacher has told me what a fine student you are."

No one had ever called him simply Dino before, and for a moment he wondered who that was. Then his smile spread across his freckled face.

"Can you take us inside?" Ezio said. "We want to talk to Signorina Sanfilippo."

Little Dino led Ezio and Donna to the door, where Fausta had pulled the curtains apart to watch, then ran back to his chores. He had not said a word.

"Signorina Sanfilippo?" Ezio said as Fausta opened the door. "Do you remember me? I'm the partisan who was outside the Cielo during the war. Maybe you don't remember my name. It was Sparrow then."

"Ah yes, Sparrow. I remember now. You were at that party that Rosa gave after the war. I don't think I talked to you that night. I mostly sat in a corner. Many people were still avoiding me for what I did at the Cielo. They still invite me to their annual parties, but I don't care to go …"

Her voice caught and she wasn't able to finish.

"I remember how brave you were when we fought with the Germans, Signorina Sanfilippo. I'll always remember that. Now I'd like you to meet my friend, Donna Fazzini."

"It's an honor to meet you, Signorina." Fausta wiped her hands with the towel she carried, shook Donna's hand and led her guests into the dark sitting room.

All the shades were pulled, making the room cool but also impenetrable for anyone coming in from the bright sun. When Ezio and Donna's eyes finally adjusted to the dark, they saw a pair of dark brown overstuffed chairs, a sofa with heavy tables at either end, and dozens of framed photographs on the walls. Two bookcases with glass doors stretched to the ceiling. Being deaf, Chiara didn't wake from her slumber on one of the chairs.

Fausta herself blended into the severe setting. Her black hair was pulled back into a bun, the collar of her black dress was buttoned tightly around her neck, and her sleeves extended well over her hands. Spectacles hung on a chain around her neck, and her only adornment was a jeweled necklace, perhaps inherited from the Contessa. Ezio thought Fausta looked much thinner than he remembered.

"I'm afraid I don't have guests very often," Fausta said. "I don't think I can offer you anything but water."

"Water is just fine," Ezio said. "Thank you."

When Fausta returned from the kitchen with three mismatched glasses of water, to which she had hurriedly added lemon slices, she found Ezio and Donna looking at the books.

"Many of these books were Signora Vallentini's. I imagine you knew her as the Contessa. She was a lovely, lovely woman, and she took me in when my house was destroyed. So generous. She liked to read romance novels, that's why there are so many there. I like more serious works. I've read *The Divine Comedy* so many times. It reminds me of Signor Silva. He loved the book so much …"

Fausta couldn't go on.

"Signorina," Ezio said, "we've come to ask you a favor. We wonder if you can help us."

Once again, Ezio described his search for a collaborator of the Sant'Anna massacre and how he had found the name of Amadeo Mazzella as someone who could help. Did Fausta know anything about him?

Fausta's eyes widened when Ezio mentioned the name. "Signor Maffini, Signorina Fazzini, I think I should tell you my story."

Like Donna, who had told of her violation by four Germans the first night she met Ezio, Fausta started at the beginning. But unlike Donna, who had remained calm throughout, Fausta interrupted her story with tears, anger, hands that gestured and lips that trembled. She held on to the arms of her chair, covered with doilies.

"My father was one of the leading Fascists in this region," she began. "Not just here in Sant'Antonio, not just Reboli, but stretching all the way to Lucca. He got his instructions from people in Florence who got theirs from people in Rome. He conducted the meetings. He recruited new people. He saw that everyone knew about the party and what it stood for."

She paused to take a drink of water.

"Growing up, I was so proud of what he was doing and so proud of being his daughter. He looked so handsome in his dark suit with the red and black armband. Mother and I would look at him and we would just shake, we were so proud. It's too bad that Mother didn't live to see him longer.

"Every time Mussolini spoke on the radio we would sit together in the living room and listen to his speech. Father would smile and tell us there was going to be a new Italy. When the *Fasci Femminili* was formed before the war, Mother and I were the first to join. We were so anxious to help poor women, to help in clinics and hospitals, to urge them to have more children. We didn't want them to work in the factories."

Donna smiled faintly.

"I myself, though, was working in the thread factory in Reboli during the war," Fausta continued. "Our family needed money and it was all I could find. I was so anxious to serve the Fascist cause, I would do anything. Anything."

She paused to sip from her glass.

"Take your time, Signorina," Ezio said.

"When Mussolini asked everyone to help in the cause, I felt so helpless. I wanted to do something. And then the manager of the thread factory became interested in me. I don't know why. You can see I'm not a beautiful woman, I never was. Signor Aldonzi was a leading Fascist in Reboli. He knew my father well. They went to the same meetings. Signor Aldonzi was married and he had eight children. He said his wife was so busy with the children, she couldn't take care of his needs."

She pulled out a lacy handkerchief from her sleeve and wiped her eyes.

"Signorina, if you don't want to tell us …," Donna said.

"Yes, yes, I must. So he asked me to comfort him. Well, I was so foolish I thought maybe this is what I could do. I could make Signor Aldonzi happy and I would be doing it for the cause. And so it began. Every week, sometimes twice a week. In the storage room on the second floor, between all the brown boxes."

There was a look of pure disgust on Fausta's face.

"And then Signor Aldonzi wanted me to do some horrible things. And he didn't just ask me, he forced me. You see how I wear my clothes? High collars, long sleeves? The rope burns have now healed, but I still can feel them, sometimes I think I can see them."

"Oh, Signorina," Donna whispered.

"But I continued to do it. It was what Signor Aldonzi wanted, and I was a member of the *Fasci Femminili*. It was my duty. And then one day he brought another man with him. He was from Camaiore. I suppose Signor Aldonzi had told him about me. They both did it."

Donna clenched her hands tightly together.

"And then a third. A big fat man who smelled. He was from Pietrasanta. Imagine, all the way from Pietrasanta. And you know what his name was? Signor Amadeo Mazzella." She spit it out.

Chiara stirred in her chair, stretched and turned on her other side. No one spoke for several minutes.

"Yes, Amadeo Mazzella. I remember the name because he dropped an envelope on one of his visits. I've always kept it. So you see, I know Amadeo Mazzella. I know him all too well!"

If it hadn't been for the thick bushes and trees in front of the house, Fausta's scream could have been heard across the street.

"Signorina," Ezio said. "I don't know what to say. I'm so sorry."

Donna reached over and held Fausta's hand.

After a while, in which these three victims of war sat in silence, Ezio asked, "Signorina, I know this was so long ago, but do you have any idea where we could find Amadeo Mazzella now?"

There was a look of grim determination on Fausta's face.

"After the war, when I realized what a fool I had been, what fools all the women in the *Fasci Femminili* had been, I decided to do something about what had happened. My father had died in the war, he never knew what those bastards had done to me, and I could do what I wanted. There were other women who were also violated and who also realized what fools we were. So we set up a committee. We would keep track of these bastards. We didn't know what we would do with them, but at least we would know where they were.

"We connected with the other women throughout Tuscany. We called each other, we wrote letters. I kept a list of every one of the bastards. We know!"

She paused and closed her eyes for a long time before continuing.

"Signor Aldonzi fled to Argentina. Yes, this man who claimed to be so good left his wife and eight children behind. The man from Camaiore went to Trieste. And Amadeo Mazzella? We know exactly where he is. He's in Barga. He's a captain of police there. We know!"

Fausta spit the words out.

"Barga!" Ezio said. "In the Garfagnana. That's where we are going now. Signorina Sanfilippo, you don't know how much you have helped us."

"I wish you much success, Signor Maffini. I hope you find Mazzella and that other bastard."

Little Dino waved wordlessly at the gate while Fausta watched behind her curtains as Ezio and Donna drove away. Then she noticed a man half hidden by a tree across the street.

"The postman," she thought to herself. "He's already delivered the mail. Why is he still hanging around here?"

PART TWO

CHAPTER 18

▼

Officially, the spectacular stone footbridge at Borgo a Mozzano in the Garfagnana region of Tuscany is named Ponte della Maddalena. But no one calls it that. It's the Devil's Bridge, and its story is one villagers happily tell disbelieving tourists.

In the fourteenth century, they say, a master builder was contracted to build a new connection across the Serchio River. Instead of a horizontal bridge, he decided to make it arched, and the work went slowly until he realized he could not make the deadline the villagers had given him.

One evening he was sitting on the banks of the river and looking mournfully at the uncompleted bridge. He was desperate. What would his reputation be if he failed to complete the bridge on time?

Suddenly, a tall, well-dressed merchant stood next to him. The man told the bridge builder that he could finish the bridge that night, but there was one condition. The merchant demanded that the builder give him the soul of the first person who crossed the bridge when it was completed. The builder agreed, and the next day the villagers had their beautiful bridge.

When they congratulated the builder, he brushed their compliments aside. But he told them that no one should cross the bridge until sunset. The builder then rode his horse to Lucca and was received by the bishop.

"What am I going to do?" the bridge builder asked. "The devil wants the soul of the first person who will cross the bridge."

"Let no one cross the bridge," the bishop said. "Fool the devil. Send a pig across first."

The builder found a pig and let it cross. The devil was furious that he had been tricked, and he threw himself into the Serchio. Many say the devil was never seen again, but there are those who insist a green shadowy figure is visible just below the surface on All Souls Day.

Outsiders might point out that similar stories are popular for bridges in dozens of towns in Europe, with six or seven elsewhere in Italy alone, but the people of the Garfagnana ignore these protests. Their story, they insist, is the only true one.

The story of the Devil's Bridge is not the only one that flies frequently from farm to farm, hamlet to hamlet and mountaintop to mountaintop in this land that has changed so little through the centuries. Villagers also tell the story of the little girl who went into a deep tunnel under the highest of the mountains. She lost her way and still wanders around in there. Or of the grandmother who gave poisoned mushrooms to her family. She didn't know they were poisoned and after all of her family died, the grandmother disappeared into the forest. Or of the young brothers who found an underground lake and dared each other to swim across. They both drowned. And, more recently, there was the story of a ghost boy who had somehow survived a massacre.

The people of the Garfagnana have always been like the Apuan Mountains that loom over them—full of fear and fantasy. It is not a large area, but a compact stretch along the Serchio River north of Lucca. It is a region where the forests are so dense and the mountains so dangerous that it can hide many secrets. It can also conceal people. Someone, they say, could hide in the Garfagnana for years and never be seen.

Antonio Denato thought of the story of the Devil's Bridge every time he climbed to the top of the old hay barn on the farm where he worked. He remembered seeing the bridge for the first time when he arrived here eleven years earlier. That was the only time he crossed it. But if he stood atop two hay bales in the northeast corner, he could see just the top of the bridge. The Serchio looked like a strand of green thread snaking through the valley. There were many times when he wanted to join the devil in its turgid waters.

On this sweltering June day on which not a blade of grass stirred, Antonio climbed down from the hay bales and settled back against them. Everything was still. He took off his cap and eyeglasses to let the sun wash over his cheeks and beard and the gaping hole where his left eye had been.

Quiet.

Up here, he couldn't hear Fabiano yelling at him to clean the stables, feed the pigs, cut some hay. He couldn't hear Sabina screeching at the chickens. And he couldn't hear the incessant chatter of their young daughter.

Quiet.

"Antonio!"

Damn. He hurriedly put his cap and eyeglasses back on.

"Antonio!"

He turned on his side. Maybe she would think he was asleep.

"Antonio! I know you're up there!"

First a wicker basket, then her frizzy red hair, still in curlers, emerged from the opening in the roof. Then her head and shoulders. She wore a flimsy blouse over her tiny breasts.

"Antonio!" Graziella gasped for breath as she lifted herself out of the opening and on to the roof. "I knew I'd find you here."

Antonio made no comment but turned to face her. A plain, pudgy girl, he thought, still with baby fat. She had put on lipstick, but it ran clumsily onto one cheek.

"Look, I brought you a treat. I made some plum tortes this morning."

She lifted the basket and opened the towel. The smell of warm plums in freshly baked dough drifted over the roof.

"Don't you love my plum tortes?" If Graziella had read any books or seen any movies, she might have known that this was a provocative statement. But she was too young and too naïve to understand any other meaning. She sat down next to him and leaned back on the hay.

"Thank you, Graziella." He moved away a little and pulled his cap to his eyeglasses. "That was kind of you."

"Don't you love it up here?" She handed him a torte. "It's so quiet. I remember when I was a little girl I used to climb up the rope ladder and sit up here for hours and hours. You were working in the fields or something. Mama never knew where I was. I could hear her calling and I wouldn't answer. I just stayed up here. Sometimes I'd bring a doll or two and we'd play house, but I don't play with dolls anymore."

She tried to see what was behind his thick glasses but his cap concealed his eyes.

"Mama gets mad at me sometimes. She says I should do more work around the house. But I think I do a lot. I do all my chores. And after I'm through I have time to look at my movie magazines. I have six now. I bought them in Barga with my allowance. I don't read too well but I like to look at the pictures of the Hollywood stars. Cary Grant. Jimmy Stewart. Tyrone Power. Oh, I love Tyrone Power! He's a dreamboat. That's what the magazines call him, a dreamboat. I cut out one picture and pinned it on my wall so I could look at him before I go to sleep. It's right next to the picture of the Madonna that Mama put up. Maybe some day I can go to Barga and see a Hollywood movie."

It was easy for Antonio to tune out her singsong voice as it went on and on.

"I haven't been to Barga since March 15, 1954. Papa had to go and buy something for the tractor and Mama and me went along. That was more than a year ago. I remember the date because I wrote it in my diary. I keep a diary every day. I told you that, right? Tonight I'll write about how I talked to you today."

Antonio took a bite from the torte.

"I never go anywhere. I don't see anyone either. Just my Papa and Mama and my little cat, Fedoro. And you, of course. I wish we had a telephone and I could call my friend Natalia. Well, she was my best friend at school but I haven't seen her for a long time. Papa said I don't have to go to school anymore. I miss school. I liked going there. But it takes so long to walk down to the village. Papa says we're even too far to get a telephone, but sometimes I think he just doesn't want to pay for it. Same with a radio. We used to have one, but it broke. Anyway, he says we don't want to know what's going on in the world. There's too much bad stuff going on in the world."

Antonio nodded.

"I'm glad I can talk to you, Antonio."

Antonio made a slight grunting noise. Poor Graziella. No one to talk to. She tells the same stories all the time.

"But you know, you never say anything. I keep asking you questions and you never tell me about yourself and what you did before you came up here."

"There's nothing to tell."

"Oh, I'm sure there's a lot to tell. I mean, you're so old! You must be as old as Papa, right?"

"No, I'm thirty-eight."

"Papa is fifty-three. Or fifty-four," she said. "You look old. You've probably traveled all over, right?"

"No," he said quietly.

She was asking new questions now.

"And you were probably in the war, right?"

He could feel sweat underneath his cap. "No! Stop asking questions, Graziella."

The girl didn't seem to hear him.

"When did you come to work here? It must have been about fifteen years ago."

"Eleven."

"Eleven. Well, it's 1955 now, so that was, that was ... My teachers always said I was bad at math."

"1944."

"1944. I think the war was still going on then. I'm thirteen now, so in 1944 I was, I was ..."

"Two years old."

"Two! No wonder I don't remember when you came here. I don't remember that at all. I don't remember anything about the war. Oh, I remember one thing my Mama told me. She said one time we were bombed! Well, not really, but Papa said there was bombing all over around here and we had to go into the shelter next to the pigsty. That was before Papa fixed it up so that you could live in it. Papa and Mama and me went in there and we stayed a whole day and night. We didn't have food or anything and we had to go to the bathroom right outside. Mama said they could hear the bombs on the next hill but they didn't bomb us. I'm glad. I don't know what I would do if that happened again. I know one thing, I'd take Fedoro with me. He would be so frightened if we left him at home and there was bombing."

Graziella took another bite from her plum torte.

"I wish you would tell me stories about your life, Antonio. I am very interested. Antonio? Antonio?"

Silence.

"Of course if you don't want to tell me that's all right, too. But I think you must have ..."

Her voice drifted off. Antonio had tried to block out his life from his memory for so long. It was like someone else's now, not his. But he remembered when he made a decision that determined the course of his life.

CHAPTER 19

▼

It was 1927, and he was ten years old. He was sitting at his father's feet, begging him to tell him the story again.

"Please, Papa," he pleaded. "I have to write the report tonight!"

Ugo Donatello put down his grappa and looked at the boy. Another long day at the factory. He could barely keep his eyes open and now the boy wanted to hear the story again.

"Go ahead, Ugo," Lidia said, putting down a dish. "He needs to write the report for school tomorrow. Why he couldn't have written this before now, I don't know. But make it short. Don't exaggerate like you always do. And, Angelo, when you're finished you're going straight to bed."

Rain splattered the dirty windows of the third-floor flat. Although it was only 7:30, the room was dark, lit only by a dim bulb above the kitchen table. Ugo leaned back in the chair next to the stove and stretched his legs. His boots, coated with white marble dust, stood straight at his side. He folded his strong muscled hands. Marble dust lingered in the crevices of his fingernails.

Ugo always had a hard time refusing his son. He had been forty-six when Angelo was born. He and Lidia had thought they would never have children. Now, look at him, as sweet as one of those curly haired little angels in a painting in the church. Ten years old now, and the boy still looked up to him like he was a god.

"I remember it like yesterday."

"Yeah!" Angelo shouted. His father always started the story this way. The boy sat up straight, his eyes wide open.

"You see, when I came home from the war there were many people unhappy. Not only unhappy, they were angry, they were mad!"

Angelo found this the boring part, but he started to write on his notepad.

"People on the farms wanted more help from Rome. People in the factories, like me, wanted higher wages. Even here in Pietrasanta. We didn't have much food. Many days, we only had bean soup for supper. You were too young to remember that. Workers were striking all over. In fact, one time we staged a strike at Stupendi."

"At your marble factory? What did you do?" Angelo asked, knowing the answer.

"We just stopped working. The manager was furious. He told us to go back to work. Everyone, even the *artisans*." As he always did, he spat out the word. Ugo's job was to unload the huge chunks of marble when they arrived from the quarries. He never stepped inside the workrooms of Stupendi Marbleworks.

"We just stood around in the back and smoked and told stories."

"This only lasted four or five hours," Lidia said.

"No matter, we made the point."

"You still didn't get more money."

"Lidia, stop interrupting. Anyway, it was like there was a civil war going on in the country. The Socialists and Communists weren't doing anything. The king was too afraid to do something. So when Mussolini stepped in, everyone was happy that we had a leader who could make some changes. He formed the Fascist party. All the men wore black shirts and pants so they were called the Blackshirts."

Angelo giggled at this.

"Anyway, in October 1922, he asked people who supported him to march to Rome and show support for the Fascist party. Then the king would listen and Mussolini would be given the power.

"So Flavio and Nuncio and me and all the other men on the loading dock decided to go along. Hell, we didn't have anything to lose. Oh, one of the guys refused. Big Red. Big Red the Communist. I said why don't you come along and he said he didn't trust Mussolini. That Big Red. Always thought the Communists could do everything. And not many people then said they were Communists. They were afraid. But Big Red wasn't. He told everybody."

Ugo drank some grappa.

"Of course, we didn't have any black shirts so your mother did the next best thing."

Lidia sighed. "I took his good white shirt and I got some dye from the cleaners and I turned that white shirt as black as the devil. My hands were black for a month."

Angelo laughed. "My teacher is going to like that part."

"So Flavio and Nuncio and me and all the other guys met early in the morning in front of the Duomo. It seemed like all the men of Pietrasanta were there. Everyone was cheerful, slapping each other on the back. I guess we didn't think about what was ahead. We weren't dressed for this. We wore black shirts, or something like that, but we should have had warmer clothes and we sure as hell should have had better shoes."

The rain was now pouring into the cracked window over the sink. Lidia, a good half foot taller than her husband, reached up and stuffed a towel into it. "I wish you would fix this window sometime, Ugo. It's been broken for three months."

"I'll get to it," Ugo said. "So old Saladino, he was the head of the Fascist party in Pietrasanta, told us to get into a line. Well, we didn't know how to form a line. And we didn't know how to march. So we just sort of grouped together and walked out of the Piazza del Duomo and down Via Sarsanese. We were singing and laughing, having a good time."

At this, Ugo began to sing the Fascist hymn. Even though he was a small man, his deep voice could be heard out on the street three stories below.

Giovinezza, Giovinezza,
Primavera di bellezza
Della vita nell'asprezza
Il tuo canto squilla e va!
E per Benito Mussolini,
Eja eja alalà.
E per la nostra Patria bella,
Eja eja alalà.

Youth, Youth,
Spring of beauty,
In the hardship of life
Your song rings and goes!
And for Benito Mussolini
Hip hip hooray.
And for our beautiful Fatherland,
Hip hip hooray.

Angelo always laughed when he heard his father sing the Fascist anthem.

Lidia picked up a pair of Angelo's pants and started mending the knee. "Maybe you should tell Angelo what you were drinking."

"What did you say?"

"I said maybe you should tell him what you were thinking."

"I was *thinking*," Ugo said slowly and forcefully, "I was thinking how good it was that the people were finally taking control of things. We were going to have a good life after all these years of misery. So it didn't matter if our legs were tired and our feet were blistered."

"Papa," Angelo said, knowing what the answer would be, "you didn't walk all the way to Rome, did you?"

"Most of the way."

"Only a part," Lidia interjected.

"I said *most* of the way. From Lucca to Siena there were trucks that took us. And then from Grossetto to just outside of Rome we were on trains. We just got on the trains and pushed the passengers off. A few times we had some donkey carts for the men who couldn't walk so fast. But for the rest of the way we walked. And we walked. You should have seen us. The man up in front carried a big flag. As we got closer to Rome, we started chanting. 'Rome or Death!' and 'Viva Mussolini!' The college students were having a great time outshouting each other.

"And we were hungry! Sometimes farmers gave us something to eat, sometimes we cooked pasta in big pots with water from the streams. We didn't have any forks so we ate with our bare hands. It was terrible!"

"Yuk!" Angelo said. He wrote some more in his notepad.

"Oh, and you think it's raining hard here now? You should have seen it then! Pouring rain all the way. No hats, no raincoats. We were drenched. At night we would find some sort of shelter, in a barn or someplace, and in the morning we would start out again. And cold? This was late October, remember. At night we were so cold we thought our asses would freeze off."

"Weren't you afraid the army was going to shoot you?"

"Nah. There were too many of us. And we were armed. We found some weapons."

"Right," Lidia said. "Tree branches, legs from tables …"

Ugo laughed. "I'll never forget this one guy. He carried a big slab of dried salt cod. What I wouldn't give to see him hit a soldier on the head with a dried salt cod."

"Tell us how you smelled," Angelo said after they had all stopped laughing.

"We smelled like shit. Well, why not? We didn't take baths for a couple of weeks. But also, we didn't have latrines. So we went by the side of the road and some of these guys, they couldn't wait and they had accidents."

Lidia laughed. "I can imagine how the beautiful women of Rome rushed up to see all these men smelling of shit."

"Don't laugh. The beautiful women of Rome greeted us with flowers and kisses. They hugged us and said they were on our side."

Lidia looked up from her mending. "Angelo, why don't you ask your father where that great leader, Mussolini, was all this time?"

"Where, Papa?"

"He was in Milan getting ready to take over the government."

Lidia laughed. "He was in Milan going to the opera with his mistress."

Angelo raised his hand. "What's a mistress?"

"Never mind!" Ugo shouted. "Don't write that down. Lidia, I told you to stop interrupting! *Il Duce* was in Milan because that's where he had his headquarters! He was waiting for the king to tell him to come to Rome and form a new government! And he did. Remember the date, son, October 29, 1922. The most important date in Italian history!"

Ugo was out of breath and took another drink of grappa. Lidia put aside her mending and picked up her knitting. The room grew quiet for a few minutes, and when Angelo felt it was safe, he asked, "And what happened that day, Papa?"

"It was a glorious day. The king gave Mussolini the power to form a new government. After all those terrible years, we had hope again. And we were all so happy. Oh, Angelo, I wish you could have been there." Ugo's eyes glistened.

"We were supposed to march into Rome but it was more like a parade. We were singing and shouting. You know I had never been to Rome, but I had seen the pictures in school, just like you're seeing them. So it was just like I had been there before. We gathered at the Piazza del Popolo, such a beautiful place, the tall obelisk, the fountains. You walk in between these two churches that look just alike.

"And then we walked up Corso Umberto. Such a long street. People were lined up on both sides, cheering us. And then we got to the Piazza Venezia. They had just built a big monument to the first king of the united Italy there. What was his name, Angelo?"

"Victor Emmanuel!" Angelo knew his history.

"Yes. It's huge and all white. Some day people will say it is one of the finest monuments in Rome. And finally, we went all the way to the king's palace, the Palazzo del Quirinale. I'll never forget it." Ugo wiped his eyes.

"What else did you see, Papa?" This was Angelo's favorite part of the story.

"Oh, the next day we were so tired but that didn't stop us. We went all over. We saw all those places I thought I'd never see. The Colosseum, the Forum, the Spanish Steps, the Trevi Fountain, the Piazza Navona. Someone suggested going to the Vatican to see the pope but nobody wanted to go."

"How many, Papa? How many men marched on Rome?"

"They came from all over. Sicily, Naples, all over the north. There were maybe sixty thousand men who marched on Rome that day."

"More like twenty thousand," Lidia said.

Ugo turned to his wife. "It doesn't matter how many!" he shouted. "We have a better life now because of what Mussolini, this great man, this son of a blacksmith, is doing."

"Yes!" Lidia was shouting now, too. "A better life! *Boh!* Now we have bean soup every day! Now we get a new pair of shoes every two years instead of three! Now you make so much more money at the factory. Not a *lire* more! *Boh!*"

Ugo stood up. "Lidia, that's enough! I told you to shut up."

Lidia got up and started to put the dishes away. Ugo went behind her.

"I'm going to bed," he said into her ear. "You'd better be in there in five minutes."

Ugo stormed into the next room, slamming the door. Lidia continued with her mending. After exactly six minutes, she put it down.

"Finish your report, Angelo," she said, smoothing her son's hair. "You always write so well. And so fast! I don't know where you get it."

She went into the bedroom.

Angelo sat the kitchen table and began to write his report. By the time he had finished and put his notepad in his backpack for the next day, the yelling in the next room had stopped, the bickering had turned into laughter and then the laughter evolved into soft moaning. Angelo lay on his trundle bed next to the stove and stared at the dirty ceiling.

"Now I know what I want to be when I grow up," he thought. "I want to be just like my Papa. A hero. Imagine, he walked all the way to Rome. Well, most of the way. And all the women of Rome hugged him. And he saw all the important places, places the whole world knew. When I grow up I want to be a Blackshirt."

CHAPTER 20

▼

He had never been in such a beautiful place, except for maybe the Duomo in Pietrasanta. The marble walls, the stained glass windows, the tall pillars, the high ceilings, the heavy wooden tables and benches. Angelo couldn't move for minutes after he entered the courtroom, not until his mother pushed him into the row of benches at the back.

They were both tired after the long bus ride from Pietrasanta to La Spezia, and now they had to wait for the magistrate to finally appear and start the hearing. And wait. And wait. The room was stifling and Angelo's suit coat, which fit last year when he was fourteen, felt like a straight-jacket. An inch of frayed shirtsleeves showed at his wrists.

"Mama, can I take my coat off?"

"No, leave it on." Lidia herself felt suffocated in her heavy black dress on this August day.

In the first row, men from Stupendi Marbleworks also looked uncomfortable in clothes they would wear only to church, if they went to church. Angelo recognized his Papa's friends, Nuncio and Flavio, on one side and the man he knew only as Big Red the Communist on the other. Big Red was leaning forward, his head almost in his hands.

Finally, the magistrate appeared, all in black and looking very bored. It was clear he wanted to get this over with as quickly as possible. A young woman carrying a notebook took her place at a long table at his side.

The magistrate picked up a piece of paper. "We are here in the matter of the death of Ugo Donatello in Pietrasanta last month, on 15 September 1932."

Lidia flinched and she grabbed Angelo's hand.

"It appears to me that this was an accident, but we will hear all the testimony."

"Mama," Angelo whispered, "he's already made up his mind."

"Shhhh."

"Let me call the first witness, Nuncio Nori."

Hesitating, Nuncio walked up to the magistrate's table.

"Signor Nori, where do you work?"

"Stupendi Marbleworks."

"And what is that?"

Nuncio nervously clasped his big calloused hands over his ample belly. "It makes ... it makes copies of famous statues out of marble."

"Very large pieces of marble, I gather?"

"Yes."

"Like the David and the Waking Slave? I've seen them."

"Yes."

"All right, Signor Nori, please describe the incident." The magistrate leaned back and closed his eyes. Angelo was sure he had fallen asleep.

"We were taking this big slab of marble off the truck and the crane suddenly tilted and it fell on poor Ugo."

Nuncio wiped his eyes with the back of his hand.

The magistrate stirred. "All right, that sounds like an accident to me."

"Wait!" Flavio stood up. "Sir, your honor, your excellency, your eminence, there is more to it than that."

The magistrate did not like this turn of events. "All right," he sighed, "tell us what more there is to this."

Flavio's hands trembled. "Just before this, there was a terrible scene. You see, Ugo and Big Red, that man over there ..." Big Red straightened and glared at Flavio. "Ugo and that man over there never did like each other. Ugo was one of the most important men in our party ..."

"What party is that?" the magistrate interrupted.

"The Fascist, of course." Flavio gave a small salute. "Ugo had been active ever since the march on Rome in 1922. He had given his own time, he helped organize meetings and distributed information. He was in front when we had parades. He ..."

"All right, you've made the point."

"But Big Red here, he was a Communist, always has been. He's always been sore that the Fascists took over. He was always criticizing everything they did."

Flavio paused for breath. He had never talked so long before.

"So Ugo and Big Red would go at it. They would be working, unloading the marble, and they would be shouting at each other. Sometimes it was just in fun. And it was sort of comical with Big Red being so big and Ugo being such a small man. Big Red could have picked him up if he wanted to. But at the end of the day they would slap each other on the back and go home. I don't think they ever went to an *osteria* for a beer or a grappa like the rest of us, though."

Lidia and Angelo listened to this with fascination. They had never heard this about Ugo before.

"Well, on this day, they were going at it pretty hard. They were calling each other terrible names. I never heard them like that before. And then Big Red went up to Ugo and pushed him …"

Big Red stood up. It was clear why he was called Big Red, brawny and well over six feet with a ruddy face and a shock of bright red hair. "He pushed me first!" he shouted.

The magistrate pounded his gavel. "Sit down! Sit down! You'll have your turn. Go on, Signor … whatever your name is."

Flavio wiped his face with a red handkerchief. "Well, they both started pushing and shoving and yelling at each other. The rest of us were just watching."

"You didn't make any attempt to stop this?"

"Well, no," Flavio sputtered. "But we were cheering for Ugo. All the rest of us are Fascists, too. Except for Big Red."

Big Red made an obscene gesture.

"Then Ugo and Big Red started fighting. Ugo hit Big Red in the chest and Big Red punched Ugo in the face. And they started swinging. It looked like they were going to kill each other."

Lidia burst into tears and Angelo put his arm around her.

"Then the boss came out and yelled at them to stop. Finally they did. And the boss told everyone to go back to work. So we did. Well, Ugo was in his usual place on the ground near the truck and Big Red was up on top of the crane. I could tell he was still mad because his face was all red. That's why we call him Big Red."

Big Red tried to say something but the magistrate stared at him.

"And then?" the magistrate asked.

"Well, all of a sudden, the crane swerved and the marble fell off the chains and it fell right on top of poor Ugo."

Lidia and Angelo both sobbed uncontrollably.

"So you see," Flavio said, "it wasn't an accident! Big Red did that on purpose!"

"It was an accident!" Big Red shouted.

"All right, all right," the magistrate said. "Come up here and tell your story. What's your name?"

Big Red lumbered to the magistrate's table. "Franeschetto Finocchietti."

Angelo wiped his nose with the back of his hand and tried not to snicker.

"Tell us what happened, Signor … um … Signor Finocchietti."

"Yes, it's true, Ugo and me had a disagreement before the accident. But I was over it. And if my face was red it was because it was a hot sunny day. I was up on the crane and I made a move to lower the marble. But that crane had been giving me trouble all week. I reported it to the boss but he didn't do anything about it. In fact, I reported it twice. The levers and the switches were all rusted and I couldn't get them right. But on that day I lifted the marble up and I thought it was going to work right, but then suddenly the crane swerved and the chains fell off and …"

Big Red's shoulders shook and everyone waited for him to continue.

"The marble fell." He could barely be heard.

The room was quiet for long minutes. Lidia held Angelo's hand. The young woman at the table fanned herself with her notebook. The magistrate looked first at Nuncio and then at Flavio and then at Big Red. The magistrate was a Fascist, and he knew he should have Big Red bound over for trial. But that would mean weeks of more boring testimony and August was just too hot for that.

"All right, it is clear. This was an accident. Case dismissed." The magistrate stood up and swept out of the room, his black robes flying behind him.

"It wasn't an accident!" Angelo leaped up from the bench, shouting and pointing at Big Red. "It wasn't an accident! That Communist killed my Papa!"

Lidia pulled at his sleeve. "Angelo, sit down."

"It wasn't an accident! You killed my Papa!" His voice cracked and he was in tears. "I'm going to get you, you Communist! I'm going to get all you Communists!"

From that day on, Lidia knew that her son had changed forever from the angel-faced little boy she had always known. He didn't do his chores and often he skipped school. He stayed out late with boys who smoked and used bad words.

Trying to appease him, Lidia gave him the bedroom that she and Ugo had shared, and she took the little trundle bed in the kitchen although she was much too big for it. She said she wanted to be near the stove to do the cooking.

Angelo became more active in Balilla, the Fascist youth organization, especially the field training with real weapons. He turned his new bedroom into a Fascist shrine, and on one wall posted a drawing of the boy from Genoa for whom the organization was named.

On another wall, he hung a poster with a sketch of Mussolini hugging a little boy. Underneath was the caption: "Benito Mussolini loves the children a lot. The children of Italy love *il Duce*. Long live *il Duce!*"

All around the room, at the top of the walls, he inscribed the motto of the Balilla: "I believe in Rome, the Eternal, the mother of my country. I believe in the genius of Mussolini and in the resurrection of the Empire."

Near his bed, Angelo kept copies of the Fascist youth magazine *Gioventu Fascista* and each night poured over its articles and cartoons. He kept a notebook, copying phrases and sentences that he liked from the magazine and attempting his own drawings.

He was fastidious about his Balilla uniform, black shirt, black cap, black shorts, gray socks, which he kept neatly folded on top of his dresser. They were next to a framed photo of Mussolini and one of Ugo, taken twenty years ago, in a cowboy costume. The rest of his clothes lay in piles around the room.

Lidia hated to go into his room to make up his messy bed. It reeked of cigarette smoke.

She started getting called in by his teachers. He was teasing the girls, getting into fights and bullying little kids, especially Big Red's five-year-old son. Lidia tried to get Angelo to behave, but he just laughed at her.

"I'm grown up now, Mama! I'm fifteen years old!"

Once, he brought home the rifle the Ballila used in weekend training. He thought he could hide it in a paper bag, but it was pretty hard to conceal a fourteen-inch carbine. Lidia was scared to death.

"I have to clean it," Angelo said, and stomped into his room.

Lidia wished Ugo were here to discipline his son. Ugo had never done that, because there was no need. Of course, if Ugo were here now, Angelo wouldn't be acting like this. She prayed every night and she lit candles in the church that Angelo would be his former self.

This went on for three years. Angelo could have waited to be drafted into the army, but on his eighteenth birthday, in 1935, he went down to the office in Pietrasanta and enlisted.

"I'm doing this for Papa," he told his mother. "I'm going to kill Communists. You'll see. I'm going to be a Blackshirt. I'm going to be a hero!"

CHAPTER 21

▼

The last place Angelo wanted to be on Christmas Eve was a godforsaken outpost in a barren Ethiopian desert. God, he wanted to be home. His father may not have paid much attention to Christmas, especially after he started wearing black shirts, but he tolerated Lidia's little decorations and certainly enjoyed her extensively planned Christmas dinners. Angelo could still smell and taste the tortellini, the little chicken, the white beans with sage and finally the pears and cheese. He could never figure out how she managed to produce such a feast.

And he remembered the little *presepio* his mother set out on his dresser and how he liked to arrange the figures of Mary, Joseph, the Baby Jesus, an angel and, especially, the cow and lamb. And then, after midnight mass at the Chiesa di Sant'Agostino, he would get a present, always a new pair of socks that Lidia had made.

After his father was killed—assassinated by a Communist, he always said—his mother didn't pay much attention to Christmas. She didn't take the *presepio* out of the box, and Christmas dinner was no different from any other. He thought she probably spent the day in a corner, knitting and crying softly. He wasn't certain, since he was out drinking with his friends and didn't come home until after midnight.

Now here he was, in 1935 in a makeshift barracks and the smallest soldier in the company. He didn't like the three other soldiers who were around, but they were the only ones who paid attention to him. Sergio was always talking about growing up in Siena and how great it was. Giacomo, on the other hand, didn't have a kind word to say about Perugia, where he was born. Rinaldo claimed to know everything about everything, but always wanted some inducement to reveal what little information he did have.

All of them were in their late twenties, had traveled in Italy and France and, to hear them talk about it, had conquered some of the most beautiful women in the world. To them, Angelo was just a boy from a small town who didn't know his right foot from his left and a ready object for their teasing.

"Hey, *ragazzo*," one of them would say, "have you written to your mother yet today?"

Angelo tried to ignore their dirty talk, which was growing louder with every bottle of cheap but highly potent Ethiopian beer they consumed. He knew they wanted him to join them, but he got sick every time he drank the stuff. He took out the box that his mother had sent him for Christmas. A bag of crumbs that he thought must have been biscotti. A little brown spiral notebook with lined pages. An orange pencil. And, best of all, a woolen cap. It was made of bright colors, mostly blue, but also patches of red and green and yellow.

"She must have used up all her old yarn," he thought as he pulled the cap on. He tried to write a little more of his thoughts in the notebook. The others would tease him even more if they found out he kept a journal.

Angelo had been crammed with the others on the ship coming over from Naples in July. As hot and steamy as the converted liner had been on its journey down the Red Sea, it was even worse when the ship finally docked at Massawa. Temperatures of more than a hundred degrees baked the flat and barren landscape.

"So this is the Second Roman Empire that *il Duce* is always talking about," Giacomo sneered. "Looks like a hell hole to me."

Angelo wanted to punch him and throw him off the troopship. "Fuck off!" he shouted. "We're here to ... we're here to ..."

"To what?" Sergio said. "Get killed by some half-assed aborigine?"

Angelo raised his arm and was about to hit Sergio when their sergeant came up, separated the three of them and ordered them to shut the hell up.

"For Papa, for Papa, for Papa," Angelo kept repeating to himself.

Angelo didn't understand all the reasons why Mussolini wanted to invade Ethiopia. Some said it was to avenge a defeat Italy suffered at Adowa in 1896. Some said Mussolini wanted an empire like the United Kingdom and France. Some said it was to gain control of the Suez Canal. And some said it was simply because Ethiopia was there for the taking.

Few people believed Mussolini when he said he wanted to expose Ethiopians as a barbaric people, "sunk in the practice of slavery."

It didn't matter to Angelo what the reasons were. When he boarded the troopship, Mussolini's address to his Blackshirt division from the back of a truck at Eboli still rang in his ears. "You will be strong and invincible," *il*

Duce had shouted, "and soon you will see the five continents of the world bow down and tremble before Fascist power."

Angelo began to shake, he was so excited.

"Yes!" he wanted to shout. "For Papa!"

Angelo was surprised, though, when Mussolini said he had "powerful armaments that nobody in the world suspects." What were Mussolini's secret weapons, he wondered.

The division's first stop was in Asmara, in Eritrea just north of Ethiopia. What had been a dusty group of houses had suddenly expanded into a tent city with the arrival of thousands of troops. It had two movie houses but, more important for these soldiers, a place called the Casino, and it was here that Angelo lost his virginity. Since there was a line of soldiers waiting outside, the session was short.

"That bitch charged me ten *lira* for *that*?" he said afterwards to Rinaldo, who had preceded him.

But on the night of October 2, he and the other soldiers sprang from their barracks when they heard church bells ringing and saw searchlights flooding the Governor's Palace and the Fascist Club. When hundreds of men started singing, Angelo burst into tears.

> *Giovinezza, Giovinezza,*
> *Primavera di bellezza*
> *Della vita nell'asprezza*
> *Il tuo canto squilla e va!*
> *E per Benito Mussolini ...*

Angelo couldn't wait to see some real action, and he thought that would happen now as they prepared to cross the border into Ethiopia and reach the outskirts of Adowa.

"I don't care why we're doing this," Angelo told Sergio as he cleaned his carbine for the fourth time one night. "I just want to do some fighting."

"Well, be a big hero if you want," Sergio said as he left the barracks. "I'm just going to see if they've got a good whorehouse around here."

Starting on October 3, Italian planes bombed the countryside, sending terrified villagers to the hills. Having never heard anything more powerful than a rifle shot, they might have been more afraid of the noise than of the bombs themselves.

"When are we going to invade?" Angelo kept asking his sergeant. "When are we going to invade?"

"When we get the orders, Private. Don't piss in your pants."

Finally, on October 6, the orders came, and the Eighty-Fourth Infantry Regiment of the Nineteenth Division under the command of General Nino Salvatore Villa Santa lumbered toward the town. Sweating under the blazing sun, Angelo felt his heart pounding. His first battle. "For Papa, for Papa."

But when they looked around, they found Adowa was empty. The Ethiopian forces had fled to the mountains.

But that didn't prevent a parade to make the occupation official. Colors flying, the Italian troops marched noisily through town. Their general and a group of journalists brought up the rear. Their song echoed in the hills.

Giovinezza, Giovinezza,
Primavera di bellezza
Della vita nell'asprezza
Il tuo canto squilla e va!

"Now this is the way to fight a battle," Giacomo told Angelo as they walked down the rocky street.

"Damn," Angelo said. "This is not the way. I wanted a real fight." Tears flowed down his cheeks.

The division band played as they paraded through the streets, deserted except for a few bewildered civilians who bowed their heads. Outside the Coptic church, with the sun glinting off its corrugated iron roof, priests had put on their colorful robes. "Your religion will be respected," Villa Santa told them. "There will be no more bombing."

And for Angelo and his fellow soldiers in the coming months, there was no fighting, either. While other units of their regiment moved to the south and more victories, not all of them as easy, his unit was assigned to occupy Adowa.

It was dreary duty. Some civilians came back to their tiny homes, but many stayed away. Angelo and the others spent their days casually patrolling empty streets, firing at birds and replacing posters of Emperor Haile Selassie with those of Mussolini. At night, they went to the only bar and played *scopa* or *briscola*, always ending their card games with angry arguments.

And they drank beer. Bottle after bottle. Angelo had never drunk so much beer before and none as bad as this. The others took advantage of his drunken state, and he did some things he could never remember the next morning. The others would point at him and snicker.

"Remember how you climbed to the top of the stockade at the end of town?" one would ask. He did not.

Homesick and depressed by the lack of action, Angelo grudgingly followed Sergio, Giacomo and Rinaldo to the bar on Christmas Eve.

"It's Christmas!" Giacomo shouted as they walked through the flimsy door. "Let's get drunk."

The room was filled with so much smoke Angelo could hardly see. Soldiers packed the long bar and the tables to the side. Girls from the neighboring establishment sat on laps and licked the infantrymen's ears before escorting them outside. There was a lot of singing. Christmas songs, Neapolitan love songs, dirty songs.

Angelo and the others found a place in the corner and took out their cards. Soon a line of a dozen empty beer bottles stretched along the edges of the table. They had already starting arguing about their cards when the place suddenly grew quiet and a crowd formed around a corporal who had just entered. Angelo tried to hear what was going on. Sergio went over to investigate and returned red-faced and out of breath.

"It's not good," he whispered.

"What?"

"Mussolini, that fool, has used mustard gas."

"Shit!" Rinaldo said. "Where? When?"

"Two days ago. There was this battle at the Takkaze River. Southwest of here. Thousands of those bastard warriors. We had tanks. They climbed on our tanks. Carrying spears, can you imagine? So then planes came down low and sprayed mustard gas. The bastards were screaming."

"No!" Angelo cried. "It's not true!"

"Stupid goddamn fool," Rinaldo said. "Doesn't *il Duce* know?"

"No!" Angelo said and covered his face with his hands. "He wouldn't do that!"

"Now he's in trouble," Sergio said. "Doesn't he know how people will react to this?"

"No!" Angelo whispered, took out his handkerchief and blew his nose.

In Balilla training, Angelo had put on gas masks and had a little training in chemical warfare. But that was in case gas was used against them. He never thought Mussolini, his great honorable hero, would use it against the enemy.

The others were describing the effects. "Huge blisters," Sergio said. "Pain you wouldn't believe," Rinaldo said. "People die right away," Giacomo said.

"No, they don't!" Angelo shouted. "They don't die. Not always anyway. It's mainly to scare people."

"Tell that to those people who just got sprayed," Rinaldo said. "You can defend your hero. Me, I'm having another beer."

"Me, too," Sergio and Giacomo said together.

The line of beer bottles grew as the night went on. At the bar, the singing had stopped and the soldiers who hadn't left with the girls were now drowning their disgust and loneliness in beer. And falling over. And throwing up.

"Let's get out of here," Rinaldo said. "This place smells like shit."

A pale moon outlined the four drunken soldiers staggering down the street, each holding a bottle high in the air. One or the other fell, had to be picked up, and fell again. Sergio threw up in the middle of the street. Rinaldo went to a stone wall to relieve himself.

Angelo's head hurt and his stomach churned and his legs felt like strands of spaghetti.

"Hey," Rinaldo said, "let's have some fun with the kid." He and Sergio were staggering along behind him.

"Hey, *ragazzo*," Rinaldo cried. "I bet you can't run to that house over there."

"Oh, no?" Angelo tried, but he was laughing so hard he fell on his knees about ten feet shy of the mark.

"Hey, *ragazzo*," Giacomo said. "How about climbing over that tank?"

Angelo struggled up the side and stood swaying on top of the turret. Then he fell off, his laughter mixed with tears.

Now arm in arm, the four bedraggled soldiers turned a corner and stood in front of the circular Coptic church. The corrugated roof shone in the moonlight.

"Hello, church!" Rinaldo yelled, and fell to his knees.

"Merry Christmas, church!" Sergio waved his arms.

"Hey Angelo," Giacomo shouted. "See the top of the church? I bet you can't climb up there."

"Bet I can." Angelo's voice was slurred. "Ten *lira*?"

"Ten *lira*? You have to be joking. That's as much as a whore!"

Angelo pointed to the top. "Well, look at it. A hundred feet high."

"Shit! No more than forty."

"Climb it!" Sergio shouted.

"Climb it!" Rinaldo echoed. "Giacomo, you're not going to have to pay this."

Angelo staggered to the side of the church. Looking up, he estimated that there would be three levels to climb. Over one arch, then over another, then to the top. He dropped his beer bottle on the ground and grabbed a pillar at the side. Slowly, he shimmied to the first level, stood up and waved down.

"Good boy! *Bravo ragazzo!*" the other three shouted.

Angelo waited five minutes, then pulled himself up the corrugated roof, inch by inch. He reached the second level but was afraid to let go of the arch.

"Good boy! *Bravo ragazzo!*"

Inch by painful inch, he made his way the last ten feet, sliding back twice but regaining his hold. Finally, he was at the top. He pulled himself up, balanced himself precariously on the top runner and waved to the three figures far below.

"A hero, *ragazzo!* You're a hero! … hero! … hero! …"

And that was the last Angelo heard as his beer-soaked shoes lost their grip. Suddenly, an excruciating pain pierced his left eye and seared to the back of his head.

CHAPTER 22

▼

After five days, Angelo came out of his stupor long enough to scream and shout curses that the good nuns at Pietrasanta Hospital had never heard before. He was quickly given another dose of morphine.

On the seventh day, he felt a pounding in his head and burning in his eyes. He was able to sense the presence of someone near him, fiddling with tubes.

"Don't move."

That was all he heard.

On the eighth day, he could feel a hand on his wrist. It was soft. He went back to sleep.

On the ninth day, he awoke with a terrible headache and screamed. He wanted to cry but for some reason couldn't. He tried to open his eyes but everything was black.

"It's all right, it's all right." The voice was feminine, distant, old.

"Where am I?" He didn't recognize his own voice.

"You're in a hospital in Pietrasanta. You were brought here from Ethiopia."

Every inch of his body hurt. "What's wrong with me?"

"You've been badly injured. It will take some time. You just need to rest now."

"I can't ... I can't see."

"You have bandages over your eyes. In time you will be able to see again, at least with your right eye."

"Not the left?"

"It had to be removed."

Angelo tried to find the source of the soft hand. His left arm was immobile. He tried the other and grabbed on to two fingers.

"I don't have an eye?"

"In time you will have a good right eye."

"No-o-o-o-o-o-o-."

"Rest now."

"Wait. Is the war over?"

Her voice grew colder. "They're still killing each other."

She removed the restraints but gave him another shot of morphine.

Then the nightmares began and they kept on, day and night. He was falling, falling, falling into a black abyss. He could hear yelling. Suddenly something seared his eye and he could no longer see.

Four days later, he was still in terrible pain.

"Private," the older voice said softly. "You have to stop cursing so loud. There are other patients here."

"I hurt all over. Tell me what's wrong with me. Please."

The response was a litany. His left eye had been removed, his right eye badly damaged. His left wrist and his left leg were broken. His spine was fractured and his ribs cracked. A bladder infection required a catheter.

After two weeks, the voice announced that he had a visitor. Still in her heavy black dress, Lidia was led by two nuns to Angelo's bedside. She reached out and touched his arm, screamed and had to be half-carried out of the room, sobbing.

Over the days, the headaches subsided and the pains in his back and chest decreased. He was propped up in bed, with his eyes still covered in bandages and his left arm and leg still in casts.

"How are you today?" The voice was different, younger, softer.

"How the hell do you think?"

"Please open your mouth so I can take your temperature."

He made no move.

"Please. Open your mouth."

She pushed his jaw down and stuck the thermometer into his mouth. "Please. Don't bite on it. Thank you," she said, examining it. "Still high."

"Well, what the fuck do you think it would be?"

She held his right wrist. "I need to take your pulse."

A pause.

"Still racing."

"Fuck! Fuck! Fuck!"

"Let me fix your pillow."

"Leave the goddamn pillow alone!"

"Please, Private Donatello, I just want to help."

"Well, don't try. Just leave me alone. Now what the hell are you doing down there?"

Angelo's face turned crimson below the white bandages.

"I have to adjust the catheter."

"Well, hurry the hell up. Where the hell am I anyway?"

"You're in Pietrasanta Hospital. You have been here for three weeks. You were brought here from Ethiopia."

"And you, you're a goddamn nun?"

"No, no. I'm just a volunteer."

"You sound young."

"I come here after school every day and volunteer."

"You mean you don't get paid?"

"This is what I want to do. It's the least I can do for our soldiers."

"Right. Somebody should do something for us."

"You were hurt very badly."

"You don't have to tell me. Bloody Ethiopians."

She adjusted the pillow. It was cool against his feverish head.

"You know how I was wounded."

"I've read the report."

"Then you know I was a hero. I'm a goddamn hero."

"I've read the report."

"Then you know."

"I told you, I read the report. I think you should rest now, Private Donatello. You've been through a lot. Perhaps I'll see you tomorrow."

"What's your name?"

"Daniella."

"Daniella what?"

"We can't give out more than that. Just Daniella."

Two weeks later, lighter casts were placed on his arm and leg and the bandages on his right eye were removed. His vision was blurred and he needed drops four times a day, but at least he could see the long row of beds. White, everything was white. The walls, the ceilings, the beds, the sisters who moved silently from bed to bed. When he moved his head and tried to look, the pain in his right eye was unbearable. He screamed, and a nun came running.

"Don't move your head, please, and especially don't move your eye." She held his arm tightly. "Your right eye is still connected to the left. It doesn't know it's not there anymore. It will get better. Don't move."

He gripped her hand until the pain subsided.

After lunch, Daniella arrived as usual. She wore a white dress, and a large linen cap covered her blond hair. She was younger than he had imagined, with pale skin that highlighted her dark eyes. She was thin, with small breasts. Although his only experience was with the whore at Asmara, he imagined he would always like a thin girl with small breasts.

She adjusted his pillow, took his blood pressure and temperature. The catheter had been removed.

"I have to put the drops in your eye."

That was a struggle. Angelo cringed and squirmed each time she tried.

"I thought you were a big war hero," she teased.

"Not when my eyes are concerned."

She put the eyedropper away and sat at his side.

"The doctor says that tomorrow you'll go to surgery again."

"For what?"

"They're going to straighten out the hole where your eye was."

"So I'm going to have a big hole there?"

She held his hand. "They're going to get you a big pair of glasses."

"What the hell for? I won't be able to see with them, will I?"

"No, but it will make you look better."

"I'm not going to wear a pair of goddamn glasses and pretend my eye is still there. My eye is gone, gone forever." He turned on his side and tears flowed from his right eye.

"Angelo, please. Tomorrow they're just going to do the first step. You'll need to go back a couple more times."

"Oh God!"

"Angelo, you'll be sedated. It won't hurt. Really. Another soldier came in last month and had this done. He already went home."

"Daniella, I'm not going to do it! I'm not!"

"Well then, do you want people to see a big bloody hole? That's what it is now, you know. Is that what you want? Is that how you want people to see you?"

"Yes. I don't care. I don't care about anything. I want everyone to see what those damn Ethiopians did to me."

"The Ethiopians did this to you?"

"Yes. Yes they did." He turned his head away again. His whole body was shaking.

"It's all right, Angelo." She smoothed his hair. "It's all right."

Daniella held his hand until his tremors eased.

"Daniella?"

"Yes?"

He tried to speak. She leaned close to his face.

"I'm afraid," he whispered.

"Would it help if I were with you in the operating room?"

"Please?"

"Of course."

With the resilience of an eighteen-year-old, Angelo was sent home after thirteen-and-a-half weeks. Lidia had refused to return to the hospital after the first aborted visit because she was afraid to see her son in such a terrible condition. Now, except for the loss of his left eye and the fact that he needed a cane to walk up to the third-floor flat, he seemed well enough, and she spent her days hovering over him.

"What can I get you? Are you warm enough? Cold? I made some fresh bean soup, the kind you always liked. Let me help you into that chair. Should I open the window? I'm sorry it's still broken, your father never did fix it." At this point she usually burst into tears and lay down on her trundle bed. The heart palpitations she had suffered since Ugo's death were increasing.

Angelo responded to his mother's ministrations by spending most of the time in his room and lying on his bed. He picked up copies of the Gioventu Fascista but it was difficult to read with one eye. He didn't even want to write in his notebook.

At night, in the neighborhood osteria, he told anyone who asked, and some who didn't, how he was injured. The battle at Adowa, he said proudly, and as the night went on, his actions in this ferocious battle became more and more heroic.

On a late afternoon in February, when the icy rain froze the towel stuffed into the kitchen window, the downstairs bell rang. Lidia called down and asked who was there.

"Daniella."

"Daniella? Daniella who?"

"Daniella Lisi. I knew Angelo from the hospital."

"One moment." Lidia went to Angelo's closed door. "There's a Daniella Lisi downstairs. She says she knew you from the hospital."

Angelo got up from his bed faster than he should have and a throbbing pain stretched from his head to his lower back. "Mama, Mama, send her up."

Opening the door, Lidia looked at this young girl with some apprehension. Too thin, she thought. Too pale. Still, she's pretty enough.

After the awkward introductions, Angelo found it difficult to talk to Daniella in the kitchen with his mother standing there. He invited her into his bedroom, closing the door behind them. She noticed immediately that he wasn't wearing his eyeglasses. They were on the dresser. His face had sunken in and the hole was black. But she didn't flinch.

"I'm afraid there isn't any place to sit," he said, "except here on the bed."

"That's all right. I just came to see how you were."

"I'm all right. My back bothers me sometimes. Sometimes I have trouble pissing. You don't want to know all the details."

"Of course I do."

"No, no you don't. Anyway, I'm all right. Bored mostly. I go down to the piazza once a day to get some air," he lowered his voice, "and to get away from my mother."

"I'm sure she just wants to take care of you."

"Too much."

As if on cue, Lidia pushed open the door carrying a tray of coffee and cookies. She couldn't find anywhere to put them, so she set the tray on the floor. She smiled at Daniella and closed the door.

Daniella looked around the room, still with its Fascist decorations. "You were in Ballila?"

"Yes, I was very active. And now I'm getting active in the Fascist party here. I started going to meetings."

"I was in Ballila, too, because I had to. I didn't like it. All they told the girls was how we had to be good wives and mothers. I don't want to be a good wife and mother."

"Oh," he smiled, "you want to be a bad wife and mother?"

She blushed. "No, no. I mean I just don't want to get married and have children, at least not yet. I would like to be a nurse, but it costs money to go to nursing school and we don't have it."

"Why did you come here, Daniella? I wasn't very nice to you in the hospital? Do you visit all of your patients?"

"No, no. This is the first time." She blushed some more.

"Then why?"

She bent down, took two biscotti and gave him one. "I don't know, Angelo. Maybe it was because you weren't so nice to me at first and then it seemed that after I got to know you better ..."

"I'm sorry, Daniella. I shouldn't have treated you that way. No matter how mad I was."

"I know you were in terrible pain."

"That can't explain everything."

Now she poured some coffee. "And you know another reason? You were so scared that day when I put eye drops in your eye. Eye drops! Here you had gone through a war and you lost your eye somehow or other and you were afraid of eye drops! And you were so scared of having the surgery. You suddenly seemed so young, so vulnerable. I wanted to hug you."

"Why didn't you?"

"Someone would have seen me. I would have been fired. But I wanted to, Angelo, I wanted to."

"I'm glad, Daniella."

They sat on the bed, their hands almost touching. Angelo was about to put his hand on hers when she pointed to the eyeglasses. "Don't you ever wear them?"

"I told you I wouldn't, and I haven't worn them since the hospital."

"Suit yourself."

"I just want everyone to see what the Ethiopians did to me."

"The Ethiopians. Is that why you go to the piazza?"

"Of course. The little kids come up and I scare them."

"That must be a lot of fun for you."

"Yes."

"Scaring kids?"

"They call me *Occhio unico*, One-Eye."

"Well, of course."

CHAPTER 23

▼

Angelo had a hard time persuading Daniella to marry him. In the months after that meeting in February, Angelo and Daniella spent almost every evening together, walking hand in hand along with dozens of other residents of Pietrasanta around the Piazza del Duomo and then, perhaps, going to the cinema.

Almost every Sunday they walked up the steep and winding path to the top of the mountain and the little village of Sant'Anna di Stazzema. Daniella's widowed aunt lived alone in a tiny hut in one of the hamlets that made up this sprawling isolated village. Angelo and Daniella arrived in time for *il pranzo*, but after the pasta and the fresh vegetables, they explored one hamlet after another and then the forests and caves in the mountain beyond. Angelo had never been in Sant'Anna before, and he wanted to see every inch of it.

"This," he would tell Daniella as they surveyed the countryside from the top of Sant'Anna, "is the safest place in the world. If we lived here, we wouldn't have to worry about anything."

"Just getting up and down the hill," Daniella said, putting her arm around Angelo's waist and squeezing it.

There was no question that Daniella had tamed Angelo's rebellious spirits. He treated his mother better and even fixed the window over the sink. And although he had never been in love before, he was truly in love with Daniella.

She learned to love him, too, and was willing to put aside her dream of becoming a nurse. But there was one thing she did nag him about. Why wouldn't he wear his eyeglasses?

"I want everyone to see what the Ethiopians did to me," he would reply.

"Yes, of course," she would say, and look away.

He proposed on November 16, 1936, almost a year after his injuries. They had gone to see *Camille*, a tearjerker with Greta Garbo, and Daniella was still misty-eyed as they sat outside the *trattoria* in the piazza. Angelo took a cue from the movie and was his most romantic.

"Daniella." He held her hand. "You know what that movie made me think about? That life is short, that we have to live every moment of it."

"Do you think I'm going to die?"

Angelo blanched. "No! No! Daniella, if something happened to you, I don't know ... I don't know what I'd do." He gripped her hand harder. "You know I love you and you love me. Let's get married!"

Daniella looked away. "I don't know, Angelo. You're only nineteen and I'm seventeen. I don't know if Papa would allow it."

"He likes me, doesn't he?"

"He's impressed with your war hero story."

Angelo let go of her hand and sat back. "Why do you always call it a story, Daniella? It's true. It happened."

Daniella sighed. "No, Angelo, it's not true. Remember, I read the report in the hospital. You were drunk and you fell off a church roof. That's what happened. Why don't you admit it?"

"Admit what?"

"That you made up this story!"

Angelo bent forward and put his face in his hands. His shoulders began to shake.

"Angelo? I'm sorry, but it's the truth. Why go on with this made-up story?"

His shoulders shook even more.

"Angelo, what about those soldiers who were with you? Aren't you afraid that they're going to come here and tell everyone the truth?"

He looked up. "Sergio is from Siena and Giacomo is from Perugia and Rinaldo is from someplace outside of Viterbo. They're not going to come up here."

He started to sob and leaned forward again.

"Angelo? It's all right. It doesn't matter to me how you were hurt. What does matter is that you admit it to me. If you want other people to think that's what happened, well, that's up to you. But please be honest with me."

He took out a handkerchief and blew his nose.

"Angelo, I have to say this. I can't, I won't, marry you until you admit the truth to me."

With his face buried in his handkerchief, she could barely hear him. "I wanted to be a hero."

She rubbed his back. "I know, I know."

"I wanted to be a hero for my Papa."

"It's all right."

"He would have fought in that war. He was devoted to *il Duce*."

She rubbed his hair. "And so are you."

"Papa was killed by a Communist. I want to kill Communists."

"Angelo, you're not making any sense. The Ethiopians aren't Communists. And you know as well as I do that Mussolini should never have invaded their country."

Angelo straightened up. "Daniella, don't say that. He had every right. He knew that ..."

She put her fingers on his lips. "Please, let's not get into an argument about this invasion of Ethiopia. It has nothing to do with your injuries. Again, please admit to me what happened."

Angelo sat back. It was almost dark now in Piazza del Duomo and the only people remaining were a few drunks who were swinging around the Column of Liberty. It was a long time before he answered.

"All right."

"Yes?"

"My buddies and me were in this bar. We had too much to drink, yes. And then this guy came in and he said Mussolini had used mustard gas. I didn't want to believe it. Mustard gas! Do you know how awful that is?"

"Yes, I know. And I know he used it."

Angelo started pacing in front of the *trattoria*. "All of a sudden I was asking myself. What was I doing there? Why was I in that war? Not that I was doing anything in Adowa. We didn't have anything to do, we were bored. So that night I started drinking and drinking, and these three guys kept telling me to do things and I did them and then they told me to climb up to the top of the church and I was so drunk I did it. And I made it, Daniella, I made it. But then I fell. The doctor told me I fell about forty feet and there was this jagged piece of corrugated iron that stuck out from the roof and it pierced my eye."

He sat down and sobbed some more.

"I'm not much of a hero, am I?"

She stroked his back. "Angelo, you are a hero. You enlisted in the Army, you went to Ethiopia, you were ready to fight."

"Yeah."

"Well, I think you're a hero."

"Yeah."

"And look at it this way. If you hadn't been in the hospital, we would never have met and I wouldn't be marrying you."

It took Angelo more than a minute for this to sink in.

"You mean you're going to marry me?"

"On one condition, Angelo. Will you promise?"

"I'd promise anything for you, Daniella."

She leaned down and kissed the top of his head. "That you wear your eyeglasses at our wedding."

And two months later they were married. Lidia sat in the back of the room at City Hall and cried softly into her handkerchief because it wasn't at Chiesa di Sant'Agostino. Neither Angelo nor Daniella had thought of having a church wedding. Their wedding picture shows Daniella seated next to a white pillar and Angelo wearing dark glasses and his father's suit. "You look like some Hollywood movie star," Daniella said.

She moved into Angelo's room and before they even went to bed she took down the posters of Ballila and Mussolini and threw away the copies of *Gioventu Fascista*. She opened the window and told him he was not allowed to smoke in the flat. And then they made passionate love.

Lidia was so happy that Angelo had found Daniella that she tried to keep out of her daughter-in-law's way. That was almost impossible, considering that the kitchen was barely big enough to hold two people, let alone three. But Lidia and Daniella shared cooking and laundry duties and Daniella left every afternoon, happy that she could support her family by working at the hospital. Every day, Angelo said the same thing when she left: "Don't meet any soldiers who have lost their eyes!"

Little Ugo was born eight months later. Angelo and Daniella were sorry that Lidia did not get to see her grandson. Her heart, weakened by the strain of her husband's violent death, Angelo's subsequent behavior and then his terrible war injuries, finally gave up, and she died early one morning in her little trundle bed. Her greatest regret was that Angelo didn't receive a medal for fighting the battle at Adowa.

After Lidia's death, the flat became a little more bearable, and when Little Ugo was born, the trundle bed had a new occupant. With only one eye and one good leg, Angelo spent the day at the baby's side and reported on Little Ugo's every smile, gurgle, poop and throw-up when Daniella returned from the hospital.

"My Papa would be so happy if he could see you," he would tell the baby.

"And your Mama, too," Daniella would add.

When Mussolini entered the war with Hitler in 1940, Angelo felt constrained and stifled. Every morning he pushed Little Ugo's buggy to the piazza so he could read a newspaper in the *trattoria*. Every night he sat next to the radio, trying to get a few sentences clear through all the static.

Daniella pretended not to hear when he swore at the bad news and yelled when some sort of victory was announced.

One night, after they put Little Ugo to bed, Angelo sat down with Daniella at the kitchen table.

"I saw somebody today," he said.

"Who?"

"Big Red. Big Red the Communist who killed my Papa. I don't know where he's been, but I haven't seen him since that day in the courtroom at La Spezia. He was walking down the street with some other men. He came up to me and said he was sorry about my eye. But he had this smirk on his face. And then he started laughing, Daniella, he started laughing."

"He laughed at you?"

"Yes. Do you think he knows, Daniella? How I lost my eye?"

"I don't know, Angelo, but it doesn't matter. Who cares what Big Red knows?"

Angelo reached over and held Daniella's hand. "It brought back all those feelings I had. Why I joined the Blackshirts. Why I wanted to kill Communists."

"You'd kill somebody? Oh, Angelo!"

"Communists, yes. Not anyone else."

"Oh, Angelo!"

"Now there's a war, and I know I didn't like Mussolini using mustard gas, but he's still a great leader, Daniella. He's going to make Italy a great nation, a world leader. We won't be this weak country anymore."

"What can you do?"

"I don't know. But I don't think I can just sit here and take care of the baby anymore. I have to do something!"

"What? You have one eye, your left arm isn't very strong and you still limp a little. You can't join the Blackshirts again."

"I don't know. But I have to do something. I'm still a Fascist. I still want to kill Communists."

"Angelo ... Angelo...."

CHAPTER 24

───────▼───────

"Mama," Little Ugo cried. "Why is Papa dancing around like that?"

"He's just happy, dear." Daniella herself didn't seem very pleased.

"But why, Mama, why?"

"He just heard some news on the radio."

For a half hour, Angelo had kept his ear to the brown box on the dresser and now, on June 30, 1944, it was time for the evening news to be repeated. Through the static and the pops and the frequent silences, the announcer's voice could intermittently be heard. Angelo sat up straight and turned up the volume.

"*Il Duce* signed Decree 446.... All members of the Fascist Party will join the *Brigata Nera*.... Black Brigade ... Task ... to fight ... bandits and outlaws."

Angelo grabbed Daniella and whirled her around the kitchen. "Did you hear that, Daniella? Those bandits and outlaws? They're the damn partisans, the Resistance. They're the Communists! The goddamn Communists!"

"I know."

"Now I can do something, Daniella! I can do something! I can join! They want all members of the Fascist Party to join!"

"*Brigate Nera?* The Black Brigades?" Daniella said. "Oh my God, now we have something else besides the Blackshirts. Black, black, black. Everything Mussolini wants is black."

"No! That's not true. I don't know why he called it that. But don't you see, Daniella? Now I can go find the Communists. I heard Big Red has a *banda* up in the hills. Maybe I'll even be able to find him."

"With only one eye? With a bad leg?"

Daniella broke away, but Angelo continued to dance around the tiny room. "He said all Fascists must join. I'm a Fascist. They'll take me."

Angelo had been waiting for this day for four years. Frustrated, discouraged and increasingly dispirited, he had listened to the broadcasters report ever-increasing disasters for Italy in the war. The Army was listless and ineffectual. Hitler controlled Mussolini. The Allies were invading from the south. Mussolini was deposed. No, Hitler set him up in a shadow government to run northern Italy. The Allies captured Rome and were heading toward Tuscany.

Now, from his hidden headquarters at Salo, Mussolini finally had given men like Angelo a chance to do something for their country.

"Don't you see, Daniella?"

"Yes, I suppose so," Daniella said as she went to the sink and started washing the dishes.

Angelo held his wife's shoulders. "I know you're worried, Daniella. But I'll be all right. And it won't be long. Really, it won't be long."

"I just don't like the way you talk, Angelo. Just go and do it. But come back soon. Please?"

He kissed the back of her neck.

Both of them knew that the war was coming closer. Since the Germans had occupied Pietrasanta, food was scarce, schools were closed and the hospital had been moved for fear it would be bombed. Every day, Daniella had to walk miles to the new location, inside an abandoned mine.

And both Angelo and Daniella knew that there were partisans in the mountains who were becoming more and more of an obstacle for the Germans. One recent Sunday, after lunch with her aunt, they had taken Little Ugo into the crevices of a forgotten forest and discovered the remnants of a campsite.

"Communists!" Angelo said. "And not too long ago."

Three times, Angelo set up a tent in another dense woods and he and Little Ugo stayed out all night under the stars. Each time Angelo thought he heard partisans moving in the hills.

"You don't have to be afraid of the forests," Angelo told his son. "Just be careful of the people in the forests."

"I'm not afraid," Little Ugo said. "I'm not afraid of anything."

Angelo taught Little Ugo how to make a campfire out of branches, what berries were good to eat, how he could crack chestnuts and, yes, how he could steal corn and tomatoes and zucchini from farmers' fields. He showed him how he could hide in piles of hay and how he could get directions by watching the sun and the moon and the stars.

"Only eight years old," Angelo said. "You're a brave little boy."

Little Ugo beamed. "Like my Papa!"

For once, Italy worked with efficiency in setting up the *Brigate Nera*. Forty-one brigades were established throughout the country. They were small units, with only 200 to 300 men each. They wore badges with a death's head along with black shirts, gray-green pants, black caps or berets.

Angelo went down to the recruiting office in Pietrasanta as soon as it opened. In the window was a large poster showing a grim-faced soldier bearing a carbine like the one he carried in Ethiopia. Underneath the words: *Pronti, ieri, oggi, domani al combattimento per l'onore d'italia.* "Ready: Yesterday, today, tomorrow to fight for the honor of Italy."

"When can I start? Where should I go? Where's my rifle and ammunition? I'm ready!" he told the jowly bald-headed man behind the desk.

"Hold on, hold on." The man looked at Angelo and didn't like what he saw. "You want to join the Black Brigades? You only have one eye! What are you, crazy?"

"My one eye is better than two of yours!"

The man stood up. "You're not off to a good start here, young man!"

Angelo stepped back. "I'm sorry, I'm sorry. It's just that this is what I want to do. I want to find those partisans. I want to find those Communists!"

The man sat down again. "How old are you?"

"Twenty-seven."

"Where did you lose that eye?"

This was no time for lies. "I lost it ... I lost it when I was drunk and fell off a church roof in Ethiopia."

When the man finished laughing he handed Angelo a folder. "All right. Fill out these papers and come back."

The process didn't take long after that. Angelo was given a brief physical, and his eye exam showed perfect vision in his right eye. Although his left arm was weak and he still walked with a slight limp, the doctor checked off all the necessary places on the chart.

"We're taking a chance here, son," the doctor said. "You'd better not prove me wrong."

In contrast to the casual training Angelo received before being sent to Ethiopia, the Black Brigades prepared their soldiers rigorously, though it was more psychological than physical. They were fighting for the honor of Italy. The partisans were against Italy. The partisans had to be destroyed.

For Angelo, partisans meant Communists, no matter that many were Army deserters, Socialists, Catholics, Yugoslavian refugees, strikers and students with no particular political leanings. The honor of Italy meant killing Communists and anyone who was helping the Communists.

At the end of the weeklong training, Angelo returned to spend one last night at home. No one spoke over dinner, except for Little Ugo chattering about what he wanted for his birthday. Daniella washed the dishes and Angelo silently put them away. Then he sat in the straight-backed chair where his father once spent the evenings, and, like his father, sang to his son. This time, it was the song of the Black Brigades, but since Angelo did not have his father's strong voice, it was more like a lullaby.

Chi siete? Io non lo so.
Chi siamo, ve lo dirò:
siam le Brigate Nere.
abbiam la forza di spezzarvi il cuor.
Siam stati nel Piemonte e in Lombardi
aper rompere la schiena dei ribelli,
Abbiam lasciato i morti per la via con sulle labbra i nostri canti belli.

Who you are? I don't know.
Who are we, I'll tell you:
We're the Black Brigades
We have the force to break your heart.
We were in Piedmonte and Lombardy to break the spirit of the rebels,
We have left them dead on the streets with our beautiful songs on our lips.

Daniella knew that her husband had reverted to the angry, vengeful person she had known in the hospital. As they lay in bed, after she reluctantly let Angelo make love to her, he knew he had changed, too.

He brushed his hand on her cheek and found it moist. "What's wrong?"

"You're going away tomorrow."

"Yes. I can't wait."

"That's what worries me."

"What?"

"You've changed, Angelo. A few weeks ago you seemed happy enough just being with me and Little Ugo. Now you just want to go off and kill people. I don't like this Angelo. I want the old one back."

He looked over at the photo of his father on the dresser. "Just for now, Daniella. Just for now. This will be over in a few weeks and I'll be back. I'll be back and be the same person I was before. I promise. I've just got to do this now. I've got to, Daniella."

She turned over on her side, her back to him.

"And I'm worried about you, too," he said. "Things are getting worse here. Pietrasanta used to be safe."

"Not anymore."

He stroked her back. "Maybe you should go away."

"Where?"

"Maybe Sant'Anna. Other people from all over are going there. It's too isolated. You could stay with your aunt for a while. Little Ugo would like that. There'd be other kids there."

"She doesn't have room."

"I guess not."

Daniella didn't sleep all night. Neither did Angelo.

The next day, after kissing Daniella and tossing Little Ugo in the air one last time, Angelo climbed to the top of Mont Meto, south of Pietrasanta. He had told the brigade leader that he was familiar with this area and now here he was, twenty-seven years old, with one eye, leading two young members of the Black Brigade who were just as cocky and foolhardy as he was.

The patrol was dangerous. The forests were almost impenetrable, the hillside slippery, and the caves murky and sodden. Worse, the partisans had set dozens of landmines.

For four days Angelo and the others searched, twice setting off landmines but avoiding them at the last minute. Once, they saw a half dozen men run behind a farmhouse and into the woods but then lost them. Another time, two men in trees fired at them but Angelo and the others managed to escape.

At dusk on the fourth night, Angelo saw a flicker of light in a clump of trees across a farmer's cornfield. Then another light flickered on the opposite side. Angelo's heart raced just as it had when he entered Adowa. Finally, he would be in a battle. "For Papa!"

"Quick," he whispered to Carmine, only nineteen, and Santo, eighteen. "Follow me."

With Angelo in the lead, the three men crawled through the withered cornstalks to the edge of the field.

"Not so fast, Carmine," Angelo said. "Stay down, Santo."

They weaved their way on the hard dirt between the cornstalks. The cornstalks swayed, and their movements caught the attention of five partisans on the right. Storming across the field, the partisans fired.

"Stay down, Santo!"

The partisans fired again. Santo fell. Angelo reached out to grab him but then a bullet whizzed past his head. Carmine turned around and tried to fire.

Two more shots from the partisans. Carmine collapsed. Angelo wanted to stay with his comrades but the partisans were approaching.

"Damn! Damn! Damn!"

From the other side, not more than twenty feet away, a big man with broad shoulders and a shock of crimson hair emerged. He aimed his rifle at Angelo.

"Big Red!" Angelo shouted as he raised his rifle and fired. The bullet hit Big Red squarely in the chest and he fell forward, his arms twisting underneath him like paper clips. Then a young man ran out of the bushes.

"Papa!" he cried. "Papa!"

Angelo fired again. The boy fell on his father's body.

Angelo knelt frozen in the cornstalks. He couldn't tear himself from the sight of the first two people he had ever killed. Big Red's face was contorted in agony and his right hand still clutched his rifle. The boy clung to his father's body until he, too, was lifeless.

Suddenly, the other partisans fired at Angelo. He didn't have time to think and he was running out of ammunition. And so the brave member of the Black Brigades who wanted to be a hero for his father crawled sobbing out of the field and clawed his way into the nearby woods. Deeper and deeper, until he found a cave where he could hide. And as the moon shown over the bloody cornfield, Angelo collapsed against a damp wall and cried.

CHAPTER 25

▼

With more German soldiers arriving in Pietrasanta every day and with more bombings in the nearby villages, Daniella hadn't been sleeping well, and she awoke with a start. Someone was moving in the kitchen and it wasn't Little Ugo turning over in his trundle bed. When the bedroom door cracked open and a shaft of light came in, she leaped up in bed, grabbed the only thing handy, a book, and tried to scream, but no sound came out. Then he entered.

"Angelo!" she cried. "What are you doing here?"

"Shhh. Be quiet." He quickly closed the door.

"Angelo! You're supposed to be in the mountains. Why are you here? Oh, my baby, you're trembling. Come here."

Although the midnight heat was suffocating on this August night, Angelo crept under the sheet. It was soon damp with his sweat. Daniella hugged him.

"Angelo, what's wrong, what's wrong?"

"No-o-o-o-o."

"Tell me, Angelo."

"No-o-o-o-o."

"What?"

"Daniella, it was terrible. I thought I could do it easily. And I did. He had his rifle aimed at me, and I shot him. I should have been happy, but I wasn't. And then I killed his son, too, his boy. I used to bully that boy when I was in school and he was just a kid. Now I killed him, I killed him. I didn't have to do that. I didn't ..."

Angelo's body was wracked with sobs.

"Who? Angelo, who?"

"Big Red and his son." His voice was a whisper.

"Oh, my God."

"I didn't know what it was like to kill, Daniella. I just raised my rifle and I did it."

"Oh, Angelo."

"Big Red died right in front of me. I swear he was looking at me. And the boy. The boy was grabbing on to his Papa. He must have been still alive. For a minute, I wanted to go up to them, not to see if they were dead but to see if I could do something. Daniella, I'm a member of the Black Brigades. I shouldn't have those feelings. I should have been glad I ..."

He couldn't go on. Daniella took him in her arms. Her husband had killed a man. No, a man and his son.

"And then, Daniella, and then the other partisans came running and I had to run and I ran into the woods and I found a cave and I stayed there and ..."

"Angelo, Angelo ..."

"I'm not a hero, Daniella. I'm a coward, a bloody coward."

"No, no ..."

"I can't go back, Daniella, I can't. I can't do this anymore."

She wiped his forehead with the sheet. "It's all right, it's all right. You wanted to take revenge against Big Red, right? He killed your Papa. At least that's what you've been telling me all these years. So you finally had revenge. You did your job. What you were supposed to do."

Daniella stared at the wall. What was she going to do? Her husband was a killer. Now he was deserting the Black Brigades. What would happen if they found out?

Both of them were still awake when sunlight starting filtering into the room. They lay on their backs, their hands folded across their chests, staring at the ceiling.

"What are we going to do, Daniella?"

"I don't know. Angelo, it's gotten so much worse here this week. They're bombing just outside Pietrasanta. Ripa is destroyed. So is the bridge north of here. There have been atrocities, women and children killed. The soldiers are on the streets all the time. Now we hear the SS is coming. I don't let Little Ugo out of the house. I'm afraid to go out myself."

"All right, then, it's settled. You have to go to Sant'Anna. Your aunt will find some place for you. Daniella, this is going to be over soon."

"How can you say that?"

He waited. "I can't."

"And what about you?"

"I'm going to stay here. I'm not going back, Daniella, I'm not going back."

"They're going to find you here!"

"No, they won't. They're all out in the mountains. They won't care about me."

Both Angelo and Daniella were sobbing when they finally separated.

Daniella and Little Ugo were exhausted when they arrived at her aunt's in Sant'Anna. She had carried a satchel of clothes and supplies on her back, he had pulled his little red wagon with toys he insisted on taking along. Giuseppina Rossello was not pleased to see them. Frantically running from the cupboard to the stove to the table with coffee and some hard bread, she alternately wiped her eyes on her apron and on a towel.

"I don't know what to do. There are so many people in Sant'Anna now I don't know how many but you see there are an old Nonna and her daughter and three *bambini* from Busana and they are staying in the place where we keep the tools and there isn't enough food and I went to the *bottega* and Adamo said he didn't have any more olive oil and how can I cook without olive oil. *Santa Maria*. And now you're here and I don't know where we can find a place for you and Little Ugo, oh my, he's grown so much since you were here last, here have another piece of bread you look hungry, oh my, I don't know what to do, Daniella, I don't know what to do. *Santa Maria*, all you saints pray for us!"

Daniella put her arm around Giuseppina's frail shoulders. "Don't worry, don't worry. We can find room. We can sleep on the floor."

"The floor! The floor! You're not going to sleep on the floor! I won't allow you to sleep on the floor, *Santa Maria!* I'll find some place, you can't go back to Pietrasanta, everyone says it's terrible down there and at least the Germans can't find us up here."

"Auntie," Daniella said, "what about in back? Where you used to keep the cow? That's empty, right?"

"*Santa Maria!* You mean the stable? Daniella, I can't let you sleep in the stable. The cow slept in there, it's not clean and it smells like a cow."

"It will be just fine, Auntie, just fine. You just take care of yourself now. Here, sit by the window for a while. Little Ugo and I will just put our things out in back."

Shortly after midnight on August 12 Angelo heard the door being bashed in at the entry downstairs and then heavy boots stomping to the third floor. In a minute, three uniformed soldiers pushed the door to his flat open and stormed in, their rifles aimed. Seeing the SS insignia on their collars, he cowered in his bed.

"Donatello! We knew you were here. Come with us!"

"No! No, I can't!"

"What the hell do you mean you can't? You're a Black Brigade, right? Now get your ass out of bed and come!"

Two of the soldiers pulled him from his bed and forced him to put his clothes on.

"What's going on? Why me?"

"The lieutenant has a job in the mountains. You know the mountains better than any of us. Put this on." The sergeant handed him a clumsily knitted mask with small eye openings.

"Why?"

"You don't want anyone in Pietrasanta to know what you're doing."

Not knowing why, Angelo grabbed his eyeglasses from the dresser and stuffed them in his pocket. He hadn't worn them since his wedding. He pulled on the woolen cap his mother had knitted for him so long ago. He needed to hold on to something from his youth.

Down the stairs, out into the street. Fourteen men were lined up, all wearing masks and bent over with rifles and ammunition on their backs. The soldier at the side threw more weapons on Angelo's shoulders. "Carry this!"

Down the street, up the hill. "Where are we going?" Angelo asked the frightened boy, not more than sixteen, next to him.

"I heard Seravezza."

"To do what?"

"I don't know."

When Daniella looked up through the gaping holes in the roof, she could count the stars in the eastern sky and catch a glimpse of the moon. With Little Ugo curled up against her, she couldn't move or she would fall off the piles of hay she had improvised into a bed. Across the way, she could hear her aunt snoring and one of the *bambini* crying.

"Oh God, we've hardly gotten here and I can't stand it already." She wanted to be home, back in Angelo's arms.

In a moonlight that was almost as bright as day, Angelo could make out familiar landmarks. The little shrine to the Virgin Mary. The abandoned tractor in the field. The clump of trees where he had to stop to repair Little Ugo's wagon.

"This isn't the way to Seravezza! This is the way to Sant'Anna!"

He felt the blow to the back of his neck before he heard the seething whisper. "Shut your goddamn mouth up!"

"No! I can't go there!"

Another blow, this time harder.

As they neared the top of the mountain, at the spot where he and Daniella used to look back down on the valley, Angelo was forced to the front of the line.

"All right, Donatello, lead the way."

He was drenched with sweat. "I can't!"

"What do you mean you can't? You will!" This time a blow across the chest with the soldier's rifle.

When the sun finally banished the moon from the heavens, August 12 began as a beautiful day in Sant'Anna. The sky was a brilliant blue and cloudless. The chestnut trees and oaks glowed with dew. The flowers around the square in front of the little church sprang to life.

Because it was Saturday, women rose early to bake enough bread for both Saturday and Sunday. Some tended to the pigs and cows in the sheds behind their houses. Daniella was glad daylight had come. Maybe it would be better today.

By the time they reached the clearing, moonlight had faded and the first rays of the sun lit the forest. Angelo could make out dozens of men in formation. He could see the SS emblem on their collars. A lieutenant was talking to them.

"The people here are traitors. They are helping the enemy, the partisans who are fighting us. They cannot claim innocence. We have warned them over and over."

"My wife! My son! They're innocent!" Angelo cried. Another blow from the sergeant. He fell to his knees.

"Now it's time to teach them a lesson. Our aim in this operation is to stop these people from helping the Communists."

"The Communists, yes." Angelo bent over on his knees and cried. "But not my wife and son!"

The lieutenant droned on and on. The sergeant pulled Angelo to his feet.

"This is what you have to do, Donatello. You know this country. There are many ways we can get to the village. You show them the most direct path. You have to lead the way."

"No! No, I can't!"

"Damn it! Get moving!" Another blow to the neck.

Angelo struggled forward. His eye, filled with sweat and tears, could hardly see the path. He followed his instincts more than anything else. He saw the spot where he and Little Ugo had camped. He stumbled on. He made out the tree where he and Daniella had enjoyed a picnic. His bad leg was starting to hurt. He reached the top of the hill.

Now Daniella heard something different, sounds of heavy boots trampling distantly in the forest. They were coming nearer. She lay frozen, afraid to move or to wake Little Ugo. She wished the baby next door would stop crying.

Out of breath, Angelo stopped.

"That way?" The sergeant pointed to a winding path between an outgrowth of bushes. Angelo was so tired his head dropped to his chest.

"All right." The sergeant motioned to the lieutenant.

As the SS rushed by him, Angelo crumpled to the ground, praying he would be trampled.

6:15 a.m.: In the hamlet of Il Colle, one of many that made up Sant'Anna, three soldiers burst into Emilia Turrini's hut, shot her dead and then slaughtered her eight children. The oldest was sixteen, the youngest three months. Then they poured gasoline on the straw roof and lit the fire.

6:20 a.m.: Elsa Benotti was about to deliver her first child when four soldiers invaded her house and shot her. Then one took his bayonet, sliced the baby from the womb and let another soldier shoot it in the head.

6:30 a.m.: Father Ignazio, the parish priest, went from room to room in the parish house, filled with refugees. "Pray, pray, pray," he called, and then, "Hide, hide, hide."

6:40 a.m.: In the hamlet of Vaccareccia, soldiers forced more than a hundred women and children from their homes and into three stables. Then they threw grenades inside and locked the doors. The explosion flattened the stables.

6:50 a.m.: In the hamlet of Franchi, soldiers filled the Pierini house, killing Angelo, his wife, Filomena, who was four months pregnant, and two little girls. Then they threw bombs on the bodies and flames surged through the house.

6:55 a.m.: Refugees huddled in the schoolhouse. "Why did we come here?" a woman from Uzzano cried. "Why did we think this was such a safe place?"

7:10 a.m. Daniella could hear the soldiers storm through the door of her aunt's house. "*Santa Maria* save us!" was all she heard before the gunshots and the screams of the family from Busana.

"Little Ugo! Wake up, wake up!"

The boy rubbed his eyes. "I was sleeping, Mama!"

"Never mind. Some bad people are here. Get under the straw! Hide!"

"I'm afraid, Mama!"

She kissed him. "Don't be afraid. You're a strong boy. Remember that your Papa and your Mama love you."

Three soldiers knocked down the makeshift door with their rifles. Daniella lay on top of the hay, her arms outstretched. She could feel Little Ugo wiggling beneath her.

Bullets riddled her body and the hay pile. One soldier lit a match while another poured gasoline.

8:15 a.m.: Bands of soldiers went to the priest's house and the school, forcing the people inside into the square in front of the church. When all of the surviving villagers—more than 130—were in the square, the soldiers circled them on three sides and blocked off the fourth. Twenty soldiers dragged pews from the church, surrounding the villagers.

The priest came running out of his house. He stood next to a young woman, Angelica Marchetti, and her two young sons. She wore a yellow dress.

"No! No! No!" the villagers cried.

The soldiers raised their rifles. Like a deck of cards, the villagers fell to the ground, one on top of another. Soldiers soaked the pews with gasoline and soon fire engulfed the square.

At the top of the hill, the fifteen hooded men forced to come up from Pietrasanta clung to each other in horror. Then Angelo tore off his mask and ran down the hill and into the smoky ruins.

"Daniella! Daniella! Little Ugo! Little Ugo!"

The smoke was so intense, and the village so spread out, that he didn't know where he was. Through the crackles of the flames he heard a harmonica playing.

"Bastards! Bastards!"

Terrified, he watched as, laughing and singing, the soldiers climbed back to the top of the hill. He saw them point rifles at the remaining fourteen men and push them down the hill to the rear of the church. Then he heard fourteen rifle shots.

For four hours, Angelo wandered from hamlet to hamlet in Sant'Anna, not knowing where he was and trying to make his way through the smoke.

"Daniella! Little Ugo!"

At last he found what he thought were the remains of the hut where Daniella's aunt lived. Behind it there was nothing but a pile of ashes and what looked like white stones but he knew were bones. He was unable to move for more than an hour, but stood immobile, his arms at his side, his teeth clenched. If he had looked up, he would have seen a young man kneeling on another hill, also overcome with grief, watching him.

"Angelica!" the man cried. "Angelica!"

And then Angelo put on his eyeglasses and ran into the woods.

CHAPTER 26

▼

The Allies liberated Pietrasanta in September, about a month after the massacre at Sant'Anna di Stazzema. The war-weary people not only had to cope with the tasks of recovery and with the danger of ubiquitous landmines, but also with the loss of relatives and friends in the killings. Almost everyone lost someone close, and some lost entire families. There were many trips up the mountain as they tried to identify what little was left of the remains. Some were never identified.

People could, however, identify the fifteen men who helped the Germans. Their relatives were often shunned, and they stayed secluded and ashamed, assuming a guilt of their own. How could they have allowed Stefano to be taken away like that? Why didn't they prevent Guido from leaving? And on and on. For the fourteen families whose sons were shot to death behind the church, there were no answers. But at least they could go to the cemetery and light candles and pray for their loved ones.

But the stories about the fifteenth soon spread from the *trattoria* in Piazza del Duomo through the streets along the railroad tracks to the workrooms of the marble factories and then throughout the whole of Tuscany. Since Angelo Donatello wasn't killed with the rest, and since he apparently had escaped, he must have taken part willingly. Suddenly, someone recalled seeing him going down the steps of his apartment building to join the others a little past midnight on August 12. Why was he wearing a mask? Someone else was certain he saw him in the group going up the mountain. And finally someone saw him leading the entire group. If he was leading, surely he was more than an accomplice. He must have been the leader of these so-called "collaborators."

Since he was missing, he became the main target for blame. Everyone knew he loved Fascism, adored Mussolini and hated the Communists.

"Remember, he killed Big Red!" someone would always say.

"And his son!"

And although Big Red had not been well-liked in the town in life, he now assumed heroic stature, especially with the loss of his son.

There was, however, the mystery of why Angelo's wife and son had gone to Sant'Anna to stay with her aunt just before the massacre.

"What kind of man would send his wife and son to Sant'Anna before the massacre?" someone would ask. "He must have known what the Nazis would do!"

"What kind of man? An evil man," someone would always respond.

Even the priest declared that there was no redemption for such an evil, evil man.

No one lit candles for Angelo Donatello.

The stories grew and grew, and *Occhio unico*, One-Eye, became the most despised man in all of Tuscany.

Since Angelo was an easy scapegoat, this meant that some of the people could ignore or deny their own complicity. They could forget how many of them had become friends with the Nazis and how they looked the other way when atrocities were committed in nearby villages. The Nazis were gone, the Allies were here, and it was time to make new friends.

In all their stories and gossip, people could not explain where the bodies of Angelo's wife and son were. Daniella, people said, was probably that pile of bones behind what was left of her aunt's hut. The son? No one knew. But a few years later, when an old man picking mushrooms thought he glimpsed a frail boy with no hair on his head and dressed in tatters in a forest on Mont Gabberi, the legend of the *il ragazzo fantasma* began. And once begun, there was no end to the dubious sightings and the expanding story of the little "ghost boy."

Everyone knew that even though the Germans were still attacking civilians indiscriminately, they were all but defeated. It would only be months before they would finally surrender. The partisans were encouraging their older members to return home and let younger ones continue to fight. And so, in Pietrasanta, a small group met every week at the Casa del Popolo: Rico Fazzini, whose left arm was badly hurt in the war; the gnome-like Filippo Parisi; the tall Leonardo Ciamino, and the man they called *il rospo*, the toad.

Like other groups of former partisans throughout northern Italy, they planned methods of retribution for the Nazi and Fascist atrocities. But how could they avenge the massacre at Sant'Anna if they couldn't find their main target? Angelo Donatello had completely disappeared.

"*Occhio unico* must have fled to Germany," one or the other would say.

"Bastard!" the others would agree.

What they didn't know was that for weeks, Angelo Donatello could not bear to leave Sant'Anna. During the day, when relatives and friends started to arrive to identify the remains and clean up the area, he stayed hidden deep in a forest cave. After dark, he slowly emerged and found scraps to eat from the fields on a deserted farm. Then he crept down to the ruins of the stable where Daniella and Little Ugo had stayed. Throughout the night, often under the moonlight and sometimes in the rain, he simply knelt and wept.

Then the major cleanup began, and people came from all over to clear the rubble and smooth the scorched earth. They took as many bodies as they could find and dug a wide and deep grave in front of the church. Angelo stood on a hill and watched as they gently lowered the bodies, one by one, and covered the massive grave with dirt. He wept some more.

In a month, Sant'Anna was a barren landscape. Stumps of trees and bushes. Shells of a few houses. Fields laid bare. It was time for Angelo to leave. He knew he could not go back home but didn't know the extent of the hatred toward him until he heard four men talking outside his cave.

"I heard someone in Lucca saw *Occhio unico*" … "No!" … "Someone saw him near Pescaglia" … "No, at Massarosa … Bastard! … "We'll kill him!"

"God in heaven," Angelo cried. "I'm everywhere."

He couldn't stay in this cave and he couldn't return to Pietrasanta and now he couldn't go anywhere in Tuscany. He had no family, he knew no one.

Disconsolate, he tried to figure out a place where he could go. Then he remembered a Fascist meeting he attended after his return from Ethiopia and his ignominious injury. A burly Fascist had boasted of how he had traveled all over Tuscany in the party's cause. He said he had gone as far as Florence and sometimes to Lucca, but his favorite place was Reboli, where he had a friend who owned a thread factory. Everyone wondered why the man smiled and grew wistful when he began to describe a tall woman who worked there.

Angelo talked to him a little after the meeting. The man said he was moving to a place called Barga in the Garfagnana where there was still an active Fascist organization.

"Why?"

"I'm going to become a police officer," the man boasted. "You know what I can do then, right?"

"Maybe some day I'll join you," Angelo said.

"If you ever need help, call on me. My name is Amadeo Mazzella."

Angelo never forgot it.

The first thing Angelo needed to do was replace his Black Brigade uniform, and clothing on the line of a burned-out hut solved that problem. Although it was still a hot and humid September, he covered his head with the woolen cap. Normally clean-shaven, he had by necessity let his beard grow. With the addition of his thick eyeglasses, which he had kept in his pocket all this time, he did not look like "*Occhio unico.*"

Usually, someone going from Pietrasanta to Barga had three choices. The longer route would go southeast, first to Camaiore, then to Reboli, then to Lucca and then north into the territory of the Garfagnana along the Serchio River and finally to Barga. Angelo could not risk taking so much time.

Another was to the northeast, through many mountains and villages and then to Vergemoli and Gallicano and to Barga. He feared that the Germans were still plundering in that area.

And so he could only choose a more direct, but far more treacherous, path due east through the thickly forested Apuan Mountains. He had no map, but simply used his instincts and the placement of the sun, the moon and the stars to guide his way.

Starting before dawn one morning, he followed the Cordoso River through chestnut woods and then stood frozen as he looked down on what was left of the village of Farnocchia. Just days before the Sant'Anna massacre, the Nazis had destroyed the village after partisans had killed eight German soldiers.

Angelo started climbing. And climbing. To the top of Monte Forato's twin peaks where a huge hole in the limestone provided a view of the entire valley. Standing at the edge of a cliff and spellbound by the landscape below him, he did not see the figure behind him until it was too late. The man grabbed him around the waist. Angelo struggled. The man held on tighter. Angelo broke loose. His shoes, worn thin, were useless against the slippery rocks, and Angelo fell fifteen feet into the branches of a chestnut tree.

The next thing he knew he was on the ground and the man, tall and wearing a floppy hat and with a band of ammunition across his chest, was standing over him. The man carried a rifle.

"You're not a German!"

"No! No!" Angelo cried.

"Good. Here, you lost this."

The man handed Angelo his eyeglasses and disappeared into the chestnut grove.

"A partisan! A Communist!" Angelo thought.

The climb down the mountain led him through glorious pristine forests and then, in stark contrast, hamlets and small farms that stood naked and forlorn. In one area, smoke still rose from the ruins of what must have been an enterprising farm. Angelo hurried past what looked like three bodies lying in a field. Crows were pecking at the remains.

It was almost dark as he trudged on. He was now deep into the Garfagnana, and the smells of chestnuts and mushrooms hung in the evening air. He cracked open a few chestnuts and found some wild berries. A cold cave provided shelter for the night and he fell asleep despite gunshots in distant hills.

The forests were even thicker the next day and it took an hour just to get over one small hill. He went past a hamlet where only broken walls remained of almost all the houses. No one was around. Then Angelo saw an old woman in a rocking chair in front of her house. She was holding a bundle and moaning.

By the time he crossed the Freddana River and reached the medieval village of Pescaglia, he was desperately hungry. He didn't have any money, but thought he could find something, even if it were in a trash can. Afraid to be seen, he edged down a nameless street against the stucco walls.

It was then that he saw three men ahead of him, on the opposite side of the street. They too were edging along the walls. Each carried a rifle. Angelo saw their destination: The church of San Giovanni Battista. Even with one eye he saw a movement on the roof of the church. A shot, and he saw one partisan crumple on the street. Another partisan fired. Angelo heard a scream from the church roof and a body fell to the ground. Another movement on the roof, more shots from the street and two more bodies plunged from the roof. Then silence.

The two partisans rushed to their fallen comrade. Angelo felt he could not just stand by and ran over to their side.

"Can I help?" he asked.

"He took a shot in the shoulder. He'll be all right."

Angelo looked down. "Thanks," the partisan said. Angelo dashed up the street and out of the village. He needed time to think.

And rest. He had traveled another full day and he needed sleep more than food. He found an old stable at the edge of the farm and collapsed on a pile of hay. When he awoke the next morning, he looked straight into the barrel of a rifle. The young woman holding it, however, appeared more terrified than he was.

"Monster! Monster!" she cried.

Angelo realized then that he had taken his eyeglasses off. He hurriedly put them on.

"No! No! Please put the gun away."

She lowered the gun but still kept it aimed at his legs.

"Please," he said, "I'm an army deserter." (which was true) "I lost my eye in a war." (which was also true, if not complete)

She put the gun on the ground and bent down. She looked about twenty-two, he thought, almost as old as Daniella. Suddenly, he didn't want to talk anymore and didn't care if she shot him. He turned over, his shoulders shaking.

The young woman didn't know why the man was crying, but thought the least she could do was get him something to eat. The hard bread she brought out was better than any he had ever eaten, and he devoured three small cups of black coffee. Angelo looked at the darkening sky and said he had to leave. She pointed the way to the road leading to Colognora and stood and watched, her gun at her side, as he slowly disappeared from her sight.

Angelo skirted Colognora. Except for a limping dog, its left rear leg shattered, the town appeared deserted. Then he saw a dozen crows descending into a stable behind what remained of a thatched hut.

Now he knew he was approaching the Serchio Valley. Down, down, down the mountains and hills. He came to fertile flatlands nourished for eternity by the river. And then before him was the most spectacular bridge he had ever seen. Built of stone, it arched high across the Serchio, which flowed gently underneath. He couldn't move, and suddenly felt very lonely. He wanted so desperately for Daniella to see this with him.

Pulling his cap down and his collar up, he made his way through a handful of people crossing the bridge to Borgo a Mozzano. He dared to ask an elderly man directions to Barga and was pointed north.

Despite the pain in his leg, he was running now, and his feet accompanied the cadence of his thoughts. "Have to put Pietrasanta behind me. Have to forget about the Black Brigades. Have to start over. Have to start over."

But then he thought about Daniella and Little Ugo and knew how impossible that would be.

Suddenly, Barga towered before him, an ancient hilltop city crowned with a medieval Duomo. He had never seen a city this large or this old. Again, Angelo wanted Daniella to be at his side as he climbed the steep streets and entered its ancient walls. The cobblestone streets were empty and eerily still. Then, from around the corner, eight German soldiers marched in lockstep directly toward him. Ducking behind a wall, he tripped and fell.

"Damn!"

He thought his leg had healed, but a sharp pain shot up through the shin and above the knee.

The soldiers went by. Angelo struggled down the street and noticed a woman peering out the window.

"Where is the police station?" he whispered. She pointed to the left.

Hobbling to the stark building with a small sign, *Carabinieri*, he found the bell at the side of the door.

"What do you want?" a voice called through a small opening.

Angelo's voice was hoarse. "I'm looking for Amadeo Mazzella."

A long pause.

"Who are you?"

"Angelo. Angelo Donatello from Pietrasanta."

Another pause.

"How does he know you?"

"He gave a speech at a Fascist meeting and said if I needed help I could contact him. Please! I need help."

Another long wait, and then the door opened.

The burly Amadeo Mazzella looked at the straggly visitor.

"I talk to a lot of people. I don't remember talking to you."

"Please!" Angelo said, and he took off his glasses.

"Ah. *Occhio unico*. Come in."

CHAPTER 27

▼

About a year after he started to work at Fabiano Guerini's farm high in the Garfagnana, Antonio Denato found a notebook that Graziella didn't want anymore and decided to write his thoughts down, just as he had as a schoolboy and as a young soldier in Ethiopia. They were simple thoughts, not even sentences. Only recently had he picked it up and wrote this: "When you only have a past, you don't have a present or a future."

He surprised even himself when he read it. He had never been a good student, certainly not a thoughtful one, but this seemed to summarize how futile his life was, then and now.

Day after monotonous day, including Sundays, he did his chores on the farm. Night after lonely night, he sat in the wooden chair near the stove, staring at the blank walls or jotting a few thoughts in his notebook until it was time to go to bed. Then he awoke to another dreary day. He rarely went beyond the borders of the farm, and then not far.

Only when he escaped to the quiet at the top of the hay barn did he feel some sort of relief. He especially liked it when the sun burned his face and the pit that once held his left eye.

When he first arrived he thought it would be a temporary job. But days stretched into weeks and weeks into months and months into years and he had no reason or desire to leave. And he knew, too, that, because of who he was, he could not leave.

Antonio seldom smiled and certainly never laughed. All his tears had been shed. And over the years every emotion had seeped out of him. Whenever he looked back now, in 1955, eleven years after Sant'Anna and arriving at the farm, he was confused. Who was this "Angelo Donatello" that he used to be? A new name, a new life, but still without a future. He thought of the times he sat at his father's knees and heard his stories. He thought of the angry

belligerent teenager who became an angry belligerent Blackshirt. He thought
of his time in Ethiopia and how he lied about his injury. And when he was a
Fascist and then a member of the Black Brigades. How could he have been
so naïve, so trusting of a leader who disgraced the country Papa had loved so
much? There wasn't much to be proud of.

Then he thought of the love and life he shared with Daniella and the
joy they had with Little Ugo. But he could not bear to think of the climb
to the top of the mountain and what happened after that. He found it all
incomprehensible.

Despite Fabiano Guerini's frequent yelling, his employer seemed
reasonably pleased with his work. Antonio didn't expect that after their first
encounter. Amadeo Mazzella had given him some new clothes and driven him
to the farm in one of Barga's sleek police cars. He had never ridden in such
luxury, and after days of climbing, dodging and running from Pietrasanta, he
almost fell asleep on the cool leather. Amadeo, however, needed to talk.

"The farmer you'll work for, he's a friendly farmer."

"You mean a Fascist."

"One of the best. Can't do much way out in the Garfagnana, though."

"What am I supposed to do?"

"Whatever he tells you. There's a lot of work on a farm. And you're young
and strong, right?"

"Yes."

"But you'll have to stay on the farm," Amadeo warned. "You can't leave
it."

"I know."

"We're going to have to tell him who you really are."

"Do we have to?"

"Yes. He has to know that the Communists will try to find you. After all,
everyone in Tuscany seems to know that you are *Occhio unico*, the man who
helped the Nazis at Sant'Anna."

"I know."

"So you can't be recognized. You'll have to wear those eyeglasses all the
time. Keep your beard long. And let your hair grow longer."

"I know."

"And you have to change your name."

"What? Why?"

"As I said, we don't want Fabiano to get into trouble. Now what name do
you want to use?"

After many alternatives were discussed, "Antonio Denato" was chosen because it was close to his real name and he didn't want to lose his identity entirely.

When they arrived at the farm, the new "Antonio" sat in the car while Amadeo and Fabiano Guerini discussed his future. It was clear Fabiano was not pleased.

"You bring me a one-eyed man with a bad leg and you say he's going to work my farm?"

Antonio didn't hear the response, but then there was much whispering and Fabiano kept looking over at him and pointing.

"No!" he heard him say. "No! No! No!"

Then he saw Amadeo lead Fabiano behind the shed and could hear no more of their conversation. When they returned, Fabiano trudged obediently behind Amadeo, who opened the car door and introduced Antonio to his new employer.

Fabiano grunted. His wife, Sabina, came running, with their two-year-old daughter clinging to her apron.

"Mama!" Graziella cried. She pointed to Antonio's eyeglasses. "Mama!"

"Shhh. He probably has something wrong with his eyes so the glasses keep the sunlight out."

Antonio had to sleep in a cave while the shelter next to the pigsty was converted into adequate living space. When it was finished, it was what one would expect a converted shelter next to a pigsty would turn out to be. A stove with a rusty grid. An old mattress on a pallet. An improvised table made out of a box, and a wooden chair. Sabina tried to make it a bit more comfortable with a red print tablecloth and a yellow pillow.

And so it began. Fall turned into winter and there was always work to do. He mowed the hay, chopped wood, gathered vegetables, milked cows and fed the pigs. Fabiano let Antonio work on his own but almost always in his sight. When Graziella was old enough, Sabina sometimes sent her over with a bowl of soup or a loaf of fresh bread. Once, Antonio had taken his eyeglasses off and Graziella ran screaming back to her mother.

When Antonio first arrived, Fabiano spent many evenings sitting by the radio, trying to decipher what the news broadcasters were saying about the war through the static and interruptions. In the spring of 1945, with Germany's losses growing and Mussolini's efforts failing, Fabiano became increasingly depressed. Most nights ended with a glass of grappa thrown across the room before he stomped up the stairs to bed.

When the war officially ended on May 8, Fabiano spent the day chopping wood and yelling curses. Sabina, Graziella and Antonio stayed as far away as possible. For Antonio, the end of the war meant nothing at all.

Graziella became a frequent visitor, and when she was about seven, she climbed up to the rooftop out of breath.

"Antonio! Antonio! Guess what?"

"I can't imagine."

"Mama said she was out in the woods picking mushrooms and suddenly around a corner she saw a boy. A boy with a pink and brown face and a bald head. A bald head! And, Antonio, he was wearing rags! She said he ran away as soon as he saw her."

"A boy like that in the woods? Is she sure?"

"She's positive. But Papa says she imagined it. He says it was probably just her imagination.

"How old did she think the boy was?"

"She didn't know. She said he was very small. Do you believe it, Antonio? Do you think there really was a boy out there?"

Antonio thought of his own struggles in the Garfagnana. "No, no. Impossible. She must have seen something else."

After Graziella left, Antonio stared into a sky overcast with threatening clouds. What if there was a little boy out there? No, not possible. He thought briefly about Little Ugo.

Last month, a runaway pig trampled his eyeglasses, cracking a lens and breaking off the stem. He always felt naked without them but the tape wouldn't hold when he tried to patch them up. Could he risk going to Barga? It's been eleven years. Surely the Communists wouldn't still be looking for him. He would have to find Amadeo Mazzella and see if there was a friendly eyeglass repairman.

With his battered truck, Fabiano drove Antonio down the winding mountain path and crossed the Serchio at Ponte a Moriano. Antonio had a few momentary pangs when they drove past the Devil's Bridge and then when he saw Barga rise above them. He remembered when he wanted Daniella to see these with him. But that was long ago, and he was too nervous now to think of anything besides getting his glasses repaired.

Not wanting to be seen with *Occhio unico*, Fabiano waited impatiently in the truck below Barga's walls. Antonio ran to the police station, where Amadeo made Antonio wait in the shadows for an hour.

"Shit!" Amadeo said when he finally emerged. Once burly, Amadeo was now balding and stuffed into his black uniform. He was sweating profusely.

"I thought I'd never see you again. I hoped I'd never see you again. What the hell do you want?"

Antonio took off his broken glasses and held them up.

Amadeo stared at the deformed face. "All right, follow me."

Amadeo put on his own dark glasses. They walked to the top of the street, but Amadeo insisted that Antonio stay twenty feet behind. After crossing Via Roma they turned down Via Madonnina. Amadeo told Antonio to stay outside when he entered a dingy shop with a sign saying *Occhiali.*

"Go in," Amadeo said when he returned fifteen minutes later. Looking frequently behind him, Amadeo hurried down the street and back to the police station.

In the cluttered back room of the shop, a wizened man of about eighty grabbed Antonio's glasses and put them on a workbench. He quickly replaced the lens and the stem and nervously handed the glasses back to Antonio. "Go!"

Antonio furtively made his way back down the hill to Fabiano's truck. He was in such a hurry that he didn't see an elderly man look up from his newspaper at a table outside Barga's Casa del Popolo.

"… and then the other day when I was playing with Fedoro, he did the cutest thing. He reached up and he put his paw on my cheek like he was going to …"

Graziella droned on and on. Antonio let the hot sun warm his face.

"Antonio! Antonio! Are you listening to me?"

PART THREE

CHAPTER 28

▼

"Ezio, we have to talk," Donna said as they pulled away from Fausta's house. She waved one last good-bye to Little Dino as he stood by the fence.

"I know."

Ezio drove the Fiat down the narrow road and onto the highway that led from Sant'Antonio to Reboli. "There's a little park along the river. We can stop there."

No one else was around, and they parked the Fiat and sat at a picnic bench. The Maggia had never been a big river, but this summer it was particularly shallow. Still, with a few fish glinting in the sunlight, it bubbled over the smooth rocks on its way to the Serchio in Lucca. During some of his bad times in recent years, Ezio liked to walk up and down its banks and find the solitude he so desperately needed.

"This isn't good," Donna said.

"I know. A police officer? What could be worse?"

"Ezio, this Amadeo Mazzella will be able to find out everything about you. He probably has already. That you're a schoolteacher, not a journalist. That you went to Pietrasanta and met with Communists rather than going to see him. And, oh, yes, that you're traveling with a beautiful woman you picked up along the way." She made a face.

"Donna, don't make a face. That last part especially is true."

"So what do we do?"

Silently, with his finger, Ezio traced the "*Ti amo*" that had been etched on the picnic table many years ago. He wondered who had written "I love you" and to whom.

"Well," he finally said, "I can't stop now. I—we—have come this far. What can I do except go to Barga and pretend that I'm a journalist looking for *Occhio unico* and ask Amadeo Mazzella to help? That's what I told that

Fascist in the *osteria* in Florence. I'll have to stick to that. But there's a bigger question. What about you? It's one thing for me to be in some sort of danger. But I don't want to put you through that. I can drive you right back to Pietrasanta, you know."

"Are you joking? You're joking, right?"

Ezio smiled. "I thought you'd say that."

"There is this, though," Donna said. "How are you going to explain me?"

Ezio pondered the question. "Um. Think you could be my assistant?"

"Since when do journalists on a tiny newspaper in Reboli have assistants?"

"Especially beautiful ones. I don't know." Ezio's finger seemed stuck on the "*amo*" on the table. "Wait. I know. Some papers have photographers. Could you be my photographer?"

"If I knew how to take pictures."

"Well, they'll never see the results. We can stop at my rooms in Reboli and I can pick up my camera."

"You know, there's another thing. Mazzella is going to want proof that you're a journalist. You're going to have to show him something. A business card, a recommendation letter, a few articles you've written. No, Ezio, obviously you can't bring *A Time to Remember*."

Ezio laughed. "No, I guess not. The memoirs of a partisan would not impress a Fascist police officer. I haven't written any articles and I don't have a card. Well, I guess I could write my own letter."

"Make it good. I'll help."

Ezio parked the Fiat just outside of Reboli so that he could take Donna on his favorite walk along the Via Bellini. He pointed out the copy of the Della Robbia Madonna on the wall of the Bandini house. They crept past Signora Franconi's fat gray cat, asleep as usual next to the geraniums. And then they stopped in front of the abandoned German tank and the plaque, "We must never forget!"

Donna clutched Ezio's hand. "I know how you feel, Ezio."

"I know you do. I wish more people remembered. The other day I found two of my students swinging on top of this like it was a trapeze."

"They were just being kids, Ezio. They weren't even born when the war ended. They don't know anything about it."

"But they should, Donna. I should have taught them better."

She turned to him and her eyes flashed. "Ezio, It's not your fault. You can't expect everyone to feel the way you do. I know that's hard to accept, but that's the way it is. You feel guilty for leaving Sant'Anna. Then you feel guilty for not going back to Sant'Anna. Now you feel guilty for not teaching the kids right. Guilt, guilt, guilt. Let it go, Ezio."

"You sound like Paolo."

Now she smiled. "Good. I'm glad."

They walked to the piazza in front of the Chiesa di Sant'Ignazzio. There they encountered Signora Antonelli and Signora Piazini, still swathed in black and still gossiping. The elderly widows stopped and stared. Ezio Maffini, that nice schoolteacher, walking with, what, a woman?

"*Buon giorno*," Ezio said, bowing slightly.

"*Buon giorno*," Signora Antonelli said, grabbing her friend's arm and quickly moving her along the cobblestones. They looked back and pointed.

"Who were they?" Donna asked.

"Just some nice old ladies who would like to see me married. They always whisper '*Povero sfortunato*' when they see me."

"Looks like you've got quite a reputation here."

Since he had been away for four days, Ezio's rooms were stuffy and he quickly opened the shutters. This immediately increased the din of the Vespas on the street below.

"Um," Donna said, "interesting view." She looked out at the bell tower of the Chiesa di Sant'Ignazio, the red tile roofs and the blinking sign of the *farmacia*.

"Not as nice as yours in the country," Ezio said. "And you don't have those Vespas."

"I guess you didn't notice the sweet smell of pigs that wafts over our house," Donna said, running her finger over the edge of the dresser. "This is a nice room. I imagine you have a lot of visitors."

Ezio knew what she was getting at, but decided to remain elusive. "It gets rather warm in summer."

She looked at the bed. "I can imagine. Hot probably."

He reached up on the top shelf of the closet and pulled down a box with a camera.

"It's a Ducati Sogno. I gave it to myself after my first year of teaching. It cost a month's salary, but it was worth it. I love it. I've taken a lot of pictures in the Garfagnana actually. Some people think it's like a Leica, but it's smaller. Look, it can fit in my pocket."

Donna handled the camera gingerly. She had never owned one, let alone used one. "I guess I'll have to practice if I'm going to be your photographer."

"We can take some pictures in the Garfagnana," Ezio said as he shoved some dirty laundry aside and pulled out an Olivetti from the floor of his closet.

"I bought this typewriter when I wrote *A Time to Remember*. It cost me another month's salary."

Donna leaned over his shoulder as he began to type, two-fingered style. "You'd better have some sort of letterhead," she said.

"Hmm. The paper is supposed to be owned by *Movimento Sociale Italiano*." He typed that at the top of the page.

"You'd better give an address. Not here, of course."

"I don't know. Oh, well, how about the *farmacia*?" He typed in Via Scalabrini, 5, Reboli, Tuscany, Italy.

"Mazzella will never guess."

Debating back and forth, Ezio and Donna finally came up with the body of the letter.

To the Reader of This Document:

This is to certify that Ezio Maffini is a journalist and Madonna Fazzini is a photographer for the regional edition of *Il Popolo*. You will recognize this as a direct descendent of *Il Popolo d'Italia*, the venerable newspaper founded by our beloved Benito Mussolini.

Your cooperation and courtesies in regard to their quest for information are greatly appreciated.

Your humble servant,

Signor Giorgio Gallo
Direttore
Il Popolo

They both had trouble figuring out a name for their illustrious editor and finally chose one of the most common in all of Italy.

Ezio put the letter in an envelope. "Do you think this is going to work?"

"No."

Suddenly, Ezio realized that he should have kept his pistol and rifle from his days in the *banda*. He would probably need them now. But after the war he got rid of everything that reminded him of those terrible days. All he had was a small pocket knife that he had as a kid. He put it in his pocket.

"All right," he said, "Let's go." He loaded film into the camera and grabbed some clean clothes. Signora Antonelli and Signora Piazini were standing silently in front of the Chiesa di Sant'Ignazzio when Ezio and Donna ran down to their car.

"*Buon giorno* again," Ezio said. The women took long looks at Donna, nodded to each other and hurried off.

"I think they were waiting to get one more glimpse of you," Ezio said. "In an hour it will be all over Reboli that I have a girlfriend."

"Good. That will do wonders for your reputation," Donna said.

It wasn't far to Lucca and they were able to take the *autostrada* around the city. While Lucca's fabled walls preserved its medieval buildings and atmosphere, the outskirts were becoming like any other Italian city, with ugly flat-roofed factories spreading across the landscape.

"Someday I'll take you inside those walls and you can see what a beautiful city it is," Ezio said.

"I keep thinking how little I've seen of Italy," Donna said.

"I'll take you other places, too."

Ezio wondered why he made such a promise to a woman he had known only a couple of days, but he was glad he did. Soon, they were driving north, along the east bank of the Serchio and through tiny villages.

"Are we there yet?" Donna teased.

"Soon. Just be patient." Ezio grinned.

They were both silent as they slowly entered the world of the Garfagnana. Even more than the countryside they saw from Pietrasanta to Sant'Antonio, this was entrancing and somehow even enchanted. But it was also forbidding. The mountains, verdant green for the most part, seemed to glow in the July sunlight as they stretched thousands of feet into the brilliant blue sky. Stony ridges dared anyone to climb to the top. A few small farms clung to the hillsides. Small villages clustered around churches. There was no breeze and the only sound was the sputtering Fiat.

"Impressed?" Ezio asked.

"I've never seen anything so beautiful. This seems like a different country."

"I've always thought that it is. Strange, mysterious."

"A place," Donna said, "that could hide someone for years."

"And where ghost boys roam the mountain tops," Ezio said. Donna ignored the invitation for a comment.

Ezio drove on, slowing down through the sleepy villages of San Annuziata, San Pietro a Vico, Saltocchio.

"What bridge is that?" Donna pointed to the left.

"It leads to a little village called Ponte a Moriano. They say that those mountains up there are the most dense in the Garfagnana."

"A good place for the monster to hide," Donna said.

"Right. Bastard!"

Donna stuck her head out of the window. "My God, did an eagle just fly over us?"

Ezio tried to see. "You're probably right. This is the only part of Tuscany where there are eagles. There are other birds of prey around, too."

"So *Occhio unico* has been hiding in these mountains, we don't know for how long, with eagles and other birds of prey flying around," Donna said. "You know, sometimes I think we're on a wild goose chase, and I don't mean one of those birds of prey."

Suddenly, Ezio slowed down almost to a stop. "Look to your left."

Donna held her hand over her mouth. "Oh my God! That's fantastic. In fact, it's more like a fantasy. That's the most beautiful bridge I've ever seen."

And so Ezio told Donna the story of the Devil's Bridge. He didn't know it all; it was something about the devil wanting the first soul that crossed but then he was tricked and then he drowned.

"Want to experiment with the camera?"

The afternoon sun sent dappled stripes across the bridge and onto the river below. The bridge itself rose majestically over the river, with a few tourists taking pictures from the top. For someone who had never held a camera before, Donna proved unusually adept. Ezio said she must have seen too many movies. She focused from the front and then from the side. She lay in the grass and shot upwards, and she was about to climb a tree when Ezio interrupted.

"You're going to get dirty!" he cried.

Donna brushed her dress, a pretty blue that was her favorite. "I guess I'm not dressed for tree climbing today." She looked back at the bridge as they continued north. "I wish we had time to walk over to the other side."

"Not today," Ezio said as they got back into the car. "We'd better get to Barga. And, you know, we'd better start playing our roles. Remember, I'm a journalist and you're a photographer."

"Right. I'm a photographer and you're a journalist."

Suddenly, she burst out laughing.

"What's so funny?"

"Ezio, did you ever see the movie *It Happened One Night*?"

"That old one with Claudette Colbert and Clark Gable? Sure, a couple of times. The cinema in Reboli doesn't get many new movies, so it keeps playing old ones, especially from Hollywood."

"Now don't laugh, but they remind me of us."

Ezio stared at her. "Oh, sure. I'm a brash young journalist just like Clark Gable. Wait. So you think I look like Clark Gable? Well, thank you! Nobody's ever said that to me before."

"Well, sort of. The same hair. Strong, masculine. No mustache, though. And you don't smoke. But of course you are a brash young journalist."

"Right. And you're an heiress who bosses everyone around. What does he call her? A brat?"

"Well, not that part. But I was thinking of the scene where they go to a place to spend the night and there are two beds so he puts up a sheet or a blanket or something to separate them."

"The walls of Jericho!"

"Right." Donna smiled. She looked out the window and after waiting for what she thought was a decent amount of time she asked, "So what are we going to do tonight?"

Since they left Pietrasanta that morning, Ezio and Donna had carefully avoided a discussion of sleeping arrangements. Ezio was torn by the twin emotions of guilt and desire and he thought of a yellow dress every time he looked at Donna, so pretty and seductive. For her part, Donna knew she needed to respect Ezio's feelings even though she had strong ones of her own.

After hesitating for a long while, in which he didn't take his eyes off the road, Ezio said, "I guess we'll just have to see what they have."

"Yes."

Donna was again speechless when Barga loomed ahead of them on the hilltop. Schoolteacher and historian that he was, Ezio gave a brief account. Founded as a castle before the year 1000 by the Lombards and then became a walled city. Known in the Middle Ages for making silk threads that were sent to Florence. For a time it was part of the Florentine dominion. Later it became part of the Duchy of Lucca. The Duomo at the top? It's known as the *castello*.

"Thank you, Signor *Professore*."

Since cars were discouraged from going into the old part of the city, they parked in the lot below and carried their satchels up the steep winding path to the entrance, looking behind them all the way. Once, Ezio thought a man was following close behind, but he went into a *bar*.

Ezio knew of the Pensione Leonardo on Via Crochetta off Via Roma. Breathless after the climb up the narrow alleys, they arrived just as the spindly matron at the desk was about to lock the door.

"All right, you can come in." She scrutinized them over her glasses. "Will you want one room or two?"

Ezio and Donna looked at each other.

"Well, I have two rooms adjoining, and there's a door in between."

"Fine!" they said together.

An hour later, as Ezio was ready to crawl into his narrow bed, he stood at the adjoining door and called out, "Everything all right behind the walls of Jericho?"

"Just fine, Ezio."

"Remember, I'm a journalist and you're a photographer."

"Right. I'm a photographer and you're a journalist. I'll see you in the morning."

CHAPTER 29

▼

When they turned in their room key the next morning, Ezio and Donna asked the woman at the *pensione* desk if she knew where Barga's Casa del Popolo was. She thought for a while. Across from the Church of the Annunziata? No. Near S.S. Crocifisso? No. She didn't have time to think anymore. "Ask someone else." She went into the laundry room.

They didn't have any better luck on the streets when they asked the next two people. A middle-aged businessman shook his head and continued reading his copy of *Giornale di Barga* as he followed a dog on a leash. A woman outside a flower shop gave a half-dozen answers and went back inside.

"There can't be many Communists in Barga," Ezio said.

Then a portly priest munching a creamy *pasticiotti* pointed north. "Palazzo Pancrazzi."

Whether he dreaded the moment when he would finally meet Amadeo Mazzella or whether he just wanted to be in Donna's company longer, Ezio decided to take the long way to the palazzo. He helped her up the steep and narrow streets, peering down into the alleys along each side. At the top, they faced the Duomo looming over the entire valley.

"It does look more like a castle than a church," Donna said.

They were more enthralled with the view, starting with the tile rooftops below them and reaching far beyond into hills that seemed to stretch into infinity. Donna wanted to climb on the protective wall, but Ezio pulled her back.

"No point taking a risk," he said. "You wouldn't have a chance if you fell down there."

"All right, Ezio. I'm a big girl. You don't have to protect me all the time."

When they reached the piazza in front of the sixteenth-century town hall, there were so many people milling around and talking that they didn't find the Casa until they turned the corner. There, a small sign in a window announced the presence of Barga's small Communist cell.

"There was a huge sign in Pietrasanta," Donna said. "You're right, there can't be many members here."

Four elderly men were hunched over *scopa* cards in the middle of the room, cigar smoke rising to the tin ceiling. Ezio approached the table and tapped one of them on the shoulder.

"Excuse me. We've just come from Pietrasanta. Um. Do you know a man named Cabbage there?" He had a hard time getting the name out.

"Cabbage?" the smallest man whispered. "You mean Rico Fazzini? The one who fought near Pietrasanta?"

"Is he dead?" another said. "God in heaven. Poor Cabbage. *E morto!*"

All four took out handkerchiefs, all of them red, and wiped their noses.

"No! No!" Ezio said. "He's not dead. He's fine. He sent me here because he thinks you can help me."

After blowing their noses again, the four invited Ezio and Donna to sit down. They had been partisans in another *banda*, but they all knew of the exploits of Orfeo Tolosi ("*Il rospo*, the Toad!"), Leonardo Ciamino ("Tomato!"), Filippo Parisi ("Radish!") and especially Cabbage.

"He's my father," Donna said.

Now the men were even more impressed. The famous Cabbage had such a beautiful daughter. Since each of the men wanted to relate his own experiences with the partisans during the war, it took a long while for Ezio and Donna to tell them the reason for their visit to Barga. But when they said they heard that *Occhio unico* had been seen, the men knew the story immediately.

"I was the one!" a husky man named Bertrando del Rosso shouted. "I was the one who saw him! I was sitting out there on that chair reading *Gazzetta dello sport*. It was the day after Rocky Marciano knocked out Don Cockell. The ninth round. May 16. That's how I remember. Well, I happened to look up. There was this man running past here. Right outside." He pointed to the street. "And I knew who he was immediately. Look!"

Del Rosso pointed to a poster on the wall. It showed the same drawing of a man with a woolen cap and dark glasses as the one in Pietrasanta. Underneath were the words *Occhio unico*.

"We've all memorized that poster," del Rosso said. "So I knew right away."

If del Rosso's chest could have gotten any bigger at this moment, it would have popped the buttons on his blue flannel shirt.

"Well," said a man named Edidio Peligni, "he may have seen *Occhio unico*, but we used my car to follow him. My 1946 Fiat."

"And I went, too," said Innocenzio Ferrara.

"And me, too," said Tino Vestini.

The four excitedly described how they stumbled and ran as best they could after *Occhio unico* down to a parking lot and saw him get into a truck. They climbed into Peligni's car and followed the truck down the hills from Barga and then along the Serchio but the Fiat kept sputtering and popping.

"Your car's no damn good, I don't know why you bought that piece of junk," Ferrara told Peligni.

Peligni was about to punch Ferrara when del Rosso stood up to describe the rest of the chase.

"That truck kept going faster and faster." He waved his arms. "Peligni tried to go faster. The truck went faster yet."

"And the road was winding," Vistini said.

"Then," del Rosso said, "we got to the bridge over the Serchio at Ponte a Moriano. And then, right there, right there, in the middle of the bridge, Peligni's car died. Died. *E morto*." Del Rosso sat down and held his head in his hands.

"So we lost him," Ferrara said, looking ominously at Peligni.

"But we know," Vistini said, "that the monster is on the other side of the Serchio."

"So near and yet so far," del Rosso said.

"Stop saying that," Ferrara yelled. "You say that all the time!"

Ezio tried to interrupt the bickering. "You've known that *Occhio unico* is across the river but you haven't done anything to find him?"

Del Rosso explained that they were all old and disabled, and the men pointed to useless arms and legs, casualties of the war. And unlike in Pietrasanta, there were now very few partisans in Barga. The men all agreed, however, that the word had been spread that the monster of Sant'Anna had not fled to Germany after all.

As the men leaned forward to listen, Ezio explained why he had come. They had a hard time believing that such a young man would still be interested in finding *Occhio unico* and that, incredibly, he had heard in Florence that the monster had been seen and had been given the name of someone who could give them information.

"Amadeo Mazzella! The captain of police!" the four men shouted together.

They all said they were not surprised, claiming that they knew Mazzella was a Fascist and wouldn't doubt that he had this kind of information. But they wondered how Ezio and Donna could get him to talk.

"He's not going to believe that you're just a journalist," Ferrara said.

"This is a trap, my young friend," del Rosso said. "Be careful. Be very careful."

"I know," Ezio said, "but I have to do this. I have to." He paused. "Tell me, Signor del Rosso, what did *Occhio unico* look like when you saw him?"

Del Rosso scratched his head. "Look like? Oh, I don't know. I recognized him from the drawing on the wall. But he was shorter than I thought. I always thought he was a big guy but he's this little, this little ... runt."

The other old partisans laughed.

"What was he wearing?" Ezio asked.

"Oh, let me think. He had a plaid shirt on, the kind farmers wear. And old pants, brown, I think. Oh, and the cap, like on the poster. I remember his cap because it had all these colors, blue, red, green. He had this cap pulled down over his head, but I could still see that he had eyeglasses on."

"Of course he had eyeglasses on," Ferrara said. "He's *Occhio unico*."

"Did he say anything?" Ezio wanted know.

"No, no," del Rosso said. "He was just running."

"Did anyone else see him?"

"Um. Let me think. Well, this woman helped him up when he fell down."

"He fell down?"

"He was crossing just by the statue in the piazza when he must have tripped and he fell. This woman, an old woman, I don't know who she was, she was all in black, helped him back up."

"Do you think he said anything to her?"

"That's the strangest thing. Here's this guy, this monster, and he got up and he seemed to be saying *Grazie* to her. Imagine. *Grazie*. I couldn't believe it."

Ezio and Donna asked the men where they could find Amadeo Mazzella and thanked them for their kindness. They said they were staying at Pensione Leonardo and promised to return. As they were about to leave, Donna pointed to a hulking man they hadn't seen before. Wearing a bright orange shirt and red plaid pants, he was sitting in a corner, reading a newspaper and smoking a cigar. Then they noticed that his left arm must have been amputated below the elbow. His sleeve was pinned up to hide it.

"Who do you think that is?"

"I can't imagine," Ezio said. "He looks like he may have been a boxer."

Ezio was unusually quiet on their way to the police station and almost bumped into a street sign for Opera Barga.

"Something wrong?"

"I don't know, Donna. All these years I've had a hard time imagining *Occhio unico* as a human being. He was some sort of huge monster that didn't have any features. In my nightmares, he's just a dark shadowy figure. Now someone talks about how he's a little guy, and he wears a cap and a shirt and pants. And he falls down. And then he gets up and thanks the woman who helps him? I don't know, Donna, I just don't know what to think."

"I know," she said. "I'm having a hard time with this, too. I mean I've heard the stories about how he was a young man in Pietrasanta, but that didn't seem to be the same person who turned into *Occhio unico*. You're not having second thoughts, are you?"

"No, no. Not at all. No!" Ezio said. "This just makes this man all the more, I don't know, real."

"Yes."

"Well, what can we do? He's still the man who helped the Germans kill five hundred and sixty innocent people, right? We have to remember that."

"Yes. A monster. Yes."

Before long, Ezio and Donna found themselves outside the stark building with a sign saying *Carbinieri*. Ezio pushed the bell at the side of the door. A long wait.

"If somebody was wounded, they'd be dead by now," Donna whispered.

Finally, a voice called through a small opening. "What do you want?"

"We are looking for Amadeo Mazzella," Ezio answered.

"Who are you?"

"I am a journalist and I was referred to Signor Mazzella to get some information."

Ezio and Donna spent the next half hour walking back and forth in front of the building, taking turns waiting in front of the bell. They admired the old villa across the street, badly in need of repair but still open for tourists. They counted the pots of geraniums that lined the entrance. They watched an elderly woman carrying shopping bags as she slowly made her way back home.

Then the door opened. His black uniform may have fit a few years ago, but now Amadeo Mazzella strained every inch of the woolen shirt and trousers. His black tie seemed to strangle him, and his ruddy face was sweating all the way back to his receding hairline. He offered a plump moist hand.

"A journalist? Well, well, come in. I've been expecting you."

CHAPTER 30

▼

Seated side by side in front of Amadeo's desk, Ezio and Donna had a long opportunity to study the framed certificates on the wall and the photos of Amadeo with various dignitaries on his otherwise empty desk. Amadeo eyed one and then the other of his visitors. He spent a long time examining Donna, from the brown curls that framed a face that could have been created by Raphael down her pale blue dress to her firm breasts and back again.

"Well," he finally said. "I thought you'd be here sooner."

"You did?" Ezio said. He could barely get the words out.

Amadeo's small eyes narrowed. "Oh, yes. When we had word that you were coming, I thought that you would be here a few days ago."

"I'm afraid we were delayed," Ezio stammered.

"Perhaps," Amadeo said slowly and deliberately, "we could have talked longer if you had come when expected." He pulled out a cigar from a box at the side of his desk. "But why do you want to talk to me? I'm just a minor police officer in a small town."

"Sir," Ezio hesitated, "I am writing the true story of Sant'Anna di Stazzema and I was told you might be able to help me."

Amadeo took a long time lighting his cigar. "Ah, Sant'Anna di Stazzema, Sant'Anna di Stazzema. Oh, my, I haven't thought about that unfortunate incident for some time."

Ezio stiffened. Donna tried not to look at him.

Grasping the arms of his chair, Ezio continued. "I know there were many articles published at the time in the press, which as you know is mainly Communist. I want to tell people what really happened there."

"What really happened?"

"Yes." Ezio swallowed hard.

Amadeo leaned back. "Yes, I know that the press was all over this story at the time, but they told only one side. *Corriere della sera, La Repubblica, La Stampa,* they all told lies or they were too lazy to write the real story. I remember one article, I don't remember where it was, about these two sisters who had gone to Sant'Anna from someplace, I don't remember where, and they died in the fire. Well, no one reported that these two women were prostitutes! Prostitutes! Can you imagine that! Prostitutes! Both of them! And no one wrote a single word about that."

Amadeo wiped his face and pointed a finger at Ezio. "How can a journalist, someone who is supposed to present the entire truth, justify that? Can you answer that, Signor ... Signor ... what is your name again?"

"Ezio Maffini, sir. I am the writer and Signorina Donna Fazzini takes photographs for our newspaper."

"What a pleasure to meet you, Signorina."

"I'm sure it is," Donna said.

Just then a short, dark-skinned young patrolman entered the room, placed a piece of paper on Amadeo's desk and quickly left. Amadeo looked at the paper and threw it in the wastebasket.

"So sorry for the interruption," he said. He lowered his voice. "So you see what kind of policemen we have here? We are getting so many now from the South ... Naples, Calabria, even Sicily. They say they can't find jobs there so they come up here! Well, why don't they look for jobs there, I ask you. They come up here and they try to be policemen and they don't know their ass from a hole in the ground, if you'll pardon the expression, Signorina. None of these men become officers, of course, because we wouldn't have it. I'll tell you, Italy would be better off if these people would stay where they belong. Ah, there's nothing like Tuscany, is there, Signor Maffini?"

"No, sir."

Amadeo wiped his face again. Ezio and Donna sat motionless.

"So," Amadeo said, turning to Ezio, "Signor *giornalista,* where do you live?"

"Reboli, sir.

"Ah, Reboli, a fine little town, a fine town. I have visited it many times. I had a good friend there, Signor Aldonzi, a fine man, lovely wife, beautiful children. Eight of them, I believe. But I believe he no longer lives in Reboli. Do you know the thread factory that he owned? No? A fine business. I often visited there. He had lovely women working there, if you don't mind my saying so, Signorina?"

Donna winced. Ezio focused on a framed certificate above Amadeo's head. Remember to breathe slowly, he told himself. One, two three....

"I remember one in particular," Amadeo droned on. "Her name was Fosca or Fausta or something like that ..."

"Sir ..." Ezio put his hand on the left side of his head. Donna reached over and held the arm of his chair.

Amadeo dropped ashes on the red carpet on the floor. It already had many burn holes in it. "And you, Signorina, do you live in Reboli also?"

"No, no," Donna said. "I'm from Pietrasanta."

"Pietrasanta! I lived there for a few years during the war. I have many friends there, too. But Signor Maffini, you say you are a journalist. How do I know that? Do you have a business card or some articles that you have written so I know for certain who you are? Just a little formality, of course."

Amadeo smiled slightly, and Ezio pulled an envelope from his pocket. "No, sir, but I do have this letter from my editor. I assume that will suffice." His hands trembled as he handed it over.

"Ah. *Movimento Sociale Italiano*. What a fine organization. I have been to some of their meetings. Excellent meetings, good discussions. And I know so many fine gentlemen here in Barga who are members. There's Signor Malandra, he owns a printing shop, and Signor Fassio, he rings the bell at the church, and of course Signor Santori, he owns a fine restaurant just off Piazza del Comune. You must go there for the *agnello di bosco*, such wonderful lamb, and the *vitello ariana*, the finest veal in all of Tuscany. I go there myself perhaps once a week to have it. You can see that I enjoy it."

He patted his formidable stomach.

"Oh yes, I had a little incident with the heart two years ago, but I'm fine now, just fine. The doctor said I should go on a diet. A diet! Do you think I need a diet? Life is to enjoy, isn't that so? We are Italians!"

Ezio was getting nervous. "Sir, the letter ..."

"Ah, yes, the letter. Hmmm. Yes. Hmmm. Ah, *Il Popolo d'Italia*." He looked up. "What a fine newspaper that was. My father used to read it to me, and then when I got older I read it by myself. Do you know what the slogans were on the masthead when *il Duce* founded it? No? I'll tell you. 'He who has steel has bread' and 'A revolution is an idea which has found bayonets.' Imagine. This was in 1914, Signor Maffini, 1914. That's what *il Duce* believed. What a great man, a great man. My father told me how people would accost newsboys who were selling *Il Popolo d'Italia*, they were so anxious to read it. Oh, how I missed the newspaper when unfortunately it ended in 1943. I remember one editorial *il Duce* wrote. It read ..."

"Sir, the letter ..."

"Ah yes, the letter. Hmmm. Ah, Giorgio Gallo. Giorgio Gallo. I believe I was introduced to Giorgio Gallo once."

Ezio and Donna froze. Ezio began to sweat.

"Yes, of course, Giorgio Gallo. Yes. It must have been on one of my visits to Reboli."

Amadeo put down the letter and smiled at Ezio. "How long will you remain in Barga, Signor Maffini? You must stay a few days at least. You must see the theater, I don't know what they are performing now, but they're very famous, and oh, yes, Opera Barga, they do such fine work. And you can't leave without going to the *Sagra*. Do you know what that is? No? Every week we have this big community dinner, it's called *Cena in Vignola* and it's in the vineyard below the Duomo. There is so much food, so much food, and the wine! And the money always goes to a good cause. And also ..."

"Sir, I'm afraid my editor, Signor Gallo, would like me to complete the article as quickly as possible. So if you could just answer a few questions ..."

"Oh, I'm sure Signor Gallo wouldn't mind if you were a day or two past whatever deadline you have. No, not mind at all. Tonight, Signor Maffini, Signorina Fazzini, you must come to my house and we will have a little dinner. Just a little dinner. My wife," he lowered his voice, "is not, if you can believe this, a very good cook, but she does what she can, and our children will be at home, too. Lovely children, a little lively sometimes. You'll like them. And we might invite a few friends. I think, Signor Maffini, these friends will be of assistance to you. Here is my address."

Amadeo wrote his address on a piece of paper, stood up and crushed his cigar butt in a glass ashtray.

"I will see you at 8 o'clock, Signor, Signorina." His tone was now menacing. "That's 8 o'clock."

Ezio and Donna were about to leave when Amadeo stopped them and pulled a camera out of a desk drawer. "Signor Maffini, Signorina Fazzini, there is one favor I would like from you. I would like to have your photograph taken. Then we can show how even in little Barga we have distinguished visitors. We have this new camera that develops a photograph in a minute. Look, it's called a Polaroid. What won't they think of next?"

He smiled a thin smile. Confused, Ezio and Donna had little choice but to stand against a white backdrop and let another policeman take their pictures. Amadeo made no attempt to show them the finished products.

"All right," Amadeo said. "8 o'clock."

Ezio and Donna couldn't run fast enough down the stairs and out into the street. Both were breathless.

"You're having a headache, right?" Donna held his arm.

"Yes, I need to go back to the room. Need darkness, cold towel."

Hours later, when Ezio's tremors ceased and his headache eased, Donna changed the cold towel on his forehead for the fourth time.

"Feel better?"

"A little. Thanks."

"You scared me."

"Donna, that was the first headache I've had in days. That evil, evil man."

She held his hands in hers. "I know."

"The worst thing? 'Unfortunate incident!' How could he say that about the cold-blooded massacre of five hundred and sixty innocent people? How could he say that?"

"I know, Ezio, I know. It was all I could do not to get up and slap him across the face."

"And all that other stuff. On and on and on. The policemen from the South. The veal at the restaurant. The wonderful members of *Movimento Sociale Italiano*. How great *il Duce* was. On and on and on."

"And don't forget about Fausta! The bastard!"

"Oh, Donna. He showed absolutely no remorse for what he did to her. He sounded rather proud of it. The bastard! The evil bastard!"

"That's when I wanted to slap him again."

Donna took the towel from Ezio's head and replaced it with her cool hand. They remained silent in the darkened room. When she opened the shutters to let in some air, they could see the top of the Duomo in the distance. Church bells rang seven times.

Ezio got up and began pacing from the window to the dresser to the bed. "And, Donna, we didn't learn a damn thing. Not a damn thing. We're no closer now to finding *Occhio unico* than we were a week ago."

"And in another hour we're going to meet some of his dear friends. What kind of a trap is that?"

CHAPTER 31

▼

Donna changed into another dress, white, low cut and with a blue sash around the waist.

"If I knew we were going to such an important party, I would have taken my third dress," she called from her room. "I own three, you know."

"I have four shirts," Ezio said.

"My, I'm impressed."

Standing in the doorway between their rooms, Ezio suddenly wanted to take her in his arms. The dress fit close where it should, her hair was smooth and shiny and her face was a little flushed.

"You look beautiful," he said. "Amadeo's friends will be most impressed."

"I don't know if I want to impress them. But this might be useful." She smiled her half-smile.

Ezio had rinsed out his sweaty shirt in the tiny corner sink and hung it on an improvised clothesline in his room.

"The walls of Jericho?" Donna asked.

"It's a pretty small wall."

As they were leaving, Ezio grabbed his Ducati Sogno and stuffed it in his pocket. There might be an excuse to take photos of these men, he said, and that might prove useful later. How, he did not know, but he wanted a record. He also said that although he might have been passive that afternoon, he was going to be more aggressive this evening. Then he made sure his little knife was in his other pocket.

Because they got lost twice in the maze of Barga's streets, it took them thirty-five minutes to reach the Mazzella villa and they barely made it at 8 o'clock. It was on the outskirts of the old city and dated back to the early 1800s. Three stories high, with a red tile roof and cream-colored walls, it

181

stood far back from the street and was encircled by a wrought iron fence. A large family crest shone in the evening sunlight above the door.

"Welcome, welcome," Amadeo shouted as he came out the door and down the path to greet them. Three pudgy children, two boys and a girl, raced ahead. Immediately, dirty fingerprints decorated Donna's white dress. One of the boys tried to take the camera out of Ezio's pocket.

"Little Amadeo, Riccardo, Immacolata, go help your mother." No apology.

Amadeo had exchanged his black woolen uniform for an equally tight black silk shirt and black pants. The shirt was open to reveal a mass of white chest hair on which rested a gold medallion of the Virgin Mary on a chain. Ezio was certain the back of the medallion contained the initials of the *Movimento Sociale Italiano*, just like Franco's in the *osteria* in Florence. Amadeo's face and scalp glistened with sweat.

As the children pushed and shoved their way back into the house, Amadeo took his guests on a tour of the gardens in back. Manicured yews, potted lemon trees and boxwood lined four terraces that surrounded two reflecting pools. Huge statues, which Donna recognized as products of Stupendi Marbleworks, stood at the four corners with small statues of dogs and cherubs in between. Stone urns dripped with ivy and tumbling roses. Cobblestone walks led visitors between immaculate landscapes of flowers that surrounded topiary trees. There was a faint scent of jasmine.

"It's just a little something that we like to keep up," Amadeo said. "The children aren't allowed back here, of course."

He lowered his voice and both Ezio and Donna wondered what secret he would reveal this time. "I have one of our new policemen, he's from Palermo, come over every weekend to take care of it. He's not supposed to be here, so he's glad that I'm doing this for him."

"It's magnificent," Ezio said.

Two men, drinks in hand, were already in the garden.

"Signorina Fazzini, Signor Maffini," Amadeo said, "I want you to meet two very good friends."

Calvino Bastiani, perhaps about sixty, was tall, thin and white-haired and wore a three-piece pinstriped suit even on this warm July night. A gold watch chain hung out of his pocket. He had a neatly trimmed beard.

Orsino Nardari was probably in his early seventies. He smoked a thin cigar and had chosen a colorful ensemble of a navy blue jacket, pink shirt, red tie and green trousers. On his jacket was a badge with a prancing black horse on a yellow shield with green, white and red stripes at the top. Ezio and Donna immediately recognized this as the symbol for Ferrari.

Both seemed more interested in Donna and her cleavage than in Ezio.

"Signorina Fazzini, Signor Maffini," Calvino said, bowing to both of them. "It is such a pleasure to meet you. We hope you enjoy your visit to our lovely city. If there is anything we can do to make your visit more enjoyable, please don't hesitate to ask us."

Orsino said much the same thing.

"You know, Signor Mazzella," Ezio said, "it would be wonderful if my photographer could take some photographs of your garden. Perhaps we could even publish them in the newspaper. I would certainly send you copies."

Amadeo beamed. "Of course! Take as many as you would like." Donna aimed the camera from several angles until Ezio stopped her.

"You know, Signor Mazzella, a photograph with all three of you in the center of the garden would certainly be a wonderful addition to your collection."

The three men stood in various positions until Donna ran out of film.

"Thank you so much," Ezio said.

"This young journalist and photographer," Amadeo told his guests, "are looking for information for a most interesting article. I am very excited about this because as you know we in the public eye are always looking for the truth to come out. We must never hide anything from the public, so to speak. I remember the time when one of our police officers, very high ranking, too, could have been involved in a bit of a scandal. He was a very kind gentleman and he owned a villa, a small villa to be sure, on the outskirts of Barga in which young women who came from other parts of Italy, many of them from villages in the South, could stay for as long as they liked and be charged very little rent as long as they were available for other services for police officers, if you know what I mean."

Calvino and Orsino smiled knowingly.

"So when the *Giornale di Barga* found out about this place, they wanted to write a big article about how public funds were being used to maintain this villa, and that police officers should not be involved in this sort of thing. Well, our captain sat down with the journalist who was going to write the article, a young fellow, not very experienced in these matters, if you know what I mean, and the captain told the journalist everything, how these were poor women were working very hard as maids for the police officers and if they didn't have this employment they would have to go back to their villages. I remember the conversation very well because three other officers and myself stood behind the captain as he was describing all this to the journalist. Well, of course the journalist understood and no article was ever published."

Amidst all the sighing and nodding, Ezio was determined not to let Amadeo control the conversation as he had in the afternoon. *Occhio unico, Occhio unico*, he kept thinking. He had to find out more.

"Sirs," Ezio said, "the article that I am writing, the one Signor Mazzella so kindly referenced, has to do with the event at Sant'Anna di Stazzema on the twelfth of August in 1944. Are you familiar with that event?"

"I remember something vaguely, oh, that was so long ago," Orsino said. "Something about a fire that killed a dozen or so people. Terrible thing."

"No, no," Calvino said, "it was something else. There was a group of Communist partisans there, dozens of them, I believe, and they descended on this little village and they killed many, many people, I don't know how many, for no reason, no reason at all."

"Not a fire?" Orsino said.

"No, no. Partisans. Communist partisan bastards."

Ezio stepped closer. "Well, as you can see, people do not remember or know everything that happened at Sant'Anna that day and I would like to write an article that has all the facts in it. As Signor Mazzella so correctly said, the public has a right to know these things."

"Yes, yes," Amadeo said. "I remember another case where ..."

"And now," Ezio interrupted, "I have been working on this article for some time and have most of my information, but I would like to talk to one of the key witnesses of this ... this incident."

He could hardly get the word out and Donna stiffened at his side.

"I understand that this witness now lives in the Garfagnana. As you know, this is a very large area and I do have to complete my article in short order. Since you have so many friends and know so many people in this area, I would be pleased if you could help me locate him. His name is Angelo Donatello."

Amadeo, Calvino and Orsino showed not a sign of recognition. Then a young woman, in a black dress with a white apron and cap, came out of the house with more drinks.

"Damn! Damn! Damn!" Ezio said it under his breath but it was clearly audible.

"Ah, Maria," Amadeo said, "thank you so much."

While Maria, stone-faced, moved her tray from one guest to another, Amadeo whispered to Ezio, "She's a lovely girl, the wife of the patrolman who takes care of our garden. She is so pleased to be part of this arrangement, too."

Ezio tried three times to get his question answered but was interrupted each time by a long story that Amadeo suddenly remembered or by arguments between Calvino and Orsino. Then Maria returned to announce that dinner was ready.

The dining room seemed to stretch from one end of the house to the other. A long table, covered with linen and candlesticks, was centered on the marble floor. Family portraits in heavy gold frames lined the deep red damask walls. Thick drapes hung beside stained-glass windows. The warm air, thick with the scent of decaying flowers, reminded Donna of a funeral she had recently attended.

Little Amadeo, Riccardo and Immacolata were already squabbling loudly over who was going to sit where, and Riccardo spilled a glass of water all over a chair. Amadeo swatted the boy on the back of his head. "All right, now you sit in it," he shouted, and Riccardo stifled tears as he covered his face with his hands.

Having forced all three children to sit down, Amadeo introduced Ezio and Donna to his wife. Giovanna Mazzella was a small thin woman who looked much older than her thirty-five years. Her eyes were vacant and her skin sallow. She wore a dark green dress with no jewelry and had tied her black hair back into a bun. Donna said later that she looked like she had endured many of Amadeo's infidelities.

Giovanna wordlessly shook their hands. Amadeo pointed out where everyone should sit, and Maria entered with the antipasti, deep-fried squid. Then the long meal began, stretching for hours and becoming more animated as the night went on. Linguine with basil pesto and tomatoes followed the squid and Donna hoped that was the end of it. Then plates of grilled breast of duck with peas, artichoke hearts, string beans and prosciutto arrived. And then the salad, romaine with roasted pine nuts. And finally bowls of pears and apples.

Through it all, glasses of wine were quickly emptied and refilled. Amadeo opened a bottle of grappa, Calvino told stories about his career at what he called an important bank in Lucca and Orsino described his days as a race car driver and then owner of a Ferrari dealership in Lucca.

Ezio and Donna declined even a glass of wine, and at one point, Ezio tried to steer the subject to Angelo Donatello. He was quickly interrupted when Calvino dropped his fork on the floor and shouted at Maria to bring him another.

Giovanna picked at her food and rarely looked up. She had not said a word all evening. The children were not silent, however.

"She kicked me!" Little Amadeo shouted.

"You kicked me first," Immacolata cried.

Amadeo got up and pulled their ears. "Now behave!" He sat down again, wiping his forehead. He was sweating profusely and held his hand to his chest for a long minute, something only Ezio and Donna seemed to notice. Giovanna kept on picking at her food.

Sweating and wiping his face and scalp even more, Amadeo was in the midst of an interminable story about his adventures capturing a pair of pickpockets from Albania when Little Amadeo stood up and smashed a piece of duck on Riccardo's head. Immacolata immediately joined in the fray.

"Now stop that!" Amadeo shouted. "Maria, put them to bed!"

Bawling and brawling, the children were taken upstairs. The room was quiet for a moment while Amadeo, Calvino and Orsino peeled their pears and apples and Giovanna sat silently with her hands in her lap.

"Well," Amadeo said, pointing his knife at Ezio, "I want to compliment you on your book. *A Time to Remember* is a very interesting account of your life as a partisan."

Ezio blanched. Knowing his cover had been blown, he could only mouth, "Thank you."

"Yes, we know all about you," Amadeo continued. "A journalist? How could you think we would believe that story? We are not fools, you know."

Donna reached over to hold Ezio's hand.

Amadeo continued to point his knife at Ezio. "No, we know you are a schoolteacher and that the signorina here works in a marble factory in Pietrasanta. We know you were delayed because you stopped in Sant'Antonio and Reboli. Ah yes, Reboli, lovely town."

He went back to peeling his pear. Ezio didn't know what to say.

"We know all about your Communist background," Amadeo said. "And of course, we cannot allow you to look for Signor Angelo Donatello."

Calvino and Orsino smiled broadly.

Both terrified and furious, Ezio knew there was no point in trying to continue the pretense. He leaned forward. "Well, then, Signor Mazzella, why don't you tell everyone here why you know Reboli so well?"

Amadeo glanced at his wife, still sitting quietly and staring at her hands. "Reboli? Why I used to visit there during the war. My good friend owned a thread factory there."

"You didn't go to see your friend," Ezio shouted. "You went to see the women working there!"

Amadeo's face reddened, and he began to sweat even more. "Well, of course, I walked through the workrooms ..."

Donna tried to hold Ezio back, but he was standing now and pointing his finger at Amadeo. "And upstairs? Maybe you'd like to tell your wife what happened upstairs?"

For the first time, Giovanna looked at her husband.

"Tell her," Ezio continued, "about a woman named Fausta Sanfilippo. Tell her what happened on the floor upstairs. Tell her about the ropes you tied her with. Tell her how you raped this poor defenseless woman over and over and over …"

"Ezio, please …" Donna whispered.

Amadeo stood up, waved his arms and began shouting unintelligible curses. Calvino and Orsino rushed from their chairs and grabbed Ezio, but he wouldn't stop shouting. "And tell her that Fausta Sanfilippo can still see those rope burns and that she knows exactly where you have been all these years!"

Giovanna now rose and attacked her husband with her fists. On his head, his face, his chest, hitting him again and again.

"*Animale! Animale! Animale!*" she screamed over and over.

Calvino and Orsino rushed to Amadeo's protection, pulling his wife away from him and wiping his face, now as red as the damask walls. Ezio and Donna ran out the door, not seeing Amadeo when he slumped in his chair and his head crashed onto the table.

CHAPTER 32

▼

Neither Ezio nor Donna slept that night. They had hurried home, looking behind them every step of the way, and bounded into Ezio's room. A sliver of a moon lit the steeple of the Duomo, and Ezio quickly closed the shutters. In the dark, they sat huddled on the bed and relived the events of the day and evening.

"Oh, my God," Donna said. "This was like some horror movie, only made by Charlie Chaplin. I'm still shaking."

"Me, too." Ezio held her tight. He was well aware that he had not held a woman like this since he and Angelica had made love the night before he left Sant'Anna. He discounted the few girls he had had since then. Somehow, he thought, this didn't seem strange, but there were too many other things to think about now.

"Well," he said, "now everyone knows we're not a journalist and a photographer. I imagine all of Amadeo's friends are looking for us now."

"Not to mention the entire Barga police force," Donna said.

"Afraid?"

"Yes."

"Me, too," Ezio said.

"That doesn't sound like Clark Gable."

"Hate to disillusion you, Miss Colbert, but I'm not Clark Gable. Donna, I won't let anything happen, I promise."

"Protecting me again?" She smiled and gripped his hands. "Thank you."

"Maybe you wish you hadn't come?"

"Are you crazy?" Donna said. "I wouldn't have missed this for the world. Too bad it's ended like this."

"I'm having trouble believing it's ended, Donna."

"I don't know what else to think. We'll never be able to find *Occhio unico* now."

"I guess so. Let's wait till morning, before daylight. We can get to the car in the parking lot and get out of this goddamn town."

Donna put her hand on his cheek. "I'm sorry, Ezio. I'm sorry it has to end this way."

"I am, too. Eleven years waiting for this. Then some hope. Now nothing."

They lay on the bed, holding each other. Sleep eluded them, though one or the other occasionally drifted off into a dreamless soft stillness.

At 5:30, just as the first rays of sunlight filtered through cracks in the shutters, loud banging on their door brought them upright.

"Oh, God," Donna said. "They've found us."

"Open up!" It was the voice of the *pensione's* matron. "There's someone here to see you!"

Before Ezio had a chance to get to the door, the woman had turned the key in the lock. The door opened and a hulking man wearing a bright orange shirt and with a cigar clenched in his mouth pushed his way in. Ezio and Donna recognized him immediately as the man reading the newspaper in the Casa del Popolo yesterday.

"Come with me!" the man shouted, waving his good right arm at them.

"Where? Why?" Ezio cried.

"It's not safe here. Come! Now!" The man held the door open as the matron fled back to her desk.

Still wearing her white dress, now wrinkled and dirty, Donna made an attempt to go into her room to get something, but the man stopped her.

"There's no time! Come!"

They followed the man out into the street where his dented Fiat was still running.

"I thought cars weren't allowed up here," Ezio said.

"*Boh!*" the man said. "You think policemen in Barga are awake at this hour?"

Noticing their concern about the car, the man patted the hood. "I bought this used two years ago. A fine car. Very little trouble at all."

The man edged into the front seat. That was difficult, because the car was too small and the man too large. He was stuffed against the steering wheel, barely able to move. Looking over his shoulder to see if anyone was watching, Ezio joined him in the front seat. As she was about to crawl into the back seat, Donna saw a man on the opposite side of the street look at them. The man then ran around the corner.

"Well," she thought, "maybe he had to pee. Let's hope so."

"My name," the man finally said as the car groaned down the hill, "is Vittorio Izzo. I saw you yesterday at the Casa."

"How can we thank you?" Ezio said, relieved.

"You're in bad trouble, my boy," Vittorio said, skillfully maneuvering the car with one hand. "Everyone in Barga knows by now that Amadeo Mazzella is dead and ..."

"He's dead?" Donna cried.

Vittorio opened the window, flicked cigar ashes into the wind, and closed it again. "His head in a plate of artichokes, the people are saying. It doesn't take long for a story like this to get around. I got a call from Edidio at 4 o'clock. Bertrando had called him. They knew where you were staying."

"Thank you!" Donna cried.

"There aren't many people who will say a Hail Mary for Amadeo Mazzella," Vittorio said. "They'll be drinking a lot of toasts in Barga tonight."

"We gathered he wasn't very well liked," Ezio said.

"That's not the point. The story also says that you two Communists got him so upset that he collapsed and died."

"Us? Us?" Ezio shouted. "We're to blame for this bastard's death?"

"That's the story. And Mazzella may have been the most hated man in Barga, but he still had—has—a lot of Fascist friends. And that's why you have to get the hell out of here now. Just relax. I'm going to take you someplace where you want to go."

"Which is?"

"The other side of the Garfagnana. Where *Occhio unico* is supposed to be."

Ezio and Donna were now totally confused, but they had little choice but to sit back in this rusty Fiat and let this crazy man take them away. Who was he and where was he taking them?

The car seemed to be having trouble in its gas line, and Vittorio pounded his foot on the accelerator, resulting in more popping and sputtering.

"Sometimes it takes a little while to get going," he said.

It was a gloomy day, with black clouds coming over the mountains from the west. With Vittorio driving as fast as the car would allow, they quickly passed Loppia and Fornaci di Barga and were on the highway south along the east side of the Serchio.

"I wish we could cross the Serchio somewhere close," Vittorio said. "But the Devil's Bridge is only for pedestrians. We have to drive down to Ponte a Moriano to cross."

For several miles, they were stuck behind a farm wagon. Vittorio couldn't pass it because of oncoming traffic, and the driver ignored Vittorio's blasts on the car horn.

"Move to the side, *cretino!*" Since Vittorio's windows were now closed, the farmer could not have heard him even if he wanted to obey. When they finally had a chance to pass, there was a lively exchange, with "*cretino*" being the mildest of the epithets.

At the Devil's Bridge, Vittorio had to slow down again, this time for the tourists taking early morning photos.

"Didn't you ever see a bridge before?" Vittorio shouted, this time with the window open. This caused a large American to come up to the car and say a few things they were fortunate not to understand.

Donna looked back at the bridge as they passed it. "Whatever else happens on this trip, if I ever get back to Pietrasanta, that's the first thing I'm going to tell my Papa about."

Ezio turned around. "The first thing?"

"Well, maybe second."

The car's engine continued to pop and sputter, but Vittorio tried to assure his passengers that everything was fine.

A little farther south, as they escaped the storm clouds, Vittorio pointed to the rocky hills across the river. "See that? That was part of the *Linea Gotica*, the famous Gothic Line. The Germans built this big defense all across northern Italy and ..."

"You don't have to tell me," Ezio said. "My *banda* was right by the Gothic Line over near Pietrasanta."

Vittorio put his hand on Ezio's knee. "I'm sorry, my boy. I forgot that you were a partisan. I heard you talking yesterday at the Casa."

"That's all right. It was a long time ago."

Vittorio explained that in this part of the Gothic line, a narrow entry led to a labyrinth of tunnels and caves and then out at another side. It was here that the Germans reconnoitered and stored their weapons. Now water seeped through the walls and ceilings and it was inhabited mostly by rodents.

"*Boh!* I suppose someone could hide in there," Vittorio said, taking another look in the rearview mirror, "but he wouldn't last long."

Just past Piaggione, they ran into a roadblock.

"Shit!" Vittorio muttered under his breath.

A young policeman stopped the car and ordered Vittorio to show his driver's license. Ezio and Donna couldn't understand why the policeman then grinned.

"You're Vittorio Izzo?" he said. "The famous boxer?"

"Well, yes, but we're in a hurry and ..."

"Vittorio Izzo! I can't believe this. You were my hero. When I was growing up I had your picture pinned to my wall. I told my father I wanted to be a boxer and ..."

"We're really in a hurry," Vittorio said.

"Vittorio Izzo! Wait till I tell the guys at the station I stopped Vittorio Izzo. And my Papa, too."

He handed the license back and just as Vittorio started the car again the policeman walked to the other side. "Wait. You've got another passenger."

"Yes, this is my friend. He's sick. We have to get him to a hospital."

Donna by this time had crouched on the floor of the back seat while the policeman scrutinized Vittorio's passenger.

"You look familiar," the policeman said. "Wait. I want to get a photograph I have in my car."

The policeman had not gone two feet when Vittorio pounded on the gas pedal and the Fiat sputtered and plowed through the barricade, scattering wooden splinters all over the road. The policeman quickly got into his own car and gave chase. Up and down the winding hills, Vittorio soon lost ground to the newer, faster police car. Then Vittorio came upon an ancient dog of no particular heritage that had decided to take a nap in the middle of the road. He swerved to one side and got past just as an equally ancient farmer, with only one leg, hobbled slowly onto the road, poked the animal awake with his crutch and followed it to the other side. The policeman was left behind, honking and waiting.

It was not long before they were at the bridge to Ponte a Moriano. "This is where Edidio and the others saw *Occhio unico* cross the river," he said. "So we know he's on the other side somewhere."

CHAPTER 33

▼

On the western side of the Serchio, Vittorio drove north along the winding roads and through the ever-higher hills. Finally, near Sabatana, he suddenly veered off the road and stopped the car deep in a grove of chestnut trees. The storm clouds had moved on, but the day was hot and humid.

"We can take a break here," Vittorio said, edging out of the car and collapsing on a fallen tree trunk. He was breathing heavily. Ezio and Donna stretched and joined him.

"No point worrying about grass stains on this dress," Donna said. "It's ruined."

"Again, we want to thank you," Ezio said. "I don't know what we would have done if you hadn't come."

"What we would have done," Donna said, "is go back home."

"No! No, you can't do that," Vittorio said. "We need you."

Sweating and brushing his close-cropped head with his thick hand, Vittorio took out another cigar, put it in his mouth and lit it, all in one swift movement with one hand.

Ezio and Donna had a hundred questions to ask Vittorio, but they knew they had to proceed at his pace, not theirs. After all, he was their rescuer. But, realizing that Vittorio wasn't in the best of condition, Ezio wondered why he had put himself in danger by helping them.

"Let me tell you a story," Vittorio said. He eased himself onto the ground and leaned back against the tree trunk.

"Do you know what these letters stand for?" Vittorio pointed to the initials "P.C." embroidered on the pocket of his orange polo shirt. Neither Ezio nor Donna could make a guess.

"Primo Carnera, of course."

"Oh, of course," Ezio said. "The boxer. I know."

Vittorio puffed long on his cigar. "Primo Carnera was the greatest Italian boxer in history. He was born near Udine. Do you know where that is?"

Ezio knew that it was near the Adriatic, near the Alps.

"Beautiful town," Vittorio said. "My hometown, Udine. I was born there. I walked by his house every day. A humble little home, just like him. You know one reason why I like him?"

They did not.

"He was huge. Six feet, eight inches tall. Two hundred and seventy-six pounds! Imagine, two hundred and seventy-six pounds! Do you know what he had for breakfast? No? I'll tell you. This is what he had for breakfast."

Vittorio counted it out on the stubby fingers of his only hand. "A quart of orange juice, two quarts of milk, nineteen—nineteen!—pieces of toast, fourteen—fourteen!—eggs and a half pound of ham! I read that in the newspaper. You know what they called him? No? The Ambling Alp. They called him the Ambling Alp!"

"So you decided to be a boxer, too?" Donna asked.

"There was a gym in Udine. I trained there. But I was never as good as Primo. Do you know his record?"

He answered the question himself.

"Eighty-seven wins, fourteen losses and one no-decision. And you know what, sixty-nine of those wins were by knockout! A fine man, a great fighter. From my hometown. Me, I didn't last that long, forty-eight wins, thirty-two losses, but thirty-five of my wins were by knockout."

"That's very impressive!" Ezio said.

"*Boh!*"

Vittorio puffed on his cigar. "I used to follow Primo's career in the newspapers. In the United States he beat Jack McAuliffe, the great Jack McAulife. Then King Levinsky and then, on June 29, 1933, one of the most important dates in boxing history, he knocked out Jack Sharkey and became World Heavyweight Champion. Round six, a knockout. Imagine, this guy from Udine, my hometown. Tears were running down my face when I read it in the newspaper."

Donna thought Vittorio's eyes were glistening even now.

"Oh, I know there was a lot of talk about his fights being fixed, but what fight wasn't fixed in those days? Jack Dempsey, Max Baer, Gene Tunney, you think their fights weren't fixed? *Boh!*"

Ezio and Donna couldn't help but wonder where all this was leading.

"But you know what I liked the most about Primo?"

They shook their heads.

"On June 14, 1934, I remember the date well, Primo was to fight Max Baer. Now Baer was half-Jewish and the year before he had defeated Max Schmeling, Hitler's favorite. You know about that?"

Both Ezo and Donna knew this.

"Well, Primo had a broken ankle, but he still went into the ring with Baer. Primo fell down twelve times—twelve times!—and every time he got up. Now I liked Baer, too, but Baer took advantage of Primo. It took eleven rounds to defeat Primo, such a courageous boxer he was. He had a broken ankle!"

Donna was certain now that Vittorio had tears in his eyes.

"Now he lives in Los Angeles, California. California! Imagine. From my hometown, Udine."

They waited for more, and finally Vittorio said, "You know why I told you the story of Primo Carnera? I'll tell you why I told you this story. I like a man with courage, a man who fights for what he believes in, a man who can fight even if he has a broken ankle. Do you understand?"

"Yes, of course," Ezio said.

Vittorio put the stub of his cigar against the tree trunk. "When I heard you talk at the Casa del Popolo yesterday, I couldn't help thinking what a courageous man you must be. Here is someone to admire, I thought. Just the man we need to find *Occhio unico*. He has been free for so long and nobody is doing anything about it. Those old guys you met yesterday, they don't do anything. Sit around and play cards and smoke cigars and drink beer, that's what they do. *Boh!* I wanted to go find him but you see ..." He pointed to what was left of his left arm. "Yes, the Germans did that. Landmine. Three men in my *banda* killed. And my heart isn't so good anymore. But never mind that.

"Now here you two come, all the way from Reboli and Pietrasanta. Hell, I don't even know where they are. But you want to do something, you want to find *Occhio unico*. Now that's what I like, that's courage. That's like Primo Carnera."

Vittorio was obviously moved by all this, but so were Ezio and Donna.

"Signor Izzo," Ezio began.

"Call me Vittorio."

"Vittorio, there were two other men at the dinner last night. With Mazzella dead, aren't they going to be looking for us?"

"Of course! What do you think! You think it's only the Barga police force? The Barga police force couldn't find a thief if he robbed the police station. No, it's the Fascists we have to worry about. They're organized. I bet they already have people looking."

"One of them was very dignified," Ezio said. "Calvino Bastiani. He said he had a bank in Lucca."

"The other one scared me more," Donna said. "He said he used to be a race car driver and then he owned a Ferrari dealership in Lucca. His name was Orsino Nardari."

Vittorio shook his head. "Not good. Not good at all."

"What do you think they'll do?"

"Bastiani has some henchmen, but he likes to keep his hands clean," Vittorio said. "I'm more worried about Nardari."

"Why?"

"Well, I've heard that old Nadari has maybe ten or twelve Ferraris. Only Ferraris. Export, Europa, all kinds. He doesn't drive them anymore, just puts them in his garage. He hires a man full time just to polish them and keep them in good shape. Can you imagine? Spending all that money on cars. *Boh!*"

Vittorio took out another cigar and slowly lit it.

"Nadari could afford any kind of car. Masereti, Alfa Romeo, American cars. But he only buys Ferraris. Do you know why? No? Well, it's not because Nadari is from the same town as Enzo Ferrari. Modena. That's over by Bologna. Now there's a town with a lot of Communists. Lots of Communists. Red Bologna, they call it. I would love to go there sometime and …"

"Why does Nadari only buy Ferraris?" Donna asked.

"It's because of the name on the car. Enzo Ferrari."

Vittorio wiped his forehead with the back of his hand. As the day had progressed, thick humidity began to envelop the entire valley.

"Enzo Ferrari was a Fascist. Well, that's what everybody said, anyway. You know, here was this guy who put shoes on mules in the first war, but then he became a famous car racer and Mussolini liked that. So what did Mussolini do? He made Ferrari a knight of something called the *Cavaliere dell'ordine della Corona d'Italia?* Do you know what that is? Hell, I don't either. But Nadari thought it was a great honor, and so because Mussolini liked Ferrari, he only buys Ferraris."

"I thought Enzo Ferrari tried to make good after the war," Ezio said, "trying to shed his reputation as a Fascist."

"Didn't everyone?" Vittorio asked. "Was Enzo Ferrari somebody like Primo Carnera? Never! Primo was a courageous man. Primo Carnera fought Max Baer eleven rounds with a broken ankle. Now that's courage. From my hometown, Primo was. Udine."

Increasingly, Ezio and Donna wondered why Vittorio told them this long Ferrari story.

"Because," he said, "one of Nadari's Ferraris could overtake my little Fiat in three seconds. He's probably on the road right now."

"You think so?" Donna said.

Vittorio slowly got to his feet. "I didn't tell you that we were being followed for a half hour back there. That's why I stopped, to let whoever it was go the other way. Now we'd better go."

CHAPTER 34

▼

In the oldest and wealthiest section of Barga, Orsino Nardari picked up the phone, careful not to wake his young mistress who was snuggled in their eighteenth-century bed.

"*Pronto!* Orsino here ... Yes, Calvino ... No, of course not ... Yes, I've been thinking what to do now ... first, we have to spread the word ... the Communists provoked Amadeo and then he died ... They're responsible ... It's just like they killed him ... Tell your barber and in an hour it will be all over the Garfagnana ... *Ciao.*"

Orsino crawled back under the thick comforter and pulled the young woman to him. But in two minutes they were interrupted when the telephone ran again.

"*Pronto!* Orsino here ... What? ... What? ... Uzzi the boxer? Of course I know who that is. Everybody in Barga knows him ... What? ... Bastards! ... South along the Serchio and across to Ponte a Moriano? ... Rusty old Fiat, right ... Don't worry, I'll find him. *Ciao.*"

Orsino pulled on the pink shirt, green pants and navy blue jacket that he had dropped on the floor in his haste to get into bed with his mistress only a few hours earlier. He ran down to his garage, filled with eight Ferraris of various models and years. The question was which one to choose.

"I want," he told his serviceman, "the fastest car I own."

"Yes, sir," Sabastiano said.

They walked quickly up and down the aisles amid cars that were polished to a blinding shine. Sabastiano suggested the 250 Export. Orsino rubbed his hands over its smooth finish and remembered its introduction at the Paris Motor Show two years earlier, but then he moved on.

"How about this one?" Sabastiano asked.

Orsino looked at the bright red model and stroked the shield with the prancing horse on the hood. "Yes, the 250 Europa GT. I love this car. Reminds me of when I was racing."

"You were a legend, sir."

"Oh, not a legend. But I won a few races. Yes, this one. Now, Sabastiano, make sure this is in the finest condition. Quickly. I may be in the most important race of my life."

As they headed still farther north, the hairpin turns and hilly roads made it hard for Vittorio to see in the rearview mirror. That may have been why he didn't see the bright red 250 Europa GT that was coming up three cars to the rear. He was also too busy holding the wheel and trying to keep the car on the road.

Vittorio tried to gain speed, but his car kept balking. There were now only two cars separating the Fiat and the Ferrari. One of them turned off toward Arsina. Vittorio looked into the rearview mirror.

"Shit!"

Both Ezio and Donna turned around. They could see a new 1955 Fiat right behind them and then the red Ferrari to the rear. Donna realized why the man on the Barga street had run away.

Vittorio tried to go faster. The car sputtered. The 1955 Fiat turned off at San Concordio d'Moriano. The road narrowed, and huge black chestnut trees formed an arch overhead. Below on the right, the hillside dropped off into a ravine.

The Ferrari was now racing toward Vittorio's Fiat. Vittorio couldn't get the car out of gear.

"Damn!"

Ezio tried to help his one-armed driver steer.

"Damn!"

The Ferrari was even closer.

Donna crouched on the floor in the rear. Ezio held on to the steering wheel. The Fiat was shaking violently. Vittorio floored the gas pedal but couldn't gain speed.

Yards became feet and feet became inches. Vittorio tried desperately to avoid the mighty car that was about to strike from behind. Then, as Vittorio took his hand off the wheel and Ezio leaped into the back seat on top of Donna, their car smashed through the trees and plunged down into the ravine, coming to a smoky rest in a muddy ditch.

In the same instant, the faithful Sabastiano yelled to his boss, "No! Sir! Sir!" but the Ferrari left the road, plowed into the largest of the chestnut trees and burst into flames.

Using his elbow, then his fists and then his small pocket knife, Ezio punched out the rear window of the Fiat, trying to prevent splinters of glass from falling on Donna. He crawled out first, and then pulled Donna from the wreckage. They opened the driver's door and tried to rescue Vittorio, but it was clear that he was crushed between the back of the seat and the steering wheel. Shards of glass from the broken windshield had pierced his forehead, and his only hand was a bloody pulp.

"What should we do?" Donna said. She was crying.

"We'll have to leave him. And we'd better get out of here quick."

Ezio patted Vittorio on the shoulder. "Good-bye, my friend. You were a very courageous man."

"Like Primo Carnera. From Udine." Donna picked up his bloody hand and kissed it.

Ezio had protected Donna from injury by covering her with his body when the car crashed. Somehow, he escaped with only a bruised back.

"Maybe no one will know we were here," Ezio said, covering their footprints with branches.

They couldn't go back to the highway, so they plunged into the forest. There were no paths and nothing to tell them where they were or where they were going. It wouldn't have mattered if it were sunny or cloudy because the trees were so thick that no sky could be seen. They had only a faint realization that it was the middle of the afternoon. Ezio wished he had brought his watch along.

"Let's stop, Ezio," Donna said. "I need to rest."

"I do, too."

Breathless and shaking, they sat on a fallen tree trunk. Ezio put his arm around Donna and she put her head on his shoulder. It was one thing to see Amadeo Mazzella fall dead before their eyes, but it was quite another to see the kind and generous Vittorio Uzzi forced off the road and murdered just as surely as if someone had pushed a knife into his back.

"Poor Vittorio," she said.

"I know. One of the most courageous men I've ever known. I wish I had been in his *banda*."

"He didn't even mention that," Donna said. "He was probably a great hero and we'll never know."

"I hope somebody finds him soon. I really didn't want to leave him."

"And," Donna said, "that they take him back to Udine."

They remained quiet for a long time. Donna rubbed her fingers on the wire bracelet on Ezio's wrist. He didn't pull his arm away. Then strange sounds that began in the distance came nearer. Ezio said it must be a dog from a nearby farm.

"That doesn't sound like a dog to me," Donna said.

"I remember a fox I heard when I was hiking around here once," Ezio said. "I guess it could be a fox."

"Let's think it's a dog. I think we should go."

They stumbled in the opposite direction, trying to find any sort of path in the rapidly darkening forest. Impossible. What must have been a mile later, a strip of what looked like a girl's slip on the ground gave them hope that surely someone must live around here. They searched for a path or footprints or at least smooth areas in the forest bed. Nothing. They could only conclude that a pair of lovers had found the space at some point in the past and perhaps had been equally lost.

Tripping and crawling, they edged deeper into the forest. They were now so tired they knew they had to stop for the night.

"How about here?" Ezio asked, looking at a space under a growth of huge bushes.

"Not quite the *pensione*, but this will do," Donna said as she shook out her hair. "And look, here's a place to hang a sheet. If we had a sheet."

This time, Donna's humor was forced, and she knew it. Besides being exhausted, she was afraid.

"Every bone in my body hurts," Ezio said, easing himself down on the bed of grass and leaves they had improvised. "I'm so tired I don't think I can sleep."

"My fingernails hurt," Donna said.

"My toenails hurt," Ezio said.

They lay on their backs, side by side but about five feet apart.

"I used to love to sleep just outside the shop on the Piazza Santo Spirito when I was a boy," Ezio said. "My mother and father would let me, but I know my father kept opening the door to see if I was all right, or if I was still there."

"I tried to sleep outside a few times," Donna said. "But the smell of the pigs drove me back into my bed."

"It seems so long ago."

"It was."

"Before the war," Ezio said. "Before everything started happening. Scared?"

"Terrified now," she said. "I'm really not the strong woman I pretend to be, you know."

"Well, in case you haven't noticed, I'm not Clark Gable."

"I'd rather be with Ezio than Clark any day. Or night."

They grinned at each other.

They could have said more. If they weren't exhausted, they could have talked through the night. In his sleep, Ezio instinctively edged over to the sleeping woman next to him. She turned over and put her arm around him.

CHAPTER 35

▼

Leaving his isolated farm in the Garfagnana, Fabiano Guerini drove his truck down to the village of Mastiano to buy a brace for a plow that had broken. Afterwards, he stopped at a *bar* for an espresso, a special treat since he hated Sabina's coffee so much.

Sipping his coffee and dreading the drive home to Sabina's screeching and Graziella's chattering, Fabiano heard a whisper of "Communists" among three elderly men at a nearby table. He leaned closer.

"Everybody's talking about it. Now they say they're over by ..." Fabiano couldn't hear the rest.

"I heard they were seen at ..."

"No, it was ..."

"I heard they were looking for someone named Denato," the first one said.

Fabiano could wait no longer. "Excuse me," he said, "but did you say Communists are looking for someone named Denato?"

"Didn't you know about this?" one of them said. "Where have you been?"

And then the three of them, overlapping and with hands gesturing wildly, proceeded to tell Fabiano an amazing tale of how an important police official in Barga had died after being provoked by two very large Communists in his home.

"Where are these Communists?" Fabiano asked. "Have you seen them?"

"No," one said, "but everyone knows they must be around here."

Slamming his unfinished espresso on the counter, Fabiano rushed out of the *bar* and to his truck.

Back at the farm, Antonio was taking a break from chopping fire wood and leaned back against a hay bale on top of the barn. It was cloudy, as it had been for several days, but the wet humid air felt good against his face. Others might complain, but he liked the feeling of drowning, even if it were only in smothering air.

"Antonio! Antonio?"

"Damn!"

The wicker basket emerged first from the opening in the roof, then Graziella's red hair and then her pudgy body.

"I looked in back but you weren't there so I knew you were up here," she said breathlessly. "Mama wanted you to have a piece of this walnut torte she made last night. I didn't want to give it up because it's really good but she said she wanted you to have it."

Graziella took the torte out of the basket and handed it to Antonio.

"Just Mama and me are home now. Papa went down to Mastiano to get something for the plow. I could have gone along but there's nothing in Mastiano. Nothing. And I don't have any money anyway."

She leaned back against the hay bale next to Antonio.

"I wish I could go to Barga. Papa never wants to go there. Even Mama said she would like to go there sometime. You know she's worn the same dress for about a week now. But I shouldn't talk, I don't have many blouses either."

She ran a comb through her frizzy hair.

"Oh, Antonio, I have to tell you what Fedoro did last night. He is so cute, I just love him. We were playing with this string, and I was pulling it through the house and he was running after it but I kept going so fast that he couldn't catch it and then I didn't see him anymore so I thought maybe he had given up but then he popped out from behind a chair and grabbed it. He knew all along that I was going that way and he popped right out. He is so smart. I just picked him up and hugged him and hugged him. That made him throw up like he does sometimes when I hug him but I know he loves me."

Antonio tried to tune her out.

"Antonio, remember the other day when we were talking about the war and you didn't say anything when I asked you if you had been in the war so I asked Papa if you had been in the war and he didn't say anything either."

Antonio sat up straighter.

"I mean, most men were in the war at that time, weren't they? I was thinking that maybe you were in the army or maybe you were one of those, what do they call them, parmesans, or something."

"No, I wasn't a parmesan, Graziella."

"Oh, well then you must have been in the army. Papa was in the army, but he didn't do any fighting. I think they sent him to some place where he was a guard over some bad guys. Did you do any fighting, Antonio? I bet you were very brave."

"Graziella," he muttered, "don't you have to do some chores now?"

"I didn't do the dusting yet but Mama's so mean today I don't want to go back down there yet. She was mad because Papa didn't eat his breakfast before he went to Mastiano and she had just baked this good bread and made some espresso for him. A lot of time he doesn't eat breakfast even though she has it on the table for him and she gets so mad."

Antonio's hands were shaking as he reached for the torte. "This is very good, Graziella. Tell your mother I said so. So tell me more stories about your cat."

"Oh, I don't know. The other night he found a mouse in the woodshed and he brought it into the house to show us, and Mama screamed and Papa said he was going to shoot him the next time he does that. But then I started crying, and I know Papa will never do that."

"I've seen him chase after the chickens. He seems like a very nice cat."

"He is. But you know, Antonio, I was wondering about the war. I don't know what got me interested in this all of a sudden. We didn't even study it in school so I really don't know anything about it. I know the Germans and these parmesans or whatever they're called were all over in this area and there was a lot of fighting. I heard Papa tell Mama one time that the Germans were always blamed for things they didn't do and that the parmesans were actually the real bad people in the war. I don't know. What do you think?"

"I haven't thought about the war in a long time, Graziella."

"Well, when you were in the war, did you shoot guns and everything? Oh, Antonio, did you ever kill anyone? I don't know how someone could kill somebody else. I mean we're all people, right? I could never do that. I would start to cry if somebody told me I had to kill somebody else."

Antonio suddenly thought of the moonlit night in a cornfield long ago. Even now he could see Big Red emerge from the trees. He came closer and closer. Antonio could see his rifle. Antonio raised his own gun and shot. And then Big Red's son came out. 'Papa,' he cried. In the fury of the moment, Antonio fired and the boy fell on top of his father's body. How could he have done that? Antonio shuddered and his hands shook. For so many years he had tried to avoid thinking about that night, the night that changed his life.

"Antonio, are you all right? You're shaking all over."

"I'm all right, Graziella, but I think I'll go back down now."

Just as he got up, the clouds that had grown darker through the morning suddenly opened and they were both drenched. On the ground, Graziella ran to her house and Antonio to his little shelter next to the pigsty. It was raining too hard to do any work now.

Graziella arrived just as her father drove up. Covered by a piece of plastic, he ran to the house, lugging the brace for the plow.

"Where is he?"

"Who?" Sabrina said. She was trying to repair a tear in a dress but the sewing machine kept getting snarled.

"Denato, that's who!"

"I don't know. Probably working out back."

"He's in his shelter, Papa," Graziella said. "I was just talking to him and it started to rain so we both came inside."

"Graziella, go tell him to come here."

Graziella looked out the window. "Now, Papa? It's pouring out."

"Graziella, I told you to go get him and bring him here. Now!"

"Yes, Papa."

Graziella sloshed her way through the muddy fields that had suddenly turned into rivers. She had holes in both of her rubber boots and she could feel the water rising to her ankles. The wind whipped her umbrella inside out and then broke the frame entirely. She was soaked by the time she got to Antonio's shelter.

"Graziella! What are you doing here! Come inside!"

"Papa wants to see you right away." Graziella's tears mixed with the rain on her face. "He's very mad. I've never seen him so mad."

Antonio's old woolen cap and tattered raincoat weren't much protection as they dashed across the field to the house. Fabiano was waiting in the kitchen, his arms folded across his chest.

"You're going!"

"What? But … I don't understand."

Sabina stood up from the sewing machine. "Fabiano, what are you talking about? Where is he going? It's raining. He can't go out in this …"

"Shut up, Sabina! Antonio, or whatever your name is, you can't stay here anymore. You're going. Now!"

Graziella burst into tears and clung to her mother. "Papa, why? Why does he have to go? He's been so good here. I need him to talk to, Papa. He's the only …"

"Shut up, Graziella!" Fabiano lifted his arm as if to slap her but Sabina held him back. Fabiano turned to Antonio.

"In Mastiano. Everyone is talking. Two Communists were in Barga looking for you and they killed a police officer because he wouldn't tell them where you were. You know what police officer? That Mazzella that brought you here. Now there are Communists all over the Garfagnana and they're looking for you. Well, they're not going to find you here."

"Papa!" Graziella cried.

"We've kept you hidden all these years, ten, eleven now. Nobody has known where you were. Nobody has known what you did at Sant'Anna. Well, they're not going to come here and find out now. Get your things. You're going! Now!"

Antonio was speechless throughout all this. What could he say? Shoulders bent against the rain and the fury of Fabiano's words, he slowly went out the door and trudged back to his shelter. In the kitchen, Fabiano began to unpack the brace for the plow. Sabina sat at the table, staring at the torn dress in her hands. Graziella looked out the window, crying.

CHAPTER 36

─────────▼─────────

Ezio awoke a little after 5 a.m. when he heard a soft rain falling from trees just behind where he and Donna lay. Bushes and a giant chestnut tree protected them, at least temporarily. Brushing his hand over his forehead, he felt the edge of the wire bracelet and held his arm out to look at it.

"Damn."

Ezio had been so involved with finding Amadeo Mazzella, with their escape from Barga and with Vittorio's violent death that he had thought about Angelica only briefly for two days. Two days! He had never gone a day without the image of a young woman in a yellow dress holding the hands of her two children far from his mind.

The horrible sounds and smells of Sant'Anna had been a part of his life for eleven years.

Now, two days had gone by. Was it because of his relentless search for *Occhio unico*? Certainly that was part of it. But, he also knew it was because of the lovely woman still sleeping in his arms.

Donna stirred, and he smoothed her hair. As she settled back, he couldn't help comparing her to Angelica and remembering how Angelica had slept in his arms one night in the mountains outside Sant'Anna. Angelica was taller, with long golden hair and features so fine that her face seemed to glow with an inner light. Ezio remembered how her laugh brightened any room she was in. Her eyes were always bright. Donna was shorter, with brown curly hair. She had larger breasts and hips, but her hands were small. He liked the way she smiled, and her funny comments, but her eyes seemed sad.

And so when Ezio began to think about Angelica now, he realized that he was confused and conflicted by an issue he had avoided, perhaps even consciously, since he met Donna. Rubbing his hand over the bracelet, he realized how much he still missed Angelica and wanted to be back in

Sant'Anna and hold her in his arms again. He remembered the walks in the woods and their picnics with the boys. And he remembered their nights of passion before … before … He couldn't bear to think about the massacre.

But then when he looked down at Donna he began to ache.

"Good morning." Donna's morning voice was soft and low. She moved just a little bit away from his arms.

"Good morning." Ezio had trouble finding his own voice. "It's raining."

"I can hear."

Ezio sat up and stretched his arms. She held her hands over her breasts and when Ezio looked down he was tempted to kiss her. He knew where that would lead, and she knew what he was thinking.

"All right," she said, "I'm getting up." She stretched her back, and then sat down opposite him. The ground was filthy, but she no longer cared about her white dress.

"And now?" she asked.

"Well, first we wait until it stops raining a little," Ezio said. "Then we try to find a path to a road. Then we try to find a village. Then we try to find something to eat."

"Oh my God," Donna said. "We haven't eaten since that night, that night at dear Amadeo's."

"And you thought you'd never eat again."

"I didn't, but now I'm famished. Do you have any money? I don't."

Ezio took out his wallet, crushed and dirty in his back pocket. He counted the big bills. "I think I have enough for two very small *panini*."

"That will be fine. And after that?"

"Then we try to hitch a ride or if we have any *lira* left over take a bus back to Barga. I hope we can get the car without any trouble."

Donna reached over and held his hand. "So this time it really is over?"

He took both of her hands in his. "I don't see what else we can do, Donna. We have no way of knowing where *Occhio unico* is. We're likely being followed by a bunch of Fascists and the Barga police. There won't be another Vittorio to rescue us. Yes, it's over."

"I'm so sorry."

"Well, I am, too, but as you keep saying, we can't control things. I guess I've learned that lesson at least."

"And now *Occhio unico* will remain free forever."

"I guess so," Ezio said. "Maybe that's a good thing. You know how I've been feeling since the other day at the Casa del Popolo."

"That he might not be such a monster, but just an ordinary man."

"Yes. Even though he helped kill five hundred and sixty people. Oh, Donna, I'm so confused."

"I know, my darling."

Ezio dropped her hands. "What? What did you say?"

Donna blushed. "I'm sorry. That just came out. I didn't have a right to say that. I'm sorry. Forgive me." Her face was flushed and her eyes moist.

Ezio smiled. "No, no. I'm glad you said that. You know, we've been together for days now …"

"… and nights …"

"And nights. Well, sort of. I'm recognizing my feelings for you, too. I've just been afraid of saying anything."

She looked into his eyes. "Let's go slow, Ezio. We didn't even know each other a week ago. I know you still have strong feelings for Angelica. I want to respect that. Let's go slow."

He gripped her hands and pulled her to her feet. They embraced for a moment, then both pulled apart.

"I think the rain is stopping," Ezio said.

Although the rain had ended, the clouds threatened to open again as they crawled out of their improvised shelter and tried to determine where they were. No clue. Forests all around them. Only a slight trace of a path leading up a hill.

They followed it for what seemed like miles, pushing their way through clumps of wet bushes. One or the other would fall and the other would come back and they'd start over again. Ezio cursed himself for not bringing a map along, though that would have been of little use here. But when they finally got through the last patch of sticky branches, hands bleeding, they couldn't believe what they saw.

A small, perfectly kept cottage with a thatched roof stood in a clearing. A short path outlined with broken bricks led to a tiny garden. They could see ripe tomatoes and zucchini. No one was around.

"Food!" Ezio whispered as he started to crawl toward the garden.

"Stop!"

The voice was deep, and Ezio and Donna first saw the man, who appeared to be in his late thirties, emerge from the little house, and then a woman who followed close behind. They were dressed pretty much alike, with plaid shirts, patched brown trousers and heavy boots caked in mud. The man used a cane.

"Please!" Ezio called. "We've been in an accident, we're hungry and we're lost."

Hobbling, the man came forward and looked at both Ezio and Donna carefully. "Come into the house."

CHAPTER 37

▼

There was only one room, but it was apparently big enough for this couple. A stove on one side, a bed on the other, a table in a corner with four chairs. Under a window was a small table and on it a menorah. The furniture was old, but the place was spotless.

"Who are you?" the man asked. "Where are you coming from? What kind of accident?" One answer led to another question and another and another, and finally the whole story, from Pietrasanta to Barga to the terrible accident, came out.

Peppino and Livia, as they introduced themselves, remembered hearing something about Sant'Anna years ago but didn't know that Italian Fascists had helped in the massacre. And they certainly didn't know that the main collaborator might have been living in the Garfagnana, perhaps nearby.

"Near here?" Livia asked. "What's his name?"

"He was Angelo Donatello before the massacre but he must be using another name now," Ezio said. "We all know him simply as *Occhio unico* because, well, because he has only one eye."

Peppino and Livia looked at each other and shook their heads. "We don't go very far from here," Peppino said. "We don't know many people. I don't think we can help. You were looking for someone who is supposed to be somewhere?"

"We were," Ezio said, "but we're lost and we don't know where we're going and we don't know how to find the man we're looking for and we don't know his name."

When he summarized it this way, Ezio knew that they should never have begun this futile quest.

"So," he added, "we want to go home but we don't know how to get there."

211

"But you must have something to eat," Livia said, "You're probably starving." She pulled a pan from a hook on the wall and lit a piece of paper in the wood stove.

"But first," Peppino said, "let me take you out in back." There, they found a pump to wash the grime off their hands and faces and a *cesso*, between a chicken coop and a pigsty, to take care of other needs. When they returned, the smells of fried tomatoes and zucchini filled the little room. Livia was frying eggs in another pan.

"We live on tomatoes and zucchini and eggs at this time of year," Livia explained as she added some warm bread to the table. For Ezio and Donna, this was better than the extravagant meal they had at the Mazzella villa.

Peppino cut more bread. "I can't tell you what to do, but I don't think you should give up now. We could have given up a lot of times in Germany."

"You were in Germany?" Donna said. "During the war?"

Peppino put down the knife and rolled up his sleeve. On his left arm, Ezio and Donna could see the numbers 3629 and then two more that they couldn't read.

"That's my souvenir of Germany," Peppino said. "Auschwitz, actually. And this is another one." He pointed to his right foot, now just a stump.

And then Peppino and Livia told their own story. They were students, had gotten married and were living in a tiny apartment in Florence when Mussolini ordered the deportation of Jews.

"I've always heard that Mussolini had a benevolent attitude toward Jews, aside from his racist policies, of course," Ezio said as he devoured more zucchini.

"A lot of people think that, but it's not true," Peppino said. "Jews were deported. Lots of them. Our apartment was so small. But they found us."

"Yes, they found us," Livia said. Just as Donna had described her rape, she said it calmly, as if it had happened to someone else. "First they sent us to the internment camp at Fossoli, and then to Auschwitz."

"We didn't see each other all the while we were there, ten months and twelve days," Peppino said. "I don't know how we lived through it. We saw others being taken away. I won't tell you everything. You've heard it all by now, I hope. There were only about 7,500 of us left when the Soviets liberated the camp. January 27, 1945. I remember the date as well as this number on my arm."

When they returned to Italy, they said, they refused to go back to Florence. It was not a good place for Jews and it was too big. They traveled around and thought for a while that they might live in Lucca, but even that was too big for them. So then they found this little tract in the Garfagnana.

"There are still some people who don't want us around here," Livia said, "but we ignore them. It's pretty safe. And with the pigs and the chickens and the garden, we have everything we need here."

"When the seasons are good, we have a lot of food," Peppino said. "When they are bad, well, we wait for another good season."

He leaned over and took his wife's hand.

Peppino saw Donna looking at the little table. "We found the menorah at a market in Lucca," he said. "There aren't any temples around here, so we just pray and read the Bible by ourselves."

"You seem so calm and peaceful," Donna said. "Aren't you still angry about what happened to you?"

Peppino looked at his wife. "I suppose at first. Some people said, well, so many people were killed, you're lucky to be alive. Ha! We lost all our families. We almost got killed ourselves. How could we not be angry?"

"But over the years," Livia continued, "we learned to live with it. It happened. We had new lives now."

"And," Peppino said, "if we stayed angry, what would that do? Honor those who had been killed? I don't think so. So we read the Bible. We tried to find comfort there."

"That was very hard," Livia said. She cleared the table and put the dishes into the tiny sink.

"We looked and looked, chapter after chapter," Peppino said. "There were all these things like eye for an eye, get revenge. How were we to get revenge for the killing of six million of our brethren?"

"And then we found the story of Joseph," Livia said.

"Joseph?" Ezio said. "As in Joseph and his brothers? What has that got to do with the Holocaust?"

"We weren't sure at first," Peppino said, "but then we read the chapters over and over, and there are nine chapters in Genesis about this. Imagine, nine chapters. But we read how Joseph's brothers were so cruel to him, how they threw him in a ditch, stole his clothes, sold him into slavery. But then after he was freed and after he became governor of Egypt, he forgave them. Forgave them everything. It seemed to be a story meant for us."

Since the Old Testament was rarely mentioned in the Catholic school she attended, Donna didn't know what he was talking about, but Ezio had studied parts of the Bible at the university.

"I know the story," he said, "but I don't understand how this relates."

"If you read the chapters," Peppino said, "you see how hard it was for Joseph to forgive. He went back and forth, back and forth. And yet he finally embraced his brothers and showered them with gifts, even though they had been so cruel to him. And I thought of our guards, one of them anyway. I told Livia about him. He was cruel, very cruel, but sometimes I could see the horrified look on his face as he boarded people on to the trucks. I realized he didn't want to do what he was doing. He was under orders, he couldn't help it."

"So we thought a lot about him," Livia said, still standing next to the sink. "We thought, well, we can't see him as this totally evil man. We have to see him as a man under orders. He would have been killed if he hadn't followed orders."

"But let me be clear," Peppino interrupted. "We haven't forgotten. We can never forget. We will always remember. But we try to forgive. Otherwise, well, otherwise, we could not go on."

The room was quiet for a long time. Ezio thought of *Occhio unico*. Also a man, and perhaps under orders? He hadn't thought of that.

"So are you suggesting that we forgive *Occhio unico*?" Ezio asked. "How in the world would we be able to that? He helped kill five hundred and sixty people!"

Peppino got up and ran his hands over the menorah. "We can't tell you what to do. You have to decide."

Ezio looked at Donna. She nodded.

"All right. We won't go back to Barga. But we're going to need help. I suppose in these little villages we won't be able to find a Casa del Popolo."

"The best place is probably Cira," Peppino said. "It's pretty far from here, but I think you'll find help there. Just a tiny village, but I know there are Communists there."

"And how do we get there?"

Peppino tore off the side of a brown paper bag and found a stubby pencil.

"Let me make you a map," he said, drawing a line. "Go down to the base of the hill here. You could, I suppose, follow the road there, but if Fascists are following you that might be dangerous. So follow this stream. You'll go through some pretty thick forests, and then you'll see a broken little shrine to the Virgin. I'll draw an X. Why does Italy have so many of these things? Turn left, this way. It's going to be rough, but eventually you'll get to Cira. But be careful!"

Ezio shook Peppino's hand and Donna kissed Livia.

"I wish we could help you more," Peppino said. "But with my bad leg …"

"I think you've helped us very much," Ezio and Donna said together.

As they walked down the path from the house, with the map in Ezio's back pocket, Peppino suddenly called out. "Wait! I just thought of something."

The something was the time, in the middle of May, when Peppino made one of his rare trips to Barga. On the way back, his old car, which had balked all the way, stopped in the middle of the road. Peppino was trying to crank it into running again when a truck halted just behind.

"I remember this guy cursing and cursing. Get off the road, he kept shouting. Well, I couldn't. I couldn't get the car started. But the guy kept cursing. I went back and tried to explain, but he kept yelling and cursing. Said he was in a hurry to get back to his farm. Anyway, there was another man in the front seat. His hired hand, I guess. But a little guy, not like what you'd expect from a hired hand. I remember thinking, why does he have his cap pulled down so far? It was a funny cap for a farmer to wear, old with a lot of colors. And he had dark glasses on. I wondered why he had dark glasses on such a cloudy day."

CHAPTER 38

▼

As usual, beer and wine and grappa were flowing at the rear table of the Osteria del Ponte in the Oltarno in Florence and, as usual, the talk was of soccer and women and cars and soccer and women. All of the young men except Roberto had been working that day. All wore their usual black shirts, open at the neck, and black pants.

"Did you see those two girls sitting under the Cellini on the Ponte Vecchio this afternoon? Skirts up to here?" one of the men said. "They said they were from Paris and didn't know the city and wanted someone to take them around."

"So you did?"

"Yeah, but it turned out they were from Calabria. I dumped them at the Piazza della Signoria. Calabria!"

"You mean you don't know a girl from Paris from a girl from Calabria?" Roberto said. "I mean, the accent alone."

"I wasn't listening to the accent. I was mostly looking."

One of the men promptly doused his friend with what was left in his glass of beer. The others roared and asked for another pitcher.

"You still betting on *Fiorentina* in the championship, Roberto?" one of the bearded men asked. "You're not even working. How are you going to pay us?"

"Simple," Roberto said. "I'm not going to have to pay. They're gonna take it."

"Hey," one of them said rather blearily. "Wonder where Franco is. I don't have any money for the bill. He'd better come."

"He's never this late," Roberto said, filling his glass again. "Must have met one of those girls from Paris."

"Or Calabria."

But then Franco staggered in. It was clear that he had stopped at another *osteria* first, and probably two or three.

"Hey, Franco, my friend!" one of the other men said. "Sit here, have a beer. We'll let you pay."

As the discussion of soccer and women and soccer and women continued, Franco sat strangely quiet but that didn't prevent him from ordering a beer, then wine, then grappa.

"I shouldn't have done it," he slurred during a lull in the conversation.

"What? To a French girl?" Roberto said. "Hell, she'll go back to France and tell everyone how great Italian men are. You did her a favor, you did our country a favor, and I bet a lot of other ..."

"No. Not that." Franco slammed his hand on the table. The others sat back. They'd never seen this usually reserved friend so upset.

"Can you tell us what, then?" another asked, trying to be as quiet as possible so that the family group at the next table wouldn't hear.

Franco emptied his glass with one long swallow. "Roberto, your friend from Reboli ..."

"Ezio? The guy I brought here that night? Nice fellow. The ... the ... journalist." Roberto looked down at the table.

"He's not a goddamn journalist! Don't try to fool me."

"Sure he is. He writes a lot of articles. I've read a few of them." Roberto tried not to smile.

"Stuff it, Roberto. I knew right away he wasn't a journalist when he was here. I could see right through him. Writing an article about Sant'Anna. Wanted another source. Bullshit!"

"Well, what did that have to do with you?" Roberto said. "Why didn't you just ignore him if you didn't believe him?"

Now Franco looked down at the sticky beer-stained table. "I wanted to impress everyone in the *Movimento Sociale Italiano*. They were telling me I've got to do more, got to do more. So I told him, I told him ..."

"What?"

"He wanted to know where he could find *Occhio unico*. He didn't say that. He just said he wanted to find a witness to Sant'Anna. Bastard! I knew right away who he was looking for."

"*Occhio unico*?" three of the men said together. The most famous Fascist collaborator was still a legend all over Tuscany ten years after the war. But everyone knew he was in Germany.

"*Occhio unico*. So I could tell right away your friend was a Communist ..."

Roberto swirled around. "Ezio's not a Communist! Well, not a big Communist anyway."

"He is a Communist, Roberto! A goddamn Communist. So I found out a contact and told him to go to the Garfagnana. I knew that if he found that person, that would be the end of your friend Ezio."

"What?" Roberto shouted.

"The *Movimento Sociale Italiano* would take it from there."

Roberto got up and lunged toward Franco. "You bastard! You dirty bastard!" The others pulled him back down.

"Never mind. It didn't happen. Nothing happened to him. I got a phone call this morning. The story is all over Tuscany. No! Instead, your friend, this well-known journalist Ezio, killed the guy I led him to. Maybe not with a gun or a knife, but the guy had a heart attack. And you know who he was? A police officer in Barga! An important police officer!"

In their drunken state, the others couldn't comprehend all of this.

"And he had help!" Franco continued. "A woman. From over in Pietrasanta."

The others found this hard to believe. This nice guy, this seemingly gentle man who knew a lot about soccer if not about women, couldn't have killed anyone. Could he? But Roberto remembered Ezio taking off in a hurry and later he heard from his mother that Ezio had stopped in Sant'Antonio with a beautiful woman. Imagine, Ezio with a beautiful woman. And the woman worked in a marble factory in Pietrasanta.

"And that's not all," Franco said. Now another glass was emptied. "There was another man, a really respected man in Barga. He was a race car driver. Orsino Nardari. You know the name?

"Of course," two of the men said.

"Well, Nardari found out about it and chased your friend Ezio. There was this long chase. From Barga down the Serchio and across to Ponte a Moriano. And then Nardari crashed into a tree. Dead. Dead in an instant."

Franco was sobbing now.

"So now two important men of the *Movimento Sociale Italiano* are dead. And it's all my fault. And the members of the *Movimento Sociale Italiano* here are furious with me. They think I betrayed them. I was only trying to make an impression. I tell you, on the way over here, when I looked down at the Arno ..."

Normally, a confession like this would have resulted in considerable back-slapping and comforting words: "No, no, it's not your fault, it's not your fault. Don't do anything foolish. Everything will be all right." Instead, the others stared down at the table or drank some more beer or looked at the memorial to the Torino soccer team on the far wall. No one said anything.

"They're gonna kill me," Franco whispered.

"No, no, they're not," one of the others said. But he didn't sound very convincing. These things were known to happen, especially in Florence.

"Franco," Roberto said, "where is Ezio now? Is he with this woman? Were they killed in the chase, too?"

"No, goddammit. Their driver was killed but they must have escaped. At least their bodies weren't found anywhere. They're probably looking for *Occhio unico* on their own."

For the first time, Franco smiled. "That's all right. I know that members of the *Movimento Sociale Italiano* will find them."

Roberto put down his glass, got up and went to the pay phone at the rear of the *osteria*.

After many rings, a sleepy Paolo answered the phone in the kitchen.

"Roberto! Why are you calling this late? It's after midnight." Paulo tried not to wake Lucia, who had turned over when he got up, or Little Dino, who was always a light sleeper.

"No! No! No! No!"

Now Lucia stood by his side. "What is it? Who died? Maria? Oh, I knew she didn't look well today. No, Marco? Rosa said he couldn't sleep lately. *Santa Maria*, pray for us." She frantically paced around the kitchen table as Paolo's face lost more and more color.

"No," Paolo said. "No, no, no. I don't know. Let me think. I'll talk to Lucia. I don't know. I'll call you back."

Paolo told Lucia the incredible story, and tried to find what was terribly wrong with it. Surely Ezio, Paolo's wartime comrade and longtime friend, could not kill anyone. And this woman? Lucia said she seemed so nice, so kind, when Ezio brought her here. And they seemed so much in love they wouldn't be going around killing people. Where did this story start? Something must have happened.

And where were Ezio and Donna now, especially with a bunch of Fascists looking for them?

"What are we going to do, Paolo?"

"I don't know, Lucia. Ezio and Donna are up there in the Garfagnana. Do you know how dangerous that is, even without the Fascists? How can they survive that?"

"*Occhio unico* seems to."

They had somehow forgotten the original target of all this. Now, it was more important to rescue Ezio and Donna than to find the collaborator.

For long hours, they sat at the kitchen table. Lucia made coffee, but neither of them drank much. Paolo got up and paced the room and sat down. Lucia started cleaning the stove. The first rays of sunlight filtered through the window when Paolo remembered what Ezio had said. "I'm going to need help. I can't do this alone."

"Lucia," Paolo said. "I'm going up there."

"No!"

"I have to."

Lucia's eyes filled with tears. "You can't, I won't let you. There are people ready to kill up there."

"Ezio said he would need help, Lucia. I have to go."

"But where would you go? You have no idea where they are."

"I don't know, Lucia. I don't know."

They stood holding hands in front of the kitchen window. The mimosa tree glowed in the early sunlight.

"Well, at least take somebody with you," Lucia said at last. "You can't go alone."

"Maybe Roberto?"

"If he's sober," Lucia said. "And awake. My brother always sleeps until noon."

"He said he'd be willing to help. I'll call him back, I'll call him right now."

Before he had a chance to pick up the phone, it rang again.

"Oh, my God!" Lucia said. "What is it now. They're dead. I know they're dead."

"*Pronto!*" Paolo said into the phone. "Adolfo! Did your brother call you, too?"

Lucia tried to listen.

"No. No. I know it's impossible. Somebody made this up. Yes. No, I don't know where they are but we've got to find them, we've got to find them before somebody else does."

Paolo wiped his forehead. "I'm going to go, I'm going to go this morning. You will? Great, Adolfo. Can you leave right now? I'll meet you at the bus station in Lucca. I'll call Roberto, too."

Paolo put the phone down. "Adolfo says he's glad to take a break from the university."

"Yes, a break to get killed."

"Now, Lucia, it won't be so bad. I'll call Roberto right now."

A sleepy Roberto answered the phone after seven rings. But he readily agreed to leave right away. They would meet Adolfo at the bus station in Lucca at 8:30.

Paolo got a map from a kitchen drawer and spread it on the table for Lucia to see. "All right," he pointed to Sant'Antonio. "We'll drive north along the west side of the Serchio, see. We can make it to Ponte a Moriano by ten. Then we can go to some villages. Here. Garafolo. Del Monte. Malatesta. Scarano. Cira. There are so many. I wish I knew this region better."

"What's going on?"

Rubbing his eyes, Little Dino stood in the doorway. He wore a blue-and-white gondolier t-shirt and blue shorts.

Even though he was ten years old, Lucia picked him up. "Oh, nothing, Little Dino. Your Papa and I were just looking at this map. Papa is thinking about going on a little trip for a few days."

"Really? Can I go?"

"I'm afraid not, Little Dino," Paolo said. "It's just a little trip to the Garfagnana. I won't be long. I'll tell you all about it when I come back."

"The Garfagnana? I always wanted to go to the Garfagnana."

"Always? Little Dino, you're only ten years old."

"Ever since I was little. Really."

Lucia put him down. "You're getting too heavy for me, Little Dino."

"But can't I go? I really want to go? Please!"

"Not this time," Paolo said. "I'll tell you lots of stories when I get back. Besides, you have to take care of Fausta's flowers, don't you?"

Little Dino stood silently in the doorway. His lower lip trembled. "Please?"

"It'll be just for a few days, Little Dino. You'll hardly know I'm gone."

"Please! I'll be good. I won't say anything." A large tear ran down his brown cheek.

"I know that, Little Dino."

"Please!"

Paolo patted Little Dino on the head. And then he went to the closet in the bedroom. From the back of the top shelf he pulled out the box containing the pistol and bullets he had not used since his days in Ezio's *banda*.

CHAPTER 39

▼

Rosa, ever vigilant at her window, heard the car doors slamming in front of Lucia's house early in the morning. There was only one thing to do.

"Lucia!" she called, wiping her hands on her apron as she crossed the grass. "What's going on? Did someone die?"

Lucia put a bag of cheese and bread and apples into the trunk of the car. "No, Rosa, it's much worse than that."

Like the others before her, Rosa could not believe the story. Poor Ezio. *Povero sfortunato*. Poor Donna. Such a beautiful woman. *Santa Maria!*

"But Lucia," Rosa said, "why is Paolo packing the car? Where is he going?"

When she heard the response to that question, Rosa grabbed her friend. "No, Lucia, you can't let him. It's too dangerous."

"What am I going to do, Rosa? Paolo says he has to go. Remember Ezio said that he was going to need help. And remember what you yourself said, Rosa. You said you wanted to help, too. We all said we would."

Rosa wiped her eyes on the apron. "Yes, but I didn't think it would turn out like this. I didn't. I just thought maybe I could make some pasta or something. Should I get him something to eat to take along? I've got some cookies, some bread."

"No, Rosa, I've got plenty for him."

"But what can I do? I'm just an old lady. What can I do?"

Lucia put her arms around her. "It's all right. Sometimes all some of us can do is stay home and wait and hope."

"And pray, I guess." Rosa surprised herself when she said this because her attendance at mass was not regular now that she didn't like the new parish priest. She didn't pray much.

Next door, however, another woman was saying her daily prayers. Hearing the voices outside even in the midst of the third decade of the Joyful Mysteries of her rosary, Maria hobbled to her door and then down the stairs. Lucia repeated the story she had told Rosa. And then, "*Santa Maria! Santa Maria! Santa Maria!*"

Lucia led her inside so that she could sit down. Gina and Pietro were already there, Gina wringing her hands and Pietro silently staring at the people going back and forth.

Paolo made his way through the living room with a suitcase badly tied with a rope. Still wearing his gondolier t-shirt, Little Dino followed closely behind, tears streaming down his face. Lucia took him into the kitchen.

"Papa will be back in a few days, Little Dino. He'll be back soon. You be a good boy."

Little Dino nodded.

In a corner, Maria was reciting the rosary and was on the third decade of the Sorrowful Mysteries. "They made a branch of thorns and put it on the head of Our Savior. The blood ran down from his eyes. They put a reed in his hands ..."

"*Permesso?*" Now Annabella was at the door.

"I could hear Maria crying from my house. Did someone die?"

Again, the story was told. Again, more hand wringing.

"All right," Paolo said, returning to the door after closing the trunk of the car. "I'm going. Adolfo and Roberto should be at the bus station when I get there."

While the others tried not to look on, he took his wife in his arms. "It will only be for a few days, I'm sure."

"You know, Paolo, that's what they said when we had to go up to the Cielo during the war," Lucia said. "It was three months before we came back down."

"No, it won't be three months. I promise."

"You know you can't promise, Paolo."

"I promise. I'm sure Ezio and Donna are fine. We'll find them."

Paolo reminded Lucia that Ezio had led a whole *banda* in forests during the war so he knew how to get around. "We just always followed him. He seemed to have an instinct on where to go. He knew how to escape from danger."

"Now he has to escape from Fascists."

Paolo kissed his wife long and hard. He wiped away the tears from her eyes when they separated and then wiped his own. As he got behind the steering wheel he patted his pocket to make sure the pistol was still there.

Watching the car leave, Lucia hugged Gina who hugged Rosa who hugged Annabella who leaned down to hug Maria. Pietro stared straight ahead. Then Lucia turned around.

"Little Dino? Little Dino? Are you in the kitchen?"

He wasn't in the kitchen. "Little Dino! Where have you run off to now?" She went out to look in the garden. "Little Dino!"

It was when Roberto and Adolfo were getting into Paolo's car at the bus station in Lucca that Adolfo saw a freckle-faced boy under a blanket in the back seat.

"Shhh," Little Dino whispered, putting his finger on his lips. "Don't tell Papa."

"I'm afraid you've been discovered, Little Dino," Adolfo said. "Paolo, did you know you have an extra passenger back here?"

Paolo was so angry that Roberto put his hands over Little Dino's ears so he couldn't hear the expletives. But then, as always, Paolo relented when he saw Little Dino's grin.

"I'll tell you, Little Dino, when you want something, nothing stops you."

Paolo ran into the bus station to find the pay telephone. At the other end, Lucia was in turn furious and relieved. Paolo had to hold the phone away from his ear. He promised not to let Little Dino out of his sight. Meanwhile, grinning widely, Little Dino got in the front seat so he could sit next to his Papa.

In the Garfagnana, Antonio had left his shelter on Fabiano's farm, but the rain was so heavy that he could not possibly continue. And although he kept his cap pulled low, his eyeglasses were so filled with rain he couldn't see. He found a cave only about a hundred yards away.

The cave was dank and bug-infested, and he was visited during the night by rats that he thought were as big as the pigs he had cared for. There wasn't much to unpack because there wasn't much he had taken, but he did take a knife from the drawer and at the last minute stuffed his worn notebook into his back pocket.

He hardly slept, and when he did, there were nightmares about climbing another hill long ago, about falling down, about keeping vigil beside a pile of white bones.

"No! No!'

Fortunately, no one was near to hear his screams.

When he woke, it had stopped raining but the sky was overcast and he knew he had to move on. He was leaving when he heard noises in the wet grass nearby. He pulled out the knife.

Now the rustling came nearer. He crouched back in the cave.

"Antonio!" It was only a whisper.

"Good God!"

"Antonio, I know you're there. I saw you when I went out to feed the pigs."

Antonio crawled out from the cave. "Graziella, what are you doing here? Your Papa will be very mad at you if he finds out."

Graziella crept to the cave through the mud and grass. "He won't find out. Really. I didn't think you had gone far because it was raining so hard last night. I didn't sleep all night, Antonio. I was so worried about you."

"Thank you, Graziella, but you have to go back home now."

"I know."

"Good-bye, Graziella. Thank you for everything you've done for me. And thank your mother, too. No, then she'd find out you were here."

"I just brought you a few things. And I like to bake, really."

"You've been very kind. I've enjoyed our little talks. I hope you can find someone else to talk to now."

She sat down in the grass and began to cry. "No, I won't. There's no one else around here. There's no one else I can talk to, Antonio. You're the only one."

He wanted to hold her, perhaps even kiss the top of her head, but he dared not. She had to go home.

"Antonio, I know I'm only thirteen years old and you're, well, I forgot, but I know you're so old and I know there couldn't be anything between us, but to me you are like Tyrone Power. You are a dreamboat! Lately, every night before I fell asleep, I looked at the picture of Tyrone Power next to the Madonna but instead of seeing Tyrone Power I saw you. Isn't that strange, Antonio, I saw you. It was like you were my dreamboat."

"Graziella, you have to go home now."

"I know." She pulled up the bottom of her dirty blouse and blew her nose.

Antonio was desperate. "Tell you what, Graziella. If I ever get out of here, I will write you a letter. Is that all right? It will be a letter only between you and me. And you can keep the letter forever."

"Will you write to me, Antonio, will you?"

Antonio knew there was no chance that he would ever write a letter to her or anyone, or that he would even get out of here alive.

"Yes. Yes, Graziella, I will."

"Oh, Antonio, thank you. I will look for the postman every week. He only comes once a week, you know."

"Not yet, Graziella. I won't be able to write yet."

"Can I answer you?"

"I don't think I'll have an address. I don't know where I'll be,"

"Well, maybe I'll write about this in my diary. No, I'd better not. Mama sometimes looks in my diary. She got mad at me when she found something I wrote about you and it wasn't mushy or anything, it just said that I had talked to you on top of the hay barn and she got so mad about that."

He stood up and helped her to her feet. "You have to go, Graziella."

She didn't dare look at him. "I know you're not going to write to me. You're just saying that to make me feel good."

"Please go, Graziella."

"I won't have anyone to talk to anymore. No one." She wiped her tears with the back of her hand. She didn't move. Antonio held out his hand and she took it. He knew she was about to fling herself in his arms so he took his hand away and stepped back.

"Good-bye, Graziella."

"Good-bye." She got back on her knees and crawled back through the grass and the mud. He could see that her shoulders were shaking.

Antonio couldn't stop thinking about Graziella as he left the cave. What will ever become of her? She has no friends and she'll be stuck on the farm all her life. Her father and mother will die and she'll be left all alone with this decrepit farm. Well, he thought, maybe a Tyrone Power will come along and rescue her.

"Got to move on, got to move on," he kept saying to himself.

As he climbed one hill he thought he heard a movement to the left, pulled out his knife and stayed perfectly still. Nothing. As he crawled along an abandoned railroad track he thought he heard noises below. Nothing.

For whatever reason, his leg bothered him more this morning than at any time since he broke it in Adowa. Looking back on it now, he wished he had died when he fell from that church roof. That was child's play. Now, if Fabiano was to be believed, hundreds of Communists were in these mountains and forests looking for him.

"Got to move on, got to move on."

That was difficult, considering his bad leg and the thickets of woods he had to crawl through and the rocky hills he had to climb. At least it had stopped raining. He spent the entire day moving, but he didn't know where he was and didn't know where he was going. He also didn't know what he would do if he saw someone.

Deep in the forest, he suddenly came to a passageway through the trees to his right. It seemed obvious that he should take that route. No, he thought, if he were being followed he would easily be found. Fallen tree trunks obstructed the way to the left. Still, this was the way he had to go. Climbing over one after another, he moved slowly on, tripping, falling, not knowing where he was going.

And then he fell fifteen feet into a ravine.

CHAPTER 40

▼

Ezio felt as if Peppino had handed him a gold watch with one hand and punched him in the stomach with the other.

So *Occhio unico* might be somewhere near, maybe very near. Now they wouldn't, couldn't, leave and go home. The search could again go on. That was good.

But what if Ezio didn't want to confront this monster now? If this man were only a man, what would Ezio do if he found him? That was bad.

Standing in front of Peppino and Livia's little house, Donna also worried as she saw the mixture of joy, relief, anxiety and confusion cross in waves over Ezio's face. He remained quiet when Donna told Peppino again, "Thank you so very much for everything. We're going to try to find Cira."

Peppino and Livia waved as Ezio and Donna made their way down the brick path. Even down the hill, they took longer than they expected, mainly because neither of them had good shoes and the forest bed was still muddy from the rain. When they reached the stream, Donna suggested that they stop briefly for a rest. Ezio had not said a word and followed grimly behind as Donna led the way. Donna tried to respect what he was going through, but she knew they had to discuss this before they went much farther.

"You're not having second thoughts now, are you?" she asked as they found a little grassy spot to sit.

"You know what I'm thinking."

"Yes."

"Very confused, Donna. I'm very confused."

"But we have to remember this, Ezio. Whatever else has happened, we have to remember why we started this. We have to find *Occhio unico* and at last see that justice will be done for all the people killed at Sant'Anna di

Stazzema. He was a Fascist. He was a monster. He may be a little guy, he may wear a silly cap, but he's still a monster."

"I know," Ezio said, "but I can't help thinking of Paolo and Little Dino. Donna, do you think this guy went on picnics with his wife and played with his son?"

"Ezio ..."

"Do you think he bought him gelato?"

"Ezio ..."

"Took him for rides?"

"Ezio, please stop ..."

"Helped him with his homework?"

"Ezio, please stop tormenting yourself. We're not going to be able to go on if you're in such torment. You know, maybe I shouldn't say this, but didn't you start all this in honor of Angelica? How are you going to get rid of all this guilt otherwise? You're doing this for justice, yes, but you're doing it for yourself, too. And for her."

"I don't know, Donna, I just don't know. I've been thinking of what Peppino and Livia were talking about. The Joseph story."

"You mean you're thinking of forgiving the monster? Oh, Ezio."

Ezio silently traced circles in the sand with a broken stick. "I don't know. I'm not much of a religious person, you know. I hardly ever go to church."

"That's all right. I don't either."

"But I did take courses in university. There are other stories, too, not just Joseph. The sermon on the mount. The story of the prodigal son."

"I know those," Donna said. "The good nuns at Santa Felicita's School always talked about the prodigal son. The father who forgives his son who has been such a bastard. Whenever this one girl would hit me, the nun would say, 'Remember the father who forgave his son. Forgive her, forgive her.' I'd never forgive her. I'd hit her back and then I was the one in trouble."

"So I shouldn't forgive the monster?"

"I can't tell you what to do, Ezio. All I know is that you've been tormented by this man for so long, you have to somehow confront it. If that means confronting the man himself, then I think you should do it. You don't have to forget this terrible massacre and what he did. There's a difference between forgiving and forgetting, you know."

Ezio's circles in the sand kept getting smaller. "I'll never forget."

"None of us will. At least those of us who lost our loved ones."

Ezio was now poking holes in the sand rather than making circles. "Sometimes I think I'm a coward. Maybe I'm afraid to do this now."

Donna was exasperated. "Oh, great. Now you're having guilt about your guilt. Ezio, please. Let it go."

Ezio looked up. "And if we find him, what do we do? Kill him? I've only got a little pocket knife and who knows what he has?"

"We'll have to face that when we find him," Donna said.

"If we find him." He threw down the stick.

Donna got to her feet. "Let's go."

The route along the stream was, as Peppino predicted, more dangerous. They climbed in and out of ravines and tried to avoid the branches that kept hitting them in the face. In a gully, Donna suddenly stopped.

"Did you hear that?"

"What?"

"I thought I heard something over there."

They stood frozen, but the only sounds were the soft rustling of leaves overhead and occasional bird songs.

"My imagination, I guess," Donna said as they began to pick their way through the brush again.

"Stay here," Ezio said as they approached a hill. "I'm going to look up ahead and see if there's something there. Maybe we're not on the right path."

Donna was kneeling, rubbing a bruised elbow, when she saw something move to her right.

"Oh, my God!"

Not more than twenty feet away, in the shadows of the forest, there appeared to be a slight form next to the trunk of a chestnut tree. It was so small and thin it could have been a frail girl. Its face was pink and brown and its head was bald. It was dressed in rags.

Donna waved. "Hello!"

The figure hesitated, and waved back. Just then an eagle, screeching so loud Donna's ears hurt, swooped down, its eight-foot wingspan gracefully winding through tree branches. Donna screamed and Ezio ran back and took her in his arms. In seconds the eagle had flown back into the darkening sky.

"It's all right," Ezio said. "The eagle's flown away. But I didn't see anything."

"Ezio, I saw him! I saw *il ragazzo fantasma!*"

"You're kidding. Where?"

"Right over there. He was standing by the tree but when the eagle came down he disappeared. Ezio, don't laugh. I know. I saw it. I saw *him*."

Ezio went over to the tree and looked around it. Maybe, just maybe. There were small indentations in the grass. "I don't know. Maybe. But who or whatever it was, it's gone. We'd better go."

CHAPTER 41

▼

He wondered now whether he should have gone up to her. The lady seemed nice enough, reminding him a lot of his mother. She was just kneeling there, she couldn't have hurt him. But her dress was all dirty, and so was her face. His Mama would never wear a dirty dress like that.

For the first time in a long time, he thought maybe he'd like to talk to a real person again. Not a man, no. He never wanted to talk to a man again. Not after what happened. But maybe a woman like his Mama. But then the eagle came down and that must have been a warning for him not to get too close. So he came back to the little home he had created in this long tunnel.

It was nice back here in the corner. Sometimes it was too cold in winter, but when it was hot in summer he could come back and it would be so much cooler. He could light one of the candles he found behind a church and even read a little. Since he only went to the third grade, he couldn't read very much. He had found some books in a trash pile on a farm and he liked to look at them. *Storia d'Italia.* He thought that was boring, what he could read of it, but he liked to look at the maps. *Decameron.* He couldn't read or understand any of that but there were interesting drawings inside. *Pinocchio.* That was his favorite. The back cover was torn off and some of the pages were ripped, but it had funny pictures. When he felt all alone sometimes, he would read that book.

He remembered his Papa and his Mama reading that book to him when he was very little. He thought he could remember it by heart. His Papa and Mama also helped him with his homework. He liked to play ball with his Papa. He remembered his Papa used to throw him in the air and he would be so scared but it would be so much fun and his Papa always caught him.

He had to be careful, though, so that he wouldn't land on Papa's face and hurt his eye. There was a terrible hole there. Mama always told Papa to wear his eyeglasses, but he never did.

He missed his Papa.

He missed his Mama, too. He remembered the bean soup she used to make. Sometimes he could still taste it. He remembered when she put him to bed and she said a little prayer with him and he would fall right to sleep. He remembered the little trundle bed.

It was so long ago that sometimes he couldn't quite remember what they looked like. He wondered where his Mama and Papa were now. Papa had stayed at home when Mama took him away that day and he never saw his Papa again.

But he didn't remember much about that day. He knew he took his little red wagon and a lot of toys and they climbed a big hill and they stayed with an old lady and there were a lot of people running around. He remembered how he and his Mama had to sleep in the back of the house on some hay and it smelled really bad and he couldn't sleep. And then he remembered his Mama waking him up and telling him to hide right inside the hay because some bad men were coming and he felt his Mama lying right on top of him.

And he didn't remember much of what happened next but there was a lot of screaming and bangs and he couldn't find his Mama and he was crawling through some logs that were on fire and it smelled really, really bad and there was smoke all around and he couldn't see.

And he remembered crying. Crying.

And then it was dark outside but there was still so much smoke it didn't matter. And it smelled even worse, a stinky smell like when his hair caught on fire that one time when he was little, only much, much worse. And then he didn't remember anything else until later. Much later.

He was in a bed in this old house and there were things all over his face and then he heard a woman ask him how he was. He said he couldn't see and she said he had bandages over his face because he got burned in a fire and his hands and legs and feet were burned, too.

The lady sounded old but her voice was nice and she fed him some soup and he was very, very hungry. And he remembered he slept a lot and then one day the lady took off the bandages and he could see that he was in a little room and he could look out and see chestnut trees and olive trees in the distance and just outside there were two pigs and some chickens and a horse. The farm must have been high in the mountains because he could see eagles every once in a while.

And he missed his Mama and Papa so much and when he asked the lady about them she just started to cry and told him not to ask anymore because they were gone and he wouldn't ever see them again. And then he cried even more and the lady held him in her arms and her breasts smelled like sweet powder like his Mama's.

Sometimes he asked the lady how he got burned but she wouldn't tell him. She said the burns had hurt him real bad and she didn't want him to look in a mirror but sometimes he did. It scared him. His face and hands and feet were pink and brown and other colors and his eyes were sunken and his lips were swollen and he was bald because hair wouldn't grow on his head. He didn't want anyone to see him and he wondered if it would ever change.

The lady was nice to him and she let him do what he wanted and he told her when his birthday was, 15 November. She made him a little cake but she was sorry she didn't have any money for a present. Soon it was Christmas and she gave him a little toy. And then it was summer and he liked to run outside but the lady told him not to go too far because he might get lost and because he might also scare people because of the way he looked.

But sometimes he just wanted to run and run and run. A few times he saw someone but he tried to stay behind a tree so they wouldn't see him.

He remembered when his birthday and Christmas came again and he knew he was getting stronger but he still wasn't growing. But he didn't care. He would always be short like his Papa and his grandfather. He found that he didn't think about his Mama and Papa so much anymore during the day, just at night before he went to sleep.

And then it was summer and his birthday and then Christmas and one day the lady told him he had been at her house for five years. He knew he was thirteen years old but he didn't know what that meant. He had come to like it there. Sometimes he did a few chores, but mostly the lady let him play and run outside. And she made good bean soup, like his Mama's.

The one thing he didn't like was the old lady's brother who came to visit sometime. He lived all by himself on the next farm. He was fat and smelled of grappa and he would always pick him up and hug him and kiss him and he didn't like that at all. But he only came once in a while so it wasn't so bad.

Then a terrible thing happened. The old lady got sick and she stayed in bed for a long time and he had to get his own meals and clean the house and he didn't mind that but he didn't know what to do when she started moaning and crying. So he ran over to her brother's farm and told him and the man came and stayed with the lady for a couple of days but then the lady died. And some men came and took her away in a big box.

And then the man said he should come and live with him in his house. It was smaller and not very clean like the lady's house and the man said he had to help with the cleaning and also to feed the pigs and chickens. He didn't like that very much but after his chores he still had time to run in the forests and lie in the grass and look up at the sky and watch the clouds and the birds and the eagles.

And there was only one bed and he had to sleep with the man. He didn't like the way the man kept his arm around him when he was sleeping but he was so tired at night he didn't care much about anything.

Then one night he felt the man's hand on his back rubbing up and down and he was awake then and he felt the man putting his hand down his underpants and feeling down there. And he knew his Mama wouldn't like that because she had always told him never to touch himself down there. And then he felt the man feeling his bum. He didn't know why the man was feeling his bum.

He didn't remember much after that because it really hurt and he started screaming but the man didn't pay any attention to him and the man was making bad noises. And then it was over and he tried to sleep but he couldn't.

The next day the man smiled at him and was really nice and he gave him some nice food to eat but that night the same thing happened. He wanted to run away but it was so cold out now and anyway the man kept smiling at him and giving him good food to eat. But every night it was the same.

And this went on night after night and his bum was so sore that sometimes he couldn't sit down but the man was nice and gave him good stuff to eat. But he still had to do the chores and feed the pigs and the chickens before he could run and run and run.

He stayed through the whole winter and the summer and another winter. And almost every night it was the same thing.

One day he was running in the hills and he found this fantastic tunnel under a big hill where he could run in one side and run out the other. Sometimes he would do it again and again and this was so much fun. And one of the best parts were the guns he found laying here and there in the tunnel. Old guns, rusty ones. He liked to pretend he was shooting them, but he never did it outside of the tunnel. His Mama was afraid of guns but he knew his Papa wasn't.

And one night after the man did the nasty thing and fell asleep he knew it was a good time to go away. And that's what he did. He jumped down from the window and he ran and ran and ran and he never looked back.

He made a little home in the tunnel and he could find enough to eat if he looked in the big cans in back of farmers' houses or if he took things from the gardens. The first winter he was alone he didn't have enough to eat and he was almost thinking of going back to the man but he knew he couldn't do that. So after that when it started to get cold he collected some apples and plums and zucchini and other stuff from gardens and he made a little place in his tunnel where he could keep them. He always seemed to find something to eat in one of the farmer's bins. He knew of one farmer especially that threw a lot of stuff away. And he knew his clothes weren't very good. When one shirt or pants got too old or torn he would just take another one from a clothesline. Nobody saw him. He never wore any shoes.

When it was daytime he liked to walk and run through the woods and if there was a grassy place he would run and run and run and he would feel so free. And he liked to lie on the grass and look up at the sky and count the clouds and wonder where they were going. And the sun felt good on his face and hands and head, which still didn't have any hair.

And there was a fox nearby and at first he was afraid of the fox but then he started giving him scraps of food and the fox came around and started eating it. And he called the fox his friend and sometimes when he slept under a tree the fox would come and sleep nearby. He thought the fox was protecting him.

He wasn't afraid, though. He remembered his Papa telling him not to be afraid in the woods, and he wasn't. Not even of the eagles that lived in a nest in a tree near the top of the mountain. He liked to go up there but not too close and when the Mama eagle had little babies he watched as they grew and then they flew away. He liked to think the eagles were his friends, too. Sometimes he missed the boys he used to play with in that town where he lived. He couldn't remember their names anymore and he couldn't remember the name of the town anymore.

Sometimes he thought he would like to talk to someone but every time he tried to get close, the person would run away. He didn't want to talk to just anyone. Especially not a man. Sometimes when he was running or maybe just skipping through the woods he would see someone and they must have seen him because they would act real peculiar and point and scream and run away. He didn't have a mirror anymore but he could see what he looked like in a stream.

Last year he was up on the hill where he liked to go because there was this beautiful bridge over a river and he would have liked to cross it but that would mean seeing people. But when he looked the other way he could see the top of a hay barn and there was a man and a girl and it looked like they were talking. The man reminded him of his Papa but he wore eyeglasses and his Papa never wore eyeglasses.

He had never seen a young girl like that and he felt different than he had ever felt before. A kind of tingling feeling he didn't understand. He wanted to climb down the hill and then up on the roof of the hay barn and talk to her but the man was there and he was afraid of the man. And anyway he thought the girl would be frightened if she saw the way he looked so all he could do was sit on the hill most every day and see if the girl would be on the roof of the hay barn. And he was happy when she was there because he liked to look at her. She had red hair. He'd never seen a girl with red hair before.

He never knew when his birthday was anymore but he figured he must have had four of them since he left the man's house so that would make him nineteen years old now. He knew his name was Little Ugo because that's what his Papa and Mama and everyone called him. But he didn't feel like he had a name anymore. He didn't even feel like a boy anymore. He just felt like a spirit, or maybe a ghost.

CHAPTER 42

▼

Through what seemed like never-ending forests, Ezio and Donna trudged on. Finally, they reached the little shrine, which was indeed broken. Someone had stolen the statue and the wooden shell was splintered. Worse, someone had written an expletive on the side.

"All right," Ezio said, "which way do we turn?" He reached for the map in his back pocket.

"Shit!"

"Not there?"

"I must have lost it."

"Great." Donna turned and walked away.

"He said to turn right, right?" Ezio called after her.

"I'm sure he said left," she called back.

"You sure?"

"Well, now I don't know. Oh, Ezio."

Ezio ran his hand over his hair. "I think right. Let's go."

Donna trudged obediently behind as they made their way through more forests, though this time there was a clearly defined path.

"We must be getting to Cira soon," Ezio said. "Peppino said it would be far, but I didn't think it would be this far."

"Seems like we've been in these forests for days if not years." Donna brushed tree leaves from her hair and shoulders. "I'm not complaining, but I do wish I had brought another dress along for our glorious adventure in the woods."

"I wish I had a razor," Ezio said, rubbing his chin. "And a clean shirt. I bet I smell."

"I'm not even going to consider answering that question."

Now the trees grew less dense, with vast meadows spread out among the hills. They could make out an actual farmhouse high above. And then from somewhere, a church bell rang six times.

"The Angelus," Donna said. "Even I know that. It's 6 o'clock. I didn't think it was that late."

"We must be near Cira."

Soon, they found a better path, and that led to a dirt road that led to a paved highway.

"I wonder," Donna said. "I thought Cira was a tiny village. Think this is right?"

"Shit!"

They stared at the sign: Malatesta.

"Well, how the hell did we wind up here?" Ezio said. "Damn!"

"Yes, damn!"

"All right, Donna, say it."

"I told you so? Why should I bother?" For the first time since they had begun their journey, Donna's voice was hard and low.

While Ezio checked the knife in his pocket, Donna ran her hands through her hair and smoothed out her dress. They tried to be just friendly visitors as they walked past the frame houses, the gelato shop, the *bottega*, and the butcher shop and wound up in a miniscule piazza. It had a statue of a war hero in the middle and a forbidding church at the side. No one was visible.

"Everyone's home getting ready for dinner, I guess," Donna said.

"Well, let's try the *bar*."

Only the proprietor was inside, a small, thin man with a sliver of a mustache and long black hair. Ezio asked for two *panini* and tried to engage the man in some casual conversation about what was going on in Malatesta that night. The proprietor said he had no idea and nothing ever happened in Malatesta.

"Just wondering," Ezio said. "Say, do you know the way to Cira?"

The proprietor looked his customers up and down. A straggly man and woman who looked like they'd slept in the forest for days. "Cira? That Communist town? Take that road out there. Leads to the Serchio."

He hurriedly made the sandwiches and collected his *lira*. Ezio and Donna had just settled down at a little table when Donna looked up. "He's making a phone call. We'd better get out of here."

Clutching their sandwiches, which were now dripping tomatoes and mozzarella, Ezio and Donna fled the little shop, crossed the piazza and walked quickly past more houses to the outskirts of town. Then they began to run.

Just as the paved highway turned into another dirt road on the other side of town, a small black car roared from behind. Their *panini* tossed aside, Ezio and Donna made a dash for a grove of chestnut trees about forty yards from the road. They hid behind a huge tree and held their breaths as they heard the car's door slam shut.

"Don't make a move," Ezio said

"How could I? I'm frozen to this spot."

Gradually, they could hear someone approaching. Then they realized that there were two people, coming from different directions.

Ezio took Donna's hand. "We're going to have to make a run for it. There's more forest over there. Hold my hand."

They ran through tall thick grass, with Ezio pulling Donna and with both of them frequently falling.

"Am I hurting you?" he asked at one point.

"I didn't plan to use that arm again anyway."

"There's some sort of old barn up ahead. Let's see if we can make it."

Crawling and crouching, they were almost to the old dilapidated structure when a bullet whizzed past Ezio's head.

"Faster!"

They managed to get inside just as another bullet hit the side of the barn door. Ezio saw a small enclosure at the rear that was filled with hay.

"Quick," Ezio whispered, "get under this stuff."

Donna picked up armfuls of hay, dug a hole in the middle and covered herself up. A few feet away, Ezio did the same. Two minutes later, they could hear the muffled voices of two men who seemed out of breath.

"They've ... they've got to ... be ... to be here someplace."

"I told you ... they went the other way ... they're not here ..."

One of the men picked up a long stick and started poking the hay piles that covered the floor. But they didn't get to the back of the barn where Ezio and Donna remained frozen, desperately resisting the urge to sneeze.

"I told you ... there's no one here ... we should have gone up that hill ... you never believe me ... you ..."

Even after the voices faded into silence, Ezio and Donna did not move. Finally, Ezio tore through the hay and carefully lifted himself up. Poking around, he found Donna and freed her from her smelly prison.

Ordinarily, Donna could have been expected to make a wry comment about always wanting to play in the hay. Instead, she silently tried to get strands of hay out of her hair, her dress and her shoes.

"If we didn't smell bad before, we sure do now," Ezio said. "I reek."

"No comment," Donna said.

They knew they were lost again, that darkness was descending fast and that, with pistol-toting Fascists somewhere nearby, they could not leave their hiding place. Now, besides being exhausted and discouraged, they were experiencing the first tensions between them. Donna sat on the floor, her back against the wall and held her knees close to her. Ezio stood by the window, watching a half moon move over a distant hill. They remained in their separate worlds for a long time.

"You're mad at me, aren't you?" Ezio finally asked.

"I'm too tired to be mad."

"I wish you'd tell me how you feel."

Donna played with a strand of hay. "I feel ... I feel like I've gone through the wringer of our washing machine back home. Up, down, up, down."

"I'm sorry."

"I am, too."

"I shouldn't have asked you to come, Donna."

"Ezio!" Her eyes flared. "You didn't ask me, may I remind you. I wanted to come. I volunteered. I wanted to find *Occhio unico* as much as you did. Well, almost as much."

"I know, but ..."

"But what? I'm a big girl, Ezio. I'm thirty-three years old, and heaven knows I've had some experiences. Bad experiences. But these last two days have been, well ... like shit."

"I'm sorry."

"Let's get some sleep."

Donna lay on her side at the far end of the hay pile, facing the wall. "Good night."

Ezio lay facing the opposite side. "Good night."

During the night, the sounds of a distant dog—or was it a fox?—awakened him briefly, but then he went back to sleep.

He woke when sunbeams filtered through the cracks in the barn roof. Sleep and sunlight had softened their tensions, but Ezio and Donna still spoke and acted gingerly.

"Good morning," he said when she turned over.

"Good morning."

"For once, it's a nice day," he said. "Better yet, now we can tell east from west, north from south."

They fled the barn in minutes and were back on the road, with the sun shining brightly as they slowly proceeded east. They walked side by side but avoided holding hands, and they made little conversation. As they rounded a curve in the road another car could be heard far ahead.

"We'd better not stay on the road," Ezio said, and pointed to thick chestnut trees that lined the road about twenty feet away. "If we go through there we can keep an eye on the road and still be hidden."

This might have been safer, but it was also more difficult. There apparently had been a storm at some point, and fallen tree trunks littered their path. Ezio helped Donna over one after another, and sometimes she helped him. At first they didn't see the indentions in the grass near a tree line, but Ezio stopped to examine them.

"Donna, look. These aren't like those little ones we saw yesterday. These are bigger."

Donna knelt down and put her hands around what appeared to be footprints. "These are fresh. Ezio. It just rained so someone has been here! Someone has been here recently!"

More excited and encouraged than at any time since they entered the Garfagnana, they carefully walked alongside the footprints. One, two, three, four, five …

The prints went on for about twenty-five feet, and then stopped abruptly at a deep ravine. Still keeping an eye to their left so they wouldn't lose sight of the road, they balanced their way across the edge when Ezio noticed what looked like a blue mitten half way down.

"Think that's anything?"

"I don't know," Donna said. "Everything else here is wet but that looks dry."

"So it's recent," Ezio said as he grabbed branch after branch and lowered himself down.

"Got it!" He climbed back up and handed it to Donna.

"Well, it's not a mitten," Donna said as she shook the dirt out. "It's just an old cap of some kind."

"Donna!" Ezio cried. "Look at it. It's blue, red, green and yellow!"

CHAPTER 43

▼

With the old cap firmly stuffed into Ezio's back pocket, they struggled through more meadows and more forests until they saw a little village ahead and thought it safe to get back on the road.

"No sign," Ezio said. "This better be Cira."

"Hmm," Donna said. "Well, it's certainly small, like Peppino said. I wonder where the Casa del Popolo is here."

"In someone's living room probably," Ezio said.

A couple of dozen houses lined the road. A church stood far in the distance. The only business establishment was apparently behind a door with a sign saying *bottega*.

"That must be where the natives find the best bargains," Donna said. "But how are we going to find all these Communists? Do we just go up and introduce ourselves and ask all the Communists to raise their hands?"

"We'd better not. Maybe this isn't even Cira."

Their suspicions that even this might not be the right place grew as they walked down the road. They could sense, but not see, eyes peering behind shutters. A little girl ran into her house pointing at the visitors.

"Well, I know we look pretty awful," Donna said, "but I didn't know they had a dress code here."

"Let's chance it," Ezio said as he opened the door to the *bottega*. To their relief, a sign above the espresso machine read *Bottega di Cira*.

A big bald-headed man with muscles bulging from his white t-shirt was slicing prosciutto on a wooden block at the back of the store. Two women dressed in black looked over the small selection of pasta. Four men played scopa at a table in the corner. Everyone turned to stare at the visitors as they entered.

"It's them," one of the card players whispered.

"You sure?"

"I'm sure, *cretino*."

Trying to be casual, Ezio and Donna studied a display of statues of the Virgin and bleeding Christs when one of the men got up.

"You looking for someone?"

Ezio spun around. "Someone?"

Ezio and Donna still weren't sure.

"*Occhio unico?*" the man asked.

The men looked like they could be trusted. "Yes," Ezio said.

"We've been waiting for you. The whole Garfagnana is talking about you two. You don't look so big."

Donna didn't like the way the card players looked her up and down.

"Big? Are we supposed to be big?"

One after another, the card players told the stories that had spread. Ezio and Donna couldn't believe they were the subjects of these outlandish tales, heroes to some and murderous villains to others. But to these people in Cira, they were the former.

The butcher stopped slicing prosciutto and hauled down a jug of wine from the top shelf behind him. "This calls for a celebration."

The wine was barely drinkable, but Ezio and Donna managed to get some down before getting to the reason for their visit.

"Can you help us?" Ezio asked, wiping his mouth with the back of his hand. "Do you know where *Occhio unico* is?"

"We're not sure," one man said, putting down his cards. "We just found out he was staying at Fabiano Guerini's farm over by Mastiano all these years. Imagine! We didn't know that or we would have done something about it."

"Of course we would," another said.

"We could have caught him," the third said. The fourth nodded.

"But now," said the first, "we've learned that Fabiano kicked him out when he heard about the hundreds of Communists that were going to descend on him."

"Hundreds?" Donna asked.

"I guess that's you two."

"Oh."

"But we should tell you something else."

Ezio gripped Donna's hand. "What?"

"Some people were here in a car looking for you this morning."

Immediately, Ezio and Donna thought of Calvino Bastiani. He was the only surviving person at the Mazzella villa who knew they were looking for

Occhio unico. Now they were certain he and his henchmen were following them.

"What did they look like?" Ezio asked. "Was one of them tall, gray hair, short beard, maybe a three-piece suit? Looks like a banker?"

"No, no. Nothing like that. The driver was a young guy, like you only a little heavier. There was a boy in the front seat, too, maybe about ten years old. Two guys in the back seat, looked pretty much alike. Could have been cousins, maybe even brothers."

"Oh, my God!" Ezio said. "Paolo, Little Dino, Roberto and Adolfo. What are they doing here? With Little Dino! This is insane! They could be killed!"

"Well, they were asking around, the driver was anyway, and he said they wanted to help you."

"Good God," Ezio cried. "Are they going up and down the Serchio asking everyone they see?"

"No, no. They knew we were friendly here."

Ezio and Donna thanked the men for their help.

"We think we know these people," Ezio said. "How can we find them now?"

"Well, you came from the south, right?" the man said. "We told them to go over there to the west, just look in the forests near the road. And if they didn't find you, they should come back."

One of the men offered Donna a chair. Ezio stood by the window. The card players went back to their hands, although loudly arguing who was to deal next. The butcher went back to his prosciutto and the elderly women went home.

Donna watched the clock on the wall. 2 o'clock.

3 o'clock.

4 o'clock.

The card players had long gone home when the butcher said he wanted to close his shop. Ezio pleaded with him to stay open a little longer.

"All right, 5 o'clock. That's it. I mean, I hope you catch *Occhio unico*, but my wife is waiting dinner for me and I better not be late. She'll kill me."

Ezio and Donna wondered how big his wife was, considering that he weighed at least two hundred and fifty pounds.

Then they heard a car bouncing along the bumpy road.

"It's them!" Donna shouted and they both rushed out of the shop. The butcher quickly followed and locked the door.

Ezio, Donna, Paolo, Roberto and Adolfo gathered around the car. Ezio yelled at Paolo for coming and Paolo yelled at Ezio for causing such trouble. Then they embraced each other. Paolo, Roberto and Adolfo were impressed with Donna, and she with them. She shook Little Dino's hand again. Ezio described his and Donna's adventures and encounters in the forests, and Paolo complained about the futile stops his group had made along the way.

"There was a guy in Malatesta who actually laughed at us," he said.

"That was before he got on the phone," Adolfo said. "We got out of that town fast."

Ezio pulled the cap out of his back pocket. "And look, we found this."

"A cap?" Roberto said. "What's so important about a cap?"

"Everyone says that *Occhio unico* wore a woolen cap. Mostly blue but other colors, too. We found this in a ravine just back there. So he has to be around here somewhere."

Paolo asked where they should begin searching for this monster. No one knew.

"Let's just drive north along the river," Ezio said. "We can get out every once in a while and look on foot. With all of us, we can spread out."

Ignored by his elders, Little Dino stood apart, trying to get out of his father's sight. He shuffled pebbles with his left foot, then his right. He found a pretty blue one to take home to Mama. He started kicking a bright green one and kicked and kicked until he slowly walked around to the back of the *bottega*.

Suddenly he saw a movement in the trees. He took a step forward. What looked like a boy about his age was half hidden by a tree. The boy's face was all sorts of different colors and his head was bald. Little Dino took a few more steps. The boy came out from behind the tree. Little Dino waved a little wave. The boy returned it. Little Dino mouthed a silent "Hi." So did the boy. Little Dino moved closer and so did the boy. When they were about ten feet apart, the boy sat down in the grass. Little Dino sat down. He said "Hi" again. So did the boy. Little Dino patted his head three times. The boy patted his head three times. Little Dino put his finger on his nose. So did the boy. Little Dino touched his chin. So did the boy. The boy put his fingers in his ears. So did Little Dino. The boy stuck out his tongue and rolled his eyes together. Little Dino tried but couldn't quite do it. Little Dino picked up a blade of grass, held it to his mouth and made a whistle. He was very proud that he could do that, something Paolo had taught him. The boy across the way picked up a blade of grass and did the same. He had discovered this himself lying on the grass one day. Little Dino whispered, "What's your name?" The boy waited a while and then said, "Little Ugo." Little Dino said, "My name is Little Dino." They smiled at each other.

In front of the *bottega*, Paolo was suddenly aware of Little Dino's absence. "Where's Little Dino? Where did he go? He's always running off. Lucia will kill me. That kid! Little Dino! I told you to stay with me!"

There was a frantic search up and down the road and then behind the houses and the *bottega*. "He's right over there," Adolfo called. "He's sitting in the grass all by himself."

"Come on, Little Dino, it's time to go," Paolo said.

Little Dino looked behind him as he ran to the car. There was no one there.

Antonio's leg was now hurting even more. He was afraid he might have broken something in the fall into the ravine. Using his knife, he manufactured a crutch out of a tree branch, tearing off a sleeve from his shirt to bind the top together, and hobbled along. He knew he needed to get some help. Would he have to give up and try to see a doctor? The Communists would probably see him and kill him first, but he'd have to take the risk. He couldn't die out here alone.

He knew that the bridge, the one they called the Devil's Bridge, was up ahead. If he could get there and cross it, he should be able to get some help at Borgo a Mozzano. It was risky, but he didn't have much of a choice.

He hobbled along, sweat pouring down his face and into his beard. He wished he hadn't lost his cap when he fell. His shirt clung to his back. He had to stop every fifteen minutes to rest.

Atop the third hill he climbed he could see the top of the Devil's Bridge in the distance. From this angle it was even more impressive than from the top of the hay barn. Massive, it was still delicately carved. He could see the heads of a few people as they crossed. The Serchio surged beneath it.

Now he had a destination. Stumbling and falling, swearing and cursing, he struggled on and on. He was pushing himself too hard now, he realized.

"Got to move on, got to move on."

He had to find a place where he could rest for an hour. The hillsides along the Serchio were open and anyone would be able to see a bearded man with glasses struggling along with a crutch.

Then he fell again. This time, an aching, terrifying fall as he tried to cling to bushes and rocks on the way down.

"Damn, damn, damn, damn!"

He landed in a heap and lay, trying not to scream, for uncounted minutes. When he finally opened his eyes he saw what appeared to be an opening behind thick bushes. He crawled up some steps and into it. He had to leave his broken crutch behind and he realized that he had lost his knife, too.

Inside was a cave that seemed to go on forever, and although it was the middle of a sunny day, he couldn't see more than fifteen feet inside. Water dripped from the top, and the walls and floor were wet. This was more than a cave, he realized. This was part of the *Linea Gotica*, the Gothic Line.

In training for the Black Brigades, he learned all about it, how the Germans forced Italian laborers to build a defense line across northern Italy. Fortifications, gun pits, trenches, barbed wire and ditches were added to the natural defensive wall of the Apennine and Apuan Mountains. But for all of the ingenious Nazi plans, the line proved to be indefensible when American and British troops arrived. The Germans fled.

This tunnel, Antonio realized, must have been used for fortifications. He almost tripped over an old carbine in a corner. He collapsed next to it.

"Got to move on, got to move on," he kept saying to himself as he fell asleep.

CHAPTER 44

▼

Ezio was positive they wouldn't all fit, but Paolo said it wouldn't be a problem. Paolo and Roberto sat in the front and Donna sat on Ezio's lap in the rear along with Little Dino on Adolfo's lap.

This meant they could not move easily and, worse, Paolo could not see out of the rearview mirror.

"I think we must look like the clowns stuffed into a little car at the circus," Adolfo said.

"Just pray that no *carbinieri* come along," Paolo said.

"I hope the *carbinieri* have better things to do than stop a nice family going on a picnic," Donna said.

To make matters worse, the road was filled with holes, which caused Donna to bounce hard on Ezio's lap.

"Are you enjoying the ride, Ezio?" Roberto leered. Ezio blushed and held Donna tighter.

They jerked along the bumpy road for miles and then found that it led to a highway along the west side of the Serchio.

"Ezio," Donna said, "the Garfagnana looks different here than on the other side."

"This is more open. I think. So maybe it's better that *Occhio unico* was seen on this side."

"Look!" Paolo and Roberto shouted together.

Miles ahead but still clearly visible was the spectacular bridge across the Serchio. "What is that?" Paolo, Roberto and Adolfo all said together.

"The Devil's Bridge," Ezio said. Then he told the story. Little Dino's eyes became bigger and bigger. In all the books he'd read in school, he had never heard such a fantastic tale.

"But Signor Maffini," he said, still thinking he was in the classroom, "why didn't the devil just swim across? Why didn't he just get out of the river?"

"Well, maybe he wasn't very strong or maybe the current was too swift."

"I bet I could have swum it," Little Dino said.

"Little Dino, you don't know how to swim," Paolo said over his shoulder from the front seat.

"I could do it. I bet it's not hard."

Paolo smiled. "Little Dino," he thought. "He's getting bolder every day."

"Well, anyway," Ezio said, "maybe the devil didn't want to swim. Maybe he wanted to drown."

Little Dino thought about that for a long time. "I feel sorry for the devil," he said quietly.

As they drove closer, they opened the car's windows so that they could let the afternoon breezes through. The Serchio roared now. If *Occhio unico* was around here, they had better park the car and search on foot.

Paolo and Roberto went in one direction, Ezio and Adolfo in another. Donna thought she'd better stay with Little Dino even though he wanted desperately to join in the search.

"We should stay near the car," she tried to explain. "Then when they find this bad man we can drive over and pick him up."

Little Dino knew she was just trying to prevent him from going along.

Picking their way through the rocks and shrubs, Roberto found a long branch that had broken in two. "Look," he said. "What do you think this is, or was?"

Paolo examined it. Why would a tree branch have a piece of cloth around it? Even Roberto realized what it was. They looked up and saw a clear path of crushed bushes and smooth sand. "Somebody fell down here," Paolo said. "Somebody who had this crutch."

"And look," Roberto said. "Here's a knife. Well, I can use that."

Paolo tossed the branch aside, Roberto held on to the knife and Paolo took his pistol out of his pocket. It was not long before they found the entrance to a tunnel. They slipped quickly inside, and Roberto promptly tripped over a leg stretched out on the floor.

"Damn!"

Roberto felt a blow to his chest and fell backward. Paolo grabbed the assailant, pulled him forward and tore off his eyeglasses. When he saw the face, he knew immediately who it was.

"*Occhio unico!*"

Antonio broke away and hobbled into the inner reaches of the tunnel. Paolo tried to follow but kept falling or hitting his head on the low ceiling.

Behind him, Roberto kept calling, "Where are you?"

"I'm here. Ahead of you," Paolo said. "I'll keep talking so you know. *Occhio unico! Occhio unico!*"

The space ahead was eerily still.

Outside, Ezio and Adolfo continued to move north. Adolfo slipped and grabbed Ezio's arm.

"He couldn't be around here," Adolfo said. "How could anyone make it around here?"

"He must be." Ezio silently edged on.

In the middle of the tunnel, Antonio could hear "*Occhio unico!*" shouted over and over behind him. He fell, got up, fell, got up again. Turning a corner, he entered a space where there was suddenly a little light. He thought there might be an opening somewhere in the roof of the tunnel, but then he saw that it was a candle flickering on the floor. When his eye adjusted, he saw a boy, a boy who seemed very young, sprawled on a pile of leaves. A book lay in his lap. Antonio could barely make out the title. *Pinocchio.*

The boy leaped up and crawled to a corner, where he crouched down, put his hands over his head and trembled.

"It's all right," Antonio said. "What are you doing here? Are you lost?"

No answer, although the boy was clearly whimpering.

"Are you all right?"

The boy was sobbing now.

"I won't hurt you."

Loud, wracking sobs shook his whole body.

"Really."

Forgetting that he was being pursued by two men who were probably going to kill him, Antonio knelt down. He reached out his hand.

"Please?"

Slowly, the boy took his hands from his head. His back straightened, but he still didn't turn around.

"Please?" Antonio said.

The boy remained kneeling for a few minutes, then dared to look over his shoulder. Antonio saw his face.

"Oh, my God!" he whispered. "What happened? Are you all right?"

The boy nodded.

"How did this happen? God in heaven, how did this happen?"

The boy shook his head.

Antonio thought there was something about the boy, something familiar ...

"It's all right. Can you come closer?"

Antonio's voice was soft and comforting. The boy seemed to remember it from somewhere, somewhere long ago. He moved a few inches. Antonio stretched out his hand. The boy looked at it for a while, not sure what to do, and then, trusting, he reached out and put his own small white hand lightly on Antonio's.

"It's all right," Antonio said. "I won't hurt you. I promise. Can you come a little closer? Can you talk?"

The boy moved a little closer and the flickering candle lit his face.

"Oh, my God! Oh, my God!" Tears from Antonio's right eye flowed down his face. He reached out his arms. "No! Little Ugo! Little Ugo! No!"

The boy was confused. Who was this man? His voice was more familiar now. He remembered a little apartment long ago. His Mama and ... his Papa. His shoulders shook and tears flowed as Antonio took him in his arms and held him close.

"I never thought I'd see you again. How did you get out of there? Little Ugo, Little Ugo."

The boy ran his hands over Antonio's rough face, trying to avoid the pit where his left eye should have been. "Papa ... Papa ..."

Suddenly the candle began to flicker violently and then went out. The draft through the little space could only mean that Antonio's pursuers were coming closer.

"*Occhio unico!* We're coming! You can't hide!"

Antonio picked up his son.

"We have to go, Little Ugo. Some bad men are chasing me."

Little Ugo had not grown much over the years and Antonio found him almost as light as when he tossed him in the air in Pietrasanta long ago. Still, Antonio's leg was so badly injured that he had difficulty struggling through the narrow tunnel. Repeatedly, they rammed against a wall and Antonio put his hand on his son's smooth head to protect him.

"Don't worry, Little Ugo, it's all right. I'll get you out of here. Nobody is going to hurt us."

Antonio had no idea what he would do if and when he emerged into the sunlight or where they would go, but he knew they had to escape whoever was following them. Little Ugo nestled his head on Antonio's shoulder.

Eventually, streaks of sunlight glimmered into the tunnel. Antonio could hear footsteps coming closer from behind and tried to run faster. "*Occhio unico!*" At the entrance, he suddenly fell forward, still holding Little Ugo in an iron grip.

Standing above him were two men, one older and one younger, and they were soon joined by the two who had chased him.

Paolo pointed his pistol at the writhing form on the ground and cocked the trigger. Roberto clumsily pointed the knife.

"No!" Ezio shouted. "Paolo, no!"

Ezio put his foot on Antonio's leg. Antonio screamed.

"At last."

It was more of a whisper than a cry of victory. Ezio looked down at the man below him. He was short with straggly hair and a beard, wearing filthy pants and a shirt with one sleeve missing. Ezio could not stop staring at his face, sunburned and bruised, with a gaping hole where his left eye should be. The sunlight made it look even darker.

Ezio pulled the worn cap from his back pocket.

"Is this yours?"

With the bright sun in his eyes, Antonio could barely make out what Ezio had in his hands. Ezio held it closer.

"Yes," Antonio said. "I lost it."

"So you are *Occhio unico*! Or Angelo Donatello!"

"Yes."

Feelings of anger and anguish, repulsion and revenge churned in Ezio's belly and rose to his aching head. Eleven years of obsession lay under his foot. He should grab the man by the neck and strangle him. He should stomp on his chest and kick him in the head. He should take Paolo's pistol and shoot him. He should ...

But seeing him there, helpless and with a crying boy clinging to him, Ezio felt a new emotion: pity. He took his foot off the man's leg. Paolo, Roberto and Adolfo stood silently at the side, not knowing what to do. Donna and Little Dino ran up to join them. Little Dino looked at the boy in the arms of the man on the ground and pointed. "That's Little Ugo," he whispered to Donna.

"Oh, my God!" Donna cried. "It's *il fantasma ragazzo!*"

With the sun behind the dark figures that loomed above him, Antonio gripped Little Ugo harder. "Kill me, do what you want to me, but let the boy go, please let the boy go!"

"You're a monster!" Paolo said.

Antonio's hands shook. "No, not a monster."

"You are!" Paolo continued. "You helped to kill five hundred and sixty people. You helped to murder my friend's Angelica!"

"No!"

"You did! You helped the Nazis. You led them up to Sant'Anna! You carried the weapons! You showed them where to go!"

"No! No! I didn't!"

"How can you say that?" Paolo shouted. "Everyone knows you did."

"I didn't, I didn't. They forced me."

Antonio began to cry. The others standing over him were silent, now even more angry and confused. Antonio tried to say something and Ezio leaned down to his disfigured face.

"They forced me," Antonio whispered as Little Ugo clung to his Papa even tighter. "The Nazis came to my room and forced me to join in the march up to Sant'Anna. They beat me over and over."

He had to stop and breathe. "I didn't even know where we were going until we got there. Then I tried to run away but they beat me again. We were at the top of the hill and I fell down and they thought I was pointing to the village. But I wasn't, I just fell down."

"What about your wife and son?" Paolo shouted.

"I sent them there for safety! I didn't want them to stay in Pietrasanta. It wasn't safe! And now she's dead, and Little Ugo … Little Ugo … I am so guilty, so guilty."

Antonio kissed Little Ugo on the top of his head.

Ezio finally spoke. "Why should we believe you? You've been hiding all these years. That proves you're guilty, right?"

"I was afraid," Antonio said. "I couldn't go back. I'd be killed. And I'm a coward." He pointed to his eyes. "Even this is a lie. I wasn't injured in Ethiopia. I fell off a goddamn church roof, a goddamn church roof."

Ezio turned and walked away. He had to think. Why wasn't anything clear? Why wasn't he relieved that he had finally found *Occhio unico*? And why, for God's sake, was he suddenly feeling compassion for this man? Even if everything he said was true, the man was still a Fascist. Wasn't that reason enough to kill him right here? He went back and crouched beside the man.

"How can we believe anything you've said?"

Antonio wiped the tears that were running down his face with the back of his hand. Then he reached behind him and pulled his torn and dirty notebook from his pocket. "Read what I've written."

Ezio took the notebook but made no attempt to open it.

"Please." Antonio was crying. "Do what you want with me. Kill me. Put me in a prison forever. I don't care. I don't care. But take the boy someplace.

Have someone take care of him. He's so small, not much bigger than when I saw him last. His face and hands were burned, but he is all right. He needs someone to love him. Please!"

Donna looked at Ezio. Ezio looked at Donna and nodded.

"We're not going to kill you," Ezio said. "We don't know what we'll do with you. We'll take you back to Pietrasanta. There are people there who have been looking for you. And we'll see that the boy is taken care of."

Ezio reached down and tried to pry Little Ugo from Antonio's arms. A look of horror came over the boy's misshapen face. "No!" he cried and wiggled out of his father's grasp and Ezio's hands.

He began to run. Faster and faster. Antonio struggled to his feet and tried to follow.

"Stop!" Antonio cried. "Little Ugo! It's all right! Stop!"

Years of running through the forest had trained the boy to flee like a fox down the grassy slope to the river. Ezio, Paolo, Roberto and Adolfo ran after him. Antonio couldn't keep up.

"Stop!" Ezio cried.

Little Dino broke away from Donna. "Little Ugo!" he cried. "Come back!"

Donna grabbed Little Dino and he buried his face in the folds of her dress.

Tripping and falling, the boy who thought of himself as a spirit reached the bridge. No one was on it. He started running across, stumbling over the bricks and picking himself up. Then, at the other end, five men began to cross. Four were big, hefty men. The man in front was tall with gray hair and a short beard and he wore a three-piece suit.

Little Ugo froze in the middle of the bridge. He couldn't think. On the right was a man who was going to take him away from his father. On the left were men who looked bad. He climbed over the wall of the bridge. Balancing precariously at the top, he looked both ways again. Then he spread his arms like his friend the eagle and plunged.

The others could hardly see his tiny body floating just under the surface of the river when Antonio got to the middle of the bridge.

"No! Little Ugo! No!"

Antonio climbed the wall. Teetering on the top just as he had on a church roof in Ethiopia many years ago, Antonio looked down at the swirling river. In a minute, his body floated gently behind his son far past the Devil's Bridge.

CHAPTER 45

▼

A few hours later, his car again filled to overflowing, Paolo drove back to Porte a Moriano, crossed the Serchio and then headed north to Barga. No one spoke. Little Dino sat stoically on Adolfo's lap but sniffled every once in a while. Donna snuggled up to Ezio.

In the parking lot below the city, Ezio and Donna hesitated before getting into their Fiat. Bound by a tragedy they could not have foreseen, no one wanted to leave. Then Paolo put his arm around Ezio and they walked to the edge of the parking lot.

"How are you, Sparrow?"

"Angry, upset, confused. All those things."

"Relief?"

"I guess, when I sort this all out, that's what I'll feel most. Relieved that it's finally over. And relieved that I didn't have to kill this man, even if I could have done it."

"Think of how you'd feel then. More guilt!"

"I feel so sorry for his son."

"Poor little kid," Paolo said. "Not much bigger than Little Dino."

"And you know, I feel sorry for *Occhio unico*, too. I guess we'll always call him that. Very sorry."

"Sorry enough to wipe away your guilt?"

"I don't know, Owl, I don't know yet."

"I think we should be going," Paolo said. "Lucia is probably out of her mind worrying. We'll talk more about this, Sparrow. I'll see you soon."

"Thank you, Owl. Thank you for coming and for everything."

Paolo looked into his friend's eyes, which were very moist. "Take care of yourself, Sparrow. I'm glad you have Donna."

"I am, too."

The two friends embraced. When they returned to their cars, Donna was saying good-bye to Roberto and Adolfo and she shook hands with Little Dino, who smiled shyly and then went to hold his Papa's hand.

Reluctantly, Paolo and the others climbed into one car to drive back to Sant'Antonio, and Ezio and Donna got into the Fiat and headed back to Reboli.

The sun, which was so bright earlier that day, now remained behind dark, threatening clouds. Traces of lightning flickered between the mountains. Lost in their own thoughts, neither Ezio nor Donna said anything. When they passed the Devil's Bridge, though, he took her hand after she wiped her eyes.

Ezio was having a hard time sorting out what he had believed for eleven years and what he had just learned. Was anything Angelo Donatello said true? Was he only trying to save his life? No, Ezio thought. This was a man who didn't care if he died, so he must have been telling the truth about Sant'Anna.

So *Occhio unico* was not the monster they thought he was. Yet he tried to make himself out as a war hero, so he was a shameful liar. And he was a Fascist, and the Fascists were to blame for so much complicity with the Nazis during the war.

But this man said he didn't collaborate with the Nazis at Sant'Anna. He said he was forced to carry weapons and that was all. He didn't point the way. And he didn't want his wife and son to be the victims of the massacre. He sent them there for safety. He loved his wife and son and he was devastated by their loss.

Somehow, Ezio believed him. In a far different way, Ezio thought, Angelo Donatello was also a victim of this horrific event.

Ezio couldn't understand how the stories about this man started and how they were uniformly accepted as truth. Everyone, at least everyone he knew, believed *Occhio unico* committed this terrible act. And everyone said they were positive that he had fled to Germany. People, he thought, believe what they want to believe.

"Well," he thought, "some people might like to believe that the devil built the bridge at Borgo a Mozzano."

Looking out the window but not really seeing the scenery, Donna thought about how her life had changed on this trip. She had also believed the stories about *Occhio unico* and now she knew they were false. She would have a hard time convincing her father and all the others at the Casa del Popolo.

But she had also discovered something about herself. Since the rape she had protected herself with quips and jokes, hiding the hurt and shame that she had buried and tried to ignore. Now, for the first time in her life, she cared so deeply about someone else that she was willing to let down her guard, show her real emotions and express her love.

It was late when they arrived in Reboli. All the shops on Via Bellini were closed and even Signora Franconi's fat cat had gone inside for the night. Signora Antonelli and Signora Piazini were nowhere to be seen. Ezio's rooms were stuffy again and he opened the shutters to let in the evening air.

"Surprise," he said, "the *farmacia* hasn't fixed their sign yet."

"Well," Donna said, "they're probably too busy putting out the *Il Popolo*."

Ezio sat in the chair at the desk and let Donna have the comfortable, though very worn, blue chair near the window. He pulled out Antonio's notebook from his pocket and turned the pages. Most of the early pages were faded beyond legibility or obliterated by what appeared to be wet spots. "On a farm … hiding … can't be found …" "Can't think about what happened …" "Guilty, guilty, guilty …" "Liar, liar …"

Most of the sentences had evaporated.

The handwriting seemed to change in the last pages. It seemed shaky and sometimes unreadable. "… our wedding anniversary." "… 15 November. Little Ugo's birthday." Then: "12 August 1954. Tenth anniversary. I miss them so much. Why did I do it? Why, why, why, why?"

There were other entries. Sometimes the word Daniella was written over and over down the page, sometimes Little Ugo.

"Donna, listen to this," Ezio said as he put his finger on a page. "A whole sentence. 'When you only have a past, you don't have a present or a future.'"

"Not very profound," Donna said. "I mean, what does it mean? He probably heard it somewhere and wrote it down."

"I don't know," Ezio said, repeating the line over to himself. "I think it's fascinating to know that this is how he felt, and I keep thinking what a terrible life this guy must have led since the … since the massacre. I believe now that he didn't intend to collaborate with the Nazis, but he did see this terrible, terrible thing happen. With his wife and son right there, among the victims. And he had to live with that. He knew he couldn't go back, that his life was over. I don't know why he didn't kill himself long before this."

"How sad. But, Ezio, you kept saying that you saw a man run away. That was Angelo, right?"

"Yes. The man who ran away, but not because he had caused the massacre but because he couldn't have prevented it."

"Yes, very sad. So you're going to forgive him for what he did?"

"I don't know, Donna. I have to think about that some more. Maybe someday. I know I won't forget. I'll never forget."

He caressed the notebook, now a revealing link to the past. "And you know, I don't want to ever feel the way he did. I've had some good parts in my past, and some bad parts, and I've had one terrible, terrible part, too. And I've dwelled on that for so long that it became not only my past, but my present, too. I want a future, Donna, I want a future."

She could see tears in his eyes. She reached over and gripped his hand.

"And all this guilt? Can you let that go? You have to let that go, Ezio. You did what you had to do at Sant'Anna, both before and after the massacre."

"I don't know, Donna. I can't throw this off like an old shirt. But I'll try."

"And I'll try to help."

Ezio smiled. "You can be my psychiatrist."

"Well, I'm sure my fees will be lower than the guy in Lucca. Oh, Ezio, I want a new life, too. For some reason, I feel so free now even after all we've been through. I guess it's *because* of all we went through. I don't want to go back to that dreary life I've had. And I certainly don't want to spend the rest of my life at that stupid Stupendi."

They both smiled.

"I want to share my life with someone, Ezio. Dare I say that I want to share it with you?"

He moved to her side, pulled her to her feet and held her hands. "I know this sounds like a dumb Hollywood movie ..."

"Clark and Claudette?"

"No. 'Ezio and Donna.' I want to share my life with you, too, Donna. It's going to be hard for me, letting Angelica go. And it will be hard for you, waiting and watching while I let her go. But I know I have to do that, Donna. I have to do that."

She kissed his cheek. "I'll wait, Ezio. I don't care how long it takes, as long as you let me be there with you."

They moved to the only other place where they could sit, the bed. They sat side by side. Ezio put his arm around her. "I don't know what I would have become if I hadn't met you, Donna. A bitter old man, I guess. My students would hate me. I'd be like Signor Pilozi. And no one else would like me, either, not even Paolo. And you know what? I wouldn't like myself. I could feel myself getting that way. I kept saying I wanted revenge, I wanted justice, but you know what I really wanted? I wanted someone to love me again."

"And I do," she said.

"I know you do. You saved me, Donna. You saved me from becoming that bitter, lonely old man."

They kissed, long and hard. Donna ran her hand through his hair.

"I'm no heroine, Ezio. Remember I was lonely, too. My jokes? Just a way of protecting myself. I wanted someone to love but I also wanted someone to love me, too. I think even our little spat in the Garfagnana helped me to understand how much I do love you."

"I know I was trying too hard to protect you, Donna. But I think I was trying to protect myself, too, protect myself from another awful loss. I need you so badly, Donna."

Ezio stared at his wrist for a long time, and then, slowly but firmly he took the wire bracelet off. He pulled out the box from under the bed, put the bracelet in it, and put the box back.

"I swore I'd never take that bracelet off," he said, rubbing the white line the bracelet had left. "I was never going to love anyone again. For eleven years, I didn't. I knew some girls, sure, but I never loved them. Now it's different. I still feel a great love for Angelica and I'll always think of what we had. I hope you don't mind that, Donna."

"No, I understand that."

"But, like everyone has kept telling me for so long, I have to move on from there. With you, I hope I can."

Their lovemaking began soft and slow and warm. They explored each other's bodies and then they laughed and giggled and Donna said something about the walls of Jericho coming down and Ezio smiled. They fell asleep and woke and began again. And in the morning, as the sun came up over the Chiesa di Sant'Ignazio, they lay for a long time in each other's arms.

And then it was time for Donna to drive back to Pietrasanta to tell her father what had happened and to go back to work at the marble factory.

"It's going to be strange telling Papa and the men at the Casa del Popolo in Pietrasanta," Donna said. "They won't believe me. They will go to their graves believing that Angelo Donatello was the greatest villain the world has ever known."

"I'm going to go over to Florence and tell my father, too. I'm not sure what his reaction will be about *Occhio unico*, but I know what he'll do when I tell him about you."

"What?"

"He'll start to cry."

"And, Ezio, you know what my father will do when I tell him about you?"

"What?"

"He won't be surprised, but he'll cry."

CHAPTER 46

▼

In the days following, the participants in what they called the Devil's Bridge tragedy tried to resume their lives but discovered that they had been irrevocably changed.

In Pisa, Adolfo went back to his studies but found himself staring out of the window and thinking more about the Garfagnana than Galileo. In Florence, his brother, Roberto, impressed his friends with an amazing tale of how he kept *Occhio unico* at bay for hours with a tiny knife. The Fascist Franco sat glumly at the side, now only drinking the lethal grappa.

In his *pasticceria* in Reboli, Paolo smiled a lot but told of his trip only when asked. The response of his customers to what happened at the Devil's Bridge ranged from total disbelief to genuine relief. Paolo spent every afternoon talking to Ezio in the piazza.

In Pietrasanta, Donna decided to give her notice at the marble factory. She told her father she needed time off.

As soon as he returned, Ezio's first visit was to Maria, who hugged herself and cried and fingered her photo of Angelica and the boys. But then she smiled broadly when he told her about Donna. His next was to see Fausta, and after hearing about Amadeo Mazzella's untimely and unceremonious death, she opened her shades and joined Little Dino in caring for the garden. She even hummed little tunes.

After recovering from the strain of her husband's and son's quick departure, Lucia planned another party. Rosa would bring ravioli, of course, and Maria her chicken and Annabella a dessert.

Rosa and Maria and Annabella started the day by going to mass. Maria had trouble walking that far to church, but Rosa took one arm and Annabella the other and they made it. When it was time for Communion, the priest came down from the altar and gave Maria the host in her pew. Rosa was surprised that he would do such a thing and thought maybe he wasn't so bad after all.

Rosa arrived at Lucia's first, again bearing a bowl of ravioli in one hand and guiding Marco with the other. She guided him to a chair, smoothed his hair and kissed the top of his head. Then she kissed Lucia and Paolo and patted Little Dino on the head.

Annabella, impeccable as always, brought a perfectly formed chocolate cream cake on a silver platter. "I had a little time so I just made this," she said. "Francesco always used to like it so much."

Rosa took the plate and kissed her. "It's beautiful. I can never make cakes. All I make is ravioli. You must be getting tired of them."

"No!" Gina said, coming down the stairs with Pietro. "Rosa, we will never ever get tired of your ravioli. You can bring some over every day."

Having barely made the train from Florence, Roberto arrived just before Adolfo, who had taken the bus from Pisa. They kissed their parents, but Pietro stared vacantly and sat down.

Everyone was shocked when Fausta turned up at the door. "I know you would have invited me if you thought I'd come," she said. "Well, I invited myself. If you'll have me, I'd really like to be part of *il gruppo di Cielo*."

She handed Lucia a bouquet of roses and irises. "Just a few things from my garden."

"*Santa Maria*, Fausta," Rosa said. "Of course we want you here." She kissed her on both cheeks.

Maria was the last to arrive, with Ezio on one arm and Donna on the other, and it was obvious that the three of them had a secret.

Rosa, of course, quickly asked, "Ezio, Donna, you look so happy. Why are you so happy?"

"It's such a beautiful day, Rosa, don't you think?" Ezio said. "Don't you think it's a beautiful day, Maria?"

Maria beamed.

Rosa plunged on. "But, I mean, there must be a reason ..."

"Oh, Rosa," Donna said, "Maria just let us try some of her biscotti. How do you make such great biscotti, Maria?"

Maria's bosom heaved because she was chuckling so much. "Oh, you know, I just put in a little of this, a little of that." She had to take the handkerchief from her sleeve because tears were rolling down her plump cheeks.

"All right, all right," Rosa said, "if you don't want to tell us, don't tell us. But we're going to find out anyway!" She threatened to hit Ezio with a wooden serving spoon, but she was smiling.

Little Dino was again dispatched to get Maria's chicken, Roberto and Adolfo carried the big table outside, and again wine and beer and grappa made the rounds after the ravioli and chicken and various salads. Tonight, no one wanted to clear the table and wash dishes. Gina let Pietro nod off at one end and Rosa put a blanket over Marco's knees so that he could nap.

"This is like *il gruppo di Cielo*," Rosa said. "All of us who were there who are still alive. And now we have another member." She smiled at Donna as she sat next to Ezio.

"No more headaches, Ezio?" She ruffled his hair.

"No, none." He grinned.

"No more nightmares?"

"No, none."

Rosa smiled at Donna again. "I think I know why."

There were so many questions and so few answers. Helping himself to another bottle of beer, Roberto said that he had been at the *osteria* the night before and that Franco had been even more drunk than he'd been the last couple of weeks.

"He can't hold it anymore," Roberto said. "Not like me."

"Right," Adolfo said, slapping his brother on the knee.

"He's got reason to, I guess. He's lost his job ..."

"Really?" Ezio said.

"Wouldn't show up on time, always drunk. But that's not the half of it."

"Which is?" Adolfo said.

"The *Movimento Sociale Italiano* has sent him packing. Won't have anything to do with him. Last night he was crying in his beer, 'They call me a traitor, a traitor, and I was just trying to let them know how much I wanted to be part of the movement.' Poor guy, I guess. But I can't feel too sorry for him."

"Yes, of course," Paolo said. "He was just trying to help an innocent journalist from Reboli."

"Right," Roberto said. "So, Ezio, when is that article going to appear? The other guys want to see it."

"Still working on it, Roberto."

Roberto also reported that Franco had news about Fabiano Guerini, the farmer who protected *Occhio unico* all those years. "He's selling the farm and moving his wife to Barga. His wife didn't want to stay there anymore after their daughter died."

"I didn't know they had a daughter," Donna said.

"Teen age girl. She fell off the roof of the hay barn the day after *Occhio unico* left. Died instantly," Roberto said.

The others wanted to know what Guerini would do in Barga. After all, he had been a farmer all his life.

"Franco said old Calvino Bastiani got him a job as a handyman. What that really means is that he'll be another one of Bastiani's Fascist goons."

"What I don't understand," Paolo said, "is why Bastiani was on that bridge when we got there. Just a coincidence?"

"Not according to Franco," Roberto said. "Bastiani was the head of the *Movimento Sociale Italiano* in Barga and of course they were keeping an eye on *Occhio unico*. So they heard that he was across the river from the Devil's Bridge, too, and were on their way to rescue him."

"Too late, of course," Ezio said.

"The way they ran back to their car when they saw us ..." Paolo said.

"They probably thought we had three hundred Communists coming right behind," Adolfo said.

"That reminds me," Donna said. "We had our pictures developed at the photo shop. Can you imagine what they charge to print pictures?" She dug an envelope out of her purse. "Now remember, I'm not a very good photographer."

Despite her disclaimer, the photos of the Devil's Bridge and the formal garden at the Mazzella villa were quite good.

"So that's the Devil's Bridge," Lucia said. "Don't take me there, Paolo. I don't ever want to see it."

Gina put the photos in front of Pietro but he couldn't comprehend them.

Then they looked at the photos of the three men in the garden. "These must be the last pictures of Amadeo Mazzella and Orsino Nardari," Donna said, "and there's Calvino Bastiani."

"Look at Calvino," Ezio said. "Standing there so arrogant. Bastard. And you know what, because of people like him, the *Movimento Sociale Italiano* will still go on."

He had an idea. He would take Calvino's face out of the photo, blow it up into a poster, and send it to every Casa del Popolo in Tuscany to replace the one of *Occhio unico*. "Everyone will be on the lookout for this new monster," he said.

"Well," Donna said, "we have to remember the man who saved us from Bastiani and Nardari, and died doing it."

Ezio raised his glass. "Here's to Vittorio Izzo, a famous fighter to the last." Everyone else raised glasses, too. "Dear Vittorio," Donna said. "From Udine."

Rosa brought up the subject everyone had avoided all evening.

"Well, there are other people dead, too," she said. "I don't think I want to toast *Occhio unico*, because my mind is still all fuzzy about him. But the man is dead, right? And his wife. And his son. Should we have a little forgiveness?"

Donna and Ezio exchanged looks. "Yes," he said, "let's forgive."

Maria raised her hand. "I'm too old to have any hatred left. I lost Angelica and Little Carlo and Nando, but, yes, even I forgive him. And in our hearts, I think we should say a prayer for all of them."

Everyone, even Roberto, sat silently for a moment. Ezio put his arm around Donna's shoulders. She looked to see whether Little Dino was listening. He was bouncing a ball against the mimosa tree.

"I feel so bad for Little Ugo," she said. "For one thing, I can't believe he escaped the massacre. And then to live all by himself all those years."

"I wonder if he did live alone all those years," Paolo said. "He was so afraid of us. Something must have happened so that he couldn't be with people. You know Little Dino said he actually sat down with him on the grass at Cira. That's where Little Dino was when we thought he was lost."

"This has been really hard on Little Dino," Lucia said softly.

"You know," Paolo said, "it seems like he's afraid to go near a river now. Even the little Maggia. I tried to take him fishing the other day but he wouldn't go."

"He'll get over it," Ezio said.

"I hope so," Lucia whispered.

Ezio got up from the table and said he and Donna would be leaving in the morning for Pietrasanta.

"You mean you're going to leave and you're not going to tell us when the wedding is?" Rosa said.

"Rosa!" Ezio and Donna said together. Rosa smiled triumphantly.

"Well, it's hard to keep a secret around here," Ezio said, "but I guess it's pretty obvious. Donna and I will be getting married as soon as we can arrange it in Pietrasanta. And you're all invited."

Maria beamed and everyone cheered and hugged and kissed. As they went outside, Ezio stopped Donna and pointed to the hills.

"Can you see it now?"

It didn't take Donna long to see the yellow speck near the hilltop. "The Cielo? Yes!"

"Think we should buy it and fix it up?"

"We?"

"Of course."

Made in the USA
Lexington, KY
18 May 2010